PRAISE FOR
SWIMMING WITH THE SUN

With friendship and love at its core, *Swimming with the Sun* gives us a new spin on the dystopian novel, with relatable heroines and a world that feels at once familiar and fantastic.

—Taylor Hartley, *Ladies of Leora*

Full of heart, Swimming with the Sun is a cozy dystopian novel where characters thrive in the small moments, challenging their world order with honesty and hope.

—C. G. Honer, *These Gilded Bones May Bloom*

A thoroughly original and imaginative dystopian story filled with friendships, romance, and celestial occurrences. I look forward to reading more from Martel. Especially if there are more horses.

—Jessika Grewe Glover, *Another Beast's Skin Series*

SWIMMING WITH THE SUN

SWIMMING WITH THE SUN

JULIA MARTEL

MARTEL ENTERPRISES LLC

*To the curious souls who want to do
everything in their earthly lifetime.
Who fear they won't be able.
Who try anyway.*

"It is a serious thing to live in a society of possible gods and goddesses, to remember that the dullest most uninteresting person you can talk to may one day be a creature which, if you saw it now, you would be strongly tempted to worship, or else a horror and a corruption such as you now meet, if at all, only in a nightmare."

—C.S. LEWIS, *THE WEIGHT OF GLORY*

PROLOGUE

My love,

How have I ended up here, writing you words my vows forbid?

It has turned into a funny quip—a party anecdote, a nod to my eccentricity—that I was not overheated by the Enlightening. We laugh, they nod, and we all agree I was so very lucky to never feel that pain. When the great white heat of ascension befell us all, your souls were scarred with an aching—a yearning to be warmed once again.

I, instead, awoke to icy waves lapping at my waist as I lay on that pebbled beach. I do not ache, and I am not scarred. My Enlightenment was a genesis, a renaissance, an evolution.

But what drew me there, my sweet? For it was not luck.

There are not enough clovers in the fields or shooting stars in the sky to arrange what happened those days. Months of happily painting deserts and cityscapes suddenly interrupted by the calling to paint that arctic lake. It was farther north than I had ever been, farther north than pods travel. For days, my feet struck the earth one in front of the other through thick forests and craggy mountains; each step drawing me closer to that glacial body. I barely remember packing my sack, or eating, or even drinking water until I found that clearing.

Along the shore of those crystalline waters, I climbed a ledge to better see that crisp blue horizon. The handholds in the cliffside seemed carved for my grip alone. Once atop, I withdrew the supplies from my canvas cylinder and began to paint.

Something otherworldly, ancient, and profound placed me there. Near my final brushstroke, I was overcome, like all of you. The intensity of our glimpses to the ascended realms caused me to stumble, and I fell from that ledge into the iced waters of Le Grand Lac. That clumsy, inevitable dive has led me to this trouble.

But it is good trouble, dear. Trouble that might save the second generation—the generation of our young one when they finally enter the world. Sadly though, the Elders do not share my view, and I will not be able to hold your hand or kiss their forehead when that day comes.

I will continue to dream of nothing but you and our child. Letting you go is the hardest thing I'll ever have to do, but the easiest decision to make. For if I stay, I will only be putting you both in danger.

I leave you with the painting from that day and hope you will remember me fondly; for all the days preceding this one. When the world changes, away from this damned system, know it is because of what I am setting into motion now.

It will get worse before it gets better.

Have faith in me, ma cherie.

I will certainly need it.

All my love,
Charl

CHAPTER 1

From: The Variety
Recipient: Noa Lavoie
0000 hrs., 01.06.0253

ASSIGNMENT CEREMONY REMINDER: *CAVALRY*

You have completed your Assignment preparation for *CAVALRY*. Your Reassignment Ceremony is tomorrow at 0800 hrs. at *The Bowl* in *City Centre*. Dress in *CAVALRY* uniform. Bring your provided Skill Trip materials. Wishing you great expansion.

NOA

"You know we're never coming back," V murmured into Noa's ear, under the roar of a filling stadium.

He tended to lean too close and lower his voice to a hum when he spoke. The rich rumble in his tone caused the fine hairs on her neck to prick.

"Knock it off," she said, swatting him away and barely missing his face.

It was the third time he'd made this ominous threat in as many days. The other two times, back in prep class, he'd leaned over his desk and whispered in her ear the same way. But, afraid to make a scene in front of her prep instructor and classmates, Noa hadn't swung at him then. She had just sat there, head forward and still, like a compliant doe.

She didn't mind his fingertips and breath on the back of her neck. It would have been hot if he was mouthing something other than his nonsense plans to escape the Variety.

Their plans…if she wanted.

She didn't have time for this—for him. Especially today. They were minutes from meeting their Cavalry leader and leaving on their Skill Trip. She was already dressed in the ridiculous Cavalry uniform: calf high boots, wide-hipped pants, and head-to-toe khaki tones. The outfit annoyed her almost as much as V, who was still standing too close.

She should have swatted at him the very first time. Now, he was overly confident about invading her space and probably thought he was on the brink of actually convincing her.

She gave him a dirty look and turned to walk away. He rounded to her front and closed the space.

Too close.

"Come on," he practically groaned.

Fuck, he was tall. Tall and blond, but not in the sweet and sandy kind of way. The wild, almost white kind. Noa remembered the first time she'd seen it atop the head of a lanky, smart-mouthed ten-year-old. They hadn't been friends back then either, just kids who happened to attend the same lessons.

In school, V was a bully. Not to her, particularly, as she was too invisible to be the target of anyone's disdain. She hadn't planned to be invisible, but her parents had made it clear that her questions about the world were unwanted—at home and elsewhere—and, if she couldn't hide how she felt, she'd be better off hiding her entirety in the shadows of other people's light.

And V burned bright. With white-blond hair and white-hot anger, he was rude and loud and combative with anyone who dared to squint in his direction.

Until he needed something, of course.

Noa shook her head, avoiding eye contact as she stepped away. She scratched her ear, shaking out his lingering voice, and started a lap around the stadium floor. She craned her neck to appreciate the architecture. The Bowl had a unique design, sinking beneath the city rather than floating above it like the skytowers. The top of the arena began at ground level, and large concentric circles of light grey stone, acting both as steps and seating, descended fifteen stories into the ground. Around her, on the Bowl's floor (which was staged today with incredibly plush faux-moss material), new Assignments grouped along the perimeter. Not every Assignment was represented at every ceremony. Such a thing wouldn't be possible, there were far too many.

In early-development lessons, Instructors often taught a unit on the contextualization and celebration of the Variety.

One year, Noa's Instructor asked students to guess the total number of Assignments on a given date. The class had erupted in laughter as if it were possible to tally a finite number of ways humans could spend time evolving their souls.

12, 181.

Or at least that was the answer the year Noa committed it to memory.

The Variety adjusted the total number of Assignments in the Northern Province on its own. Its real-time adaptation to their needs as an evolving species was a highlight of its intelligence and unimpeachable design. It knew what was best for society because it knew what was best for each individual citizen. It could determine the number of Artists the world needed just as easily as it could determine the exact moment Noa had gotten her soul's fulfillment from being a Nurse and should become a Service Member instead.

Today, two dozen Assignments were welcoming new members. Everyone on the Bowl's floor had a soul that also needed a change. So said the Variety.

Noa hadn't seen this Reassignment coming. Her soul hadn't felt filled by the Service—it wasn't the kind of work that could ever make her soul full—but she still felt she had more work to do there. She could have made more of an impact.

The Variety keeping you guessing was part of its charm, Noa supposed.

Today didn't feel like a good day to be guessing, though. Noa wanted answers and clarity, and for someone to tell her exactly what was going on. But, as she often did, she pushed the storm of questions to the back of her mind.

Noa spotted her family where she'd left them in second-level seating. They waved to her, however her sister's wave was more of a full-body cheer. When Noa raised her arm to wave back, her heavy crossbody duffel restricted the movement of her shoulder.

She and Sami had spent hours the night before packing her Skill Trip bag. The supplies and uniforms had already been packed when she picked them up on the last day of prep-class, but she had wanted to take stock and more importantly, needed to make room for her favorite sweater and jeans.

Their mother, Chemi, had caught Noa and Sami in the middle of the sister-bonding packing session. Khaki vests, under layers, and wide-hipped canvas pants were strewn about Noa's room, giving Chemi the chance to fit in one last motherly scold.

"Must you challenge everything, Noie?" her mother had said. "They know what you need. They provide it, they clean it, they fold it, and they put it in a sac. You think you know better?"

Noa never thought she knew better.

After a fit of sisterly giggles at their mother's exasperation, she and Sami had repacked everything into the duffel including the extra outfit. They "accidentally" lost the issued sunhat to the bottom of Noa's closet, deciding she would avoid any Skill Trip activities that required her to wear the ugliest-thing-they-had-ever-seen, and clasped the bag shut.

Noa pursed her smile and broke the wave with her family. They had said their goodbyes.

Rounding the second half of her stadium lap, she focused

on the other Assignments, all at different points in their own ceremonies. Some had started earlier than others. The Archaeologists and Historians were already receiving their tokens—chisels and brushes—and preparing to depart.

Her eyes glanced upward to the stadium seats again. Thousands of citizens were in attendance, populating the rings of seating at various densities depending on the size of the Assignment cohort on the Bowl's floor in front of them. Some of the audience members were family of the newly assigned, others were just devoted Variety citizens. She wondered how many people in those seats she was personally responsible for. Or worse. How many people were not in those seats today, because of the work she had done in her previous Assignment.

Noa bumped into a herd of Welders who were stumbling across the Bowl in darkening masks and thick, protective gloves reaching their elbows. She weaved through them, priding herself on only ricocheting off two, coming out the other side into a patch of Chefs. They were the largest class in attendance and wore shiny, red coats with oversized buttons and delicate hats. They ignored her interruption and nodded obediently at their leaders' instruction.

She scrambled away and crossed the center of the stadium toward a group she didn't recognize. They wore stiff black collars and elongated grey wool sweaters resting near their knees. They stood motionless and equidistant apart, like chess pieces on an invisible board. Stranger than their orderly arrangement, all their autos were open, the projections glowing soft blue in front of each pawn. It seemed impolite to have your auto open during an Assignment ceremony, but they each had the same program running.

Noa stepped forward, hoping to hear who they were.

The gangly man orchestrating the woolen group had curly blond fringe at the top of his head and freckles that could be seen even from a distance. He wore the same stiff uniform, but he swam in it languidly, as if someone had sewn up the garment and then poured him in.

He called to his new Assignments, "Who can tell me about the symbol on your sweaters?"

Noa squinted. It appeared to be a small, spiky flower embroidered in white thread, bright against the dark grey.

A short woman whose neck was tight to her collar raised her hand. "The Arctic Seuil. A plant symbolizing wisdom and patience, originating from the Nouveau Française people of the North Coast."

The leader scrunched his thin face and gave a reluctant nod.

"What does patience have to do with being a Librarian?" He paced the platform while waiting for an answer.

Librarians, of course.

Librarians, the organizers of knowledge, touched every piece of information citizens consumed. They compiled historical notes, wrote new articles, re-architected subject matter. They authored school texts and aided in keeping Assignment preparation lessons up-to-date. They even received citizen submitted queries and daily reports, triaging them for publication. The work of Librarians probably informed most everything Noa knew. Odd she had never seen one before today.

The man snapped his head up and glared at Noa. His

eyes scanned her, likely trying to discern if she was a deviant Librarian who had dared to show up late and without the appropriate wool dress. Noa tucked her head and moved on until she was settled at the back of the Cavalry again.

Iyan, her Assignment prep Instructor, stood at the front on a raised platform, surrounded by sixty other soon-to-be Cavalry members. Iyan hadn't called Cavalry to attention yet and chatted with two other Instructors donning the signature orange Teaching robes.

Noa shifted her feet and adjusted the bag strap on her shoulder that was digging into her.

"Need to set that down already?" V appeared beside her, putting an elbow into her rib cage hard enough to hurt but soft enough to appear as a playful jest.

She kept her eyes fixed on Iyan.

"Surprised you made it all the way across the floor," V continued. "You look like you're going to fall over."

She glared at him. "Surprised you're still here." Her upper lip twinged. Noa hated him for pointing it out, but she did need to set it down. Everyone else still had their bags over their shoulders or the long straps slung across their bodies.

She didn't care. And her parents were far enough away that her manners couldn't disappoint them. She flopped it to the ground with a thud.

A short, young woman about Noa's age turned at the sound. Her eyes, big and pleading and bright against brown skin and magenta hair, stared straight at Noa.

"Are we allowed to do that?" She pointed to the bag on the ground.

Noa shrugged.

Without hesitation, the girl pulled her own bag over her head and dropped it to the ground. In doing so, the strap brushed her fluorescent hair causing the tight curls haloing her face to bounce. An older man next to the girl did not turn around but had clearly eavesdropped on the conversation enough to let his bag drop too.

Thuds rippled across the group.

"I didn't know how much longer I could hold that thing," the girl said with an animated look of exhaustion and a swipe of her brow. The exaggerated expression faded into a contagious smile and an extended hand. "Alexis, but you can call me Lex."

"Noa."

"Vitus," he jumped in, "but you can call me V."

Alexis reciprocated his greeting with a wide smile and turned back to Noa. "You're lucky you've already made friends," she said, flashing a glance to V. "I didn't meet anyone in my prep class. So much more intense than my first stint."

Iyan interrupted Alexis and all the other murmurs, waving her arms to bring focus to the platform. Alexis gave a smaller wave to Noa and mouthed "later" before turning to face the front. Noa was grateful her new peer didn't make her disobey the Instructor's call for attention by continuing their conversation.

Iyan recited much of what she had said on the last day of prep class—that the Skill Trip would be difficult. All three prep classes had learned the fundamentals of Cavalry and now had to learn the practicals. They couldn't exactly learn how to ride a horse from the text on their autos.

"In a moment, your new Assignment leader, Decker, will

take the stage. The Variety assigned Decker as a Cavalry member forty-seven years ago, and he has not yet been given his notice. He has the highest-ranking post at Main Ranch and will guide your Skill Trip with the help of a few Marshals. Finally," Iyan paused to motion for the other two Instructors to step forward, "it has been a pleasure knowing each of you. Getting to know our students is the best exercise in exposure we have as Instructors. We hope you have evolved in our presence as well." In unison, each Instructor put their hands together in prayer position in front of their chests before taking a bow, and reciting the communal prayer. "We wish you great expansion."

The crowd of new Assignments bowed their heads in reflex.

Noa never managed to hold her prayer as long as those around her, so her head was raised and her eyes already open as the three Instructors shuffled off the box stage. They were replaced by a man who appeared to have been baked on the surface of the sun. Given his age, she thought he must be Second Generation. First Generations, those alive for the Enlightening, had all passed on. Noa's parents, who were Third Generation, had told her all about the Last First celebration. It had been a solemn and holy occasion marking the death of the last Elder, the oldest living human to have experienced the Enlightening.

Although Decker didn't appear to be as old as the last Elder, he wasn't as young as her parents either. He stood with his chest out and hands on his hips, taking in each audience member with the look of a proud father. He wore a weathered version of their uniform, the sand and olive-colored fabric darker around the seams and worn lighter around his joints. Noa cracked a smile, noticing that he wore a different hat than the one they were all provided.

"Hi, Ranchers," he called out in clear expectation of an echoed greeting.

Instead, sixty mouths remained silent, and a hundred and twenty eyes blinked.

"Guess you're not a chatty group." He chuckled and tucked his thumbs into his belt loops. "I'll be leading this Skill Trip. I lead everything back at the ranch, too, but let's not get ahead of ourselves."

He laughed to himself again, and another mimicked smile crept across Noa's face. Decker was charming and warm and, for some unknown reason, Noa already wanted to be in his good favor. That was probably how he managed to stay in the same role for forty-seven years—it matched a theory her parents told her once.

When Noa was about eight, she heard a story of a Mariner who had been Assigned for sixty years. She pestered her parents for weeks asking them to explain how that could be. It went against everything she had learned about their evolution and the Variety. After throwing an impressive tantrum, her parents finally answered: Once in a while, a human provided more evolutionary value by having others experience them in a specific role, rather than collecting different experiences. The Variety knew this and would keep them in that Assignment to maximize their evolutionary contribution.

She had been certain it was placating nonsense but maybe it was true for Decker.

"You'll notice you're a small cohort compared to the other Assignment groups today. We don't get a lot of Cavalry Assignments, and this trip takes a lot of effort on behalf of our crew. Seems The Variety appreciates that fact because it only assigns us to lead it once a year. Even so, this is the biggest cohort we've had." His voice trailed off only to come back stronger as he resumed. "It'll be a difficult couple of months on this Skill Trip, but I promise: I never leave a rancher behind." He took another deep breath and rocked from heel to toe on his exhale. "You ready to receive your Assignment token?"

A few people in the crowd answered with a holler.

Decker beamed. "Come on—this way! As big as this stadium is, our tokens don't fit inside." With the energy of someone years younger, he hopped from the platform to the ground and guided them toward an exit.

Three jaunty steps in he turned on his heel and shouted. "Wait!"

All the Calvary froze.

"I can't believe I almost forgot." Decker shook his head. "Look up to those seats and find your family. Send them a wave or whatever you need to say goodbye. I never leave a rancher behind, but this may well be your last Assignment." He removed his hat, resting it at his hip, and waited for the group to follow his command.

Last Assignment. Noa investigated the stands, trying to orient herself. Her thoughts raced and her skin clammed. Where were her parents and Sami sitting again? What did Decker mean by "last Assignment?"

She knew what he meant.

Forty-seven years was way too long to be in any Assignment—even for someone as suited for it as him. Her parents were wrong.

And the rumors were true.

"Told you," V said, walking away with his bag still on his shoulder.

CHAPTER 2

TALI

"And in every human's conscious brain, the Gods, um, showed our true destiny." The teenage boy's voice cracked on the last line of his presentation.

Tali sat on the living room rug staring at a collage of holograms. The display showed each of her classmate's live silhouettes in a small amphitheater layout. The boy speaking and the Instructor appeared larger and at the front of the virtual classroom.

Tali could see her reflection in the room, too. The hologram made her round cheeks rounder, her doe eyes larger, and her long, wavy, dirty blond hair blue. Self-display didn't have to be turned on, but Tali was comforted watching herself; she could catch her juvenile fidgets before they were visible to her peers. She was thirteen now, after all.

"Very good," the Instructor said, straightening his orange blazer. "And what is our true destiny?"

The boy shrank, fiddling with his shaggy hair. "Um, to evolve."

The Instructor rolled his hand, encouraging the pupil to elaborate. "Evolve to?"

The boy's hands stuck even more stiffly to his sides, fingers curled into his palms. With his gaze on the floor, he muttered something impossible to hear. Tali wiggled to her knees on the floor, the boy's nervous energy exciting her.

She caught a glimpse of herself and stopped wiggling. Her mouth was ahead of her, though. As always. The words burst out before she knew she was speaking.

"Evolve into a soul species. He *knows* the answer, sir. We *all* know the answer. Matthieu just hates being on view." Tali paused long enough for a single inhale. "But I don't—I'll go next." She stood and smoothed her crepe tunic.

The Instructor sighed. "Tali, what have I said about interrupting others?"

Tali leaned in, eyes bouncing around her classmates' glowing virtual faces. Her friend, Ash, was covering laughs at her, and Tali shot him a look before answering her Instructor. "To not?"

"Right. Now, Matthieu, please repeat the last line of your presentation, and we will move on. And yes, Tali, you can go next."

Tali caught a smirk from her Instructor and confirmed for herself that his annoyance with her was feigned. "You've got this Matthieu!" Tali slapped a hand across her mouth and plopped back to the ground, avoiding her Instructor's disapproving eye.

Tali hadn't prepared an essay presentation like the rest of her classmates; she'd written a poem. Poetry was the only thing she liked to write. Well, except songs, but she never wrote those down.

When it was her turn, she stood again and swayed. Not nervously—she was never nervous in front of a crowd. In fact, she lived for it. She just couldn't keep from swaying, twisting, fidgeting.

Something she should have grown out of by now.

Catching herself, she stopped twirling and stood still, head bowed. Well, not entirely still, that seemed impossible, but she doubted anyone could detect her thumb rubbing the scar on the tip of her finger. She waited until the virtual classroom hushed and broke the stillness with a flourishing arm-raise to recite her poetry:

"The Gods visited me,
whispering in my ear.

special, I thought.
Chosen, I knew.

I waited, fingers twisting in my hair,
like I always do, hoping my secrets
would get caught up there too.

But,
like I always do,
I let my voice boom.

I told them what I had heard.
What I had been.
What I was meant for.

They told me—
They had heard too.
They were destined too.

I screamed—"

Tali was interrupted by the Instructor's stiff hand raise, signaling her to stop.

"What is this?"

"I wrote a performance piece instead of an essay. It still hits all the points in the rubric. Promise." She placed her hand over her heart, the way she used to make promises to her mom.

"That was not the assignment. The assignment was to write an essay, with a beginning, middle, and end describing the transition from the Advancement Age to the Variety."

"Well, see, my poem is from the perspective of a First Gen who thought they were a Chosen One or Elder, just for a second, before finding out about the Enlightening. Also, I do touch on the Variety in this next part." Tali cleared her throat to continue but her eye caught the Instructor's hand again.

He motioned for her to take her seat. "Adapt your poem into an essay and turn it in before the end of the week."

Perhaps he wasn't as charmed by her as she'd thought.

Tali's knees pretzeled her to the floor and for the rest of

the class she sat, head resting in her palms, listening to twelve nearly identical essays.

After class, Tali sauntered around the garden to pick lemons ripe enough for lemonade. Lemon trees didn't grow naturally in the rough terrain of Montana Province. In fact, until the past 200 years or so, nothing did. The great fires had wiped out nearly every essence of life in the mid-continent. But, with the Cavalry assigned to train in the desolate desert, they began taking care of the land and herding livestock in specific patterns to recycle nutrients into the soil structure—or something like that. Tali hadn't paid much attention to that lesson.

Still, the rocky red clay wasn't quite lemon-tree ready. There were large pots with citrus trees and raised beds overflowing with leafy greens around the garden. Trellises with vines creeping up, polka-dotted with red cherry tomatoes or streamed with snap peas.

After all, Andrea maintained the most immaculate garden. Andrea was a dutiful caretaker but, since half of the Marshals had left on the Skill Trip, she was pulling double herding duty which meant Tali and the lemon trees were on their own most days.

Tali kicked the sliding glass door closed behind her, her clay-stained toes leaving distinct prints. She promised herself to remember to wipe down the glass and dropped the armful of lemons onto the large kitchen island like confetti.

They rocked, rolled, and wobbled across the marble-style Sleekstone. Tali froze as she watched them, and a smile beamed across her face. She took a bow for her imaginary audience for not letting a single fruit fall to the floor.

Dancing around the kitchen to gather supplies, Tali was happy and comfortable in Andrea's house as she'd always been. It was hard not to be. The design was somehow natural and ornate at the same time—a balance Tali had recently come to consciously pursue. Andrea was a traditionalist with a formidable knowledge of history and art. The life and home she shared with Mirai, one of the Cavalry Marshals, was speckled with artisan treasures of crocheted blankets across the back of the couch, handmade tapestries hung on walls, ancient recipes that filled the house with unfamiliar scents, and hand-hammered silver rings adorned Andrea's fingers.

But the best thing at Andrea's house was her homemade lemonade. Tali had watched Andrea make lemonade every Sunday for the past six years. She'd always been allowed to help juice lemons and was promoted to designated stirrer after a single year. But it wasn't until three years ago, when Tali turned ten, that Andrea finally showed her the secret ingredient—ginger.

Andrea had taught Tali how to juice the lemons by hand, never with one of the juicing machines, and the same went for juicing the ginger. They used a small white bowl with a raised middle and bumps to grate the ginger on. The ginger juice would pool in the surrounding porcelain trench and then be poured through a cheesecloth to catch any remaining grain, a step which also ensured the secret ingredient remained secret.

This summer, Tali worked on perfecting her own recipe. She'd tried everything—different sweeteners; adding herbs like mint, thyme, or lavender; and even stirred in a spicy chili pepper once. But nothing came close to Andrea's. So today, Tali didn't experiment. She just made Andrea's lemonade and sat at the kitchen counter, drinking it slowly.

"Mind if I have a cup?" Andrea entered from the front door into the large kitchen.

Tali shrugged, still sucking her lemonade through her straw.

"Any surprises I need to know about?" Andrea raised an eyebrow at the pitcher, examining it under the light. She'd fallen victim to the chili pepper batch.

"No, your recipe today."

"Ah." She took a sip. "How was school?"

"Fine. Can we go riding tonight?"

Andrea sighed, leaning forwards to put her elbows on the counter. "This is going to be your year, love. We'll get you on a horse, I promise. But he said no riding. We can ask again when everyone's back from the Skill Trip. Maybe, after remembering how tough it is to teach those poor new Assignments, he'll be in a better mood to teach you."

"Because I'll be a natural?"

"Of course! Look at the way you dance and twirl about, feeling the rhythm of the world. Horses love genuine people—and dancing." Andrea shimmied her hips, mimicking Tali's trademark wiggle.

Tali smiled but traded her enjoyment for a more serious tone. "He's never going to let me ride," she said, crossing her arms. "I'm more knowledgeable about these horses, the herding patterns, and this land than any of these new Drops will be."

"Is that what we're calling Assignments now? Drops? Explain."

"Like you get dropped in." Tali raised her eyebrows and shrugged her shoulders as if the term explained itself. "If I can't ride, what else am I supposed to do all night, every night for the next two months while they ride back?"

Andrea scrunched her face. "You've managed to fill years at this ranch without riding. I think you can manage two more months."

Tali glared.

"We could volunteer you to help get Main Ranch ready? For the new Drops." Andrea's head of black hair, streaked with shiny silver, fell forward as she laughed at Tali's new lingo. "But, how about I cook us dinner first? What are you in the mood for?"

"It doesn't matter, we eat the same thing every night."

"We do not!" Andrea insisted with a smile.

Tali rolled her eyes the way a teenager was supposed to, but she was never actually upset with Andrea. Andrea was right, *and* she was a phenomenal cook—making dishes way better than anything Tali ever ate at her real home. But, sometimes, she just felt like complaining.

"Fine, what do we need?" Tali walked toward the sliding door leading to the garden.

Andrea opened the refrigerator and examined it. "Let's go with thyme and golden oregano. And grab some squash blossoms. I'll use them to pretty up our salad."

Before picking the herbs, Tali walked to the back edge

of the garden, which stretched south into red rocks and dry desert grasses. The transition was jarring. The garden had rows of terracotta pots overflowing with tones of sage, lime, mint, olive, and emerald all of which abruptly halted at the end of the stone patio. Beyond the patio's edge was a never-ending horizon of burned bushes and rock-formation shadows rising from stripes of scorched earth.

Around dusk each night, the desert scared Tali. The heat was predictable during the day, so was the dust and buzzing. But at night, the wind whipped recklessly and cold fell from the sky with abandon. Small animals rushed around, scattering away for the evening. Nothing was in sync or rhythm. It was all just chaos.

But fear didn't make Tali turn away. Fear told her where she needed to grow stronger. On the first night this summer, when she'd recognized her unsyncopated breathing and rustling heart as fear, she'd made herself walk out to the blackened boulder. The second week, she had reached what looked like a snake hole. Three days ago, she marked her bravery with a line in the sand nearly fifty yards from the last garden stone.

Tonight, she would challenge herself to make it a step farther into the nightmarish landscape. She stood warily with her toes at that line. She didn't want to wait another week to take another step. She wanted to be brave today. Now.

She couldn't take a step forward, though. Her body froze, not allowing her to pass the imaginary boundary she had created for herself. This must have been how Matthieu had felt in front of the class. Small, shrunken, shriveled.

That wasn't who she was. She was big, magical, and loud.

She took up space and talked so much that she imagined she had breathed the majority of the air in any room she'd ever been in. Why should it be different outdoors? Why should it be different at night? She was bold. The air was hers.

She took a few steps back, raised her hands, and ran the same steps forward. When her foot reached the boundary line, she flung her body forward and put her hands to the ground, springing herself into a cartwheel—and then another, and another. Her head looped around, her long hair gathering sand, and the momentum pushed her farther than she'd ever been.

Finally, when she was too dizzy, she let her head anchor her at the top of her rotation into a standing position. She stood still and peered at her surroundings for a new marker. What was once a thick tree trunk—now nothing more than charcoal splinters with a faint resemblance to a log—was two paces in front of her. The ground at her feet was empty.

Something howled in the distance.

Tali hurried to the stump, bent down to tap it with her hand, turned, and raced all the way back to the garden.

When she reached the patio's lights, she curled over and rested her hands on her knees to catch her breath. Her lungs filled with excitement staring at the mark of her accomplishment—a black coal smudge on her knee.

CHAPTER 3

NOA

"Do you think this is supposed to scare us?" Alexis asked.

It was odd they hadn't just walked up the stairs or taken City lifts to street level like the other Assignment groups. Instead, they were meandering the Bowl's mechanical halls in an unevenly distributed group behind Decker. The halls were clean and plain and illuminated in a counterfeit hue that emphasized how far from natural light they were.

"Decker doesn't seem like someone with that kind of malice," Noa said. They walked a few steps on their tiptoes to eye Decker at the front of the group. His stride had a playful bounce and hand gestures seemed to be a core part of his communication style. "Probably just the fastest way out of City Centre," Noa reasoned.

Alexis tilted her head and scrunched her lips, still

examining. "Probably," she said. Her suspicion was clearly unresolved, but unserious.

Noa stepped to the side and stopped to untuck her hair from the cross-body strap (it kept getting caught as she walked). Alexis paused with her, which shouldn't have taken Noa by surprise. It was a normal thing to do—basic manners, simple human courtesy. Still, it was nice not to be left behind the first chance this girl had. *Gods, I'm pathetic.*

"I have no idea which direction we're headed, though," Noa said, in an effort to keep the conversation going. They rejoined the group, farther toward the back now.

Alexis tilted her head again, toward the ceiling this time, as if she could see through it to glean their direction. Her internal compass didn't seem to find a pole and she changed the subject. "I want to know what our token is. Kind of disappointing not to receive it in front of our families, you know?"

"Your family was there?" Noa had been too disoriented to notice who Alexis waved goodbye to.

"Just my little brother; he likes to attend the ceremonies. Plus, that was probably my last one for a while." *A joke?* "He just got his first Assignment."

"First one? Hopefully something milder than the Cavalry!" Noa hated the sound of her own voice when she said something she was 'supposed to say.' She sounded like her mom.

"Hopefully not! Isn't that the whole point?" Alexis drew a coral curl from her temple and twisted it in her fingers. "He got Artist, which just—it suits him perfectly. I can't wait to read his dailies and see what he creates."

Alexis was beautiful, especially when she smiled. If she had been smiling when she first turned around, Noa probably wouldn't have noticed the pink hair first. She had dewy, brown skin, sharp brown eyes, apple cheeks, and a wide, brilliant smile. Her smile dimmed. "I wish I could be there for it."

"I'm sorry," Noa said. It was easy to empathize with Alexis. It was likely she'd miss Sami's first Assignment, too. A thick sadness rose to her throat. She coughed to brush it off and changed the subject back. "This token must be pretty good if we couldn't show it off at the Bowl." Noa raised an eyebrow with an encouraging smile, and Alexis smiled back.

They walked the corridors for a while, past doors to storage rooms and offshoots to darker halls. Eventually, Alexis broke off to talk with another group and Noa fell back, grateful for the social respite.

It didn't take long for V to appear beside her.

"Last chance, Lavoie." He gripped her arm stiffly from behind.

"Let go," she said under her breath, trying to shimmy from his grasp.

"No, this isn't just your last chance. It's mine. We're as good as dead and disappeared if we follow this clown." His head gestured to the front of the group, where Decker was leading. Except, they'd fallen farther behind and couldn't see him anymore.

Good, she thought. She wanted nothing more than to disappear after her previous Assignment, and (this way) the Variety was doing it for her.

For most of the three-week Assignment prep—on the

days she wasn't fighting with Vitus Lange anyway—Noa's thumb and pointer finger had twitched toward each other. They'd wanted to touch and open her auto, so she could stare at the message again. After she'd moved past the initial shock and confusion of her sudden Reassignment, she'd found herself reopening the note and smiling at it regularly.

She should have been sad to be assigned to the Cavalry at nineteen, knowing what she knew. If her parents or sister had ever heard the rumor that these far-off Assignments were ways to get rid of problem citizens, they had played dumb. Other than the expected worry that came with this being the first Assignment that required Noa to move out of the family home, they hadn't seemed the least bit concerned. She was grateful for that.

She was even more grateful that the Cavalry Main Ranch was as far away as she could get from the Variety system while still being able to stay in contact with her family. Plus, she'd still have access to food, clothes, her auto, and maybe even transportation. Things that weren't available if she were to abandon the Variety altogether.

And, if the rumors were true, she would never have to be involved with the Variety again. She wouldn't have to spend her life shuffled around on the whim of an algorithm. This would be her last Assignment. She'd be Cavalry for the rest of her life. That didn't seem so bad.

Vitus grabbed her tighter and pulled her back. The last of the group rounded a corner ahead, now fully out of sight. He backed Noa against the wall, towering over her. He knocked her bag from her shoulder and replaced it with his hands, one pinning each of her shoulders against the smooth Sleekstone.

"V, get off me."

"Not 'til you hear me out," he said. "You're not thinking this through."

"*You're* not thinking this through." She swiped at his arm with her hands but couldn't reach with her shoulders locked to the wall.

"I'm serious," he said, his eyes bouncing back and forth between hers. His voice was no longer buttery or smooth, it wavered with desperation.

She examined him closely. His white-blond hair was oily and unkempt; he clearly hadn't showered in days. He was close enough to her face that she could see the early sign of a wrinkle forming between his brows and smell the mint of his breath. *At least he brushed his teeth.*

"No, you're not," she said, raising her chin to him. "You've been fucking with me for three weeks. Pushing those bullshit rumors and snooping around about me."

"I had good reason to snoop—I was right about your last Assignment, remember?"

Noa flared at the mention of her time in the Service. V couldn't possibly know everything she had seen, everything she had done and risked to protect good people from the consequences of exactly what he was suggesting. Her skin flushed in anger. "You don't know anything about the Service. Or me, for that matter. You think you know enough to ask me to run away with you? You think I won't turn you in? Why? You think I'm that charmed by you?"

V took his hand off one of her shoulders to point a finger in her face. His blue eyes jumped around again but, this time, they scattered across her face as if he was taking in her every feature. She could almost see her own face in the way he was scanning her. Her straight lips, her scooped nose, the freckles on her cheeks. He dropped his pointed finger, still pinning her with the other hand, and huffed. "I know damn well you don't like me." He smiled slowly at this, confusing her. As if her not liking him was the goal. "I've been trying to be polite, and I don't care much for you either. But, your experience with the Service —"

Her face must have immediately conveyed the contempt coursing through her veins because he didn't finish his sentence.

"Look," he started again. "I need your help. You've been part of them. You can help us get away undetected and stay that way."

"I'm telling you. It's not worth it," Noa said. But her conscience betrayed her. Loud and clear, she was reminded that Britt and Eli, even after all they'd been through, would tell her she was wrong. It *was* worth it.

"Hey!" someone exclaimed from down the hall.

Fuchsia curls bounced toward them, and V dropped his grip on Noa.

"Let her go, creep," Alexis said, approaching them.

V backed off a few steps, and Noa lifted herself from the wall.

"You okay?" Alexis asked.

Noa nodded.

Alexis turned her body abruptly and headed straight for V.

"Listen to me you oily-haired, lighthouse lookin' bully, don't you ever put your hands on my friend again, got it? I don't care if she gives you a dirty look, or spits on you, or takes away your favorite toy—you'll do nothing but look the other way and carry on with your business. Got it?"

Noa's eyes and mouth were wide at Alexis' fierce response, but V seemed only amused.

Also, were they friends already? Noa didn't have many friends, well *any* really except for her sister, but she was pretty sure you needed to know someone for longer than an hour to call them a friend.

V smirked and put his hands up. "Got it."

Alexis turned en pointe to face Noa.

"Let's go, we have to catch up to the group before we lose them."

They lost them.

Alexis led Noa, with Vitus trailing, down the halls in the direction of the group. After a few minutes, they stopped. Listening for the grumbles, they heard nothing. One dark hallway after another led nowhere to no one. No luck.

V was the first to open his auto to search for a map, but there was no connectivity underground.

After a frustrating amount of time, they finally found an unlocked door leading back to the floor of the Bowl. A few lagging ceremonies were wrapping up, but the stadium had mostly emptied. The three of them climbed the stairs to the pedestrian level of City Centre.

"Now what?" Alexis asked at the top, looking around.

"Noa, I'll ask one last time. Are you absolutely sure you

won't?" V stood towering in front of her, eyes locked as if they were the only two people in the entire world.

He was serious.

So was she. She shook her head *no*.

V huffed. "Then, we head to City Fields. It doesn't take a genius to figure out our tokens were going to be our horses."

Noa and Alexis raised their eyebrows at him expectantly.

"And the only place they'd be able to stable them is at the fields' track," he supplied before heading off that way.

Without a word, Noa and Alexis agreed and followed in the direction of the fields.

A minute later, Noa double-stepped to walk next to V. "So, you're on board now? Just like that?"

V shook his head, dismissing her.

Alexis looked back and forth between Noa and V. "On board with what?" Her animosity for Vitus had disappeared as quickly as it had risen.

"Nothing," he said.

They walked silently for a long time. Besides the looks they got for their odd Cavalry get-ups in the City, Noa didn't mind the crowded streets. The flow of pedestrian traffic allowed her body to move involuntarily, letting her eyes and mind wander to her favorite subject: architecture.

City Centre was scattered with tall buildings floating stories above the walkways below. Crystalline stairs and iridescent lifts whipped around the city, extending and retracting, appearing and disappearing, zipping up and down carrying citizens from the walkways to the buildings. The hovering skytowers shaded the city and the Sleekstone material that made up each building added to the chilly atmosphere. Each structure was cold to the touch, and Noa found an excuse to cool herself against one every time she visited.

She'd race to finish shopping before her sister, resting her back on the stone while she waited. Or, she would fake a pebble in her shoe and place her palm to the icy, smooth surface as she held her balance. Most often, she would walk close to the buildings dragging her hand along behind her, as if she were collecting their chill in her skin.

She'd loved architecture and city design studies in school and was fascinated by the Sleekstone material. It made up every building, though they did not look identical. Many had facades that mimicked the appearance of Limestone, bright and clean. Others, a more serious Green Slate or Emperador Dark Natural Stone. A few of the mid-sized buildings, which were still enormous, chose earthier colors like Rusty Verona Stone or Honed Jerusalem Gold. There were even a few fashioned in Rosa Tea Stone, which appeared light pink. The Rosa Tea Stone buildings were gaudy in photos, but in person they sparkled.

However, even the sparkling Rosa Tea Stone buildings couldn't compare with Variety HeadQuarters. It was the only structure in the entire city made of Imperial White Granite Sleekstone. In the field of floating buildings, HQ was a composite of several rounded towers of varying heights attached to a large round base of steps descending to the pedestrian level of the city. It was nearly a city all its own and the only large structure secured to the earth.

Most architectural engineering texts Noa had read contained at least one chapter that fussed over the breakthroughs in safety confidence following the adoption of gyroscopic stabilization platforms on large scale structures. One to three story family homes? Those were best built on solid foundations on the ground. But skytowers? Those were safer steadying themselves in the actual sky than resting on Earth's shaky surface. Maybe HQ was too big, or had a hole in the middle that compromised its buoyancy, or maybe it was just an art thing Noa didn't understand. She didn't understand a lot of art but could recognize it when she saw it and HQs design was intricate and grand. It reflected the sun's natural light, illuminating and warming the space around it, a haven from the shadowed city beneath.

A faint vibration buzzed inside Noa's wrist. She double tapped her thumb and middle finger to check her auto. The projection appeared and her eyes rolled at the message's subject. She had to stop doing that; an immature habit left over from her teenage years.

It was from Pastor, the hooded figurehead of the Variety. Of course she'd get this message right as they were walking past shiny HeadQuarters. Pastor was nobody, or everybody—a benign broadcaster from Variety HeadQuarters used to send messages.

"Good afternoon," Pastor's voice droned. "This is a reminder that all citizens are required to partake in their Reassignment ceremony, Skill Trip, and Assignment. Your Skill Trip is about to begin. Please find your new Assignment leader right away. Wishing you great expansion." The hood bowed, and the comm ended.

Alexis approached Noa. "I'm guessing we just got the same message?"

"Oh, and from the Pastor themselves. How comforting," Vitus said flatly. He saluted HQ, glowing in the distance.

Noa ignored him and turned to Alexis. "We'll be at City Fields in like twenty minutes, it's fine."

As they turned the corner, Noa spotted her favorite building. It wasn't a giant skytower, but an individual dwelling at the pedestrian level. Kitty-corner to her family's favorite teacart, a small house with a fenced-in yard sat as if patiently waiting for her.

Whenever she was in line for drinks at the teacart, Noa used that time to examine the home. The roof was made of black slate triangles which contrasted the bright white of HQ poking out on the horizon. The house's siding was a khaki color and, up close, revealed itself to be a Polished Fossilized Coral. The front had tall windows reaching from floor-to-ceiling with glass so clear and clean it looked like running water. Noa grew thirsty just looking at them. But her favorite part of the house was the front door. A solid sheet of emerald jade broken up only by the sparkling white geode serving as a doorknob. The house was a piece of jewelry.

"That's my favorite house," she blurted to Alexis.

"Which one?" Alexis asked, squinting around.

Noa pointed and suddenly felt vulnerable that her favorite thing was about to be judged.

"It's gorgeous," Alexis said. "Though, I really imagine you in more of a farmhouse. I'm a high-rise kind of person, personally." She looped arms with Noa again, steering them a little farther from Vitus. "I bet he's an underground bunker kind of person," she whispered, giggling into Noa's shoulder.

Noa smiled.

"Wrong," Vitus said, turning around on them.

Alexis rolled her eyes. It didn't look immature when she did it. "Okay then, where *does* the human form of ooze want to live?" She'd dropped Noa's arm and put her hands on her waist, challenging V.

Vitus let out a laugh Noa had never heard before. It was loose and light. Unburdened.

"Where did you say? A high-rise? I could do that." He raised an eyebrow to her.

Alexis let out a faux-offended scoff. "As if you'd ever be invited."

"If I only showed up where I was invited, I'd never leave the house."

"I bet," Noa retorted.

CHAPTER 4

NOA

Noa had never seen a horse in real life.

In class, the diagrams demonstrating their size astounded her. The texts showed an image of a human standing between a historic, unmodified horse and a present-day horse. The present-day horse was hands taller and wider than the former.

The Librarian's annotations in her text had explained that modern horses were bred for size, loyalty, and intelligence. Historically, horses had always been trusted soldiers; however, with generations of breeding, the modern-day animals acted more like giant domesticated travel companions than brave, allegiant warriors.

"My horse better be drop-dead gorgeous," Alexis said as they rounded the last sports field and neared the stables.

"And white. They have those, you know. Did you see it in the text? White horses? What color are you hoping for?"

Noa didn't answer—her mind was focused on what they were trudging toward: a large muddy track with a long stable lining the top bend. And, likely, a pissed-off Assignment leader.

She ignored that last part and squinted at the stable. It had dozens of stalls (maybe a hundred total) with dividers between them. In front of each stall was a few extra feet of space and a bench to give riders a private area to get ready and space to store their horse's tack.

"I guess it doesn't matter," Alexis continued. "As long as our horses are friends, so we can ride together." Alexis's assuredness in their sudden friendship was as relieving to Noa as having private space to greet her giant horse.

Noa opened her mouth to finally answer about her preferred horse color, but Decker's voice rang across the field before she could respond.

"Get lost, did ya?" He waved to them from the center of the stable.

They hurried their last steps to meet him.

Alexis spoke first. "Sorry sir, we got turned around in the tunnels and made it here as fast as we could."

"That's what I get for challenging the Gods with that bit about never leaving one behind. Only losing three in forty-seven years still ain't bad though." A hint of a belly shook on Decker's midsection as he chuckled to himself.

Noa peered around him at the large stable. About three-quarters of the stalls were full, with large brown heads bobbing into view. In the stalls closer to where they stood, new Cavalry members were tending to their four-legged partners by brushing and feeding and cooing saccharine greetings to the giant beings. Some were even starting to lead their horses to the track. Despite being far behind, Decker didn't seem rushed as he instructed their small group to line up and face the stables.

"Let me give you three the gist of my speech, then one of my Marshals will take you to your stall." Decker pointed to the three Cavalry Marshals pacing the stable before continuing. "Your horses are your Assignment tokens. As with any other token, they're your responsibility and yours to keep. Between us, back when the Cavalry was more of an actual cavalry and less about ranchin', the tokens were just the saddle. But no one seemed to have any use for 'em after. They're big and clunky. Unlike these giant horses here." Decker slapped his hip to punctuate his wheezy laughter, then straightened himself into a more serious tone. "Breaking those human-horse bonds over and over again took a toll on the old herd though. These are fine creatures. Bred for loyalty. Once they are yours, you are theirs. Of course, when the Variety reassigns you, you do have to return the saddles." Decker bent over, wheezing once again at his own joke.

Noa wasn't sure if the punchline was that they had to return the saddle, or that they would ever be reassigned.

"Anyway…" Decker whistled. The command caused the three Marshals to turn and pace toward them. As they got closer, each seemed to size up Noa, Alexis, and Vitus.

Noa sized them up back. The older Marshal walked with a light step and had a soft face. He was the least threatening. The other two, a woman and a young man, strode casually and confidently, assured in their tanned and toned bodies. The woman's sleeves were rolled up to show off her muscle definition. Her hair hung neatly in a low ponytail accentuating sharp features. The man's shirt was tucked in and taut from his broad shoulders to his belt. He wore his hair shaggy, complimenting his round face and stopping just above dark eyes.

The dark eyes landed on Noa, and she flicked hers to Decker, who was speaking again.

"Just a last word or two. We have a lot of ground to cover over this Skill Trip, and you're going to have to rely on your equine partner. You'll rely on them even more once we're back at Main. You'll borrow their athleticism, their strength. Right now, they're stronger than each one of ya." Decker pointed his finger at Vitus, then Alexis, and lingered pointing at Noa. "They've just done this trip on the way up from the ranch, though, and returning with you and your gear will be tiresome. More than once, they'll rely on you to march forward. Remember how much you need them in these early days and repay the favor from time to time. Treat them with as much respect, honor, and friendship as you would a human partner."

No punchline that time.

Decker unclasped his hands and swung an arm out in the Marshals' direction. "My Cavalry Marshals for this trip are Sai, Amar, and Mirai." *Amar had the dark eyes.* "They'll introduce you to your horses and help get you settled. I'll be around supervising. We only have as much time as we have daylight to get you walking, trotting, and cantering around this track. You'll need to do a few laps of each pace. Once you have that down, we'll head out for a quick ride to our first camp and reconvene as a group for dinner." Decker waved his hand, and the three Marshals stepped forward.

Mirai approached Alexis with the grace of a hummingbird, pointed and firm in her direction yet seemingly floating. She wore the same misshapen riding pants as everyone else, but they didn't look terrible on her. As she strode past, Noa caught a glimpse of a muscle in her forearm making a defined line. Noa flexed her own wrist in different angles to see if she could create matching muscles; they were nowhere to be found.

Sai, the soft Marshal, held a neutral, borderline pleasant look on his face and took Vitus.

Amar barely moved, just shifted his weight to stand in front of Noa to claim her. She remained still as the others walked away. Amar's eyes weren't scrutinizing her now as they'd done before, they were busy scanning something on his auto. He scratched at the facial hair shadowing his jawline and neck, shut his auto, and raised an arm to direct her to follow him. Even through the thick layer of khaki, the motion displayed the muscles padding his chest. Without having to check, Noa was pretty sure she didn't have those muscles either.

When they reached the stall, he finally spoke.

"Alright, Droplet, get in there. You have to greet your horse, not me." His voice was low and firm, making no effort to ensure she could hear him as she caught up from behind.

Noa blinked. "That's it?"

"His name is Trax," Amar said. "You can use that."

Noa took small steps into the covered area directly in

front of Trax's stall and made a mocking face at Amar when she knew he could no longer see her expression. She was brand new to this and he just stood there, unhelpfully, as if she knew how to approach an animal that was several times her size.

She found the feed bucket on the ground but stumbled in her motion to pick it up and tripped over a haphazard piece of wood.

Who would leave a piece of godsdamned wood in the stupid stall?

Embarrassed, Noa looked behind her. Amar was already gone. He really didn't care that she was on her own. When she turned back, she was closer to the stall than she'd realized and found herself staring at the backside of a horse on the other side of the gate.

Trax was an entire head taller than the other horses with a dark sorrel coat that was almost black, except that his black mane contrasted slightly. She couldn't see his face yet, but she could tell he was striking. And something about his energy told her that he was certain to be wild.

She stepped back and crossed her arms to better examine his position. Trax had exiled himself to the farthest corner and faced the wall. With feigned confidence, Noa reached into the feed bucket again and held out a hand. She cooed and clicked at him—to no avail. When she reached her fist back into the bucket to rustle the feed, Trax let out a startled whinny.

Perhaps he wasn't obstinate, just hard of hearing.

She made shushing noises to calm him, and he moved to face her—but only slightly. Through one of his black marble eyes, he took a good look at her and jerked his neck back to face the wall.

Offense spread across Noa's face. Recalling some nonsense from her prep class about horses being sensitive to emotion, she threw her shoulders back, buried her frustration, and took a different approach.

"Trax, Trax. Come here, boy. I'm Noa, your new owner. Well—," she rethought the term, "—your new partner." She continued in a sing-song voice, snapping her fingers and clicking her tongue. "Come here. I've got some food for you!"

Trax ignored her.

"Come on, Trax. Come over to meet me."

No response.

"Then I will come over to meet you." She unlatched the pen's gate and was face to face with his larger-than-her hind legs. She stepped toward him carefully. "We're going to go on an adventure together and become great friends." She rambled moonily and sarcastically, so that he would hear her as she approached his head, which remained buried in the corner.

Trax's ears flickered. He clearly heard her. He even seemed to understand how ridiculously desperate she sounded and turned to take account of her. He swooped his neck and let his brawny body follow the motion. He loomed over her and tilted his head. Noa's reflection was tiny in his eye.

As tall as Trax was a few minutes ago, he was now taller. His head twitched and, in reflex, Noa's body dropped to the ground into a crouch—a significantly more pathetic stance than she had planned to greet him with. She stretched a fist full of feed in his approximate direction and turned her scrunched face away from him. Slowly, she opened one eye and determined that her position was exactly what one would define as a cower.

I am cowering to this giant creature. I am cowering to my partner.

Trax realized this was the wrong move at the same time. His heavy head swung and connected with Noa between her shoulders, knocking her off-balance from the crouch. Before she could look up in defeat, Trax's head came down for another swing, this time railing into Noa's side and jamming her own elbow into her rib cage.

She shuffled to her feet and put her back to the stall's fencing. Trax let out a cry of discontent. Noa did not want to be around for another head swing and made a dash, closing the gate behind her.

Noa dusted her hands on her pants and fled from the stall, still trying to get the knocked-out wind back inside her lungs. She peered into the nearby stalls to spy on the others—she couldn't be the only one struggling. When the immediate surrounding stalls didn't give solace, Noa paced. In the other stalls, greeting a horse didn't look so hard. The other Drops were petting noses and holding handfuls of feed. Alexis, who beamed and waved when Noa strode past, was even brushing the mane of an enormous white horse with grey freckling.

The three Marshals stood in the center of the stable's aisle, just a few stalls down. Amar locked eyes with her before walking toward her. Noa turned and raced back to her stall covering and stood flush against the wall, hoping he'd assume everything was fine and not come over.

It was definitely not the move of someone who was fine.

When Amar walked in a few seconds later, he was so focused on his auto that it gave her time to adjust to a less precarious position. He tapped his thumb and finger twice to close it and looked around to find her standing behind him.

"What kind of trouble are you getting into here?" His eyes scanned her pants, and he craned his neck to see the hay dust on her backside. She turned her body away to hide the dirt.

Noa gestured to the colossal creature stubbornly facing the wall and mumbled something about how he must have first-day jitters.

Amar widened his stance and took an invasive measure of her, his eyes rolling down, all the way down, and back up to her cheeks. She was sure they were bright red. "It's Trax who is nervous?"

"Yes," she said, fidgeting with the extra fabric at her hips and unwilling to admit fault so early. "I did what everyone else did—offered him some feed, cooed at him. And, when I went into the pen he, uh, pushed me out." She shrugged and pretended to believe the difficulty wasn't a big deal. Inside, her body corrected her outer nonchalance, as it always did. She vibrated, and her eyes tumbled around the stall trying to catch something to lock onto.

They locked onto Amar's eyes, and she was surprised at the comfort she found in them. His face didn't reflect empathy, but his eyes did—deeply. Waves of calm poured over her. Her shoulders drooped and her fingers stilled at her sides. Her only upset now was seeing his eyebrow raise and knowing he wasn't fooled by her pretend composure.

Amar broke the gaze as if it were just a passing glance and offered a handful of feed into the stall. Trax turned to greet him right away, slurping the feed in one mouthful.

Instinctively, Noa's eyes rolled.

"Did you just roll your eyes at me?"

"What? N—no," she stammered. "It was for Trax, not you."

"Watch out, buddy," Amar said to Trax, offering another handful. "She's got it in for you."

Noa laughed nervously.

"Here, you try now." Amar nodded toward the feed.

Noa swallowed and offered her hand.

Trax let out a snort and a stomp of defiance, turning back to the wall.

Amar dropped his head to stifle a laugh. "You really did not get off to a good start." He paused and let the smile fade. "Do you mind?" He pointed at the space next to her.

She shook her head, and he moved to stand behind her. When Amar inhaled to speak, his chest expanded, and his shirt brushed her shoulder blades. Goosebumps rose on her arms.

"Together," he said.

Amar moved his palm to form a cup with hers. The feed pooled together, and Noa concentrated on keeping her hand still and pressed with the right amount of pressure against his.

Amar clicked his tongue, and the noise rang in Noa's ear. Trax responded immediately, taking the feed from their cupped hands. A smile spread on Noa's face, and she bounced onto her toes, causing her body to lean fully into Amar's.

He quickly stepped back. "I think you can take it from here." He tapped his fingers together again to open his auto and pull up the day's schedule.

"We're asking everyone to move to the track soon, but you should take a few more minutes to bond with him before you take him out." He sounded official and serious again, his calm lost to the focus on his auto.

She nodded. "Thanks, Marshal."

Amar looked up, and his face gave a small, nearly imperceptible scrunch.

Did he not like being called Marshal?

He gave Trax another pat on the nose and walked out of the stall.

Once Amar was out of sight, Noa offered Trax another handful. Trax met her gaze and jerked his head back to the corner.

CHAPTER 5

NOA

Hours passed and everyone (except Noa) practiced their walks and trots around the track. A few Drops bonded with their horses quickly and were already cantering—they would be the first group to head to camp with Mirai. The second group would head out with Sai a little later. The last and slowest group would leave at the end of the day with the remaining two chaperones, Amar and Decker.

Noa was certain to be in the last group. Fistfuls of oats, hundreds of pets, a nose brush here and there—all got her nowhere.

Decker popped into the stall. "Take him for a lap."

"I managed to slip in his bit," she said, "but he won't let me near him with the saddle." Noa's face flushed hot. She was holding up the entire group.

"Just lead him then. Some horses take a little extra time to warm up, that's all."

Decker's pity felt heavy.

"Nothing to worry about darlin'," he said.

Noa managed a stiff nod. *He's only trying to help,* she reminded herself.

Begrudgingly, Trax followed Noa around the muddy track, stopping every few steps. Each time he stopped, she would beg him under her breath until he started moving again. She made herself small, hunching over more with every step and growing tinier every time someone trotted past. She shrunk to her smallest when V and Alexis cantered by.

Alexis slowed and settled in Luna, her large white horse, to a walk beside Trax and Noa. Luckily, Alexis waved V to carry on, and he abided.

"Your horse is huge," Alexis exclaimed sweetly, bringing attention to something other than the fact that Noa was not actually riding yet.

"He's a stallion, alright. A little stubborn though."

As if on cue, Trax stopped again.

Noa forced herself to ignore her anger and bite back the muttering that wanted to wiggle out of her mouth. She didn't want Alexis to see her so easily rattled. Instead, she gently brushed Trax's face, coaxing him forward.

"No kidding," Alexis said. "I got off easy with Luna. She's a dream. And white like I wanted!"

Noa forced a smile as Alexis patted the speckled horse's side.

"I'm sure you both will find your pace soon," Alexis said

and let her voice trail off.

Noa nodded, and they walked in silence for a quarter of the track—Noa on the ground and Alexis far above on her horse. Finally, Alexis broke the lull with an urgent voice as if she were spilling a secret she'd held for too long.

"V and I are heading to camp with the first group." Alexis sighed, relieved of unnecessary guilt. "I'll save you a spot for your tent?"

Noa's inner embers roared, and she had to choke down sparks before she could speak coolly. "Sure, that would be great. Thanks, Lex."

Alexis beamed and took off, catching up to V. Their group was already gathering to head out.

As Noa finished yet another walking lap, she mentally listed all the steps she and Trax needed to take before they could head for camp. The longer the list grew, the faster sparks rose in her throat. They finally came out, pouring from her eyes, hot, heavy tears gliding quietly down her cheeks.

Then flames erupted from her mouth. "This is an embarrassment," she yelled at the side of Trax's long face. "You're better than this. I am better than this. We need to show everyone that we are better than this!"

Trax didn't seem to care about their reputation and walked again, without Noa's lead.

She yanked the reins and stopped them both, standing firmly in front of Trax, dwarfed by his massive height.

She caught the eye of another Drop trotting by and lowered her voice, pulling her head in close to him. "Please. This is the first day, can't we just get through this? Can't we just put on a saddle and get to camp?"

He ignored her and continued walking, kicking up dust that stuck to Noa's face, damp with sweat and fallen tears. But they managed that entire lap without stopping, and her face began to cool. Maybe Trax had some empathy after all.

After their third walking lap, Decker helped Noa put the saddle on. As she rode her first uncomfortable lap, the sun began to set. The second group left for camp, then the third began to form.

Decker stayed by her side and filled an hour of the early evening with riding instructions like, "Roll your pelvis as an extension of his movement," and, "Don't produce the walk with your seat."

For more laps than she could count, she kept her hands "independent" and held her thighs "tight without bouncing" and directed her body to perform a million other foreign movements. Fortunately, she seemed to be able to do these movements in sync and without much effort or thought. There was hope that riding Trax could be easier than befriending him.

Too bad they'd gotten such a late start.

After rounding her first lap of trotting solo, Amar and Decker waved her over, pulling her aside just before she reached the stable. She'd been so excited to nail her first trot, she hadn't realized she was the only one still on the track.

"You have to get your canter down here before you hit the trail," Decker said. "But it's also getting late, and I don't want the others to miss the first dinner." He looked over his shoulder to the third and final group packing up. "I'll take this group to camp, and Amar will hang back to help you. I'd stay, too, but it's tradition I give a little speech at the first dinner." Decker grabbed imaginary suspenders and tipped his chin up.

The news of being left behind was an anvil on Noa's chest, crushing her.

Decker must have seen her face crumple because he clasped a hand on her shoulder. "Amar's a great Marshal. You might even make up some time on the trail and still be able to join us for dinner."

Decker smiled, the deep crinkles around his eyes forming natural folds. Noa could barely breathe through the heaviness.

Without waiting for her reply, Amar mounted his own horse and pulled next to Trax. He clicked his mouth and heeled his horse, starting both his horse and Trax forward. The effortless maneuver might as well have been a thousand anvils falling from the sky—she was buried in the weight of insecurity.

"This is Mozart," Amar said, petting his horse's shoulders softly. The motion calmed Mozart—and Noa too.

During the rest of their twilight training session, Amar didn't speak. When he needed to correct her riding technique, he spoke in grunts and points. He didn't coddle her, compliment her, or make pitying remarks that they might make it back in time for the first dinner. She knew they wouldn't. His silence was honest.

Trotting to cantering was a much larger leap than walking to trotting—the speed and movement of the canter was exhilarating. She wanted to holler out in excitement.

Soft voice, mon ange.

Nineteen, leaving home, possibly permanently, and Noa's

mother could still shush her. She bet Alexis's mom let her whoop.

By the time the sky was a singular color in darkness, Trax and Noa had held it together long enough to finally head to camp. There wasn't much city beyond City Fields and Noa was grateful. She and Trax were not quite ready to ride through crowded streets with lifts whizzing overhead. Sidewalks quickly turned to gravel paths, which led to wild fields, then trees, and then darkness.

"How are we going to find our way in the dark?" Noa's voice came out louder than she'd anticipated, and she mentally cursed herself for being the first to break their unspoken silence agreement.

Even a short way out of the city, the landscape was cloaked in quiet.

"Our eyes will adjust in a few minutes," Amar replied.

Noa was thankful for his quick response. She wasn't sure he would respond at all and maybe the awkwardness would have hung in the air for the rest of the ride.

"The horses' eyes take a bit longer to adjust," he continued, "but once they do, they can see better than us. Once you're posted at Main Ranch, you'll do a lot of your riding at night." He paused and added, "Also, this is day one, so the path to camp is straight and flat. Not much we need to see."

"Sorry we're missing dinner."

He shrugged.

"Hm," she huffed, turning away at his non-response.

She felt him watching her, hopefully noticing her dissatisfaction. Suddenly she was self-conscious again. Why did she have to be like this?

"I don't mind a quiet ride instead of the big dinner," he said. "Once you've been part of the Cavalry for a while, everything else seems loud. Especially a few days in the city and an afternoon with all of you." A small smile flashed on his face.

Noa returned his smile, relieved, and gave a quiet laugh. She wanted to ask him a thousand questions about the Cavalry. What was it like to be alone at night in the middle of nowhere? Was the desert beautiful or scary? How far could he and Mozart ride in a day? How fast could he ride? Did he love it?

Instead, she asked nothing.

Amar paced Mozart up and looked questioningly at Noa. Trax mimicked the speed and Noa nodded back to Amar.

Amar hastened again.

Upon her command, or perhaps just out of collegiality with Mozart, Trax matched Mozart's pace. Noa's entire body was strained from the day's riding. Her stomach muscles were exhausted, her arms slow, and her thighs chafed. But she didn't let up because she could finally start to feel it—a connection with Trax. At a faster pace, her body became an extension of his movement. They rode through the dark, wind cooling the back of Noa's sweaty neck, and Noa finally understood what Decker meant by "borrowing" from Trax. Trax was giving her something she didn't earn—a free ride— and she was grateful for it.

The two horses slowed and lined up to ride together again.

"Decided to finally turn it around, huh?" Amar joked.

"I guess." Noa forgot to make her voice light, distracted in recalling each awful moment of the day.

"Don't worry so much. You'll bond. And when the difficult ones finally trust you, the connection is that much better. It's a cliché for a reason, trust me."

She decided she would. "Was it difficult with you and Mozart, at the beginning?"

Amar let his head fall back, relaxed, as he examined the sky, like he might find his response among the stars. "Horses are intuitive," he explained. "If you're unhappy or untrusting, they reflect that right back at you."

She wasn't sure if he was talking about himself or her. "And you were...both?"

"Mmhmm." He rolled his head from the sky to look directly at her. He didn't look angry at her for prodding—if anything, his expression was soft.

Noa took him in, in the moonlight. His dark hair rested just above thick eyebrows that were un-scrunched for the first time all day, and his full mouth was no longer pulled tight. His dark eyes startled her now that the expression on his face matched their empathy instead of contrasting it.

"Why?" Noa asked. "Why weren't you happy about Cavalry?"

Amar looked away, took a deep breath, then released a forceful exhale like he was dragging the story up from somewhere deep inside himself. "My first Assignment was at HQ and, when I was reassigned to Cavalry... Yes, I was unhappy." He paused. "No, I was pissed." He swept his hair out of his face with one hand and let out a soft, relieved laugh.

"And why were you untrusting," Noa pressed before she could think not to; it was probably too much.

A singular scrunch returned to his face—the same one as

when she had called him Marshal. *It was too much.*

To her surprise, he answered.

"Same reason, I guess."

Noa nodded as if she understood—she did not. She knew why *she* didn't trust her Reassignment, but she doubted he had the same reason. She bit her lip, withholding what she really wanted to ask. He'd been sparse with his words all day and even kind of mean to her earlier. From a day of brief encounters, she didn't know much about him or his personality, but his calm was undeniable and infectious. She had to know.

"Have you always been this calm?"

Amar laughed, and a genuine smile crossed Noa's face. *Calm.*

"No. And it's not a permanent state." He raised an eyebrow as if challenging her.

She petted her giant horse's side. "I need to harness some of it for Trax's sake."

"Oh, I know. I saw you on the track. Yelling like that will not get you very far with horses." He paused, then added, "Or humans."

She wiggled in her jacket thinking about him watching her get upset earlier. She felt Amar read the embarrassment on her face.

"It gets easier, I promise."

When they finally arrived at camp, Noa and Amar rode past rows of canvas tents—only a few of which still had lanterns on inside. They dismounted their horses at a grove of trees. In the moonlight, they untacked and brushed down Trax and Mozart. Noa remembered most of the routine from prep class but glanced over at Amar a little too often to make sure she was following the right steps. Luckily, Trax was easier to untack than he had been to saddle. Still, Noa tied him up for the night near Luna, hoping he might learn a bit from her easy-going nature.

"I have to check in with Decker," Amar said. "You okay to set up your own camp?"

Noa finished hanging the saddle over a tree branch, picked her bag up from the ground, and turned to face him. He was standing much closer than she'd thought.

"Yeah, I'm good," she lied. She had no idea how to set up camp. "Thanks again for staying behind with me."

Amar nodded, keeping his eyes on her. Finally, he said, "See you tomorrow, Noa."

She liked the sound of him saying her name.

As he walked away, he turned back and cupped hands around his mouth to amplify his whisper, "Don't forget to stretch!"

CHAPTER 6

NOA

As soon as Amar's steps faded, Noa dropped her pack to the ground. She needed to drag, not carry, the heavy duffel.

She trudged down the aisle of tents toward a brightly lit haphazard-looking fort and the sound of Alexis' voice. As Noa approached, it was clear three personal tents were strung together, with little to no thought, to construct this messy shelter.

"Alexis?"

"Noa!" Alexis said from inside. Her arm swept a canvas panel aside, nearly knocking the whole fort down. "You made it!"

Inside, V and a few other Drops sat on the ground. Each had one hand up, bracing the shelter from collapsing, and another with a handful of playing cards.

"Be right back," Alexis told the group. "I'm going to show her where to set up." She slid on her boots, tucking the wrapping into the heel as she stumbled out of the tent. Alexis reached to grab Noa's bag from her hand. "Here, let me take that."

"Thanks. Normally I'd protest, but I don't know if I have a single muscle that isn't made of rock right now. I thought muscles were supposed to hurt the day after?"

"I know, riding horses hurts! Good thing it's fun though." Alexis chatted about the dinner Noa had missed, Decker's indulgent fifteen-minute-long speech, and mostly about the boys in the tent. Before Noa could get a word in, Alexis unclipped the tent from the outside of Noa's pack and said, "Here, this is the spot." Alexis laid out the tent footprint. Noa remembered that step from her prep lessons. "So, tell me all about your night."

"It was so awful," Noa confessed, the words tumbling out of her mouth. "Trax is so stubborn and—"

"Not Trax. Marshal Amar? Or as I call him 'Amarshal'." Alexis laughed at her clever nickname, then made suggestive eyes at Noa. "How was your moonlit ride to camp with the handsome cowboy?"

Noa thought about his calming presence and her name coming off his lips. "It wasn't like that. He was just helping my pathetic efforts."

"Sure, sure. He couldn't possibly be interested in all this." Alexis waved her hand up and down Noa's body. "Oh, or this!" Alexis held Noa's chin in her hand and released it dramatically. "Give the rest of us a chance!"

Noa curtseyed with her hands pulling out the wide hips

on her pants and laughed.

An evening with Amar had been nice but if Noa said gratitude prayers every night before bed like her parents had taught her to do, Alexis's name would have been first on the list that night.

After staking the tent, Alexis pleaded for Noa to join for cards—even going so far as to bribe her with the few snack crumbs the boys had left uneaten. Noa declined, too tired for any morsel of food or company.

As Alexis turned to leave, Noa spoke. "Hey, Lex?"

"Yeah?" She turned around but continued walking backward in the direction of the other tent.

"Thanks." Noa looked straight at her, hoping her eyes said what her mouth couldn't.

Thank you for saving me a spot. For adopting me. For being nice. For carrying my bag. For being here.

Alexis raced back the few steps and hugged her.

"Whatever, hon. See you at breakfast."

Lying in the pitch black on her thin sleeping pad, Noa listened to her surroundings. She couldn't hear the others playing cards as she had expected, only the nature around her.

Bugs buzzed against the fabric of her tent and frogs croaked in the distance. She closed her eyes and focused on the sound of the branches overhead rustling in the wind. As she drifted to sleep, the branches appeared in her mind. Toeing the line between dream and waking reality, the branches transformed from gnarled bark into silky galaxy filaments and cosmic webs. The spacey swirls performed in her dreamscape, flashing here, striking there, glowing with deep celestial greens and blues and purples.

The dream pushed on, her body frozen, but her mind tiptoeing between wakefulness and deep sedation. Her vision zoomed on a single stellar supercluster, and her bones vibrated as it began shaking. The coolness of space pressed against her flesh, reminding her of dragging fingers along City Centre skytowers.

Then, she heard it: a chorus of whispers, a symphony of pleas.

The voices crashed through her sleeping mind in waves, and she drowned in the dark, deep sea—she tried to decipher the sounds, and her waking body tried to catch a breath. After what felt like an eternity of being crushed by the never-ending swells, she finally began to distinguish some of the voices and let the others barrel past her.

I don't know if I can do this anymore, came a small, weakened voice.

I want to go back, shook a deep prayer.

He has to get better, through sobs.

Does she love me?

Show me a sign.

Just let me be okay.

Get me through this.

On and on the pleading prayers continued. With each voice, the dark sea of Noa's mind lightened. It glowed brighter until she could feel her physical body squinting in pain. The light burned white and grew hotter until she broke into a sweat. Her teeth ground until her jaw ached, and her ears filled with pressure.

Finally, the voices muffled and vanished.

Her body relaxed, and she opened her eyes. It was morning.

CHAPTER 7

TALI

Gasping, Tali pulled herself to the edge of the reservoir, crawling over reeds and algae scum until her torso settled on land. Her feet, still scrambling to push the rest of her body out of the water, couldn't find grip on the silty mud shore. She choked and reeled, vomiting lake water from the depths of her stomach as her gangly arms clutched the soil and yanked her to solid ground.

When the wheezing finally subsided, and her stomach stopped cramping from her hurls, she lay on her back and stared up at the early morning sky.

She'd swum in the reservoir plenty of times. In fact, she'd learned to swim as an infant and had only gotten stronger since moving to Main Ranch. She could hold her breath for longer than some turtles—but today, something had taken over her.

She hadn't even been diving or having contests with the turtles. Only swimming lazy laps to burn off pent up energy before the day started. Something had scared her or distracted her or—no—she'd heard something.

And she'd stayed underwater too long trying to hear it—to make sense of what had been spoken to her by such a familiar voice.

That was it. Something had been calling to her.

Or someone.

CHAPTER 8

NOA

Noa lumbered her stiff body out of the tent, Amar's words echoing in her mind.

Don't forget to stretch.

She let out a deep sigh and threw herself into a forward fold, dangling her arms and hair lazily in the grass.

While partially upside down, she slid on her boots and wrapped them up her calves like gauze. The design of the boots was tricky—two straps winding around the heel and ankle first, then up the calf. They had to be layered neatly, but once in place, were more comfortable and flexible than anything she'd worn before.

Outside, the row of tents was being packed up by tired bodies. Alexis's spot was already empty and, fearful of being in last place again, Noa hurriedly packed and headed toward the smell of a hot breakfast.

In the center of a crowd of chairs near the serving table, Alexis's head—more watermelon than fuchsia in the morning sun—bounced. Her face was blocked by V's head, also bobbing in laughter.

At the sight of V, Noa turned before she was noticed and headed for Trax in the grove. It wasn't until she was walking through the trees that her stone muscles ground against each other enough to warm and loosen.

In the distance, Luna nodded up and down chewing on grass. The tree next to the large white horse, where Noa had tied Trax, was horseless.

Noa threw down her bag. "What the—? No, no, no, no, no, no!"

Her eyes darted around the shaded field. Trax, who stood out even in a crowd of other incredibly large horses, was nowhere among them.

What did I do wrong? Did I not tie the rope correctly? Does he really hate me this much? Noa tried to force an optimistic thought. *Perhaps Amar or Decker untied him and*—but before she could form any kind of glass-half-full scenario, reality set in.

Trax's rope hung from the tree, still tied—with a gnawed-through end.

Noa scoured her surroundings for signs, clues, hope—anything. Beyond the field of trees, a thick line of bushes had a clear path stamped through it. For a moment, she considered not going after him. She imagined telling Decker that Trax had run away, and Decker taking pity on her and giving her a nicer, smaller horse.

But no, Decker wouldn't give her a new horse. Likely, he would let out his best Cavalry whistle, and Trax would come running. Noa would be the laughingstock for the second day in a row. She had to get Trax back by herself—and before anyone noticed he was gone.

Following the downed foliage, she stomped into the bushes. Trax had chosen to wade exclusively through prickly bushes, and Noa's forearms gathered scrapes as she followed his trail. She found the other length of broken rope caught in some branches and pulled it free. A few paces in, just far enough to be camouflaged, Trax stood stoically next to a large tree.

A river of lava gurgled in Noa's throat. "What? The tree I picked wasn't good enough?" she spouted. "You needed to stand next to *this* tree, out here, all by yourself?"

Trax turned his head toward her, letting her know he was unphased by her frustration.

She stepped forward and he stepped back, maintaining the distance between them.

"Don't you dare! You are coming back with me right now. We are not doing this again."

Trax turned so his hind faced her as it had in the stall. This time, though, he didn't have a corner to bury his head in. Noa walked a wide circle until she stood in front of him. She stepped toward him, and he leaned his weight backward as if he might go up on his hind legs.

"Shit."

She could not have him taking off farther into the woods,

or worse, sending a hoof toward her head. She would have to channel some of Amar's calmness before she approached again.

It was hard to remember what calm felt like. It had only been one measly day, twenty-four short hours since she left her family in The Bowl. The confidence she'd had in herself that short time ago slipped like sand through her fingers.

Noa closed her eyes, inhaled, and pulled her shoulders away from her neck the way she remembered them falling so effortlessly yesterday. The tension in her muscles released, morning air filled the deepest part of her lungs, her blood flowed and then—calm.

She opened her eyes to find Trax's nose breathing hot air onto her face.

Startled, she flinched, trying to create distance between her and the large head that had hurled at her yesterday.

"Good boy?" She reached an unsure hand out and gently stroked his face. She looped the extra length of rope around his neck and stepped backward, out of the woods. One foot, then another. Her breath hitching when she reached the end of the rope's length. Trax took a step at its tension, and she exhaled. "Oh, thank Gods."

"Where are you two coming from?" Alexis asked, brushing Luna.

"Trax didn't like the tree I picked out for him last night," Noa said, pointing to the gnawed rope still hanging from his neck. "He found his own in the woods over there."

She laughed. "How independent of him." Alexis took her brush to the side of Trax's neck and gave him pats.

Dust and pollen plumes rose from his coat. Trax leaned into Alexis's brush and a pang of resentment struck Noa's guts. She clasped a hand to her belly and shifted it away.

"I was saving you a seat at breakfast but when you didn't show I grabbed you this." From her jacket pocket, Alexis pulled an oat brick in clear wrap and handed it to Noa. "It's not as good as the hot meal but better than nothing if you're hungry."

"Starving," Noa said, making grabby hands to take it from Alexis.

Alexis stopped brushing and stared at Noa's feet. "Where did you learn to wrap cowboy slippers?"

Noa followed Alexis's gaze to the neatly wrapped, olive green fabric with a taupe sock poking through only at the top of her knee. She compared Alexis's feet and found a wrap with large gaps, making her calves candy-striped. At the top of Alexis's knee, big bunches of the fabric were tied into sloppy bows.

"Here." Noa knelt in front of her friend. "The trick is to wrap them around your ankle twice before going up your leg. Since you're smaller, you might even have to do it three times."

The elastic fabric unraveled easily, and Noa pulled the two strips to either side of Alexis's leg. Alexis dug her toe into the ground to keep her balance. She was strong, like the gymnasts Noa had treated at the hospital during her Nurse Assignment—gymnasts were always spraining wrists and ankles; another reason why she was so good at wrapping the boots, it was just like applying a flexi-cast. Noa crisscrossed the wrap around Alexis's leg and up her sock, careful to lay each pass with an even overlap. At the top of Alexis's shin, Noa stuck the strips behind her knee and gave her two pats to let her know she was done.

Alexis gave her leg a shake and widened her smile at the sight of her two very differently wrapped boots. "Ever heard of a rancher who couldn't tie their own shoes? Huh?" She did a jig pointing to her feet and laughed in a way that made Noa desperate to take herself less seriously.

While Alexis attentively tried to mimic Noa's work on her other foot, Noa untied the gnawed rope from Trax's abandoned tree and used a fisherman's knot to fasten it to the other half still hanging from his halter.

When Decker called everyone to saddle up for the day's ride, he explained that there were no mounting blocks in the trip supplies as there had been at the riding track. Instead, everyone would need to either learn running mounts or find mounting blocks in nature. He pointed to two large boulders and the mounting lines formed.

Having the two largest horses, Alexis and Noa got in line for the slightly taller boulder. When it was Alexis's turn, she aligned Luna to the boulder and braced to mount. Her eyes bounced from foot to stirrup, calculating how to bridge the distance.

V cut in from behind Noa and hopped onto the boulder with Alexis. Noa watched as he swayed a little too close to Alexis before he laced his hands together to give her an extra step into the double-rung stirrups. Alexis swung her leg around and landed in the saddle, blowing a kiss to V before gliding away atop Luna.

"Care to be a good Samaritan twice today?" Noa asked before V hopped off the boulder.

To her surprise, he nodded and stayed on the rock.

She lined up Trax on one side and stepped up next to V on the rock mount. She put one foot into V's hands, and he let out an audible groan.

Her eye roll was immediate. "I haven't even put my weight on you yet," she said too defensively.

V laughed, which caught her off guard. It was the same light laugh he'd given Alexis the day before.

Was he actually being friendly?

Noa pushed her weight into his fingers, not being particularly gentle about it, and lifted herself. She slid her other foot into the stirrup but, as soon as she tested her footing, Trax countered and pulled away from the boulder instead of leaning into it.

Noa swayed in the air, transferring her weight back and forth between the stirrup and V's hands, unsure who would give out first. Trax took a full step away and Noa fell, twisting her foot out of the stirrup just in time but knocking V off the boulder in the process. They tumbled together, landing in the grass.

"What the hell!" V pushed her off him.

Well, at least that sounds more like him. "Sorry," she said, rolling onto her knees. "Trax is a little difficult." She stood to dozens of eyes on her, including Amar's. Noa ducked her head and blushed.

"Ugh. Let's just try it again." He huffed and rose to his feet. "What?"

"Again," V repeated, which only confused Noa more.

The Vitus she knew would tell her to forget it. That Noa was on her own. Quick to temper. Quick to storm off. But kindly offering to help her again? Well, not *kindly*, but still.

What kind of magic had Alexis worked on this guy in under a day?

Trax stood a few steps away from the boulder as a line of impatient Drops and horses waited. She couldn't risk Trax throwing a second tantrum, so she calmed herself first. In front of the boulder, she repeated the routine of closing her eyes and taking a deep breath. When she opened her eyes, Trax was once again nose to nose with her.

Her eyes bugged. "That will work," she said, petting the side of his face.

They tried again and this time Noa didn't test her weight. She placed her foot firmly and swung her leg over, landing in the saddle.

She let out a "Woo!" of excitement, and a few others cheered too.

"Thanks, V. That was really—" she took a second to find the word, "*decent* of you."

He waved her off, hiding a smile. "Other people are waiting."

She couldn't believe it. He was going to stay on the boulder and help everyone in line.

Magic.

CHAPTER 9

From: The Variety
Recipient: Noa Lavoie
0000 hrs., 08.06.0253

SKILL TRIP CHECK IN: *CAVALRY*

You have successfully completed your first week of *CAVALRY* Skill Trip. Optional Daily Reports are highly encouraged during Skill Trips. Wishing you great expansion.

NOA

Noa tapped her fingers to dismiss the notification and scratched at her forearm. The Skill Trip path south was remote and had been mostly outside of auto connection; feeling its buzz for the first time in a few days made Noa's skin crawl.

Supposedly, no one else ever felt their auto except when they were supposed to. She'd asked about it every chance she had gotten after hers was implanted; until her parents told her to stop. She still examined people's palms, searching for a scar that matched the one she'd gotten from implantation.

When Noa was ten, the auto grew from her hand into her wrist and arm, as it was designed to. Only, hers clumped as it branched and left a raised bump on her wrist and a ridge on her forearm. It wasn't particularly noticeable, and she had learned to ignore it. Until it itched. Then she wanted to tear it out with a feverous desire.

"Bug bite?" Mirai asked, pulling beside Noa and Trax.

Noa stopped scratching at her arm. "Must be," she lied. Mirai had started checking on Noa regularly after she'd found her at the back of the herd on her Marshal rounds on day two.

Trax and Noa rode well together, for the most part, if they were isolated. But, as soon as they joined the group, Trax was restless and disobedient. The key was finding a riding style that gave Noa confidence and allowed Trax to feel in control around the large group.

Or at least that was what Mirai had told her.

Noa loved Mirai's teaching style. She didn't just repeat the same instructions over and over as Decker did, nor did she limit her direction to pointing and grunting like Amar. Instead, Mirai suggested and showed Noa a dozen tricks and gave her time to practice them on her own between loops until they found something that worked.

Now, a week into the trip, the wild idea that finally clicked was riding reinless.

At Mirai's command, Noa had unclipped the reins and directed Trax with her legs and hips alone. Their jilted movements had smoothed, and Noa was able to lift her head from Trax's immediate next steps and take in her surroundings.

The wind rushed past her face, stinging her cheeks and carrying the smell of dust and grass. The soft blue sky poured perfectly around them, uninterrupted by a single wrinkle or cloud. Tall, lush green pine trees barely scraped the far-off horizon, in contrast to the pale trail they followed. The grassy fields rolled in the wind, a beautifully dizzying motion. Noa anchored her sight to a large stack of boulders artfully piled like ancient ruins of an unrecognizable planet.

Her eyes started to stick at the bottom of her blinks.

"Your riding seems to be going well, but you look like you might fall asleep," Mirai said.

Noa returned a dazed half-smile. She was exhausted from yet another strange sleep the night before. "Sorry, Marshal. Just tired."

"I told you, Mirai's fine."

"After all your help this week, I didn't catch your horse's name," Noa said. "What is it?"

Mirai's horse had a chestnut coat the same color as Mirai's hair, but with one white patch on its chest. The horse was also similarly lean and toned—and an appropriate, normal height.

"This is Reyna," Mirai said. "The best equine partner a girl could have." She petted Reyna and fidgeted, straightening the reins.

The play on reins and Reyna was cutesy, but the horse was a perfectly regal-looking creature, and Noa figured that must be the connotation.

Noa thought ahead to the days and weeks of their journey yet to pass, and the tougher terrain on the horizon. "What do I do when I need to control—I mean, direct Trax? You know, more than just a wiggle or a heel?"

"That'll be up to the two of you to figure out. Every partnership is different. If you can't use reins, you'll have to find another way to communicate."

"He seems to like me when I'm calm," she said.

"Guess you'll have to start meditating then, huh? Actually, if you need calm, you should hang out with Amar, he's the Zen-master—"

"I noticed," Noa said, accidentally speaking over Mirai who was still finishing her thought. "Sorry, what did you say?"

"Oh nothing." Mirai waved her off.

It sounded like, "*Until he's not.*"

Noa bit back a question, thinking she'd better not press it. She straightened in the saddle and looked ahead to the trail group. The riders had spread out, speckling the landscape now decorated with sparse tufts of grass. Unfortunately, the horses kicked up so much dust, she couldn't spot who she was looking for.

She turned back to Mirai. "You seem pretty composed too. Is there some sort of Cavalry trick I need to learn?"

Mirai let a small laugh escape. "No, not unless you wake up early enough to practice with Yori," she said more to herself than to Noa. "The solitude mellows everyone out after a while, but that's not to say it won't rile you up first."

"Really? I can't imagine you riled. The whole Assignment

suits you so perfectly. You make it look effortless." Noa's stomach twisted with uncertainty. Her compliment might have been too forward, so she changed the subject. "How long have you been part of the Cavalry?"

"About five years now."

"And how long from 'riled up' to 'Cavalry calm'?"

Mirai's head fell back in another free laugh, and some of her silky hair escaped her braid in the movement.

"'Cavalry calm,' I'm going to use that." Mirai traded a friendly look. "When I first started this Assignment, I was resentful, upset, and—" She paused and started again. "I trust in the system. I really do. But I also know the Variety's job isn't to make each of our individual lives the best. It's supposed to allow us, as a collective, to experience as much as we can. I think that includes disappointment and pain. And when I was heading into this Assignment, I thought that was what I had been dealt."

Noa hadn't considered this viewpoint before and tried on the assumption for her own circumstances.

Her first Assignment as a Nurse had been fine. It was exciting in the beginning but quickly settled into a perfectly boring Assignment that didn't suit her at all. The Service was intense from day one and, ultimately, scared her.

If Mirai's theory was true, perhaps the Cavalry wasn't the punishment she'd guessed but, instead, a reward. Maybe this was the Assignment where she could finally experience a kind of passion and belonging. Then again, maybe the Variety needed someone to experience an entire life of boredom and anger and resentment and failure and loneliness. And perhaps she was that person.

"Anyway, I was dead wrong," Mirai continued. "And now I've put down some roots, as best as we all can, and found a new kind of happiness that I didn't have in my pre-Cavalry life."

Mirai petted Reyna, and Noa unknowingly mirrored her by petting Trax's shoulders and running her fingers through the tips of his black mane.

"It will get better for you too," Mirai said. "In the Cavalry, we like to say the days go by slowly, but the years pass quickly."

Mirai's eyes burned on Noa trying to make contact. Noa met her gaze, and Mirai softened. "I know your first couple of days have been tough, but trust me—the weeks, months, and years will fly by before you know it."

Years.

Noa's throat tightened, and she found herself holding back tears she didn't understand.

By early evening, Noa grew tired of riding alone. Mirai had taken off for rounds hours before and, though Noa and Trax were getting along better, they hadn't had the energy to catch up to anyone else.

A sliver of orange sunset was still visible on the horizon as the sky turned to a cool gloaming. The night air rushed in her lungs, stimulating her blood to pump more wildly.

Trax sped up, and the skin on Noa's arms tightened as the cold wind dried the day's sweat. Breath cycles, heartbeats, and hoof pounds created a symphony of movement. The sky darkened, and her forehead relaxed, relieving her eyes that had squinted and watered all day. She swiped at dried tears with dirty fingers.

Noa and Trax slowed in unison. She reached for the canteen at her side pocket and struggled to unscrew the cap with numb fingers. The water spilled over her hand, but she kept pouring, eager to get the dirt and dust off her palms.

She dumped the remaining water into a cupped hand and threw it at her face, using the inside of her shirt to wipe it clean before tucking the empty canteen away into the saddlebag. Her eyes adjusted to the dark night and found Amar ahead. Noa urged Trax closer to pull alongside him.

"I was starting to wonder how far back I'd have to drop to find you," he said.

"You callin' me slow?"

"Well, we're not at the front of the group, are we?" His eyes smiled. He'd joked with her a few times over the week whenever he caught her at the back of the herd.

Noa let out a pretend huff of offense. "I'll have you know that I've had private lessons."

"Must have been a great teacher," he said, his chest puffing.

"Yeah, Mirai is a talented mentor."

He clutched his heart. "Ouch."

"Look, no hands." She held them up, demonstrating the reinless riding.

"Impressive."

Her mouth bunched to one side, holding back a smile.

They rode quietly for a moment but, with her energy surging, Noa couldn't hold the silence for long.

"Can I ask you something?"

He considered and nodded casually.

"I meant to ask the other night, but I wasn't sure if it was appropriate…"

"But, now, you think it is?"

She stiffened and answered firmly, "Yes."

He turned to face her, straightening in mock importance. "Alright, shoot."

She had forgotten about his arresting eyes until they stared right at her, sparkling with the reflection of a crescent moon.

"Um, you said, you said," she stammered. She breathed and started again. "You said you worked at HQ, and that was one of the reasons you were unhappy or maybe untrusting coming into this Assignment." She paused to see if she'd crossed a line, but he showed no reaction. "I don't like to talk about it, but my last Assignment was with the Service."

"Oh." Amar's posture collapsed out of the playful form and their gaze severed.

"I know." Noa thought she'd better get her words out before she lost her guts. "It didn't end well. And, if it helps at all, I hated it."

Amar was silent then said, "It helps."

"Anyway, I guess I just wanted to tell you that, about me, before I asked you."

"Uh huh, spit it out, Noa." His tone had grown impatient.

"Do you think it's true? The rumor about placements in Cavalry?"

"How do you know about that?" Amar adjusted his seat but maintained a steady demeanor.

"Well, for one, Decker has alluded to it in his speeches more times than I've ever heard it whispered."

"Yeah, he's not as subtle as he thinks."

"But my Assignment in the Service involved a lot of casework. I had to interview hundreds of people who lived outside, and I heard all sorts of wild ideas…including the rumor that certain Assignments were used as punishments. To distance problem citizens from the rest of society."

"Hm."

"Well," Noa prodded, "is the rumor true?"

"I guess that depends on what you did to get yourself Reassigned."

CHAPTER 10

NOA

After days of riding solo, practicing riding without reins, and coaxing Trax closer to the pack—Noa could finally ride with her friends. Unfortunately, that also meant there was now an audience to witness her body sway like a jellyfish tentacle to keep Trax moving without reins. She wiggled while everyone else rode stiff and steady, but at least she could direct his movement and pace.

"Your turn," Zahira said to Noa. "Your choices are Coffee Barista, Technologist, and Mariner."

"What? Those aren't good choices," Jo protested from his horse.

Noa had figured out that Jo was the gangly blond, but it had taken her a while to tell him apart from Jash. The two looked nothing alike, but she had either blacked out or not paid attention the first time Zahira introduced them, and she'd only latched onto the detail that both of their names started with J.

Now, she could tell that Jo and Vitus were closer in appearance. Both tall and blond—but while V looked sharp, angular, and certain—Jo was soft, warm, and unsure.

Zahira, Jo, and Jash had all been in the third Assignment prep class together. Zahira was unmistakable and memorable—she was perfectly fit for her horse, Chance; both touting glimmering brown complexions, dark brown eyes, and black hair. Zahira's features were as sharp as her mouth, and her thick, arched eyebrows drew attention to high cheekbones and striking facial contours.

By contrast, both Jash and Jo had softer features on round faces—which was about the only thing they had in common. Jash was stocky and muscular with olive skin and the stubble of a beard he'd clearly started before this Assignment. Jo was fair, tall, and had no stubble to show even after a week of no shaving.

Noa shifted her focus from Jo's absent beard to the choices Zahira had laid out for her. A Technologist was a stable and respectable job, but Noa had always found micro-engineering subjects beyond boring. A Coffee Barista could be okay. She could learn intricate drink recipes and live a stable, private life. Except for all the folks she'd have to serve every day who might be needy and nosey. That might get tedious. Being a Mariner was a dangerous job; life on the open ocean conducting research, fishing, and repairing hydro-vehicles. Noa didn't know much about oceans, but they seemed far from boring or tedious.

"I would never be a Technologist," Noa started. "I would be a Coffee Barista for a short while, and I would be a Mariner forever."

"What?" Jo's jaw hung open as he stared at her. "You wouldn't want to be a Technologist ever? That's the one that I thought was the obvious forever choice. You get to work with all the systems and invent and learn all the time."

"See? It was a good set," said Zahira, sticking her tongue out at Jo. She turned back to Noa. "Your turn to pick someone and give them three choices."

Alexis and Zahira had already gone, so Noa landed on Vitus.

"Fine, but you better give me some good options," V said after she called on him.

"Your choices are Educator, Healer, or Farmer." Proud of her thoughtfulness, Noa imagined her choices would give a peek into the chooser's values. Did they care about knowledge and the future of a generation, wellness and compassion, or hard work and solitude?

"Those are the worst choices ever," V said. "I'd like to never be any of those things."

"You can't *not* choose," Alexis said. "Plus, I think what you choose will say a lot about you." She gave Noa a wink.

"Fine," V grumbled. "I would never want to be a Healer, I know that. I guess I wouldn't mind being an Educator because you always get to be right. So, I'd be a Farmer for a bit and an Educator forever." His shoulders straightened into a prideful position, settling into his imaginary future.

"That's not surprising," Jash said. He rolled his neck and shoulders as if he were easing the tension V's response had aggravated in him.

He was riding particularly close to Noa, so it wasn't her fault she noticed the cascade of muscles that flexed in his display of disagreement. *Jo the blond one, Jash the bearded one,* Noa repeated to herself. Upon closer examination, she remembered Jash. She had seen him around mealtimes when she'd had the energy to eat in company and remembered noticing he didn't seem to like V very much. She liked that about him.

"Oh yeah, and you're so much deeper? Alright, you're next." V's voice raised a decibel louder. "Your choices are Sex Worker, lowest rank Analyst at the Sleekstone manufacturer, or Service Member." V spit the words out as if he were casting these Assignments on Jash's future.

Noa refused to look at V, but she could feel his vindictive gaze burning through her on his last two words.

Jerk.

"You think those are bad choices?" Jash scoffed. "That's easy. I would never be the Analyst at the stone plant because I can't imagine I'd get much exposure or expansion from that role. A Sex Worker is literally the world's oldest profession, and I would be able to connect with so many people in a short time, and I'd be a Service Member forever." Jash beamed about his new future.

"What? Why?" Noa blurted before thinking.

A Service Member forever, he'd said. She hated that about him.

The Service was advertised as a noble Assignment, held in high regard for bringing citizens from around the world who had been born outside of the Variety into its protective, elite umbrella. What wasn't advertised—but everyone knew anyway—was that the Service did a lot more than that. They brought the Unevolving (or UEs for short) into the Variety through any means necessary. And not just those born outside of it—those who had intentionally made the choice to leave it. *Especially* those who'd made that choice.

Noa had seen firsthand the means that Service Members deemed "necessary." They were anything but noble. You had to be complicit, or just plain ignorant, to not know that.

Noa relaxed her contorted face, trying not to appear overly disturbed or curious. She could still feel V's gaze and, from the corner of her eye, caught his stupid smile as he watched her fidget.

"At the end of the day, the Service is made of people the same as any other Assignment," Jash answered. "The more good people in it, the better the Service would be, and the better the Service, the stronger the Variety, the faster we evolve. Plus, I bet you get so much exposure from that role— you'd meet so many UEs, and they'd all be strange with wild stories."

He isn't ignorant, Noa thought. *Just complicit.*

His attitude, although a little tactless, was admirable. But he was dead wrong.

Vitus laughed. "More exposure than a Sex Worker?"

Everyone replied with scrunched faces and audible groans.

"How far do you think we've been riding each day?" Alexis asked the group, changing the subject.

"Let me check," Jo said. He tapped his finger and thumb to open his auto display. "We started from City Fields so…" He mumbled some percentages and calculations. "Given that we were moving slower for the first couple of days…I'd say we have completed about ninety miles so far."

"You like numbers, huh?" Alexis laughed. "I'm glad we started off slow. If we did this pace the first few days, I don't think I would have made it."

Seeing everyone nod in agreement, Noa warmed. It hadn't just been hard for her.

"I can't believe you can even connect out here Jo," Zahira said. "My auto was acting all spotty even yesterday at camp." Zahira tapped her fingers together to check hers. "Nothing."

"I'm not connected right now. I just have the map saved, and I can tell where we are based on geographic features," Jo replied.

"Now you're just showing off," Jash said.

"Features like what?" Noa asked. She'd never needed to read a map before—or at least not one without jammy stops, pod stations, and street names.

"Like the streams and lakes, those show up on the map. And our elevation. I have a topographical view. You should save one on your own auto at the next town. I like to check mine in the morning to see what's ahead on our day: flat ground, incline, decline, mountains, lakes. Things like that. Helps me feel like I know the day's plan."

"That's brilliant," Zahira said, and Jo's face lit up at the compliment. "When's the next town?"

"Assuming our pace is relatively steady now, we'll be there in five or six days."

"Do you think we get to shower when we reach a town?" Alexis asked. "It's already been a week, and I cannot imagine what I'm going to smell like in another five days."

"I bet we all get to bathe in the lake tonight," Jo said.

"Excuse me?" Zahira blurted.

"Camp is next to a lake instead of a stream about once a week, and tonight is one of those nights. I just assumed those were our bathing days," Jo said.

"I don't care if it's a shower at the palace or a dip in the lake, as long as I get all this sweat and dust off of me," Alexis said.

"Same!" Vitus and Noa said in unison. They exchanged eye rolls and Alexis laughed.

Jash straightened in his saddle. "How about we speed things up and try to make it to camp early tonight, so we can get in a game of cards?" He and his horse, Adobe, rode even closer to Noa and Trax. He leaned in toward her. "You going to actually join us for a game tonight?"

"If I have any energy left," she said, pulling away. She was hopeful to have one full day of good riding with Trax. She petted his neck as if to knock on wood and not jinx her wishful thinking.

V pulled to the front of their group and led them away at a faster pace. "Alright, let's ride."

The group maintained their lead on the other Assignments throughout the day. Many of the others had also formed their own riding groups. A group of older Assignments rode steadily at the back of the riding train. A group of middle-aged men often sprinted past everyone in a gallop and then slowed for hours at a time falling back into the middle.

Decker and one Marshal, usually Sai, rode steady in that middle. The other two, Mirai and Amar, wove through the train checking on the riders. Occasionally, Amar would check on their group at the front. He never spoke to Noa any differently in front of the others or let on that they'd had conversations about anything more than horses and trail times. But, whenever he caught her eye, she felt like he held it for a moment longer than normal.

Near the end of the day, Amar made his final round to the front.

"How is everyone feeling?" he asked.

"We're good, man. Just ready to hop in that lake," V said, wiping sweat off his forehead.

"Ah, you already know it's a rinse day—good. We're hoping to get everyone to camp a little early, so we have more time for bathing and dinner tonight. You all up for a faster pace? You can get in and out before the crowd?"

"Hell yeah! Let's do it," Alexis called.

Zahira and Jo both hollered in support too.

Jash reached his hand out as if to tap Noa for her attention. "Race you there?"

Noa squinted and lifted a corner of her mouth, not quite smiling. Jash was cute in the late afternoon sun glow—his long brown hair stuck to his round, sweaty, dimpled face. The dust grime looked gross on everyone, but he managed to make it look rugged.

Dust and sweat suited Amar, too. Jash and Amar kind of looked alike. Noa glanced at Amar who was grimacing at an unwitting Jash. She changed her mind—they looked nothing alike. Jash looked like holding hands and city strolls and butterflies. Amar looked like hands in her hair and sprints under the stars and aching.

"Noa?" Jash repeated. "Wanna race?"

"Huh?" Noa shook away the thought before facing Jash, flushed now from more than the sun. She laughed. "Race? Do you know how fast Trax is?" she asked, not really knowing herself.

"No, but I bet I can still beat you." Jash readied himself and lined up Adobe with Trax.

"No fair, I want in on this," Alexis said, pulling Luna to Trax's other side.

V added to the line. "How about we make a friendly bet?"

Zahira and Jo joined too.

"Like what? You want my extra helping of granola tomorrow?" Noa teased.

"No," V said, shooting her an overly sour look before turning to Alexis. "How about the last one to camp has to get in the lake naked first?"

"Oh, I like it," Alexis said.

"Fine," Noa interjected, "but don't hate us when we all laugh at your naked butt, V." Noa knew she and Trax could ride fast, and she didn't care all that much about nudity.

Amar pulled ahead. "You're all getting in the lake either way, so I don't care who's getting in first. Also, I'm faster than all of you, so you'll know you're at camp when you see the giant lake and me, setting up my tent."

With that, Amar and Mozart accelerated to a full gallop in a few short strides. Mozart was not as large as Trax or Luna, but Amar rode like a professional, and they all watched as he faded into the distance.

Alexis broke their collective trance and yelled, "Go!"

The horses worked up to a canter and quickly to a clunky gallop, spreading farther apart. Amar was already far ahead, and they were not gaining on him, even with their increasing speed. Vitus's horse, Whalen, took off the fastest, and they were in first place for a short while until Alexis came up behind them with Luna. Zahira and Jo were behind them, and Jash and Noa trailed in the back.

Jash tried talking to Noa, but she couldn't hear him over the hoof beats. She steered Trax with her hips and created more space for herself. Leaning forward, she petted Trax's muscular shoulders and directed him to take off.

His hooves beat the ground, and her heartbeat increased, aligning with his. When he worked hard for her, she felt it in her own body. Sweat dripped down her neck and between her shoulder blades like she, too, was running as fast as she could.

Noa set her eyes on the horizon where the sun was just touching the earth. Her mind cleared, and she focused only on her breathing. Long inhale and longer exhale. Flames rose in her throat again—like when she'd wanted to cry on the track—but, this time, they didn't spark in anger or try to force their way out of her mouth. Instead, the heat worked its way down past her lungs, into her stomach and turned into a white-hot orb.

She could feel the phantom sun taking up space inside her body. It wasn't heavy—it was light and nice.

Her vision fogged, tranquility washing over as she bumped around on the ride. Trax's hooves flickered in her periphery, spitting up dirt flecks and dust. Birds sang their twilight songs in branches just off the trail.

The sounds faded until the world was on mute.

Ahead, the sun set on a blurry horizon, transforming into a white orb, like the one she felt in her stomach. It grew larger and floated closer, eventually taking over her vision and transporting her.

Where was she? Where had she just come from?

She couldn't remember, and didn't care, falling in love with where she was *now*. It was hot, the light searing until she couldn't withstand it. She lay back into a cold pool, plunging her body below an icy surface.

She loved it here.

It was the place of Gods and grandparents and souls and songs.

She wanted to share it with the world.

White light cast through the water's surface, evaporating the pool and a heartbreaking emptiness overcame her. The space faded from memory and the orb from her stomach, in tandem. Like a dream, she clung desperately to hold on, but the harder she tried, the faster it dimmed, and the smaller it shrank.

Heartbeats, hoof pounds and bird songs became clearer once again. Then, something muffled called to her.

Who was that?

She listened more intensely but was exhausted and gave up when the last morsel of white light was blanketed in darkness.

CHAPTER 11

NOA

"Noa! Hello? What is going on? Noa! Look at me!" Tears streamed down Alexis's face. Something was wrong.

Noa heard the words more clearly now as the sunset came into focus. It wasn't orange anymore. The sun had fallen below the horizon, and the sky was now the soft yellow and light blue of twilight. Hoofbeats and muffled words rang in her ears.

"Please, look at me!" Alexis cried. She and Luna fell behind Trax, not able to keep the fast pace.

"Alexis?" Noa whispered to herself. Her clammy hands gripped tight to Trax's shoulders, his body pounding into hers with each of his strides.

She needed to sit up. She raised her torso, and the wind whipped her face; they were going too fast. Suddenly aware,

Noa released her heels from the hold they had into Trax's barrel, and he slowed.

Alexis pulled alongside, tears still carving rivers down dust-covered cheeks."What's wrong?" Noa asked her friend, pulling her weight back until Trax slowed them to a stop.

"What's wrong? What do you mean, 'What's wrong?'" More tears filled the carved banks on Alexis's cheeks, now a shade paler than usual. Her lip quivered before she spoke. "Noa, what just happened?"

Last Noa remembered, Alexis and Luna had been far ahead, leading their pack. However, in their chaotic sprint, Noa and Trax had caught up.

Now, they were stopped at a lone oak tree at the precipice of a rolling hill that arched down toward the dark lake and grove where they would spend the evening. Alexis hastily dismounted Luna coming to Noa's side and offering a hand to dismount.

Dazed, Noa missed Alexis's hand and instead gripped her entire forearm as she dismounted. "What do *you* mean?"

Amar approached, running from the grove below, already settling at camp as he'd predicted. "What happened?" he asked. "I heard screaming." His eyes bounced between Alexis and Noa, landing on Alexis who was in tears. "Alexis, are you okay?"

"Am *I* okay?" Alexis trembled as she ushered Noa from standing to sit at the base of the large tree. "*I'm* fine, Noa is the one who—who just left this planet. Noa, what happened? You were riding so fast, then your body went limp, and your eyes glossed over, and you couldn't hear me. I thought you were going to fall off and get trampled."

Noa felt sick.

She remembered the white space.

She remembered—ascending.

To the next plane of existence. Where humanity had been told they could reach all those hundreds of years ago by the Gods themselves.

But that couldn't be true. No one had ascended since The Enlightenment.

She couldn't trust herself. Could she?

A few seconds ago, it had felt so normal and real—but now, with Alexis and Amar staring at her, she couldn't piece together what just happened. She had so clearly known the truth of her experience, and now she doubted that's what had happened at all.

"Noa?" Alexis demanded. She was loud and upset.

"I don't—I don't know. I'm so sorry," Noa stammered. Guilt sank into her for scaring her friend. She started sweating. "I don't know what happened." Her head fell back against the tree and her eyes pooled with tears. She was heavy, full to the brim with leaden blood and confusion.

Alexis moved her arm from Noa's shoulder to her forehead. "You're burning up."

Amar felt Noa's arm with the back of his hand. "Let's get you cooled off in the lake, and then you can go lie down."

"I'll set up her tent and grab her a change of clothes," Alexis said, hopping up into action. "Meet you by the lake."

As Alexis took off, Amar helped Noa stand and put her arm around his shoulder. He rested his arm around her waist, gripping just above her hip. She might have been able to walk on her own but was weak and dizzy and didn't mind the support.

As they hobbled toward the lake, Noa heard the others arrive at camp. She recalled their bet and tried to listen to see who had arrived first or last but couldn't tell. The thought of the bet made her shiver. Not because of the stakes but because that conversation felt like it had happened so long ago. Years ago. Lifetimes.

When they reached the shore of the lake, Amar unraveled from her.

"Can you get undressed?" His strong brown eyes barreled down her weak hazel ones.

"Pardon?"

"Unless you want wet clothes tomorrow, you'll need to get undressed." Amar began stripping his own clothes. Quickly and mechanically. He'd clearly undressed lakeside at twilight many times.

The near-night shadows suited his body just as well as the sun and dust had suited his face. He was all rounded muscles and angled limbs and lines—sharp and soft at the same time.

"Yeah, okay," she said, watching Amar slip off his boots.

Slowly, she took off her shirt and bent over to unravel her boots. When she leaned forward, blood rushed to her head, and she wobbled. Amar clasped her arm holding her steady, preventing her from falling forward any farther. Gripping her arm, he lifted her back into a standing position.

"Let me do that."

He crouched and unraveled her boots. His fingers touched the inside of her knee when he undid the tie and brushed her again at the back of her ankle when he slipped each one off her foot. Noa gripped his bare shoulder to steady herself.

He was already down to his underwear, and she stood barefoot and topless with only a sports bra and pants on. She unbuttoned her pants and shimmied them over her hips. She managed to pull them off without bending over to avoid needing his help again.

She went to remove her bra, but Amar made a sound.

"What?" she asked, her fingers still gripping the elastic under her breast.

"We don't—you don't have to." He cleared his throat and resumed speaking in his Marshal voice. "We're alone and you're not feeling well. It would be best if we didn't completely undress."

"I'm not a prude," Noa said defensively. And she wasn't. She had no problem getting undressed in front of others, she'd done it thousands of times in physical education lessons and Nurse Assignment locker rooms. Nudity was normal, natural. She knew that. But then again, she was relieved he'd given her an out from stripping in front of him. "Fine," she continued, dropping her hand from her bra.

Under different circumstances, she would have delighted in his intense gaze, having those eyes to herself. Instead, the worry behind his expression exhausted her.

"Let's get you into the water. You don't look so good."

She could only imagine how red and puffy her complexion was. She swiped her long, frizzy hair from her sticky forehead and nodded. She wasn't like him. Sweaty didn't look sexy on her. It made her look sloppy and sickly.

His arm found her waist again, supporting her as they

moved toward the water, his fingers now landing near her bare belly button.

"This okay?" he asked.

She wanted to lean away, not feeling decent enough to be close to him, but his skin was cool. As cool as Sleekstone in the shade. She let out a faint, "Mmhmm."

They waded in, and the water steamed as it met Noa's skin. Waist deep, Noa threw herself forward, letting the dark water cover her. Her hair fanned behind her, finally unstuck from the dried sweat.

In her swan dive, Amar lost his grip on Noa's waist but had somehow managed to keep ahold of her arm, his hand cuffed around her wrist. Noa enjoyed being submerged underwater and anchored to him. The silence beneath the lake's surface released a pressure from her mind she hadn't realized was there until it lifted.

When she was absolutely sure she was out of breath, she rose to the surface to face Amar.

He watched her intently, as if trying to read something on her face.

She happily watched him back as he loosened his grip on her wrist and finally let go of her completely.

"Are you feeling better?" he asked.

"I don't know."

How could she tell him that she'd visited the next plane of human existence—a new form of consciousness, the place some thought to be the afterlife or the next life. How could she tell him she'd just had the best experience of her life? That it was more than any of them ever knew? How could she explain that she was still coming down, and that he was the only thing keeping her suspended from crushing reality?

"I think so," she finally decided.

He put his hand on her, keeping them tethered together. In her movement she floated inches farther away, but his hand guided her back to him. They kept some distance, but their hips brushed in the water as they bobbed, and her blood rushed.

"Noa, what happened?" His voice was deep with concern. "Alexis was really upset, and it sounded bad."

A lightning storm passed through her brain as she thought of the ways she might brush off the conversation. But when her gaze rose to meet him, she wanted to tell him everything. "I don't think you'll believe me."

"I'll believe you."

Another promise.

Noa's mouth opened, but words escaped her. Her mouth fumbled but no sound came to fruition. She investigated their surroundings; it was just them and the frogs croaking in the distance.

He said he would believe her. Her dad would tell her she'd have to give Amar the chance to live up to his word. *Trust is built, Noie.*

"I think," she started. "I think I ascended."

He didn't react. Even Noa, who unwillingly logged the micro-movements and reactions of everyone around her, couldn't detect a single flinch.

Before she knew it, more words poured out. "On Trax, when I was riding, I visited, or was visited. No. No one was there—it was a place? Like a state of being. I don't know how to explain it, but I was... more. Not figuratively, either. I mean that my world, my body—I was—" She raised her hand to gesture 'up' and 'higher' and 'elevated'. Her eyes sparkled looking at her hand as she remembered.

Then, her eyes widened, welled with tears, and dropped to Amar's. In shock of herself, her palm fell to cover her own mouth. She was frightened of her own words. She sounded lost.

Amar didn't react.

That made everything worse. She went from unsure to dissociative and shaking. Through tears, she tried to find something along the shore to anchor her. Small trees with craggy roots. Glimmering ripples. Footprints in pebbly sand. A log. Her breath went shallow; this wasn't helping.

She closed her eyes.

"Breathe," Amar said, his grip tightening on her wrist. That was it. That was the anchor.

"I can't explain how I know," she continued, her shoulders dropping in resignation.

He looked above her head to a small moon and let out a deep sigh. His eyes returned to hers, and his fingers gripped her tighter. "I believe you."

Heaviness lifted from her in that moment, comforted by his single hand.

So, it had been real.

Now that she'd told someone, and he believed her, maybe she could believe it herself.

Alexis rushed the lakeshore with the rest of the riding group. Given their hurry, she must have told them what had happened. Amar and Noa pulled away from each other, and Noa felt cold in the water by herself.

Why does he believe me? The thought nagged her. Sure, she'd let him hold her in his strong arms when she was on the edge of faint and contemplating her entire reality, but they didn't know each other that well. Not *that* well. She would have to think it through later. In the sudden presence of others, she didn't want to talk anymore about what had happened.

"I guess Noa beat us to it," V said, pulling his shirt over his head at the same time as he kicked off his boots.

Alexis and V, both equally unshy, were the first to be fully stripped and swim out to Noa and Amar. Jash was next, followed by Zahira and Jo. Zahira because she was trying to cover her body as she undressed, and Jo because he was meticulously folding his clothes into a pile. Noa and Amar treaded water as everyone invaded their space in a circle under the moon's light.

"You alright?" Jash asked as he swam across the circle to approach Noa.

"Yes, how are you feeling," Alexis almost shouted. "I told everyone how you started not feeling well after you beat me here."

So, Alexis hadn't told the others the full extent of what happened. Noa smiled at her, grateful for her friend's intuition to keep the incident a secret. For now, anyway.

"Fine. I just overheated," Noa answered.

Zahira whistled. "That horse is fast! You came out of nowhere. I cannot believe you can ride so well with no reins. Especially since—" Zahira stopped herself.

"Since I was the worst new Assignment?" Noa finished for her and laughed.

"Well, yeah—sorry."

"It's fine, I can barely believe it myself. Turns out that Trax and I are good at riding fast but not so good at taking things slowly."

"I like that in a girl," V said, pulling Alexis into him with one of his arms.

Alexis ducked under the water and spat some at V when she popped back up.

"That's enough from the two of you," Zahira said, splashing them both. "We're supposed to be cooling down."

Noa shivered, and her empty stomach gurgled. "I think I'm all cooled down, actually. I'm going to head in."

"Me too," said Amar. "I have to help set up—"

"I'm glad you're okay," Jash interrupted Amar.

Noa waded past Jash. "Thanks."

"We'll be right behind you," Alexis said. "And we can help set up dinner too, Amar."

Amar got out of the water first. "That would be great, thanks."

As Noa walked behind his silhouette, she wondered if he would turn around and offer to help her...or even just look at her. She *was* nearly naked and dripping wet after all.

He didn't.

He crossed to his clothes and began to re-dress. Noa went to the pile of clothes Alexis had brought for her. She fought to get out of her wet bra and managed, more gracefully, to pull the dry shirt over her head. When her head poked out of the top, she caught sight of Amar turning his head away quickly—he *had* been looking at her.

"Sorry," he whispered.

She smiled as she pulled the top taut, happy to have caught him.

Once fully dressed, he stepped closer to her. "Are you coming to dinner? I can have Alexis bring some to your tent if you're still not feeling well."

"No, that's okay. I'll come. I'll just get my camp set up and then I'll help with dinner."

He nodded.

They walked to the open field where the new Cavalry would create their pop-up town that night. When they slowed, he stepped closer. Close enough that she could see his face in the moonlight.

"Noa?"

"You love saying my name," she said, immediately wanting to cover her stupid mouth.

Amar furrowed his eyebrows.

She hadn't meant to embarrass him. Or maybe, he didn't—no, he probably didn't think of her like that. It was all in her head. What she meant was *she* loved hearing him say her name.

"I like it," she clarified.

His brow unknit.

"I appreciate you telling me about what happened." He paused. "And I do believe you."

Her chest sank. There was a caveat coming.

"But…you can't tell anyone else."

"Oh." A familiar tightness spread through her body. She wanted to disappear. "Right."

CHAPTER 12

NOA

"Noa? You in there?" Alexis scratched at Noa's tent door.

It was still nighttime, and Noa was considering whether she'd follow through on showing up to dinner. It had been a long day.

Alexis was already crawling inside as Noa said the words 'Come in'.

She plopped in front of her, mirroring Noa's cross-legged seat and embracing her in a tight hug. Rose curls, damp from lake water, pushed against Noa's face. Alexis released but left a hand resting on each of Noa's shoulders, punctuating the gravitas of her forthcoming inquiry.

"What the heck happened today?" Her brown eyes pleaded, glazed with restrained worry.

"I think I just got overheated and started to pass out," Noa lied.

Alexis was still and steely. "I saw what happened. That was not heat-exhaustion. That was something else entirely. You went somewhere, like the real deal, you checked out. Do not lie to me, Noa Lavoie."

Alexis was one of the most playful people Noa had ever met; she laughed loud and often, she flirted, she bounced when she walked. Kind and soft.

Until she needed to be firm. Then Alexis was as solid and unwavering as an oak.

Noa readjusted to sit on her knees. "First, it's pronounced lah-vwah, not lah-voy." Alexis's cheeks flinched in the slight direction of a smile, but held commitment to the, "I'm not leaving without the truth," pout.

"Second, I want to tell you but I'm not sure I understand it yet."

Alexis shuffled to perch on her own knees, hands resting in her lap. Her expression softened as she leaned in. "You don't have to tell me anything. If you need time to figure out what you want to say or share, that's fine. But you seem like the kind of person who isn't going to share, even if you want to, unless I pry it out of you. So, this is just me making sure you know you don't *have* to sort this all out by yourself."

After a moment, Noa filled the silence.

"I'm going to sound ridiculous," Noa said. "But I need you to remember that you like me, and that I'm not a ridiculous person."

Alexis bounced with fervor. "That's not true. I like you and you seem like a very ridiculous person."

Noa fell from her knee perch back to sitting on the tent floor as she described what happened in detail. It was more than she had shared with Amar. She tried to recall and relay each sensation she'd experienced and Alexis listened, hanging off every word. When Noa finished, Alexis stayed quiet.

"Lex, please say something. I'm dying over here."

"Well, gee, Noa! I mean—" Alexis's hands rested atop her head as her large brown eyes focused on nowhere in particular as she processed. Finally, Alexis's palms dragged from the crown of her head down her face, distorting her expression into something comical, exhausted, and weird. When she released their hold, her features bounced back to their rightful place with bright and eager energy. "I knew it!" Alexis exclaimed with renewed enthusiasm. "I didn't imagine this, but I knew it was *something* and this makes sense. I think. Humans have ascended before, so why wouldn't we start ascending one by one? We thought it would be a collective thing but could be one at a time. Oh, or maybe there is a special message for you? Maybe you have to ascend to learn and share something so the rest of us can evolve?" Alexis took a breath and lay back on the sleeping bag. Her eyes darted around the roof of the tent.

Noa watched her, not ready to respond. Before she needed to, Alexis shot back up.

"What do you think riding a horse has to do with it? No, wait—more importantly—are you going to try to ascend again?"

Noa blinked. Is this how people felt on the receiving end of her relentless questioning? "What? What do you mean?"

"Humans haven't ascended in over two hundred years. If you had an ascendent experience of some sort, maybe the other realm is trying to reach you? Maybe you should report it? Also, I want to come back to my other question. What does riding a horse have to do with any of it?"

Noa was stunned and relieved and confused. She leaned over and hugged Alexis.

"Thank you. Thank you so much."

"For what?"

"For being an absolute treasure of a person." Noa squeezed her harder. "I have no idea what I'm going to do, or what Trax has to do with all of this. I need to get my head around what happened. But thank you for believing me. Seriously."

On the walk to the mess area, Noa thought about what Amar had said about not telling anyone. She'd told two people now and both times she'd felt better after. Maybe she *did* need to share what she'd experienced. Either way, Alexis was right—Noa would have to experience it again. There had to be more.

Fortunately, her thoughts about ascension halted as soon as she started stirring her assigned pot. Unfortunately, they were replaced with an alarming need for food. Horseback riding, racing, and possibly visiting another realm of consciousness had exhausted every fuel source in Noa's body. She ached for something to swallow and couldn't concentrate until the gaping canyon in her belly was replenished.

It was torture helping Amar and Alexis rehydrate and heat that night's large dinner. She stirred the gloppy pot of mashed meal, holding herself back from taking a bite off the serving spoon—or from dunking her entire head into the pot. She distracted herself by recalling everything she knew about the instant-heat chemical they added. She replayed her chemistry lessons, recited the compounds, and imagined the chemical structures. Her mind wandered but got stuck at wondering if the food would taste better cooked over an open flame.

It would, but taste didn't matter right now, only sustenance.

Noa's neck tightened and released waterfalls of saliva as she carried her bowl of unseasoned and unloved food. She devoured her helping, then sat still while the others ate their meals at a reasonable pace. She counted the seconds, waiting for the mush to make its way down and quiet her ravenous stomach.

Once her hunger abated, she was filled with an equally feverous desire to be alone—restless to be with her own thoughts. Everything felt surreal and Noa was agitated she couldn't leave to fix it. Nothing in the world could be real for her—not her friends or the crickets chirping or the sleeve of her shirt that she was now fidgeting with between her fingers—until… Until what?

You are having a panic attack.

It was her voice this time. Noa had talked herself through many panic attacks before and her dad had given her plenty of coaching. Acknowledgement came first.

Around her, people chattered between dinner bites. She couldn't follow the conversation, and her palms broke into a sweat. Why were they talking so slowly? Or were they? Noa couldn't tell. Everything was unreal and out of focus. She couldn't remember what actually happened today. Had she confided in Alexis and Amar? Was the lake real? She pulled up her sleeve to examine her clean skin. Her blood slowed and cooled—she was dust-free and washed.

The lake had been real.

She faintly recalled standing next to Amar and stirring the meal mash minutes before, but they hadn't spoken a word. Her mind flurried out of control. How had she acted? Had he tried to talk to her? Had she just stood there, stirring silently like a freak? Had she dunked her head into the pot after all? *No.*

Was she being a silent freak *now*?

Her blood heated and sped up again.

She swallowed. She wished so badly Sami was here. Her sister could always tell when Noa was starting to get on edge and could intervene, either calming her down, or getting her to where she knew she was safe.

There was no one here to help her. She needed to excuse herself but, since she wasn't part of the conversation, how was she supposed to interject just to say goodbye?

Abruptly, she stood and drew everyone's attention. They stopped chewing to watch her, waiting for the impending announcement.

"I'm, uh, going to bed. Not really feeling well again." Noa gripped her dish with white knuckles.

"You look pale," Alexis said. "I just have two bites left. Let me finish, and I'll walk you."

"No!" It came out harsh, and Alexis's eyes widened. Noa cleared her throat before continuing. "Thank you. I'm fine. I'll walk on my own. I just need some sleep." She held her breath as she waited for her friend's permission to leave.

Alexis squinted questioningly and nodded. "If you need me, you know where to find me?"

Noa returned her nod, then scampered away. She kept her head down, focused on the individual blades of grass before pummeling them beneath her boots. She longed to take off her boots and wiggle her feet on the cold, dewy, ground. *Grounding.* Could she do that now? Would that be weird? It felt urgent again, but she knew it would have to wait.

Finally, she plopped onto the damp ground in front of her tent. It wasn't until she reached to unwrap her boots that she realized she was still holding her bowl from dinner. Had anyone noticed as she walked away? She tucked the bowl into the tent's vestibule along with her boots and resolved not to reflect on her odd behavior for the rest of her night.

She laid on the grass and clenched her bare toes into the earth. It felt as good as she had imagined. Noa started to sort through the day's events but couldn't hold onto a single coherent thought.

Instead, her mind hummed blurrily, and a mild headache grew into a catastrophic migraine. The pounding oscillated behind her eyes and into her ears and the meal mash in her abdomen sloshed. She pressed her palms firmly into her eyes and concentrated on the pain. She followed it in her mind and tried to catch it. It drummed rhythmically, then flickered erratically like a lightning bolt erupting in the distance. Her palms dug deeper into her sockets, and her mind chased the pain's chaotic path.

This was what she always did when she got a migraine. She didn't run from the pain. That never worked.

Stifling pain only made it angrier.

Instead, she leaned into the pain and let it fully bloom. She wasn't afraid of it. She waded through the storm until the lightning grew into stalks and branches of pulsating energy in her nerves and veins, blossoming into her capillaries. Whatever tension had caused the storm began to subside. Finally, she released her palms from her eyes, and the rapids of pain washed over her skull, dissipating into the blackness of her mind.

Noa dreamed of Britt and Eli. She hadn't seen their faces in months, but they were clear in her mind. Their voices, their touch, their worry—as if it were all in front of her again like it had been that day. Her second to last day in the Service. Her last case.

"You don't have to do this," Britt had said, putting a gentle hand on Noa.

"You don't know what they're like," Noa insisted. "They won't stop, they'll keep looking for you. And, if they find you again, they won't—they won't bring you back."

"They're not bringing us back *now!*" Britt gasped at her own outburst, on the verge of tears.

Eli reached over and took his wife's hand. "We won't make the same mistake." He continued more firmly. "We won't. If you delete our file, they won't find us. They won't even look for us. No one will know we exist."

"They'll know I did it."

Britt extracted her hand from Eli's and tightly grabbed Noa's wrist. "You'll save our lives."

Noa twisted her wrist free and rubbed it with her other hand. She nodded and stood. "I have to go."

Her dream was painted over by her own voice.

I have to go. I have to go. I have to go.

Noa woke in pitch black to the sound of Alexis crawling into her tent next door. V whispered, and Alexis giggled as they said goodnight.

Noa had drifted off to sleep too early and was now wide-awake when she was meant to be going to bed. She tapped her thumb and finger together. On the auto projection, her fingers combed through the usual routine. She checked the time and the location. It had updated, which meant she'd connected at some point during the day, though she didn't remember feeling anything. She checked her comms, and a message from Sami blinked. She selected it.

A life size portrait of her sister glowed in blue light above her. Sami was smiling, which prompted Noa to smile back before pressing play.

"Hey Noa." Her sister dragged out her name dramatically, *No-ahhhh*. "I know it's just been a few days—or gosh, I guess over a week already—but I thought I'd say hi and let you know that it's not absolutely terrible without you at home. I've turned your room into a high-end gaming space and stolen all the clothes you left behind. Anyway, I hope that your horse is being nice to you, and that you've maybe learned to ride it by now."

Noa chuckled to herself. Sami's predictions were eerily

close to her reality.

"Anyway…"

Sometimes Sami made it sound like her words were heavy, and that she had to use her whole body to haul them out. As she towed the final syllable of "anyway," Noa watched her sister's eyes focus intently on her fingers, rolling a piece of lint. Sami looked directly into the camera for the first time, and Noa felt like her sister was in the tent with her.

"If you get some connectivity, maybe send me a comm? I know Mom and Dad miss you too." Sami leaned forward to turn off the recording, and she was gone.

Noa's tent darkened. The standard size screen, just a few inches wide in diameter, glowed dimly above her hand, which now rested on her belly.

The sight of her sister made her feel deeply buried in reality and further from what had happened. Still, when she closed her eyes and slowed her breathing, Noa could feel a trace of the sensation she'd had when she was riding into the white space. It burned lightly through her navel, almost into her stomach. Before she could fully summon it, she lost it. She tried a few more times to command the sensation but lost it altogether after trying too hard.

Still, she remembered.

Alexis was right. She needed to visit again.

She considered leaving her tent and finding Trax to ride off into the moonlight in hopes of ascension.

Trax. She hadn't checked on him all night. Who had untacked him? Tied him up? Had Alexis? Amar? She definitely hadn't.

She was awake now. She might as well find him and avoid

whatever vengeance he was sure to inflict in the morning if she didn't.

With the ties of her unwrapped boots slithering behind her, Noa walked through the long, wet grass and deep into the trees. She made out dozens of horses that were not Trax. She conceded—not wanting to deal if he had run off again—and plopped herself onto the grass. She stretched her body every which way under the moonlight, bathing in the stars, her back damp with night dew.

She cried. For a few seconds at first. Quietly. Then minutes. Quietly, then loudly, and quietly again. A few horses flicked their ears, but no one came to comfort her.

She missed her bed, and her sister lounging around her room. She missed her parents' steady

presence and their annoying probing questions. If her father had been at dinner earlier, he never would have let Noa get through the meal in silence. He would have asked question after question about her day and, by the end of the meal, Noa would have known exactly how she felt about the spectacularly unusual experience. But Noa didn't know what questions to ask herself to sort it out. So she just laid there—confused, alone, and sad.

Finally, she calmed. Her teary eyes dried as she looked to the leafy canopy, and her body slowed to its natural rhythm. She hadn't realized her eyes were closed until she was startled by a shadow blocking the moonlight.

Her eyes shot open to find Trax.

When she rose to greet him, he burrowed his head down and rested it on her shoulders, nudging her. She embraced his giant head with both arms, petting and shushing him until they were both comforted.

After saying goodnight and re-securing Trax to a tree, Noa returned to her tent and buried herself in her sleeping bag. She rolled onto her stomach and stretched her arms out, underneath her pillow.

She opened her auto once more and, this time, the map loaded. Looking ahead the way Jo had shown them, the next few days of terrain were what she'd hoped for—flat riding.

Tomorrow, she would wake Alexis early and tell her the plan.

CHAPTER 13

TALI

Tali's nose itched. She peaked one eye open. Yori's eyes were closed, and he was practicing his humming breath. She could practically feel the vibrations of his throat even from six-feet away. Her hands wriggled out from beneath her thighs (where she tucked them to keep still) and rubbed the tip of her nose until the itch was satisfied.

Yori, the senior Marshal that Decker left in charge while away on Skill Trip, let out a particularly loud hum on his exhale. He slowly opened his eyes at the sound of Tali's rustling.

"Sounds like we might be done for the morning," he noted.

Tali shot off the ground and raised her arms to the sky. She arched the top of her back and let her head fall, a high-pitched yawn squeaking out of her. Even though it was the middle of the night, she felt like anytime was the perfect time for one of those good-squeaky-morning stretches. Especially after practicing yoga and breathing on top of a mountain.

"Roll up your mat," Yori said. He did the same.

Tali rolled her woven blanket into a tight bundle and latched it to her cross-body pack.

Yoga at two o'clock in the morning wasn't the most exciting thing on Main Ranch, and hardly anyone came to Yori's sessions—likely because they were still sleeping or on midnight duty. But Tali had felt independent and grown-up when Andrea suggested she go, even if it was for the wrong reasons.

Tali had told Andrea about the weird dreams she'd been having and even some of her experience at the pond—leaving out the small detail of nearly drowning. Tali had thought Andrea would be as curious and excited as she was. Andrea was always talking about consciousness and evolutions, and Tali knew she was onto something with her own theories for what was happening.

But Andrea diagnosed Tali's flickerings—that's what she'd started calling them—as stress, boredom, and the inability to be still.

The prescription was middle of the night yoga with Yori.

Yori was fantastic at being still. Perhaps the most still person Tali had ever met. Sometimes, when she had lunch at Main Ranch, Tali would sit with the Marshals and stare unabashedly at Yori while he ate. You couldn't be still and eat, Tali figured.

Yori was bulky and muscular, but nimble in his movement.

He was quiet and polite, but his moments of silence came off as stern with most everyone. Watching him eat should have been humanizing. Tali had longed to watch a piece of tomato fall out of his mouth, or a bit of salad dressing drip onto his chin, or even for him to have a crouton fall off his fork right before he put it in his mouth. But, somehow, even chomping down green beans and biting into rolls looked refined and spiritual in his practice. It was odd.

Yori tucked his mat into his woven shoulder bag and turned to her. "What are you up to for the rest of the day, little one?"

"It's the middle of the night, Yori!"

Tali put her hands on her hips before gesturing to the star-lit horizon. The moon was thin, bright, and illuminated the landscape enough to see well into the distance. The scorched desert collided with the maintained ranch land on one end of the horizon and crashed clunkily into white rocks and sparsely pined mountainside at the other.

"And I'm thirteen," Tali continued. "I don't have anything to do in the middle of the night. Not around here anyway."

Back when Tali and her family lived near City Centre, she was too young to appreciate the city. She had always hated going into the noisy bustle of crowds with the chaos of the stairways and lifts floating and flying around. Except when her mom took her to the teacart. That was special—just between the two of them—and the only time she loved going into the city.

But now that she was older, she couldn't help but think there was probably a lot more to do with all those people around. If she'd been able to grow up in the city like everyone else, she might even have friends.

Sure, she had classmates from lessons—but that wasn't the same.

"Come to the stables," Yori said. "I'll find some work for you."

He started the rocky climb down, and Tali followed. She was much smaller than him, so her reach didn't allow her to trace his movements exactly. But, over the years she'd lived at Main Ranch, she'd climbed this formation dozens—maybe hundreds—of times and had her own path carved into memory.

"Yori, can I ask you something?" Tali shifted a foot from one red stone to another, rounder ledge.

He grunted affirmatively.

"Have you ever ascended?"

"No one has ascended yet, my dear," he answered. He pulled himself down from the final ridge and landed on flat ground before offering her a hand.

She refused it and jumped the last four-foot drop, landing with her knees crouched and a palm flat on the ground. She loved making that jump. It made her feel stealthy and agile.

She stood and dusted off her palms. "But hasn't anyone? I mean, *really*. You spend all your time meditating and praying—probably doing six or seven gratitudes a day, and you haven't even had one tiny speck of connection with the Gods?"

"That's hard to say. Which Gods?"

Tali bugged her eyes at him. "*The* Gods!"

Yori laughed.

She loved that her attitude always caught him off guard,

but she wanted an actual answer this time. "What other Gods are there?"

"There are mine, yours, and everyone else's."

"They're not all the same? Lessons say that at the Enlightening—"

Yori held up a hand to interrupt her. The gesture might have been rude, but his expression was soft and sincere. "Tali, you are special, aren't you? You have a unique personality. A rhythm that others don't seem to carry?"

She nodded.

"Well, I, too, am different. I sound and look unlike anyone else on this ranch. Anyone I've ever met. Have you ever met anyone like me?"

Tali shook her head no.

"And everyone else on this ranch. Andrea, Mirai, Decker, Sai, Amar. All different hearts, different cadences in their walks, different eye colors, different definitions of stillness—" He paused and stared at Tali's impatiently tapping fingers until she stopped and focused her full attention on him. "Different souls evolving in different ways, every day. We can accept all those differences within each other, but we must have the same Gods?"

For the first time that evening, Tali didn't seem to have a reply. She'd gone completely still.

Yori smiled. "Exactly."

CHAPTER 14

NOA

"Good morning, early bird," said Sai, the older, more reserved Marshal. He wiped his brow, straining to stir a long spoon around the oversized pot filled with mash paste. It would eventually be edible. "Would you like a breakfast bar? Hot meal will be another few minutes."

"Breakfast to-go today," Noa said, performing the nonchalance of someone who wasn't up to anything at all. "Gotta give Trax extra attention before riding. He's still fussy."

"He is a headstrong one, isn't he?" Sai gestured to the pile of wrapped oat bars. "Help yourself. Glad to see you putting in the extra work."

Noa smiled politely and piled six bars into her arms. If Sai raised an eyebrow or gave a strange look at the amount she took, she didn't notice. She was already hurrying to the trees where Alexis and V were waiting.

In her hurry, Noa didn't pay particularly close attention to where she was walking. Her toe caught a tree root, and she stumbled.

After two jaunted steps and a look of contempt in the direction of the root culprit, she caught her balance. She also caught Amar, who was leaning against a nearby tree, huffing in laughter. She straightened and promptly tripped over another root. This time an awkward lurch forward didn't save her. She face planted, knocking the wind from her lungs.

She cursed under stilted breath—at the roots, at the breakfast bars for flying from her arms, at her face—it was already burning red from embarrassment. Noa scrambled to her feet, eyes pinned to the ground scanning for the scattered bars. She hunched her posture more than the search called for, as if scrunched shoulders protected against Amar witnessing her graceless galumphing. The four bars she recovered would have to suffice.

"Ow!" Her head collided with something hard when she stood upright.

"Sorry, didn't mean to add to the damage," Amar said, one hand rubbing his chin, the other offering the two missing breakfast bars. "Hungry this morning?"

Noa rearranged the pile in her arms, the flush in her cheeks resurging. *Damn face.* "A couple of us are heading out early."

Without meeting his gaze, she could feel him scanning her all the same. She would have to look him in the eye eventually, might as well get it over with. *Dark eyes, light expression. That wasn't so bad.*

"Early, huh?"

"Trax needs the extra space, so I—"

"That's fine."

She didn't want his permission.

Amar spoke through a morning yawn. "I'll ride with you. Sai's on breakfast duty, and I'm finished packing." He grabbed the bars from her. "Who else are we riding with?"

Noa's mouth pulled to one side. "Alexis and V." She hoped Amar would magically put together that she wanted to ride with them—alone.

He did not.

Two hours. Amar rode with them for two hours. And while two hours was only a fraction of their lengthy riding days, *these* two hours accounted for almost the entire window Noa had to race ahead of the group and attempt to recreate her ascension.

Any other day she would have been thrilled to ride with Amar. In the quiet of *any other* early morning, she would have absorbed his energy and asked him a few of the thousand questions milling about her brain. On *any other* day, she would have loved hearing about Main Ranch and she would have admired Amar stumbling through an odd joke about cow-tipping not transferring to bison-tipping, or something like that. She hadn't listened well. Because today was not *any other* day. Today, her brain was filled only with strategies on how to shake him.

None of her tactics worked.

Fortunately, Marshal duties called and Amar left of his own accord, throwing an arm in the air waving goodbye as he and Mozart turned back on the trail. Noa peered over her shoulder until he was tiny on the horizon.

Alexis must have been watching for the same moment because she let out a, "Let's do this!" rally cry just as Noa turned around.

Alexis had yipped in excitement earlier that morning when she had first agreed to the plan. Apparently, her enthusiasm hadn't waned in the hours since.

"You brought him up to speed?" Noa asked Alexis, nodding to V.

Vitus answered. "She did, and I'm honored to be of service, oh Holy One."

Even dripping in sarcasm, Noa would take the extra support. Plus, she didn't have much of an option; V had been attached to Alexis's hip since they'd met and for some reason Alexis didn't mind. Plus, given his general resentment toward the Variety and his penchant for all things rebellious, Noa assumed he was probably actually glad to be involved.

"Let's do this," she said.

Noa shoved her hips forward, signaling Trax to speed up. Alexis and V raised their reins and their rumps out of their seats to work up a faster pace. The three of them spread out, and Noa moved herself and Trax to the middle.

Trax sped up to a gallop—even faster than the last time. Noa tried to find the same rhythms of hoof and heart beats. She breathed, exhales longer than inhales. Tendrils of her long hair waved in the wind. The mid-morning sun was above the horizon, but it didn't seem as bright as it was yesterday.

A few clouds dotted the sky, but none blocked the sun. The grassy plain rippled in the steady winds and trail dust kicked up around them. It all looked the same. But Noa didn't feel the same. Still, she pushed. She pushed Trax to work harder and gained a significant lead on both Alexis and V, though Luna held much closer than Whalen.

Noa held tight to the seat horn with one hand and wrapped her other arm around Trax's shoulder, petting him and cooing for him to keep going. After a while, her sternum bruised, and Trax slowed.

"Alexis, I can't." Noa pulled alongside Luna, completely out of breath. "I can't ride like this any longer. It's not happening."

"Oh, thank Gods," Alexis said, equally winded. "I was dying out there. It hurts to ride that hard. No one ever tells you that."

Noa laughed, holding a stitch in her side. "Who would tell you that?"

Alexis shrugged and smiled with a wheezy laugh.

V caught up and slowed Whalen beside them. "Damn, your horses are fast. So, what happened?"

"Nothing. I don't know," Noa said.

They tried again after lunch.

And again.

And again, in the days that followed.

Noa grew increasingly disciplined each time, routinizing the exercise. She calmed her breath, focused her gaze, and tried to connect with Trax and the earth around her.

Nothing.

Each day at sunset (Noa's last hope), she gave herself a pep talk as she and Trax paced up to the last gallop. Each detail was meticulously repeated or creatively rearranged and still, nothing.

An exhausting, painful nothing.

CHAPTER 15

NOA

"You're a snake!" Noa said. "You're lying and you did that on purpose."

V huffed, as if it were such a baseless accusation that it rendered him speechless. He was simultaneously shaking his head, throwing his arms up in shrugs, scrunching his face, and scanning the room for a sympathetic ally.

Zahira stared daggers at him. Noa could tell she was about to tell him off and couldn't wait to see it.

"Let me see if I have this straight," Zahira started, hushing everyone in the tent. "You 'accidentally' bumped your scoring cards to show four tricks instead of three—that *definitely* wasn't you just hoping we wouldn't notice. And when you were explaining the game—because you are the *only* one who has ever played before—you just happened to leave out the rule about stealing the deal. And it's just a coincidence that the pretty-shady-to-start-with rule that we didn't know anything about helped you win the last two tricks? Oh! And! You *totally* weren't ta—"

"Stealing the deal is not cheating," V said with an egotistical smile.

Jash and Jo booed. Noa booed louder.

"Babe, I think you've lost this one," Alexis said. She pointed an aggressive finger at him and gave a formal confession. "I want it on the record that although this man was my partner, I was not, nor could I have been complicit in his trickery. Mostly because I still do not understand this game."

"No way." V caught Alexis's arm, and his grin turned devilish and flirty. He pulled her forward into a twist-and-roll maneuver landing her back on the tent floor and her head in his lap staring up at him.

Impressive, Noa thought.

"If I go down, I'm taking you with me," he said. Alexis laughed and readjusted herself, still laying mostly in his lap.

"I think I've seen enough. I'm going to bed," Jo said.

"Me too," Zahira said. "Walk me to my tent?"

"I'd better go too," Noa said. She started packing the playing cards but since most were now under Alexis, she gave up. "V, thank you for reminding me why I don't like to play games." She gave him a big, phony smile. Then she peered more sincerely at her friend. "And thank *you* for reminding me that I do indeed like people."

After days of strenuous extra riding, Alexis had started dropping hints that perhaps they should take a break. That chasing another ascension is great and all, but wouldn't riding with the group again also be so much fun? And building relationships in this assignment is probably more important than most, due to the isolation, you know? And didn't Noa miss hanging around friends and eating at a leisurely pace?

Noa had said something along the lines of 'no' but reconsidered. V had remarked that Noa always scarfed her food and that she didn't like people, but his snotty comments weren't why she reconsidered. It was because, aloud, her response sounded...sad. And a bit selfish after all the time Alexis and V had spent helping her. So, she agreed they should take a break.

They. Not her.

Noa waded through the field, grabbing handfuls of wild grass for Trax. Before entering the moon-shadowed grove where the horses were tied, she paused to look up and take in the stars.

She had learned about constellations in school but hadn't seen many stars in the sky growing up. City Centre glowed at all hours of the night, polluting the natural darkness. Once, on a lessons trip to an observatory, her class had searched a virtual display of the sky for star formations. She found six that day.

Now, she didn't search for groupings and imagined forms among the stars. She just stood, appreciating their haphazardness and abundance.

Finding her steps again, she pondered the human history taught in those same lessons. For a long time, people had put weight into the stars' arrangement at the time of their birth. They believed it predicted what type of person they would be. Noa recalled reading the lessons on her auto—descriptive texts about each astrological sign, complete with birth charts and detailed maps about rising signs and moon signs, filled pages of ancient texts. The periodicals even included daily, weekly, and yearly predictions written by star interpreters.

The texts, as she read them, were swarmed with critical annotations from Librarians, explaining how and why astrology was categorized as a pseudoscience. It was a danger to their evolution, corrupting and slowing the collective ascension of humankind. Back then, Noa had wondered how people could believe in something so harmful for thousands of years.

The day of that observatory trip, Noa and her peers indulged in deciphering their own star signs and laughed as each took a turn dramatically reenacting the person they ought to be according to their birth chart. Noa (a Virgo) playfully acted out the Disappointed Goddess, unimpressed with Sagittarius's arrows and unenthused by Leo's roar.

Tonight, she didn't want to read someone else's interpretation of the night sky. But outside, among them, it didn't seem so strange to listen to the stars.

What kind of life would the stars have chosen for her if the Variety hadn't already had that responsibility? Would she have ever met Alexis or Amar? Would she have ridden a horse or helped a sick person? Maybe she would have done more. Or less. Maybe, without the Variety telling her what to do, Noa would have listened to the stars. Maybe the Variety and the stars weren't so different. Maybe the Variety was just a more intricate version of sky-telling. Maybe humans had always needed something to tell them who they were going to be.

Noa shelved the thought as she approached Trax. She had asked a lot of him over the past few days of riding so hard, and he'd become obstinate again—even without reins. Some extra breathwork would do them both good. She would need to improve their bond if she wanted to start racing on their own in the early mornings.

"Hi boy, how are you doing out here?"

He leaned into her, and she petted the side of his large face, offering him the wild grass with her other hand. He gobbled the snack and nudged Noa with his nose.

"Sorry, I didn't bring any more." She displayed her empty hands.

Trax nudged her again, harder this time.

She laughed. "I don't know what you want from me. I don't have any more treats." She chuckled at his insistence but quieted when Trax raised his head high, the way he had before striking her that first day in the stable.

Noa flinched and took a step back. Trax swung his head around in the opposite direction and pulled hard at the rope that tied him to the tree. The knot frayed, and Trax raised his head again.

"Okay, okay wait." Noa ran in front of his face and held up her hands to get him to stop thrashing. He paused at the top of his arc. She unfastened the rope from the tree. "Now what?"

Trax walked toward the field.

Better grazing. Noa rolled her eyes.

"Just for a minute."

They didn't make it to the field, though. Trax halted beneath a tree branch at the edge of the grove. He nudged Noa toward the tree's trunk.

"What do you want?" Noa looked around.

Trax nudged her again and whinnied with a stomped foot. Noa looked above and considered the low branch hanging centered just above Trax's back.

She gripped the crevice between the tree's first break. Placing a foot on a protruding knob, she hoisted herself high enough to wrap an arm around a branch. She was getting stronger, and one kick of her leg spun her up and around. She shimmied down the length of the branch until she was over Trax. Her feet dangled and the rough bark lifted her shirt. She'd have marks all along her stomach and forearms tomorrow.

Trax didn't budge when she dropped onto his back. He was massive and strong, but she thought he might have flinched a bit when an entire human fell on top of him.

She shifted around on him, trying to get comfortable. They had never ridden without a saddle. There was nothing to keep her from sliding backward, no saddle horn to grip, no stirrups. She wiggled again and Trax swung his head around into an uncomfortably craned position. His black marble eye stared at her and she swore there was condescension in his gaze.

"Oh, *that* you react to." She shimmied her hips again.

He blew threw his nostrils. He had quite enough of her.

"Okay." She conceded and urged him forward with non-wiggly hips and pressure through her heels. He blew through his nostrils again, but Noa was starting to better understand his sounds and that was more of a happy snort. Or at least one of relief that she'd stopped fooling around.

They walked along the outside of camp—away from the tents and slowly enough that no one would hear his steps. Beyond camp's perimeter, Trax picked up the pace and crossed the day trail where the Calvary had watered the horses when they first arrived at camp. A thin, rocky creek with water flowing from the mountain caps they would eventually have to cross.

Trax strutted along the creek, Noa unsettled on his bare back. When they found a slight incline, she leaned into his shoulders and gripped him, afraid she might slip at any second and likely get kicked on her way down to the hard, jagged ground.

Trax quickened into a gallop and despite her fear, Noa didn't slip backward. Her thighs held tight, and arms flexed to pull her weight forward, keeping her body in place. They ran closer to the stream, Trax's hooves kicking up cool mud. Noa forced her eyes to stay open despite their flinching at the flecks of hurling mud. She focused on the trees toward the horizon.

They were encased in a globe of stars.

The longer she peered into the nightscape before her, the more stars appeared. The empty distance between her and the heavens thickened into an ocean. Brilliant specks fell from their rightful place far away and plunked into the sea above. Some stars sank like tossed stones; others floated gently in flyleaf zigzags, streaks and swirls glowing in their wake.

Trax dodged a tree on the bank and ran in the shallow

water of the creek's bed. The jarring movement and splashing water jolted Noa from her trance. She raised her chest from Trax's shoulders, castoff spray from the creek misted her to soaking after just a few lengths—and then, she felt it.

The pang in her stomach.

Gravity abandoned her. Her spine decompressed, organs floated in her abdomen, and breath sat in her lungs with no urge to go in or out.

The stars grew brighter, glittering as they fell around her. Like heavy raindrops, they absorbed into the pores of solid rocks and echoed, colliding into hollow branches. One swiped the side of Noa's face and left a frosted burn.

With a hand on her warm cheek, Noa let her head fall back into the cradle of her shoulder blades and took in the stormy, light-streaked sea above. The sky thundered, releasing a shower of light. Whooshing star droplets drowned out the sound of Trax's hooves cracking against the rocky creek bed. Her ears plugged as the sound grew deeper until, finally, silence took over.

The hush quieted all Noa's senses, pointing her focus to a bright hole in the sky where the stars seemed to tumble from. She reached for it, unsure if it was just in front of her face or galaxies away. At the end of her arm length, a light tug from beyond lifted her inside.

There, beyond, Noa was confronted with everywhere she had ever been.

Her room back home, Sami lazily lounging in an armchair.

The campsite where her family stayed during a Variety trip.

The hospital where she served as a Nurse.

The woods and alleys where she interviewed UEs as a Service Member.

The burning scent of hospital iodine, the sweet rose of her sister's shampoo, and the dusty pine of the campsite hit her all at once.

More of her life played out before her. Noa didn't want to leave, but was exhausted by the stars, scenes, scents, and sounds. She wanted more time. It wasn't enough time to take it all in, to feel what she was supposed to feel.

Then, even more came. Her memories were overrun with places she had never visited and people she had never met.

A great plain speckled with brush and foreign animals drifting through dusty hills.

A fish swimming near her face, the waves from its tail putting pressure and salt water into her star wound. The fish wrestled with another, twisting and twirling. The two jumped above the surface and, when they crashed back down, water splashed Noa's face. She swiped her eyes with hands that didn't feel like her own.

Her gaze found a porcelain sink, and her unfamiliar hands reached for another cupped handful of water beneath the faucet. She splashed herself and dried with a towel. When she lifted her eyes to the mirror, the reflection showed a person she had never met.

Something tugged at her hand. Peering down the length of her arm, once again different, Noa found a small girl slipping a tiny hand into hers. The girl tugged again.

"Just a second," Noa said. She looked forward, hoping to catch a glimpse of whose body she was in now. But there was no longer a mirror. Instead, she stood in front of a teacart and ordered in a voice softer than her own.

Over the barista's shoulder, on the corner of the street was the Green Gem House. The house that had always been Noa's favorite. Before she had a second thought, Noa was on the doorstep, knocking.

An older woman with thick, black hair, streaked with grey, answered the door. Colorful layers of dress swished as she greeted Noa, then stood aside and extended an arm to show her in. "I'm so glad you finally made it."

"Where am I?" Noa examined her hands, once again her own, and remembered the little girl. Outside, the young girl held her mother's hand at the teacart on the corner.

"What's going on?"

The woman took Noa's hands and guided them into the living room, her skirts swishing and dusting the floor as they walked. They sat, close. The woman's eyes were watery and calm like the surface of a lake.

"You know where you are," the woman said, head bobbing in an affirmative nod.

Noa mindlessly mimicked the gesture, and her foggy mind began to clear.

She *almost* felt real again.

The ocean of stars falling and the montage of memories and being in other bodies—that had all been a hallucination, a fever dream. She was lucid now. They were sitting in the woman's living room. Several mismatched sofas lined the perimeter of the spacious room and strange collections of art and bits and tools cluttered the wall spaces—Noa liked one painting in particular. It was of an icy lake, and felt somehow personal. Like she remembered it.

"You're okay," the woman said.

Noa found herself nodding along again. "Wh—?" No words came.

The woman tilted her head as if she understood without them. "You're not alone, Noa."

She took Noa's hand again. The woman's hand was cold, but her touch was soft and light. "They can all come here. Whenever they're ready." The woman smiled, mostly with her eyes and cheeks. "Now, drink up."

Noa's head clouded again. She reached for the glass of water the woman offered and put it to her lips. Tilted back, the glass grew larger. And larger. The water flowed, over-filling her mouth, spilling onto her face and down her neck. She told her body to stop pouring but it was no use. There was nothing in her hands.

Shuddering and spasming, Noa couldn't even cough. She choked, her lungs retching for air. She outwrestled her body's innate desire to breathe for as long as she could. Finally, she knew. She would not be able to stifle the next gasp, and her lungs wouldn't find air. Only water.

A powerful wind rushed past, alleviating Noa from the incessant water. Her lungs hitched their involuntary gulp. *Air.*

It was dark, Noa was lightheaded, but as oxygen made its way back to her brain, a familiar movement jostled her back to the present. She was riding Trax through the creek.

She was *still* riding.

Noa didn't understand. She tried to force her brain to comprehend. She could ask herself simple questions. She could work backward. She could—.

She couldn't. She had nothing left.

In that begrudging but conscious recognition of exhaustion, her body seemed to sever ties with whatever autonomous programming it had been running while she was off hallucinating in StarLand. When Trax yielded to a pile of rocks in the stream, Noa's loosened grips couldn't recover.

She hit the soft mud of the creek's bank and rolled down a hill until her head collided with a sharp rock—the bash slowing her to a stop.

Warm blood spilled from the top of her head.

She shivered and began to sweat, unable to raise herself. She reached a trembling hand into her thick, bloodied hair, attempting to apply pressure. The tips of her fingers pulsed her rapid heartbeat. Fear poured out in a quick rhythm until, finally, a wave of calm set her free.

CHAPTER 16

TALI

Tali lay on the bed in the guest room—her room—at Andrea's house. The quilt was old and worn smooth from washes. She ran her hand over it and found a loose stitch to pick. Rubbing the thread in her fingers, she imagined what her own personal God might look like.

It was impossible.

At first, she imagined herself, inspired by something she'd heard her mother say when she was still around. *"We're all holy."*

It sounded true, but Tali couldn't think of herself as a God, even if her ascensions were getting more and more frequent; assuming that's what they were. She'd wanted to do more research and submit an official inquiry, but she was still a minor, and there was only so much she could do until her brother got home.

So, she kept trying to ascend and imagine the face of her God.

Sometimes she remembered everything about her ascensions—but those were typically the times where the experience led only to the white place, where it was warm, bright, and everything all at once.

She could only remember it the same way one might remember the taste of a favorite meal, or the smell of their home. It's recognizable in memory—but the actual experience has notes and dimensions the mind could never quite capture.

She thought experiencing the presence of a God might be the same way.

"Tali, dinner!" Andrea called from down the hall.

Tali rolled onto her back and rocked herself up to standing from the bed, heading to another silent dinner.

After telling Andrea everything and being assigned Yori yoga, Tali thought she'd better keep her research and experiments to herself. But since ascending was all she could think about, the dinner conversations had grown shallow and succinct.

When dinner was over, Tali cleared the table and escaped to the garden for another race against herself. Her record had grown farther into the desert, and she didn't have time to wander the garden or give herself a pep talk before she ran. It was no longer a thirty-second cartwheel sprint to the charcoal log. It was a three-minute run to the burnt cactus, then one minute longer to the hollow tree, and thirty seconds more to her recent marker—the crater with a red clay ring.

Tonight, she would run all the way to the bush line.

She knelt at the edge of the patio stones and touched the ground next to her bare feet. Her thin legs perched in a sprinter's takeoff stance. She tucked her chin into her collarbone, took a deep breath, raised her gaze for the first marker: the charcoal log. On her exhale, she launched into a run.

Her feet pounded the ground, and her heartbeat rose to meet her speed. She never knew what to do with her arms now that she was running for longer than a sprint, so she held them at her waist in fists and punched the air every so often.

Rounding the burnt cactus, her face flushed and filled with a smile. She laughed at her punches and wiped the sweat from her brow, finding her forehead hot to the touch—hot enough to burn her hand slightly. But she continued stumbling forward at her fast but now broken pace.

She massaged her burnt hand with the other and held it out in front of her body. It was soothed by the cool air rushing around her as she moved. The air grew thick, rushing with more and more density until it seemed to turn into water—and she was running in slow motion through the bottom of a sea.

The water boiled around her forehead, and she watched as a crown of bubbles floated to the surface that was the night sky. The last bubble she watched breached the surface and popped with a bright flash that transported her from her run into a comfortable living room.

She startled at her new surroundings and realized she was sopping wet. Not from her seafloor run, but from the sweat dripping down her forehead.

"Oh, honey. You're burning up. Drink this." An old woman with dark hair streaked in silver waded over to her, struggling to carry a large bucket of water. The bucket shifted in size as Tali reached for it, returning to a regular cup in her thirteen-year-old palm.

"Grandma Dia?" Tali raised her gaze from the cup to the woman.

"Oh, sweetheart." The woman clutched her chest warmly and adjusted her layers of skirts to sit across from Tali. "I can't believe you remember me. The last time I saw you, you were such a tiny little thing."

Tali guzzled the endless cup of water, her forehead finally returning to a normal temperature. "It's been so long." She wiped her mouth dry.

"And yet, only a moment." Dia cupped Tali's face softly and smiled. Then Dia's gaze shifted to the window, as if giving an instruction.

Tali stood and peered out the curtain. City Centre looked the same as she remembered. Exactly the same. Even the teacart she and her mother used to visit on days spent with her grandmother.

That's when she saw her.

"Is that my mother?" Tali blinked at the woman in line at the teacart already knowing the answer. It was her mother exactly as she remembered her. Tall with a thin face and shoulder-length black hair that flipped into a bounce around her shoulders. She was reaching for a takeaway teacup with one hand and holding the hand of a young girl with the other. "Is that me?"

Grandma Dia put an arm around Tali and used the other

to shut the drape. "I always love it when you two come to visit. So special when it's just us girls." She smiled and led Tali back to the couch.

"I wish I could have visited more often."

"You'll be back sooner than you think."

Tali suddenly felt exhausted and was grateful she was sitting.

"Now, just remember you can always come back here. Okay?" Grandma Dia took Tali's burnt hand in both of hers and rubbed her palm gently. Cold chilled Tali's hand, and then soothed. "I'm afraid you must go now. I'm expecting some company."

Just then a knock struck the door.

"Is it mom?" Tali's voice raised and warbled with emotion. "Can I see her? One last time?"

Dia leaned in and hugged Tali tight against her. Tali buried her face into her grandmother. Tali wasn't unappreciative of the time or affection she was getting from her grandmother— but if she could see her mom just one more time. She tried to reach beyond Grandma Dia to open the door, but Dia squeezed her tighter and Tali gave in. Somehow, she knew it wasn't her mother on the other side.

In the pressure of Dia's arms, Tali became a sand mold of herself and gradually softened until she lost her shape and fell toward the floor. Her body turned to dust and clouds, swept up to the sky on a gust of wind and whipping through time and space before finally floating back to the desert floor.

The wind gently re-piled her grains into a sandcastle form of her own body, becoming solid when the last piece landed on the crown of her head.

Tali wiggled her toes, and a small lizard escaped from a hole in the ground nearby. It scuttled over her foot before darting into the bush. She shuddered and wiggled, trying to rid herself of the creepy crawly feeling. Dramatics got the best of her. She continued shaking about until it was absurd, and she laughed. Unfortunately, deep belly laughs come with deep belly inhales which got her a lungful of dust. She stumbled back to the garden like a madwoman, laughing and choking on the sand cloud she once belonged to.

CHAPTER 17

NOA

Familiar eyes bore down with worry on Noa. It took a moment for her to realize they belonged to Amar. In his stare, she remembered the watery, lake-like eyes of the old woman. They were the same eyes, for a moment.

Amar cleared his throat. "Noa, are you awake? Don't move."

She was lying in the woods, back drenched in mud, but her head was positioned in Amar's lap instead of next to the bloody rock.

"I'm bleeding," she said dreamily, still fighting her way back to consciousness.

Her hand reached for the back of her head and warm blood wetted her palm. Amar cautiously replaced her hand with some balled up fabric and pressed it with a gentle firmness to the wound. Her head dropped into the cradle of his arm, and she looked up at him, realizing the bandage was the sleeve of his shirt.

"I need to get you out of here," he said. His eyes broke contact with hers and looked around the damp, empty woods.

Noa didn't want to move. She stared at the stars wishing they would fall around both of them like they had for her. Amar raised his chin to see what she was looking for.

"Noa." He brushed the sticky hair off her face and readjusted his arms to bring her slightly closer to him. "What were you doing out here?"

She shushed him but smiled, still high from her ascension.

He understood. "You could have gotten really hurt."

"I did." She smiled wider.

Her nonchalance seemed to irritate him, but the look dissipated into noticeable concern.

She wanted to reach her hand to his forehead and smooth the worry lines. She could comb his hair back with her fingers and might even let her hand rest at the back of his neck.

"Can you sit up? I need to get the horses." He carefully shifted her out from under his arm as he rose.

Sitting up, her head throbbed. She leaned forward to rest on her knees, closing her eyes at the pain. Her attention focused on the space between her eyebrows and she took a deep breath, exhaling slow, slow, slow, urging the pain to dissipate.

When she opened her eyes, Trax was by her side and Mozart not far away.

"Whoa!" Amar turned around, surprised by Trax's sudden proximity.

"He responds to me being quiet," she said. "Calm." She made exaggerated eyes at Amar.

"Huh." He scratched his head.

Amar helped Noa to her feet and juggled the horses' leads in one hand and most of Noa's body weight in the other as he led them to a boulder in the near distance. He helped Noa onto the boulder, then gave her a boost onto Mozart's back. He climbed on behind her and pulled her against him, his arm holding her steady. Noa sank into him, grateful for the support of his body as she settled in for the ride back to camp.

They rode in comfortable silence until they reached the wheat fields.

"Why did you go out there by yourself? You could have been really hurt," Amar said again.

"I *am* really hurt," Noa repeated, laughing at herself. She cleared her throat, imagining the disdainful look Amar was making behind her. "But I don't think I had a choice. Trax kind of pushed me into it and after that…it was like I went into a trance."

"Your horse made you? Come on."

She didn't like his ugly tone. Sure, Trax prodding her sounded ridiculous, but Amar didn't have to be so snarky.

"He didn't make me. You're not understanding, I'm not explaining it well. It's like I was called to, and there's something about Trax that helps me. It just happened."

"You're lying."

This silence was not comfortable. Amar loosened his grip around her waist; the sliver of distance felt like a canyon. Mozart slowly walked them to the trees where the rest of the horses waited, Trax trailing behind.

"I think you went out there knowing it was going to happen again, and you chased it," he said, finally breaking.

She thought about it. "Maybe, I'm not sure. Maybe I did know it was going to happen, but I'm glad I tried to ascend again. It's—"

"Dangerous," he finished.

He wasn't wrong. It was dangerous but something Britt had said jumped to her mind: *I wouldn't have all this courage if I wasn't meant to do something brave.* Noa smirked. Maybe she was meant to be brave, too. Take risks, face the dangers.

"You don't know what you're getting yourself into. Not to mention how sick and exhausted you were after last time. It's not worth it."

"You don't know that," she said.

"I do know that." His voice wasn't raised, but it was firm, leaving no room for debate.

Firey words rose easily to the back of her throat, ready to tell him off. She swallowed. He had literally just rescued her, and she was too tired to debate right now anyway. "How did you find me?" she asked, changing the subject.

"You're not as sneaky as you think you are."

"You followed me?"

"I've been keeping an eye on you. I had a feeling you'd do this."

Gods he was irritating—giving her permission to go riding early, watching her, rescuing her. She wasn't an incapable child. She didn't want to be ungrateful, but she would have rather limped all the way back to camp with her open head wound than stay tucked against him in that moment.

She mumbled something under her breath.

"What?" His tone made it clear he did not appreciate the passive aggressive mumbling.

"The ascension." Noa spoke louder. "You don't know." She paused, her voice even more sure now. "It was amazing. I know people use that word all the time to describe small things, but this was the most amazing place I've ever been. It's not even a place, it's a—I don't know. I wish I could share it with you, and maybe, if I keep trying, I'll be able to. Maybe I'll be able to do something important. But I do know that you can't tell me not to chase it, or that it's not worth it, because you don't know."

Amar fidgeted behind her. "Then make sure I'm there next time," he said, finally. "I know I can't go where you're going, but I can at least make sure you come back here safely. And that others don't catch you doing what you're doing."

Noa wanted to contest. He *might* be able to ascend too, according to the woman in the Green Gem House. And it might not be the worst thing for others to find out about her ascensions. This could be her chance to give people the answers, instead of asking all the questions. She could help. She would be brave and she would keep taking the risks.

Right now, though, her fire for this fight was dwindling under the weight of immense exhaustion and was extinguished when Amar reclaimed his grip around her waist.

Back in the grove, they tied up the horses. Noa felt strong enough to walk again and sent Amar to get the medical supplies. They agreed to meet by the lake's shore to get cleaned up before bed.

She sat in the rough sand and held the blood-soaked shirt sleeve to her head. It had begun to dry on the ride home and, when she removed her hand, it stayed stuck in her hair. She leaned back to stare at the stars again, wondering if they would ever look the same.

She wished Amar would have been there for it.

Or Alexis. Or her sister. Anyone.

She hadn't noticed how lonely her life had been up until now. In her life, Noa had stayed quiet, never feeling as though she had something to share. Instead, she minimized her impact, avoiding taking too much from others. Too much of their time, too much of their attention.

Now that she had something to offer, she longed for those connections. For that attention.

Amar returned with a bag and sat next to her. "Look at me." He shined a thin flashlight into her eyes.

She winced at the brightness.

"Doesn't look like you have a concussion. You got lucky."

She felt lucky, but that wasn't why.

Out of his bag, he pulled a canteen of water, sponge, gauze, and some medical drops. He maneuvered her to lie over his lap, resting her back on his thighs, leaving her head overhanging. He put a hand on her forehead to shield her eyes and poured water from the canteen over her hair. The shirt sleeve unstuck, and he removed it. He grabbed the sponge and blotted the blood from her hair, parting it to see the wound.

"It's a pretty big gash." He picked up the medical drops and measured liquid into the dropper. A cool tingling sensation spread over her scalp as he placed the drops into her open wound. From her experience Nursing, Noa imagined exactly what the medicine was doing as it hit her skin.

First, the drops would sanitize the wound. Then, they would release topical anesthesia. As she imagined this, the pounding in her head subsided. She continued mapping the drops' course of action. Next, they would heat up to cauterize the wound to stop the bleeding. A faint heat warmed her skull. Over the next day, the drops would activate her own skin cells to regenerate the skin barrier, and her wound would heal as if none of this had ever happened.

Without the pounding in her head, Noa noticed the silence of the lakeshore. This was only their second lake-side camp. The other camps had been loud with creeks rushing, woods stirring, and wind whistling through the branches and fields.

Tonight, the world stood still.

"Better?" Amar finished wrapping a proper bandage around her head.

She touched her fingers to the bandage. "Yes, thank you."

"Sorry I don't have a better way to wrap it. With your hair, I can't really use adhesive."

"It's okay, I can look like a mummy for one day."

When there was a lull in their small talk, Noa looked in Amar's dark brown, calming eyes and asked if she could please tell him about her ascension. She had gathered he didn't want to talk about it, but she felt compelled. She couldn't keep something so utterly life-changing to herself. She couldn't make sense of it by herself.

And then she was filled with regret.

Not about telling him—recounting the experience was

almost as good as living it. But because, as her mind and mouth moved at record pace, jumping to recall and describe each detail as vividly as she had felt it, Amar listened. He really listened. It was as if part of her had left her body to witness the two of them sitting on the lake shore and she could see it so clearly.

Her, wearing a bandage crown, hands gesturing wildly, rising in and out of her seat in the sand as she attempted to convey the enormity of her experience.

Him, listening.

Her, eyes on the stars above.

Him, eyes on her.

The patience he extended to her made her regret how quickly she had lost hers earlier in the night. He had been worried about her and for that transgression she had been ready to storm off into the night, wounded.

It had taken her so long to describe the star shower, being pulled into a hole in the sky, reliving her own memories, and the scenes she hadn't lived before. She was losing her breath by the time she got to describing being in someone else's body.

"One moment, I have stocky fingers sudsed with soap and as I rinse them. I look in the mirror to find the face of this man I have never met before, but I am him. I splash cupped hands of water on my face and with the next splash, I'm a young mother, holding the hand of my sweet, light-haired child at a teacart. It must have been confused with my own memories too, because I've been to that teacart before and then I was knocking on the door of my favorite little green house."

"What?"

"I sort of love architecture, and there's this gorgeous home I've always extra loved. It's over by HQ on the pedestrian level. It has dark shale Sleekstone roofing, and floor to ceiling windows that could make you drool, and this gorgeous emerald gemstone door," she gushed. "I call it the Green Gem House in my head."

Amar suddenly seemed tense, maybe bored. It was one thing for him to listen to her go on about her ascension hallucination; it was a bit much to have him suffer through her nerding out on architecture.

"I'm yammering, sorry."

"No, keep going. What happened after you knocked on the door?"

Her heart filled. She didn't realize how devastated she might have been if he had wanted her to stop sharing.

She kept her monologue to the ascension and when she finally finished detailing the woman with the swishing skirts and her near-drowning experience, Amar asked her what she thought it all meant.

She exhaled with great force, at a loss for words.

He smirked at her. "That serious huh?"

CHAPTER 18

NOA

Noa lay on her stomach, arms under the pillow she had stolen from Amar. Last night, they had stayed up talking until dawn broke. He had led her back to his tent, her hand in his and given her one of his neatly folded shirts and a pair of thermal leggings. She had fallen asleep in his arms with his hand around her waist and breath on her neck.

Now, she was alone. And something rustled outside the tent.

"Hey," Amar said, ducking inside. "Sorry to sneak out on you. Figured I'd pack up your camp and bring your bag back here, so you could change into your own clothes."

She took her pack from him. "Thanks."

"Also, I had to tell Decker about last night."

"You what?" Noa's hands stopped shuffling through her duffel.

"I didn't tell him everything. I would *not* trust that man with your bigger secrets. But you can't go walking around like that—" He pointed to her bandaged head. "—without him noticing. I told him you were trying to get in more practice with Trax late last night, had a fall, and that I fixed you up."

"And what about me staying in your tent?"

"Ah, well, that didn't come up. You might want to hurry." His eyes shifted to her bag. "I'll let you get dressed."

Amar bowed out of the tent but ducked his head back in before leaving. "Also, Alexis caught me tearing down your tent, so she knows about you staying the night here. Sorry." He zipped the tent.

He didn't look sorry.

Noa decided a few more minutes of swimming in Amar's shirt was needed before she could face the questioning Alexis would throw at her over breakfast.

After she changed, she folded the shirt and pants he'd leant her and placed them near his pack. Neatly folded on the top of his bag was his shirt from yesterday. She picked it up and examined it. It was missing a sleeve and covered in her blood. There was mud splatter all down the back and black dirt at the hem from the beach sand.

It smelled like him but also the woods, the lake, and (somehow) stardust.

It reminded her of everything from the day before.

She shoved it in her bag.

Noa found Alexis sitting under a large tree with the others, melon hair bobbing along as she laughed. As Noa approached, V noticed her and began a slow clap, prompting the group to join in the applause.

"What did you tell them?" Noa scolded Alexis once she was closer.

"Sorry, Mrs. Marshal, can't keep all your secrets." Alexis smiled and shrugged, patting the ground next to her for Noa to sit.

Noa sat and glanced around the group, trying to hide a small smirk.

"Nothing happened," she said. Even though nothing did happen, or at least nothing that they had been implying, Noa felt the familiar heat of her face turning the bright pink of Alexis's hair. "Anyway, I have more important things to talk about."

"Like what happened to your head?" Zahira said. "Trax take another swing at you or something?"

Everyone laughed.

"Well—" Her hesitation cut the laughter short. "Oh, no. He didn't," she clarified. "I checked on him last night after our card game, and he kind of pushed me into going for a ride, but I was riding bareback." She grabbed Alexis's arm, excited to tell her that it had happened again but as the words parted her lips, she reconsidered sharing with the larger group.

Alexis filled her pause with spitfire questions. "You didn't? It happened? How?"

"Slow down," Jo said. "What happened? What is she

talking about?"

Alexis turned to give Noa a sheepish look. Her big brown eyes pleaded to tell the group.

V said what Alexis was miming, "If I didn't think you were crazy, they're not going to."

V had a point. Sort of.

Noa hadn't been surprised that V believed her. He was prone to rocking the boat and upsetting things. Sometimes she thought the reason he annoyed her so much was because he got to ask the questions and say the things she held back.

Before Noa could share more with the others, Amar came up from behind and handed her a bowl of hot breakfast.

"You should eat something good this morning," he said, sitting down with his own bowl.

The group's stare shifted to Amar. It took him a moment to notice the attention.

He swallowed his bite. "What?"

They shrugged and stirred their breakfast, turning their attention back to Noa.

"So are you going to tell us or not?" Jash asked, using his spoon to gesture toward Noa's crown of gauze. "What happened?"

She felt Amar's gaze snap toward her and she turned to meet it. His face was stern and she knew exactly what he was trying to tell her.

It's not worth it.

But she knew better. And it felt so good to tell the group, so right. There was no substitute for experiencing ascension but when Noa had told Amar, her pulse had quickened and her stomach floated and she had a taste of how good it felt to let her experience live on through telling others. This time, she sharpened the cadence of the story and delighted in captivating her friends, their eyes barely blinking and mouths agape as she described the experience in detail.

They were all so enthralled, Noa thought she might have been the only one to notice Amar storming off.

She knew she should go after him.

Explain. Straighten things out. But his upset was uncomfortable, and she didn't want to deal with it right now. She just wanted to be happy. So she let him go.

Later that night, Jo, Zahira, and Noa were elbow deep in sudsy pots scrubbing bowls of dried mash. Decker had pulled Noa aside mid-day for a not-so-stern talking to about her night-riding and to check on her head bump. When she told him she was fine, he reminded her she was on the schedule for dish duty tonight. It wasn't a punishment, he'd said, just a coincidence. But if she didn't shape up, he could find more dishes to keep her nights occupied.

She didn't mind doing dishes tonight. The three of them fell into a good, quiet rhythm and Noa was grateful for the reprieve. It was the first quiet moment she'd had all day. She wasn't used to talking that much and her cheeks hurt from smiling all day.

After her breakfast confession, she'd become the center of attention and target of any fleeting question that popped into the group's head throughout the day: Could she perhaps be having seizures? *She didn't think so. Never had one before.* Did this make her a prophet? *Surely not, but also she needed to look up that word again.* Would she report what happened to the Variety in a daily report? *Not yet.* Did she think she was the first one to ascend? *Maybe.* What did Trax have to do with it? *She wasn't sure.* Was it life changing? *Incredibly.* Would it happen again? *Would it happen again?*

Noa unstuck her brain from that question by focusing on a particularly difficult spot of dried mash that wasn't scrubbing clean. Her friends had met her with curiosity and interest all day, reassuring her they wanted to do everything they could to help her figure this out. Whatever *this* was. She didn't need to worry, just scrub.

"Jo, is it true there's a town soon?" Zahira asked, blowing air from her bottom lip to loose a strand of hair from her eyes without having to use soapy hands.

"Yeah, Veraccu is in a few days, according to our pace." Jo, the lanky, normal-blonde one—seriously, how had Noa confused him and Jash early on, they could not be more different—let out a heavy sigh. "And that will be our last connectivity. After that, we'll be ghosts for the rest of the Skill Trip."

"Calm down, Hopper. That's a Library town isn't it?"

"Hopper?" Noa asked.

"Lead Developer of the auto." Jo answered. "And yeah. Why?"

Zahira looked at Noa. "I don't think you're the first. And I have an idea for how we can prove it."

CHAPTER 19

From: Samitha Lavoie
Recipient: Noa Lavoie
2053 hrs., 10.06.0253

ARE YOU KIDDING ME?
You're really going to make me write you first? Multiple times?
Rogue.
Comm me when you can. Love you.

From: Chemi Lavoie
Recipient: Noa Lavoie
1020 hrs., 12.06.0253

MISSED VIDEO COMM

From: Chemi Lavoie
Recipient: Noa Lavoie
1220 hrs., 13.06.0253

MISSED VIDEO COMM

From: Armel Lavoie
Recipient: Noa Lavoie
1320 hrs., 13.06.0253

HELLO

Call your mum and me when you can, just checking in. Hope you're safe and experiencing great things on your Skill Trip. Wishing you great expansion, dearest daughter!

From: Samitha Lavoie
Recipient: Noa Lavoie
1947 hrs., 15.06.0253

FINE. I'LL WAIT.

I'm fine by the way. Being home alone with mum and dad is a breeze. I really hope I don't have to wait 2 months to hear from you, but I guess it's worse for you since you have to go 2 months without me. So sorry for these hard Sami-less times you are facing. Love you.

NOA

The night before passing through Veraccu (the only town on the Skill Trip's route to Main Ranch) the new Cavalry Assignments finally had enough connectivity to use their autos. Most Drops dedicated the first few hours of camp that night to writing family, checking comms, and submitting Optional Daily Reports that they had logged offline. Almost everyone missed dinner.

Noa ate alone, and waited for her friends. They had agreed to use part of the night to research their mission for tomorrow. She was almost at her tipping point, leg bouncing in impatience, when Jo and Jash appeared to retrieve her to get back to the group-tent.

"We're getting better at this," Noa said, entering the make-shift canvas structure and noticing significantly less threat of collapse than the first few they'd built.

"The key is a lot of knots," Jash said, pointing to his haphazard nests of rope holding the ceiling taut.

"A certain kind of knot?" Noa asked.

"No. Just a lot."

"Mm, quantity. Sure." Noa pretended to sincerely admire the messy corners as if they were the intricate joints of a skytower.

"We need four auto projections," Jo said, matter-of-fact. He often seemed immune to the light-spirits around him. Noa wondered if that meant he was impervious to dark ones, too. "Zahira. Me. V, can you open yours? And Noa, you too."

The four of them opened their autos, making a pyramid

of projections. Jash and Alexis sat in the circle peering over Noa and V's shoulders, respectively. Jo instructed them to query the Library system for reports and articles of earlier incidents using keywords like: "white heat," "ascension," "blankness," "experience," "hallucination," "Empyrean," "visit," and "intense."

They took turns brainstorming extra key words, and scrolling through lists of reports, jovially sharing funny details they read, at first, and then growing silent in concentration.

"Huh." It was Jo who broke the silence.

"*'Huh'* what?" Jash and Noa asked at the same time. Jash looked at Noa and readjusted himself, backing up. Apparently he also hadn't realized how close they had been sitting.

Jo's eyes scanned his screen, his face glowing blue in the light as they waited.

"Jo," Zahira said. Her voice was always a little softer when she spoke to Jo.

"I found something, but I don't think I was supposed to."

Noa scooched toward him, shoulder to shoulder, and peered at his projection. It looked nothing like hers. "What am I looking at?"

Jo explained he was running an advanced query that he picked up in his previous Assignment as an Advancement Balance Officer. ABOs ensured technology was progressing at a good pace, but not so much that humans became ignorant to their souls' development, so they knew all kinds of cool tech tricks.

"This search pulls incoming reports before they are

sorted. It's supposed to be a secure line but I gave it a try and voila."

Noa only read two sentences before Jo's display was cleared.

"Go back, I was still reading." Jash said.

"That wasn't him," Zahira said. "Since it was an incoming report, I'm guessing it probably got sorted."

Jo smiled at Zahira. "Yeah, exactly. The Librarians will review it and it will either get published as an original ODR, an annotated report, or a correction. Takes some time though."

"Well what did it say?" Alexis was up on her knees.

"Someone submitted a medical daily report that sounded like what Noa described as her first experience," Jo said. "The Library has to proof everything before they publish. News stories, daily reports, text annotations—everything. If they corroborate the report as true, it will be published and searchable tomorrow. This is big. Noa, this means you might not be the only one!"

Noa's heart sank. She should be excited. She should feel less lonely, more empowered, more sane. There might be others. Humankind might be finally evolving.

All of humankind.

Not just her.

CHAPTER 20

NOA

Over the course of the morning ride, the group ironed out their plan. They needed to buy time in Veraccu to research what was happening to the incoming reports and see if there were others. They would need access they weren't technically allowed to have, so their best bet at not getting caught was to have the entire Cavalry group break there.

After several sparring rounds between Noa and V, the group landed on Noa planting the seed with Sai's crew, getting them to make the request of Decker. It had been Noa's idea to provide that extra layer of protection from scrutiny, surely they couldn't be up to anything if the stop wasn't even their idea.

Chomping down fistfuls of granola at lunch, they watched

the conversation they had engineered into taking place unfold before them.

Sai approached Decker, pointed to his group of middle-of-the-pack Assignments, who looked back at Decker with pleading pouts. The Drops who hung around Sai were mostly the middle-aged men who raced to the front, and then slowly lost speed throughout the day, often finishing last to camp. Decker nodded along, listening to the request, and finally gave an approving wave in agreement.

The group buzzed with excitement. A few minutes later, Amar, who had informally become their assigned Marshal, approached to deliver the news they already knew. Amar spoke to the entire group, but he only looked at Noa. The usual calmness in his eyes was tainted with accusation.

"Sai's group asked if we could stop in Veraccu for the afternoon. We'll have connectivity there, and everyone can check-in with their families before we hit the second half of the Skill Trip. We'll be there in about two hours of riding, spend the rest of the day in town, and camp just outside. We'll get back on route with an early start tomorrow morning."

Noa's face beamed with pride that their plan had worked so flawlessly, and she exchanged eager smiles with Alexis and Zahira. As Amar walked away, his head shook in disappointment and Noa's coat of pride felt too tight. Wrong, even. Everyone else was on board, why couldn't he be? Plus, even if he *thought* they were up to something, he didn't know what. He had no right to judge.

"I can't believe that worked," Alexis said. "Noa, you're brilliant."

"And manipulative," V added.

Noa's chest tightened more and she gave V a wicked, pointed glare. He raised his hands to signal surrender. He had become somewhat less obnoxious since hanging around Alexis, but then he'd go and make comments like that, finding his way right back under her skin.

Pulling into town that afternoon, the team eagerly dismounted their horses and tied them off the trail outside the city. Noa took a second with Trax to pet him and rest her head on his shoulder.

"Ready?" Alexis nudged Noa with the rest of the group at her back.

"Ready," Noa agreed.

The six of them felt odd and out of place in the bustling town. Amar had been right; even this smaller city felt noisy and overwhelming after a few weeks on the trail. Noa couldn't imagine what it was like to go back to City Centre after a year or more at the ranch. But today, the sound of buses, music, sneakers on the pavement, and crumpling croissant wrappers were the least of her worries.

They stopped walking to join the larger group forming in front of Decker.

"We have about five or six hours here. You'll meet back at the horses just before sunset, so we can ride to camp and untack the horses before bed. To buy you all some time, we're not going to prepare dinner at camp tonight, so make sure that you eat something here. If you need me, you can reach me on my auto. Otherwise, enjoy and tell your families about the amazing progress you've made as Cavalry members in the past month." Decker punctuated his speech with an approving smile and led the march into the city.

They might as well have been Martians. Heads turned at their worn clothes and straw, lake-water hair. Luckily, there were sixty Martians and not just six, which gave their small group some cover of anonymity.

The six of them split off and circled the Veraccu Library's block to ensure they had distance from the other Cavalry members. They went over their plans one last time and entered.

Noa, Alexis, and Jash strolled into the Library first, leaving space between each of them. Jash took a seat in the lobby and opened his auto, pretending to scroll through updates as he made sure he had a good view of the reception desk.

Noa and Alexis approached the support desk in the middle of the floor. It was staffed by only one Librarian who did not look up. They didn't greet her either. Instead, they punched their requests for level two passes into the kiosk and waited while the machine printed out two small, paper-like chips. Noa and Alexis walked to the stairwell, scanned their chips, and waited for the door to unlock.

The Librarian briefly looked up from her desk when the door unlatched but returned her nose to her auto screen just as quickly.

Moments later, Jo and V walked in—followed, finally, by Zahira. As planned, the five of them met in the stairwell and held out their paper chips for Jo to scan. Noa tried to discern what changes Jo was making as he ran the re-coding program but, before she could even identify the mechanism he was manipulating, he closed his screen.

"Done. Noa and V, your chips are only good for the sixth floor. Zahira and I will share one. It's good for all upper levels—floors seven to ten. Alexis will have the other two, one for the sixth floor and one for the upper floors. That way, she can help either of us if we need it. The upper levels were a riskier program, so I'm hoping we didn't already set off any alarms. Either way, we should start heading out. I don't know how much time we have."

They all climbed the stairwell until they reached the sixth floor. Noa and V waited at the door until the others were on the level above them before they entered.

Their Cavalry clothes stood out against the stiff grey uniforms of the Librarians. They didn't have a reasonable disguise or excuse to be on the sixth level so, instead, they decided their only option was to remain completely unseen.

They walked carefully by placing their heels down and rolling their feet to their toes to minimize any noise. Both being tall, they crouched slightly to avoid being seen above the workspace dividers.

They found one empty desk in the sea of cubicles occupied by hyper-focused Librarians, but someone could easily walk by and notice them. At the same time, Noa and V noticed the dimmed corner of the floor, which looked to have several unoccupied workspaces, ushering each in that direction. Together, they crept through the office and gave muted, overdramatic signals to each other to move this way or that. When they got close to the dim, empty corner, a light above them flickered on.

Motion sensors.

Any Librarian who looked in their approximate direction would see them creeping in a spotlight. V darted behind a supply bin for cover, and Noa dashed into a nearby hallway. She ditched her crouching position and walked normally down the corridor, looking for a control panel.

She needed to turn off the automatic light for that corner, so they could sit and work in peace. As she searched the hallway, she remembered visiting her father's Psychology office. The Psych office was much different. Each person had a cozy office filled with personal trinkets and each room had texture, color, and design. It was meant to be a comforting space. Here, the space was designed so that no one would want to stay any longer than they had to.

Noa spotted a door with a window at the center of the building. No one was in the room and she spotted something that looked like a control panel on the wall. She confidently swung the door open and was unexpectedly confronted by a small woman.

The woman gasped at the sight of Noa and clutched her heart.

Then, she laughed.

Noa mimicked the laughter.

"Oh sweetie," the woman said, "you just about gave me a heart attack."

Noa froze but the woman just looked at her warmly, patted her arm, and walked through the door, out of the room.

Hurriedly, Noa opened the latched-but-not-locked control panel. She ran her finger down the neatly labeled switch list: east corner, breakroom, north corner, Manager's suite, west Corner, kitchen, lavatories.

Noa opened her auto and checked the compass. *West corner.*

She flipped the switch and relatched the door, nonchalantly returning to the sea of occupied desks. She found V still crouched behind the supply bin and put an arm to his back.

He flinched when she touched him.

"It's me," she whispered.

He rolled his eyes. "Where have you been?"

"I turned off the automatic lights for that corner, so we should be able to work over there, now."

They looked both ways and darted for the dark corner. Hidden and safe in the shadowed cubicle, they opened a stationed Library auto. The screen shone blue, just like their personals, but had a completely different set up.

Noa cocked her head in confusion. "What the…?"

"Don't worry, I got it." V selected a few options from the main interface until he got to a screen that looked like small chips with short descriptions floating through pipelines. "I sorted the intakes by topic. Each of these pipelines has information intakes about one of the search terms that Jo gave us. This one—" V pointed to the largest tube on the screen. "—is for the term 'white,' and this one—" He pointed to another. "—is for 'heat.'" V placed a finger on each pipeline and bent them until they merged. "Now, all of these requests have those two words, but not necessarily together."

V carried on in silence adding more keywords and creating more connections.

Unable to help, Noa sank further in her chair and crossed

her arms. With every minute that passed, her throat itched to scream, but she swallowed it and waited.

"Anything?" Noa asked, combing through the three pipelines of incoming information V had finally assigned her.

"Nothing. How long has it been?"

"Almost an hour. We're running out of time." Noa rolled her head and shoulders, giving her eyes a break from the glowing blue light. "Is there anything we can do to change what we're looking for? Maybe the list that Jo gave us doesn't have the right search terms?"

"Yeah, or no one in the world happened to communicate with the heavens and report it in the last twenty-four hours."

"Why are you always like this with me and not with anyone else?"

"I am like this with everyone, you're just the only person who's offended by it."

She scoffed. "I'm not offended. You're being a jerk, and I don't see why no one else cares."

"You mean Alexis. You don't understand why Alexis doesn't care that I'm such a jerk?"

Noa narrowed her eyes at him.

His smile taunted her. "It's because she realizes, like everyone else, that we're all jerks. Even you, your highness. Actually, maybe especially you."

She frowned as his smile widened.

V pulled himself closer. "I bother you because you know you are just as selfish, manipulative, and egotistical as I am.

And you can't stand seeing it in me, because you hate seeing it in yourself."

She pushed herself away, clumsily banging her elbow on the table. V reacted quickly, holding the desk still with one hand and gripping her wrist with the other. They froze as the reverb from the table echoed through the office.

When they were sure no one was coming over, Noa shook free from V's grip.

His voice was a quieter whisper when he continued. "And you're jealous."

"Of what?"

V leaned back. His voice was still quiet, but his posture returned to its normal state—unapologetically taking up space. "Every once in a while, some of the true, darker side of you slips out, and you stuff it back inside. And every time you bury it deeper, you get a little more jealous of me because I live out here with all of my shadows on my sleeves."

Noa wondered if V grew up with a parent assigned to Psych, too. Noa's father was always lecturing on the importance of feeling feelings, but her mother would either ignore her or scold her when she got emotional. Maybe V's parents said the same kinds of things but actually let him do what they advised, rather than contradicting it. Maybe she was jealous.

Noa turned her focus back to the screen that was still searching pipe after pipe of text with no returns. "I don't have a darker side, V."

"You do. And it's the part I like best about you, by the way."

She fiddled with her long braid, eyes still glued to the

screen. She could feel her chest start to loosen and tremble with—something.

V kept going. "Like when you bowled over Alexis and me and our horses to race for days straight just so you could try to ascend again? That was classic. Who cares how tired we were—as long as you got what you wanted." He feigned soft applause for her.

"Shut up." Her body pulsed with anger now..

"No. I have more proof. Like how you roll your eyes and cross your arms at everything I do and say. You used to be able to stay so composed, but now that darkness is starting to leak through your cracks. It's great."

She rubbed the scar on her wrist, and pretended not to be bothered by him. She could still be composed.

"I think it started during your time in Service, but I want to take a little credit for breaking you open during those weeks of prep class. Every time I asked for help, you leaked. Didn't matter that I was desperate, or what I was going through—nice Noa didn't even ask."

He ran his tanned hands through his white hair. He had clearly gone further in this game than he'd meant to. He huffed and raised his gaze to her, where she patiently waited for him.

She'd never looked at V this closely, or for this long. His icy blue eyes had started to wrinkle at the edges, the lines of which had collected dust and tan lines from the rides. He bit one side of a rosy lip and rested his head on a hand, not breaking her gaze. "All of those shitty things you've done are forgivable because we get it. Everyone else in the world gets that we can all be awful, rude, petty people some of the time.

But for some reason, you can't see it in yourself. Except for when you look at me."

They stared at each other for a long moment. Noa sat in V's spite, which now looked like pity, and she recoiled, folding smaller inside of herself. She wondered if she looked smaller to him too.

Noa's wrist buzzed, and she broke away from him to read the comm that had come in on her auto.

"We have to go. Now."

CHAPTER 21

NOA

Noa and V banged shoulders as they thudded onto the last step in unison. They'd sleuthed their way off the sixth floor and into the stairwell, sprinting up to the seventh-level landing where Alexis waited for them.

"What's happening?" they both asked.

Before Alexis answered, their attention drew upward to Zahira bounding down the stairwell, barely slowing as she passed them.

"We have to get Decker," she said, her breath reverberating with heavy steps propelling her down the stairs.

"What's going on?" Noa asked as everyone followed Zahira.

"Jo got caught on the technician's auto. They're bringing him to the Head Librarian. The other technician saw me, and they're probably looking for me by now."

"Wait, Decker?" V asked. "Are you sure we have to get him involved?"

Noa thought about what Amar had said about not trusting Decker. She should have talked to Amar. She should have listened to him, or at least heard him out. Maybe they wouldn't be in this mess. Or at least they'd know how to get out of it.

"That's what Jo said to do if this happened," Alexis said as they rounded the fourth floor. "Plus, who else is going to be able to ask the Head Librarian to let Jo go?"

They tumbled down the rest of the stairs and spilled into the lobby. The front desk Librarian's head jerked up and the few others in the lobby froze.

The group looked to the door and back to the Librarian.

The Librarian's arm reached under her desk and the sound of the front door locking echoed across the room.

They were held in a conference room for an hour until a new Librarian in a stiff grey uniform retrieved them. She led them down several hallways, and they took a lift to the tenth floor.

The elevator doors opened directly into a large, sterile office. Two black leather chairs and a large grey couch sat centered in front of a massive concrete desk. One chair was already occupied—Decker, still wearing his large brim hat, sat wide-legged and leaning back, looking frustrated and out of place. His shoulders, which were usually thrown back in fits of laughter, were tense and hunched.

"Have a seat. Head Librarian Tempsen will be with you in a moment," said the grey uniform. She turned and left them alone in the room.

Noa, Alexis, V, and Zahira sat on the long grey couch.

Decker sat still, not facing them. Even from a profile view, he looked angry and exhausted.

Jash still hadn't joined them, and they had no idea where he was. Noa didn't see any reason why he would confess—as he really hadn't done anything but sit in the lobby as a lookout—but she was annoyed he wasn't sitting on the couch with them.

Noa leaned forward. "Decker?" She wanted to give a partial confession before they had company. But Decker didn't turn around. He held up a hand, silencing her before slowly lowering it back to his lap.

The door behind them opened and shut loudly.

"Decker, is it? I'm Tempsen, Head Librarian."

Noa was surprised she recognized the tall man with curly blond hair and freckles from the Reassignment ceremony at the Bowl. His face still looked tangled in a snarl and, as he moved across the room to greet Decker, he floated inside his stiff clothes.

Decker removed his hat and stood to greet Tempsen. "Nice to meet you. Apologies, sir. I believe my Cavalry members have gotten into some trouble here."

Tempsen gestured for Decker to sit again before perching himself on the desk in front of the group.

Decker stayed standing.

"Mmhmm, it does seem that way," Tempsen said, eyeing Decker. "Jo is wrapping up some questions with my Technicians, but it doesn't seem there has been any harm done today. Except, maybe, to the ego of our Security Officers."

Decker laughed softly. "When you're finished with your questioning, I'll take my troop out of your hair and hit the road. Today was only meant to be a quick break for them." Decker's tone was sharp and directed at everyone on the couch. "And I have others who still need to make it back to camp on time to get their rest."

"I'm sure," Tempsen said. "I just need to know what they were actually looking for first."

You already know, Noa thought. Something in his demeanor told her he knew much more than he let on. He was too calm, too arrogant.

"Noa?" Decker looked at her. "You seemed eager to speak earlier?"

She didn't hesitate. They had prepared for this. Jo had prepared them for this.

"There are rumors about the Variety and the Cavalry," she said. "Surely, you've heard them. Jo was convinced he could find proof. I've never been a Technician, so I don't really know what we were looking for, but Jo thought we might be able to find something if we had the same access as a Librarian." She let her voice trail off.

Tempsen's bottom lip twitched at her lie.

"Ah," Decker exhaled. "There's no substance to those rumors. Y'all should know better." His eyes narrowed at them but brightened as soon as he turned to Tempsen. "My apologies again. The Cavalry Skill Trip is a rigorous one and can be a stirring place for the imagination." Decker adjusted himself, preparing to leave.

"Hmm." Tempsen took a long look at each delinquent on the couch. His sharp glare landed back on Noa, but she refused to flinch under his prying gaze. Almost imperceptibly, he nodded to her—just as he had at the Bowl.

The door opened again, and Jo was escorted into the room by a few Librarian Security Officers.

Tempsen took a step toward Decker, pointing an arm toward the door. "Looks like we're done here. In the future, you would do well to better understand the filtering process here. It is all detailed on your autos. There's nothing we see that the public doesn't." He looked back to Noa. "I hope you found the answers you were looking for. Have a safe rest of your trip."

"Thank you, sir," Decker said. "Appreciate the kindness."

"You are all going to ride ahead and set up camp tonight," Decker said when they finally reached the horses. They'd walked in complete silence from the Library to the edge of town. "You're going to wake up early to cook the morning meal, do the dishes, and pack up. And it will repeat like that until I'm not disappointed anymore."

Noa didn't like angry Decker. She was glad Amar had stopped her from telling him about her ascension. It also sucked knowing her friends' nights and mornings were ruined for a while. Maybe V was right—maybe she was more of a jerk than she let on.

They took their punishment on the chin and rode into the

sunset weighed down by the camp supplies, extra horses, and guilt.

"I can't believe that was all for nothing," V said.

"I know," Alexis said. "Jo, I'm so sorry."

Noa steered Trax alongside Jo. "You got something didn't you?"

"How did you know?" A coy smile spread across Jo's porcelain features, only a small dimple interrupted the smoothness of his cheeks.

Alexis gasped. "Wait, you *did* find something?"

"Not just something." Jo leaned in as if they were able to huddle together on their giant horses. "I found what we were looking for."

Jo explained that he'd located the redacted information requests. The intake information was scrubbed, but the outgoing information was coded the same way each time—a pattern his smart searches caught. At first glance, he didn't think anything of the codes, as the routing information appeared to go to the upper-level Library offices, presumably, to the Head Librarian. But the Head Librarian's review code was prefaced with HLR, and these pieces were prefaced by HQR.

Again, Jo expectantly waited for everyone to catch up to what was apparently a shocking announcement.

"And?" Zahira urged, sweetly.

"HQR?" Jo gave everyone one last chance. "It stands for HeadQuarters Review."

Noa's mind spun. She knew what this meant. The Library was supposed to be entirely independent from Variety HeadQuarters. Having any information—but especially information about ascension—scrubbed from their records and sent to HQ seemed like the cornerstone violation that made for an overly controlling empire.

"What do we do now?" V asked. "Do they know you know that?"

Yes, Noa thought.

"I don't think so. I mean, they might figure it out, but they didn't seem to let on when they were questioning me," Jo said. "And I think it means we have another mission on our hands. We need to figure out why HQ is hiding this."

The weight of that comment hung heavy in the air.

Sleuthing around the Library was one thing, but taking on HeadQuarters was a much more serious risk.

"We've done enough for one day," Noa said. "Maybe we just try to get through tonight and a few mornings of dishes."

The air pressure dropped as everyone was let off the hook from planning another complicated and confusing mission of mysterious stakes. Noa's internal pressure didn't let up though. Energy rose in her throat, and she wanted to scream. She longed for a night of laughter and cards with her friends. A boring phone call with her family. A comforting hug from Amar.

Amar.

He would have some words for her. Or, perhaps, none at all.

CHAPTER 22

NOA

"Are you done with the dishes?" Noa asked Zahira, finishing another round of breakfast duty.

"Yeah, go ahead and pack them. We're going to take down the supply tent."

Noa stacked the dry bowls and put them into the saddlebag designed for dish supplies. Although Decker had made it known he was not impressed with their shenanigans, his punishment wasn't that harsh. Noa didn't mind setting up and tearing down the camp. It was nice to have a routine to quiet her chaotic mind.

Noa walked the saddlebag to the pack horses.

"Need a hand?" Amar asked.

They hadn't talked in days. Which meant she hadn't been able to explain, or look in his eyes for that calming feeling she longed for. She wondered if it was normal for couples to go from an intense connection to several days of disconnect. Then again, normal couples weren't half-human, half-oracle. Normal couples probably knew if they were even a couple.

And that was the sad truth. They weren't together. Because if they were, she would know.

Amar lifted the bag from Noa's hands and slung it over the pack horse's back.

"You make that look easy," she said.

"After you do it a hundred times, it is easy." He walked around the horse and stood next to her. "Are you going to tell me what you were doing at the Library, or should I guess?"

"I think if you guessed, you'd probably guess correctly."

"Thought so." His hand rubbed the back of his neck. "You need to be more careful. If Decker or the Library or HQ figure out what is going on."

"Then what?" Noa asked. "They're going to make me disappear?"

"Yes, Noa." His voice raised with urgency. He regained control. "You know that is a possibility. You know that there is something wrong here and something to be worried about. Otherwise, you wouldn't be doing all of this sneaking around. Otherwise, you wouldn't be assigned to Cavalry in the first place."

"You don't know that. It's all rumor and speculation and reading between the lines. I have to know. I have to know who else. And why does this have to be kept a secret?"

"You need to let it go."

Noa waited for him to say more but he was done. He ran his hands through his hair, thinking, frustrated. Worried.

"Jo found something." She explained to Amar about the other reports of ascension and that Jo had learned the information was being hidden and sent to HeadQuarters. "The others don't think Tempsen knows we found anything, but I think he does. We're already at risk. And we need to do something."

"No, you don't."

"Why? What do you know that makes you so much better equipped to make this judgment call? I'm the one who has ascended. I'm the one at risk here."

"My parents disappeared five years ago."

Noa adjusted herself closer to him, waiting for more.

"My dad was always this goofy, weird guy." Amar's eyes lit up talking about his dad. "He didn't really subscribe to the Variety. He believed people could 'evolve' following their own hearts. He was a romantic like that. And well, he worked at HQ."

"Hm," Noa huffed. Having that kind of outlook on life and being under the added scrutiny of working in HQ, she could put two and two together on how he disappeared. Or rather, who disappeared him. Noa readjusted herself to face Amar completely. "How long was he at HQ before...?"

"Three years if you can believe it. I don't know how he even made it that long. Before that he was reassigned constantly. He was an Arithmetician, an Artist in Paint, a WildLife Steward, and a Sleekstone Mason. For someone who was so against the Variety, he thrived in it. Once, he was even a Greeting Writer. I think that one made him happiest."

"What's that one?"

"You know those messages you can choose from on your

auto to send for special occasions? Like Reassignments or birthdays or for Last First ceremony?"

Noa nodded.

"He wrote those. Except, instead of keeping it heartfelt and funny, he added secret messages."

"He *what?*" Noa balked in her laughter. The idea was absurd. As if her mother could have sent the neighbor a Happy Reassignment message with ulterior motives.

"He would use a coded alphabet or even make the sentences into acrostics for what he was really trying to say." Amar chuckled to himself.

"And what was he trying to say?"

Amar shrugged. "I don't know but, whatever it was, got him reassigned to HQ. I think. And that was the end of that."

Noa didn't believe that Amar didn't know, but she didn't pry. She knew of people disappearing from the Variety. Mainly UEs on her Service Assignment. They'd told her stories of their family members disappearing without a trace after questioning the Variety. Noa could imagine that someone like Amar's father would make a great candidate for Service Intervention. She was about to concede that he might have some ground to stand on in his warning her, but he continued.

"And my mom."

"What about her?" Noa's blood rushed with nervous anticipation. He had said *his parents* disappeared. Not just his father.

"Her family—they lived outside the Variety. We didn't see them often, so I don't know—not for sure. But, to her, it was a plain fact that they had started ascending. A long time ago too. You can see why she partnered with someone as open-minded as my dad."

"So. I'm not the first person you've heard of ascending."

He tightened his lips and looked at her shaking his head. "No. You're not."

"Where is your mom's family?"

Amar rubbed his face with both of his hands, like he was tired from more than just a long day.

"Maybe that's enough about me for today."

"No way, I want to hear everything about you." It slipped out without a thought. *Again.* It was too forward. *Again.* Why did her mouth have to move so much faster than—

He stepped toward her. "I care about you Noa. I want to get to know you better and see where all of your awkward energy comes from and learn why you are always scratching at your palm, and listen to you talk about your favorite buildings. But not if you're going to keep chasing this and putting yourself at risk."

This felt a lot like they were together. Or at least like they could be.

She nodded in agreement and he quickly closed the distance between them, enveloping her in a hug she didn't know she had been craving. It hurt her heart to be in his arms. That one nod had committed her to a promise she had no intention of keeping. She wanted to keep chasing this. She wanted answers to her questions. She wanted to feel like she had something to offer, that she could make a difference. For once in her life, she had the opportunity to be brave. She had to step up—why else would she have all this courage?

As they pulled away, Noa looked at Amar and he peered

back, his gaze bouncing between her eyes and her lips. She leaned in, almost imperceptibly, but hesitated.

He didn't hesitate. He picked up where she left off and kissed her gently, raising his hand from her waist up her back.

She pressed into him, taking as much from his lips as she wanted. His warm hand found the base of her neck and tangled in her hair.

They had never kissed before and yet, somehow, she had missed it. She had missed him.

When they finally broke apart, she stared at her toes.

Two of his fingers raised her chin back to him, and her lips were met with more small kisses until they broke apart again—this time, she kept her head held high.

Both of their love-struck smiles fell.

"Do you hear that?" he asked, nodding in the direction of camp over her shoulder.

"Mmhmm."

Alexis and Zahira walked over the hill. Zahira was sobbing loudly.

Noa rushed over. "What's going on? Zahira?" She put an arm on her friend's shoulder, but it was swiped off.

"Noa, don't," Alexis warned in a hushed voice.

"This is all your fault!" Zahira's tone was sharp. Her skin paled when she raised her voice, and her eyes were puffy from crying. Even still, she was beautiful and reminded Noa of a watercolor painting—blurry and blended but luminous.

"What is going on?" Amar asked, catching up to them.

Zahira stared at Amar, not looking at Noa. "Your girlfriend got my boyfriend reassigned."

"What?" Noa didn't understand.

Zahira grunted, and Alexis filled the two of them in.

"Jo got a Reassignment notice this morning from the Variety. He has to return to Veraccu later today for transport. His Assignment is immediate with prep on site."

"What?" Noa repeated. "This can't be a coincidence."

"Of course, it is not a coincidence." Zahira spoke slowly to Noa, over-enunciating each word in condescension. "Jo went out of his way to answer your questions, and now you and that stick-figure Librarian got him reassigned."

Noa and Amar left Zahira with Alexis, and found V and Jash helping Jo pack his Cavalry belongings. Noa's heart sank.

"It's going to be fine," Jo said. "This is life in the Variety. It could have happened to anyone."

"But it didn't happen to anyone. It doesn't happen to anyone!" Noa raised her voice. "We always get notice. And, during a Skill Trip? That's unheard of."

Jo's face was full of desperate kindness. He obviously already knew everything she was saying. She didn't need to spell out the absurdity of his painful situation.

"There's got to be something we can do," Noa said.

V laughed.

"Has anyone ever contested a Variety Assignment?" she asked. She knew the answer. *No.* There wasn't even a way to make such a request. Jo would leave for town instead of riding off with them. In a few hours, he would be gone. She had torn him apart from Zahira. And what about his horse?

Would Adobe get to go with Jo? Or since they hadn't finished Skill Trip, would he go back to being a pack horse without a partner.

There was nothing left to do.

Noa hugged Jo and held back her tears, trying not to upset him anymore than she already had. "I'm sorry."

"It was my choice to help, and I'd do it again. You know what we found, and things are a bit more complicated now, but you'll figure it out." Jo looked at Amar, sternly. "All of you will. I'm not giving up and you can't either. Not now."

V pushed Noa back and took her place standing in front of Jo. "Alright, enough, we only have a few hours left with the man. Maybe you should leave that tent up, so you and Zahira can spend some time alone before you go?" He raised his brows unsubtly, which Jo ignored.

"I should go find her." He waved to Noa and Amar and took off toward Zahira's tent.

Noa, Amar, Jash, and V stood around Jo's empty tent.

"We have to fix this," Noa said. "We can't let Jo get reassigned. That's not what the Variety is meant for. We need him and—"

V interrupted. "What would you have us do? Break back into the Library? That Tempsen guy would have us disappeared or, well…" He motioned widely. "Reassigned."

"We can ask. We can at least *try*. We should go back to the Library and ask Tempsen what is going on. He's hiding something. If they think Jo knows something, and they're removing him from us because of it, maybe one of us is next and—"

"Enough!" Jash cut her off. "Noa, jeez. That's enough. This

sucks, Jo getting reassigned. He is like one of my best friends, so I think I'm more upset about this than you, but you don't see me chasing down the Variety and making it all about me. This is the way it is. Just drop it. You've done enough."

Noa felt ugly, spattered in flecks of accusation. She had been casting blame on herself but hadn't expected the others to blame her, too. If she couldn't fix this, she would have to survive her own internal guilt, and the disdain of others. She excused herself to pack her own camp. She would prepare for a day of riding alone.

CHAPTER 23

NOA

"You think the Skill Trip was hard, wait until training," Amar told Noa as they rode side by side. He had been her rare company over the last weeks of Skill Trip.

The final leg of the route had taken them through steep, rocky terrain. Now, Noa carefully maneuvered Trax down a thin mountain path speckled with uneven white rock. The trail was bordered by tall pines which, even though they didn't green until high on their trunk, were dense enough to limit her line-of-sight. Considering where she'd started nearly two months ago to what she was capable of now, she doubted training would be harder.

Noa brushed him off. "I'm sure it's so much tougher than riding a horse for the first time—for two months straight." She petted Trax's neck and sent a small prayer to the Gods above that training wasn't actually more difficult. She could barely remember that excruciating first day. Actually, she could recall it perfectly. And it made her want to flick Trax on the ear remembering how excruciating he had made that day for her. He had swung at her! She was used to his size now, but he was still giant. She withheld the vengeful thwack of her finger; he had become a reliable partner. Trax and Amar were pretty much all she had now.

"Feels like an eternity since we started, doesn't it?" Amar said, seeming to read her mind.

"I remember when I first got my Reassignment notice. I had no idea what Cavalry even was." Her voice trailed off. She was lying. Not on purpose, out of habit. The moment she had received her notice of Reassignment to Cavalry, she knew exactly what it meant. Not in the way she typically defined knowing things, but in the way that her sister and Alexis knew things—certainly, without the burden of proof. She had pretended not to think anything of it for the weeks leading up to her Reassignment ceremony, for the sake of her family. Noa had prepared herself to dispel any of her parent's concern about the sudden and long-distance Reassignment but they had never confronted the subject. *Of course they didn't.*

With greater distance between her and them now, Noa questioned why she was always doing that—shifting and shrinking to make peace for her parents. They had never explicitly asked her to. Sami didn't. Why had she always felt so compelled to?

"When I got my notice," Amar said, "I thought it was the end of the world. End of my life." He paused, lost in thought.

Noa slowed Trax. "You okay?"

"Noa, there's something I need to tell you before we get to the ranch tonight."

"Ahh, you have a wife and kids?" she joked.

"I'm serious."

Her back straightened, now supporting an uneasy stomach.

"Remember how I told you I was at HQ before Cavalry?" She nodded.

"And how I said I was untrusting?"

Her eyes narrowed, waiting for more. Of course, she remembered that. She'd been so frustrated when she hadn't understood the comment. She had forgotten to follow up on it, but her curiosity returned.

"After my parents disappeared I was assigned to HQ. What are the odds?" He asked rhetorically. "I wanted to know everything about my father's last days, but it wasn't open for discussion. They were just keeping an eye on me, testing if I was like my dad."

"And?"

Amar chuckled. "And I was Reassigned to Cavalry. What do you think?"

"Oh, yeah."

"But I lasted at HQ for a year or so and spent every day trying to learn more."

Amar explained how he'd asked around, and how no one admitted to remembering his father. He'd even found the official report about his parents summating that they had abandoned the Variety. His parents were added to the Service investigation list but nothing came of it year after year.

One day, Amar followed a lead and was caught breaking into the Pastor's office. He wasn't punished—just calmly told to return home for the evening.

"The next day, I was Reassigned. *We* were reassigned."

"Oh." Her stomach clenched tighter. "What?"

"I have a younger sister."

"Okay…and your parents are gone," she said, slightly stupefied, trying to catch up. "So that means…"

"Tali lives with me at Main. She's thirteen, too young to be on her own."

"Tali." The name floated out of Noa's mouth like a cloud. Amar's sister. "Who's watching her now?"

"The bison." Amar stared at Noa, playfully annoyed. He continued when she furrowed her brow. "Mirai's partner, Andrea, takes care of her when I'm working or on a Skill Trip."

Noa didn't know what to say.

"I know it's a lot. But you're probably going to meet her soon, so I thought I'd give you a heads up."

"A few hours heads-up? Yeah, that seems fair." Noa wanted to be mad at him for not telling her earlier, but the lack of conviction in her tone let on that she wasn't.

"I wasn't keeping it from you on purpose. It's just, Tali is all I have and…" He paused, recollecting himself. "No excuses. I'm sorry, I should have told you sooner."

He was good at apologies. Another thing she could stand to learn from him.

The last hours riding to Main Ranch were grueling. Terrain accounted for a portion of the difficulty, as the environment quickly transitioned from mountain foothills to flat, scorched desert land. Sand whipped in the wind and the hot sun made sitting in a saddle uncomfortable. The main degree of difficulty, however, came from having to confront that this Skill Trip would end with loneliness, emptiness, and nothing to show.

Noa's eyes pricked with tears. Before this assignment, she hadn't known much, so she hadn't longed for much either. She wasn't content, per se, but she was okay. Now, she knew the glory of ascension, the pride of being special and noticed, the warmth of being supported by close friends, and the drive of having something to fight for. Her heart ached for all the new experiences she now knew and was without.

Descending into Main Ranch was like reaching a salt-water oasis. Beautiful, but unhealing.

Copper, taupe, russet, and black soil deposits streaked rolling hills that were speckled with evergreen shrubs (which were more laurel than green). In the middle of the plain, a massive A-frame log cabin with large windows anchored a desert development that extended into barns, stables and cabins.

The small town backed up to a natural skyline of sandstone formations with stacks and arches replicating the shorter man-made structures plopped in front. In the distance, a particularly large formation rose high into the sky, changing color from its black charred base to a soft peach at its plateau peak.

The Marshals first led the Drops to the stables where they untacked their horses before being shown around the barns. Trax was visibly relieved to be at home in his permanent stall.

Finally, they were led to their dormitories, which winged either side of the large A-frame building.

Noa's dorm was simple: furnished with a small wooden dresser, a laundry machine for her clothes, a personal fridge, her own bathroom, and the most luxurious bed she'd ever seen in her life. Sure, it was a stiff single, but compared to her tent, it was everything. The room was not particularly spectacular, but it was hers.

Noa's shower felt infinitely long. She let the hot, clean water run over her body. She washed and conditioned her hair twice and scrubbed her feet until the water ran clean again. She took several extra minutes to clean all the dirt out from under her nails.

When she stepped barefoot from the shower and into her room, a new version of herself emerged.

Sitting in her cozy towel, she flipped through her auto. With connectivity restored, she considered calling her family. She had never returned their comm videos and certainly hadn't had time for a live call that day in Veraccu. She'd occasionally sent them a note or two, knowing the message would deploy when she had connectivity, and they would receive it moments later when she didn't.

Now, she could finally call them.

She shut her auto.

She needed to wait until things were going better, then she would call them. They wouldn't mind if she settled in for a day or two.

For the first time since she'd packed them, Noa took her favorite blue jeans and jumper out of her pack. She pulled them on to find her pants sat loosely around her waist and the jumper wore baggier around her chest. Like everyone else, she'd become a little leaner and more muscular on the trip.

She looked in the mirror, another thing she had not done in a very long time. She liked the way she looked, which was a pleasant surprise. Time away from her reflection had given her a new perspective on her features. Her cheekbones were more prominent, and her nose was still cute—from the front, anyway.

Today, she didn't just feel *good enough*. She felt *good*.

CHAPTER 24

TALI

Tali ran to hug her brother. "Oh my Gods, you stink!"

Amar hugged her with one arm, the other still holding his rucksack. He twirled her around and set her back down. She'd left Andrea's early that morning and spent the entire day waiting on the porch.

She had so much to tell him.

"I haven't had access to a proper bathroom in four months, what's your excuse?" He tousled Tali's hair.

She ducked and came up on his other side, pulling at his heavy bag.

"Here, I'll carry this."

He let her take it. "Oh yeah, did you get really strong this summer?"

Tali flexed her other arm. "Swimming, yoga with Yori,

and running." She waddled with the bag hitting against her leg as they entered the house. She dropped the pack just inside the door. "No riding though," she added with a flair of disappointment.

"That soon, huh? I thought you'd wait for me to be back at least an hour before bringing it up." Amar kicked his feet out of dust-crusted boots and peeled off his socks.

Tali followed him as he carefully padded across the house to the laundry room, throwing his socks directly into the machine.

"I don't have that kind of time. I'll look so stupid if I've lived here for *years* and can't ride as well as these new members."

"Well, we don't want you looking stupid, do we?" He started stripping off his layers to put them in the wash.

"Do you mean it?" Tali jumped and hugged her brother again.

"But you have to go through training, just like everyone else."

"Okay, I'm going to leave before you change your mind. You shower and do your washing. I'll get lunch stuff out for you to cook."

"It's so nice to be home where I can do all the laundry and cooking again."

"I know, right?"

Tali closed the door behind her and charged into the kitchen. As she started fixing lemonade with lemons she'd brought home from Andrea's garden, her mind wandered through all the ways she might tell Amar about her ascensions. She wanted to tell him everything, right away.

Especially about Grandma Dia and seeing mom.

But he'd become a worrier ever since Mom and Dad left. And she needed him to keep his word on letting her finally learn to ride. She'd have to wait until after training.

CHAPTER 25

NOA

Noa walked into the main cabin mess hall, tugging at her sleeve and stroking the scar on her palm. Moments ago, her jeans and jumper had felt like a ballroom gown compared to the riding clothes she'd alternated for the past two months. Now, her clothes felt exactly like what they were—the plain uniform of a plain girl.

She'd been imagining the main cabin for months.

Based on Decker's gruff exterior, she'd envisioned a small dingey camp kitchen with fold-out tables, low ceilings, and scuffed doors. Instead, the entrance to the hall was grand with tall, ornately carved wooden French doors. The room's ceiling was vaulted with a crystal chandelier draping from the center. Walls made of real logs were also carved with intricate designs. At the far end of the hall, floor-to-ceiling windows overlooked the mountainous foothills and dense forest.

Noa approached the large windows to examine the path they'd rode in on earlier that day. She held her hand a few inches off the window, feeling the barrier of where the room temperature gave way to the chill coming through the glass. It was all so impossible. The drastic temperature changes. That she was here. That she'd made it all the way from her home in City Centre out across that tiny tree-lined trail.

"Hey."

Noa turned to find Zahira, who had changed into black leggings that fit her snuggly and a zipped athletic jacket. Somehow her outfit looked like both sports and formal wear.

"Where do you even find a jacket like that?" *Seriously.* She thought she'd been getting better with nervously spitting out every thought in her head. "Sorry, I mean, you look great."

Zahira smiled instinctively at the compliment and looked Noa up and down, as if readying herself to return one. Instead, she just let her mouth fidget.

"Alexis mentioned inviting you to sit with us at dinner tonight."

Noa cocked her head, unsure what to do with the statement.

"I guess she thought it might be nice if I was the one who invited you. Not that you need an invitation or anything. But just like. You know, because it's been a while." Zahira's expression was hard to read, but Noa was familiar with her sharp looks and her face wasn't charged with anger.

"Yeah, it has been a while. I think it would be nice?" She inflected this as a question, hoping to get Zahira to agree.

"Mmhmm, I think that would be good."

"You do?" Noa silently scolded herself for adding additional hurdles to the social-magic Alexis was working from afar.

"Yeah." Zahira nodded, rocking on her boot-wrapped feet. "If we're going to be here for a while, we might as well start off—start *back* on the right foot."

Noa felt lighter than she had in weeks. Apparently, the anvil Decker had unknowingly placed on her chest that first day of the Skill Trip had been sitting there the whole time, constricting every breath and making every movement and word a struggle.

Not anymore.

She could have friends again. A home.

Over Zahira's shoulder, Lex gave Noa a thumbs up.

"So, how on Earth did you think ahead to plan that outfit?" Noa asked.

The two of them chatted and made their way back to the rest of the group, dropping effortlessly into their conversation. The large room filled until a dinner bell rang.

Everyone's attention turned to the door, expectantly.

Amar was the first to walk in. He glided across the room wearing black jeans and a pair of black work boots, which were cleaner and sleeker than his riding boots. He wore a simple black tee-shirt and a dark zip-up sweater.

He looked extravagant.

His beard, which had grown unruly over the journey, was now shaved close to his face. He'd cut his hair as well, although it was still long enough to run his fingers through.

Behind Amar trailed Tali, presumably. She had wavy light

brown, almost blonde curls, which hit below her shoulder blades. She was small, and her legs were still stick-thin in the way that some pre-teens are when they sprout in height, before they finish growing into their bodies.

Noa could already tell how different she was from him. Her hair was lighter, much lighter, than his and looked softer. He walked quietly and poised, like an automaton. She flapped around behind him, waving to other Cavalry members and dancing through the world.

Tali's eyes caught Noa's and, for some reason, her body shifted backward, startled.

Leave it to Noa to be socially awkward with a thirteen-year-old.

Tali stared at her, squinting, as if she recognized her.

Did he already tell her about me? Am I that easy to spot?

Tali finally broke her gaze when she and Amar found their seats beside Decker and Sai. After she sat, Tali's eyes landed on someone else, and Noa followed her gaze to see who.

Mirai.

She was gorgeous, as always, laughing and holding the arm of another equally beautiful woman.

Andrea, Noa guessed.

The woman was mature (maybe twenty or thirty years older than Mirai) and stunning. Her hair was grey but not wiry. It was soft in color and texture and landed around her shoulders. Her piercing blue eyes were full of light and laughter and love—even from a distance.

Noa could see clearly where Mirai had gotten some of her style. Or did Andrea get her style from Mirai? It was uncanny how well they fit together.

Behind them, the room flooded with dozens of others. Soon, the ballroom that was the main cabin mess hall was filled with nearly five-hundred people.

Noa had imagined the Cavalry as a small operation, and her prep class had allowed her to maintain that assumption, often quoting how rare it was to teach a Cavalry prep course. But, after years of people being assigned to Cavalry without Reassignment, the numbers added up.

The hall bustled with ranchers greeting each other with slaps on the backs and glass mugs clinking.

"Welcome!" Decker announced at the front of the room. He looked out and waved to people here and there. Each person waved back to him, excited for his acknowledgement. "Thank you, everyone, for joining us in welcoming our newest, and largest, class of Cavalry members."

Everyone applauded. The new Assignments looked at each other and smiled nervously. It was nice to be welcomed.

"As you all know, they've just arrived from the hardest journey of their lives."

Noa felt proud, and Alexis and V also stuck their chins out higher—until the rest of the room let out a laugh.

Their chins dropped.

"That's right, dear new Assignments, the Skill Trip is a tough learning curve, but we're not done yet. Tomorrow, we will begin Cavalry training which, as you might have suspected, is a lot more than just riding a horse down a trail. New members will meet here tomorrow at noon for the first day of training. It is a half day, so take the morning to get settled into your new quarters. For the rest of you, take the half day to get settled from your hangovers." Decker cackled and raised a glass as the crowd cheered. "Cheers! To the new members!"

"To the new members!" they echoed.

"To our new family!" Decker said.

"To our new family," everyone repeated.

CHAPTER 26

NOA

Putting her riding clothes on the next morning felt like a new experience for Noa. The wear on the fabric over the past two months was made apparent after the wash. She snuggled into the softer fabric, adjusted her now-normal wide-hipped pants, wrapped her boots, and headed out for her first day of training three hours early.

Outside, a wave of heat pushed into her, and the blinding sun reflected sharply against the light soil. Noa cupped a hand above her eyebrows and squinted to find her bearings.

"Looking for something?" Mirai asked, rounding the corner.

"Someone," Noa said. "Trax. I can't remember where the stables…"

Mirai pointed. "That way. That's where you'll meet at

noon, too, for training. The other way is a whole lotta nothing until you reach our houses."

"Whose houses?"

"Well, Andrea and I live together. We're the first house. After us, it's Amar and Tali. Decker lives on the other side of the stables, and Sai lives off the property, closer to East Ranch."

"Do you like living here?" Noa asked as they walked together toward the stables.

"Love it. There's an adjustment period to get used to the lack of everything." She gestured at the desert nothing in front of them. "But after you do, it's nice. Wonderful, even."

Noa nodded and took in her surroundings. The trees were few and far between, and those that stood were scarred black from the great fires. The clay ground was cracked and dusty. In the distance, flat land rolled into large rock structures, interrupted only by the spare desert bush which, at this point in the season, was bare branched.

"Think you'll like it here?" Mirai asked.

"I'd prefer more trees, but I think I can make do."

"Guess you're gonna have to, huh?" Mirai pointed to the back of the stables. "Trax is just there. I'll stay with you, if you don't mind. Reyna needs a good brush down before training."

"I love that name. Was that the name she had when you got her, or did you change it?" Noa asked.

"I chose it for her—after my sister Loreyna. She always went by Rey, though."

"I didn't know you had a sister. Younger or older?"

"Younger." Mirai's voice trailed.

"Mine's younger too. Sami. She would kill me if I named a

horse after her, though. Especially my horse." Noa laughed at the idea of introducing Sami to her hypothetical horse, Sam. She gave Trax a few pats, her hand bouncing off his coarse hair and hard muscles. She liked his name.

"Well, my sister's not around anymore," Mirai said.

"Oh, I'm sorry. Assignment? Or…?"

"No, not by an Assignment."

The silence opened a swirl of thoughts in both of their minds.

Mirai spoke first. "We were never really close. Not in the way that sisters usually are. But after she was gone—"

"That didn't really matter," Noa finished when Mirai couldn't. "Because you were sisters." Noa's heart sank. She drew a breath, and her chest tightened at the thought of reaching out to her family. All she had to do was call her sister who was alive and well and in her life. It wasn't so easy for everyone else. She exhaled but the feeling stayed, sitting heavily just under her ribcage.

Noa stayed with Mirai and spent the soft morning helping prepare the stables for training. Drops wandered in as the minutes passed. By the time she grew tired and wanted to go in for a quick break, Decker came out of the hall and announced it was time to start.

Decker gave another of his trademark monologues and divided the new members into groups with their training Marshals. They'd workout twice a day, have skill practices, and get oriented to the ranch's land during daily rides. They'd train for two weeks before they could officially be considered Cavalry-strong and start taking shifts.

Along with Sai, Mirai, and Amar, three other senior

Cavalry Marshals acted as training Marshals. Each had their autos displayed, looking over their new Assignment training lists.

One of the brutish-looking senior Marshals called Noa's name. She'd barely heard it; he'd read through his list so quickly. The man's face was tanned and smooth, even though he looked to be about the same age as Decker. His expression was impassive. Not angry, but not pleased either.

As Noa walked to her new Marshal, a blunt and loud, "Hey!" called her attention.

"Sorry," Amar said. "I didn't mean to startle you." He kept his eyes on his auto and his voice softer than the previous holler.

Noa looked at him, puzzled. Whenever she was caught off guard like this, it took her a beat to regain composure.

"I missed you at dinner last night."

"You did?" she said with a teasing smile. "Didn't think you'd notice with so many friends for you to catch up with."

He looked at her now.

When would her stomach stop dropping just because he looked at her? Probably when he stopped looking at her like *that*.

"Can I make it up to you? I thought you could come over for dinner tonight. Meet Tali?"

"I'd love to."

"Great, I'd like for her to meet you before I tell her about—" He cleared his throat. "—us. She'll probably figure it out anyway, though. She's nosy."

"Wait, you haven't already told her about me?"

"I'm not keeping it a secret. I just thought it would be

nicer for you two to meet without the context of. Actually, that's dumb. I don't know what I was thinking."

"No, no, not like that," Noa urged. "It's just, when I saw her yesterday with you, she was staring at me like she already knew me, that's all."

Amar smirked. "That's Tali for you. She's everyone's friend the minute she meets them. She's a pretty free spirit." His smirk turned into a full smile talking about his sister.

"She seems like a cool kid. It'll be great to meet her."

The brutish man grunted again. Noa bumped Amar to tell him she had to go.

"I'll tell Tali after training, then see you tonight?" he asked.

"Pick me up at eight."

"Seven," he corrected. "Tali has a bedtime."

Even with all of the warnings, Decker had still undersold the brutality of Cavalry training. The brutish man, whose name turned out to be Yori, remained curt through the entire day of drills. Since they were starting at noon, Noa had assumed training would last for just four or five hours. And for other groups, led by Mirai, or Amar, or Sai, it did. But not Yori's group—he kept them hours after the others had returned to the dorm.

Walking Trax back to the stables, Noa's thighs trembled from exertion. She was soaked in sweat and coated in dust. They had practiced herding in circles, sprinting with sudden stops, and descending steep cliff faces. Noa thought she'd gotten the hang of steep terrain in the mountains, but the desert landscape presented a different challenge.

Instead of jutting rocks, the desert presented slippery clay and crumbly sand which required the horses to use their front feet to brake and slide on their behinds down the slope, all the while keeping the rider level. The movement caused clouds of dust to engulf them, most of which ended up in Noa's mouth and the creases around her eyes.

As she put Trax away, she gave him an extra handful of oats; he had more than earned it. She deserved a treat, too, and wondered if the mess hall served dessert.

She trudged back to the dorm. As she strode the last steps, her eye caught a horse tied to the post at the end of the main entrance walkway. Their rider leaned against the fence, silhouetted by the flood light.

"Amar!" She ran to him, suddenly full of energy.

"Look at you." Amar grabbed her hand and gave her a twirl. "Yori did a number on you guys, huh?"

"You think?" Noa smacked her pants and dust plumed out. "Neat trick though. Have you been waiting long?"

"Just long enough to think you were standing me up." He pulled her, dust and all, tight against his body and kissed her. "I'm glad you weren't." He rested his forehead against hers.

They'd shared a handful of kisses over the last weeks on the trail, but there wasn't a ton of privacy. Marshal duties for Amar and self-isolation by Noa had meant their relationship was intermittent at best. One night, Amar had snuck her out of her tent, and they'd made out in a field under the starlight for hours. She was hoping for more of that tonight.

"Need to grab anything first?" He said, nodding to the dorms.

"Well, a shower would be nice."

"How about you grab a change of clothes, and you can shower at my place while I finish getting dinner ready?"

"Deal."

Noa filled her bag with a pile of unfolded laundry and tucked it under arm. She rode in the saddle with Amar just like she had the night she'd seen the sky fall. She wasn't high from an ascendant experience, but she wasn't bleeding from her head either, so she figured it was just as nice.

Mozart's steps bumped their bodies together in the same rhythm. At first, Noa flexed her core to keep her body from folding into his, but Amar's body rocked with Mozart's movements, and it didn't take long for his hand to settle around her waist. This time he didn't rest his palm gently but used it to press her firmly against him until they moved in sync.

"You okay if we ride a little faster?" he asked.

Noa nodded, and he motioned Mozart to pick up the pace.

All day, Noa had only smelled dust and dirt. Away from the ranch, she could smell the pines again. The air was cold—colder than any day they'd had on the trail—and, by the time they arrived at Amar's house, her face was blushed and raw.

Or at least, she *thought* it was Amar's house—a floodlight over the stable blinded her from seeing the structure in front of them clearly. At the front door, Noa realized why she hadn't been able to see the house. Its facade and front door were a Sleekstone with a metallic black finish.

Amar opened the oversized, industrial door and gestured for her to enter.

"Tali is probably finishing a program. Let me show you the shower, and I'll start on dinner."

They took off their shoes at the door, and Noa was embarrassed by her dusty feet on his clean floor. It was not normal to go to your sort-of-boyfriend's house for the first time covered in filth.

They walked through the living space and down a hallway. The house wasn't as minimalist as Noa had imagined. The living room had an oversized plush couch and a large canvas painting over the fireplace. The entryway even had a covered bench, haphazardly filled with pairs of Tali's shoes.

"Shower's here. There should be soap and everything in there for you, towels are just in the closet." Amar pulled one out and offered it to her. "Need anything else?"

Noa gulped and stood very still, pretending to think over what she'd need for a shower. Inside, her mind was blank. All she could think was that she was about to be naked in his house. She remembered that he'd probably already seen her naked, multiple times, over the course of the Skill Trip since they all bathed together in various lakes. But it was different here. And none of those nights had ever been as intimate as the first when he'd had to hold her in the water.

This was different.

This wasn't the trail anymore. This was the destination.

What happened here wasn't a phase or part of the journey. This was real life. This was Amar's real house. This was his soap!

Noa shook away these thoughts and tried to enjoy her hot shower. After she turned off the water, she wiped the steam from the mirror and dried her hair, then changed back into her jeans and sweater from the night before. They were day-old clothes now, but that was practically fresh given her new standards. Plus, she'd really wanted Amar to see her in her favorite clothes—in something that was actually her style—instead of a uniform.

Although, the jeans and sweater didn't feel like her style anymore. Not really.

She dropped her bag by her shoes at the door and walked into the kitchen. Expecting to find Amar, she was surprised to find only Tali, who turned to acknowledge Noa.

"It's you," Tali whispered as her sun-tanned skin paled like she'd seen a ghost. She examined Noa closely.

Noa fidgeted uncomfortably, unsure of what to do under the scrutinous gaze of a thirteen-year-old. "Hi. I'm Noa. I saw you the other night at the welcome dinner; it's nice to meet you." She held out a professional hand to the girl.

When Tali finished her seconds-long examination, she moved past Noa's hand and hugged her. The tight, around-the-neck, almost-choking kind. The same kind Alexis gave.

Noa lost some air from her lungs but managed to wrap her arms around Tali to return the gesture.

When Tali let go, she started talking—and didn't stop. Tali shared news that Amar was letting her join training. Then she asked if she could ride Trax—she'd seen him before and was sure he was the biggest horse. She asked if Noa would be willing to trade for a smaller horse and, before she could answer, Tali had changed topics to something about swim lessons.

Before Noa got a word out, Amar came in from the backyard with a handful of herbs.

"Tali, I thought I told you to finish your program and that I'd come get you," Amar said in a voice Noa hadn't heard before. A parental voice, a guardian voice.

"Big brother, sometimes you just have to live and let live," Tali said.

Noa couldn't help but let out a huge laugh. Amar smiled, seemingly pleased more by Noa's reaction than Tali's quip.

"You have to let me ride Trax," Tali said, turning to Noa and changing the subject back. "Amar, you'd let me ride with Noa, right?"

They bantered for a while about Tali starting her riding lessons until Amar shook his head and turned his attention to the wok in front of him, simmering finely chopped aromatics. The kitchen smelled like honey and garlic and spice.

"Do you want to help me cook?" Amar asked.

Noa and Tali both looked at him.

"I don't," Tali said first.

"Well, good. I wasn't asking you. You can set the table." He passed Tali a stack of plates and silverware and motioned for Noa to come stand by him. "Do you cook?"

"Not really, my parents always did the cooking. My dad, actually." Noa fiddled with some of the spices sitting on the counter, rearranging them mindlessly.

"High standards then?" Amar sounded confident he could meet them. He tossed the wok, and a rainbow of vegetables jumped into the air and fell playfully into the skillet with a sizzle.

When the meal was ready, Noa and Amar sat across from each other and Tali staked her claim at the head of the table. Tali talked through most of dinner. She was showy—clearly a performer of sorts—and had a lot to tell.

Noa forgave her bogarting the conversation as she couldn't imagine being Tali's age and without her family for so long. It was the case for many children in the Variety—especially for those families torn apart by it—but Noa had always had both her parents and her sister around. Still, it was a muscle Noa wasn't used to flexing. She listened, effortfully, as Tali filled them in on her recent life.

"Okay, I think that's enough for tonight," Amar said after they'd cleared the table and listened to Tali's third story about planting seeds in Andrea's garden.

"I'm not kidding, Noa. The sunflowers were like a hundred feet tall," Tali exaggerated and put her hands far over her head. "They're like magical stalks to the clouds. By the end of the season, I bet I could build a house on the petals." Tali stared at the ceiling as she imagined her sunflower home.

Noa thought a sky-high sunflower house would suit Tali quite well.

"I know you heard me," Amar said to Tali. "You have lessons in the morning."

"Okay, okay," she replied. "Goodnight!"

"Be right back," Amar told Noa. "I'll meet you in the living room."

He walked down the hallway with Tali to say goodnight. When he returned to the living room, he brought with him a wine bottle and two glasses. He set them on the table and settled behind Noa, who was staring up at the large canvas art.

He put his arms around her waist and kissed her neck.

She leaned into it.

"You have a nice home."

"I'm glad you're comfortable here," he said, between kisses down her neck.

"Very."

"Comfortable enough to stay the night?" He turned her around to face him and moved his kisses to her lips. The warmth from the fireplace and his lips swelled through her body.

"Yes."

The wine glasses stayed empty on the table as they rushed and stumbled over each other down the opposite hallway to his bedroom.

When Noa's calves bumped against the back of his bed, they both stopped. Amar rested his hand on her neck and leaned his forehead in that familiar way against hers. His eyes stayed closed as he tried to catch his breath.

"Are you sure?" he asked.

Noa nodded.

"I need to hear you say it. Because if we go down this road—" He stopped again and moved his hand into her hair, tilting her head back to look up at him. "Noa, if I get all of you tonight, some of you will never be enough again. If we—if we're going to be together, I want us to be together."

His brown eyes bored into hers, a shade darker than normal and steady. Wanting, but patient.

"If you're not sure, then we wait," he insisted. His weight shifted ever so slightly creating a sliver of space between them. "We can wait as long as we need to."

It was her turn to talk.

Noa reached around to the back of his neck and pulled his

face close to hers with both hands, stopping when their lips touched. Resting together, she bit his bottom lip and shifted back slightly—parting just enough distance to look him in the eye.

"I'm sure. I want to be with you."

The moment the last syllable left her lips Amar grabbed her, maneuvering her legs around his waist and rushing back into a storm of kissing.

Somewhere in the middle of it all, he pulled them both onto the bed and lay her down in the middle, taking care to move a pillow behind her head with one hand and support the small of her back with the other. Slowly, he moved his lips from her forehead to her neck, to the bottom of her sternum, which was bare from his hands pushing her sweater up either side. Noa tugged her sweater off over head as he moved farther down her belly. Before he was out of reach, she grabbed the hem of his shirt, tearing it off over his head.

Noa lay back and closed her eyes, enjoying the sensation of him working on her body. His grasp working from her ribs to her hips. He meticulously removed her jeans without ever letting a hand leave her. He came back up, his full body pressing down the length of hers. The weight of him sent blood rushing deep into her stomach.

Once there was only a single layer between them, they paused again, both breathless this time.

Before he could ask again, she answered.

"I'm sure.

CHAPTER 27

NOA

Over the ten days of training, Noa died several times.

Yori pushed their bodies well-beyond their natural limits.

Noa died on her twenty-first round of pushups and, again, when she was trampled attempting a running mount. Her heart gave out during morning sprints, and she choked to death on dust in afternoon turning drills. Stabbing pains throughout her body sent her into shock during jumping drills, and fear of doing the exercises every day until the end of time sent her into the afterlife.

But not all of her deaths that week were tragic.

She also caught fire in Amar's arms every night and drowned in anticipation the next morning waiting to tell her best friend about it.

Yori was gruff and without sympathy for Noa's noodle

arms, but he had her respect. Her proudest moment during the week was when Yori's curriculum required the group to learn to ride without reins—something she and Trax had already mastered. This went without praise, but Yori had taught her in just a few short days that praise wasn't the reward. The skill was the reward.

It was obvious why Decker had left him in charge; Noa wanted to learn everything Yori had to teach and was proud of her deaths at his hands. She needed to be reborn.

The other training groups clearly didn't train as hard. Yori's group did rounds of sprints before the others even woke up, and they practiced speed-tacking several more times per day.

Noa snuck out of Amar's house a full hour before he woke up each morning and arrived back only a few minutes before Tali had to go to bed.

Tali was often awake, tooling around the house when Noa left in the morning. Sometimes they shared a morning meal. More often, Tali kept Noa laughing and distracted as she stretched for the day ahead. Their relationship wasn't as complicated or difficult as Noa thought it might be, though it did make her miss her own sister.

She had received plenty of messages from her family but hadn't returned them yet. She couldn't imagine updating them and having to omit the most exciting thing that had happened to her, the thing that occupied so many of her conscious thoughts. *When would she ascend again?* Plus, an auto message was no way to reveal everything that had been happening. Her parents would think she had already gone mad from Cavalry training or, worse, that it was a joke, and she was mocking their faith.

Plus, she didn't even know if she could reveal such a thing over comms. Wouldn't the Library and HQ see it?

Jo would know.

But Jo wasn't there, and she couldn't put people she cared about at risk.

Not again.

At the end of the final training day, Yori gave the six of them a short speech. His group had started out with ten members, like the others, but most of his Drops had asked (begged) to be traded to another Marshal.

Noa watched Yori closely as he spoke. Since he wouldn't be giving official orders, she was hoping to spot a flash of softness in him. She was convinced he wasn't as hardened as he seemed.

"Tonight, we will all dine in the mess hall," Yori said. "It will be another celebration but, this time, you will attend as full Cavalry members instead of new Assignments. Which means you will be invited to join in the celebration, instead of being encouraged back to your rooms."

Still firm.

"At the event, you will receive your Cavalry posts. You cannot request a post transfer for one year. If you're still here then, which you will be, we can transfer you to any vacant post of your preference…"

He droned on about posts and shifts and how better shifts were reserved for more senior members. Noa zoned back in when he talked about partners.

"Some of you will have partners since the larger livestock tracks require two herders. Others only require one so, depending on your herd, you may or may not be on your own."

Yori gripped his heavy belt and looked them up and down. Noa thought about how Decker always looked at his Cavalry members like a proud father. Yori, by contrast, looked at them plainly. Possibly with some pity, as if they were players on his team who'd just lost a game.

"Physically, you will all do well at your posts because of my training. But I should tell you that the mental part of it, especially at solitary posts, can be difficult. I manage my mental health through prayer and meditation. If you'd ever like to join, I host morning meditation and yoga every day at 2:00 a.m. on Crested Peak. Consider this your open invitation."

His inviting words were spoken in a tone so flat Noa could tell no one actually went to his meditation. *So much for softness.*

He asked for sixty pushups and left them palms down in the dirt. He didn't need to stay and watch over them as they executed his order—they would do as he said whether he watched or not. Not because he was kind or charismatic or because they wanted his approval, but because they trusted that he knew what was best.

Noa lowered her face toward the ground and pushed her body up in sets of twenty. She had never felt strong—not like this.

Twenty-one, twenty-two...

Lifting her own body's weight again and again unlocked a part of herself that had been lying dormant.

Thirty-eight, thirty-nine...

Her mind rushed with excited anticipation for her post Assignment, and she expelled that energy through her palms into the dusty ground.

Fifty-nine, Sixty...

Sixty-one.

She released and rested on her belly. The ground was hot, and she lay her head on her hand while a smile shivered to her face. This was it. She was about to become a permanent part of the Cavalry family. She had Amar. And Tali. And Mirai. She could befriend Yori and become just as skilled. She could fully make up with Alexis and Zahira .

She would be able to get back to solving the mystery.

She could bring Jo back.

She could get back at Tempsen.

Her chest sparked with the white heat, and her eyes closed, trying to hold onto it as long as she could.

"What are you doing?"

Noa opened one eye.

It was V or, at least, V's shoes. She craned her neck to look at him. He stood over her with his boots purposefully too close to her face. The ascendant feeling vacated her chest.

"Just resting for a moment, it's been a long training day," Noa said. "Yori actually works us."

Noa remembered she was trying to make nice and stopped short of rolling her eyes. Instead, she stood and looked V up and down. He was dressed in his casual clothes and had already showered after his training.

"Where are you going all dressed up, Vitus?"

"Don't say my full name, it's weird. And I'm not dressed up." He shifted in his clothes. "Lex told me to find you. She meant to invite you to come with us to Mirai and Andrea's. They're holding a clothing swap for the celebration tonight. Lex is still showering but we're leaving soon."

"Sure, I'd love to go." Noa dusted off her pants, creating a small cloud.

"Keep your dirt off me. I'm already showered."

"Alright, alright." Noa swatted at the dust plumes, as if she could clear them out of the air. "You know, you look pretty good, all cleaned up."

V's eyebrows raised unenthused by the compliment.

"It's weird seeing everyone outside of their Cavalry clothes, isn't it?" Noa asked, trying to make conversation.

"You've seen me in normal clothes before."

"Ugh, you are beyond frustrating." Noa gave up.

"Okay, fine. I'll play nice. Yes, it is weird seeing people in colors other than khaki after two months."

Noa eyed him. "And the pants are really stupid."

V laughed the way he did only around Alexis. "The pants are fine. At least we all had the sense not to wear the hats." He pointed off in the direction of a few other new members. Many of the older Assignments had worn their hats on the Skill Trip and continued to don them every day.

Now, they both laughed like they did around Alexis.

"What are you two so chummy about?" Zahira asked, walking up to them with Jash in tow.

"Just at the unfortunate coincidence that we all lost our uniform hats before the Skill Trip," V said.

Zahira laughed. "Oh yeah, very unfortunate that mine blew away into a trash can right before I entered the Bowl."

Noa turned to head into the dorm. "I still need to run in and shower. Can I meet you at Mirai's?"

"Tell Alexis if she takes longer than five more minutes she's riding with you," V said.

"She'll be riding with you then," Zahira said to Noa. "She was still in the shower when we came out." They all shook their heads and shrugged, acknowledging that Alexis stuck to no one's schedule.

Noa knocked on Alexis's dorm door. "Lex?"

"Come in," she sang from the shower. "Who is it?"

"Shouldn't you ask who it is before you tell them to come in?"

"Hon!" Alexis swung her head out of the shower.

Noa's jaw dropped as she took in the bald state of Alexis's head. "Oh my Gods!"

"Do you like it?" Alexis ran a hand over her freshly shaven head. "The pink grew out, and it's not like they have more dye here."

Noa stepped forward. "I love it. You look stunning."

She shrieked. "Thanks! I'm going to wrap it while we shop the swap and surprise everyone at the event tonight."

"Oh yeah, about the swap, you're coming with me. The others sort of left us behind for taking too long."

Alexis finished rinsing and turned the water off. "Sounds

perfect, we need to catch up anyhow. I have so much to tell you."

Noa felt like shrieking, too, but it was less natural for her, so she just enjoyed Alexis's energy and agreed.

CHAPTER 28

NOA

"We don't have a lot of shopping nearby," Mirai said to the group of new members standing in her living room. The room was filled with racks of clothing that Mirai and Andrea had picked up whenever they traveled into the cities. They had curated the clothing library over years, and each new member could take a few items today. Then, a few times a year, there would be a Cavalry-wide swap where they could exchange what they had for new items.

"Grab some casual day clothes and something formal for tonight," Andrea said, pointing to an area of the room shining with jeweled gowns and silken suits.

About half of the new Assignments were in the living room. Noa wondered if the other half didn't care to come, or if no one had told them. After all, she had only found out because she'd been on the ground a little too long after pushups.

Noa gently pulled Mirai aside as the rest of the new Assignments invaded the clothing racks. "Did everyone get invited? I feel like we're missing a few new members."

"Noa, you are very thoughtful." Mirai stuck out her bottom lip. "I like to invite my trainees to have first dibs as a sort of treat. But word got out so that's why there are a few extra of you here. After this, we're bringing the whole collection to the dorms and everyone will get to pick."

With her conscience cleared, Noa started combing through the racks. There were long dresses, suits, jumpers, nice jackets, skirts, and sleek leggings like Zahira had worn. Then, Noa spotted a pair of black, faux-leather boots. Up close, they were not black but a deep purple. They had a chunky heel with tread on the bottom and ornamental lacing up the front.

Perfect.

After the boots, her outfit fell into place. She found a pair of black pants that had a wrap waist and leather accents that matched her boots. She tried them on, and they fit perfectly tight around her waist, billowy around her legs, and tight again around the ankles, so she could tuck them into the boots. She grabbed a cropped vest, a long sleeve shirt, and two cuffs for her wrists. The outfit was not a ball gown, but it was sexy and definitely an upgrade from her jeans and jumper.

"Hi Noa!" Tali called, sashaying across the room.

"Hey, are you getting some new clothes today too?"

"Yes, and I don't even have to swap anything. Andrea said

I can pick out two things." She twirled in an obviously new skirt. It had multiple layers and swept the floor, reminding Noa of the woman with black and silver-streaked hair from her ascension.

"I love the skirt."

"Thank you!" Tali bowed.

"What is your second item?"

"I don't know yet, wanna help me pick it out?"

They went through the racks and held up various items, scrutinizing them together. Noa reached for a large ball gown that she thought would be funny but couldn't pick it up without two hands, so she put her armful of things down on the ground.

One of her black wrist cuffs rolled off the pile and stopped at Tali's feet.

"What is this?" Tali asked.

"It's a cuff." Noa slid it back on her wrist. "I got two of them because I thought they looked cool together."

Tali reached and took it off Noa's wrist without asking and placed it on her own. It was large on her but she squeezed the metal band and it tightened to fit.

"It's badass," Tali said.

"Are you allowed to say that?"

Tali laughed at her, intentionally opening her mouth, and sticking it close to Noa's face. "Can I keep it?"

Noa liked the look better with both cuffs, but she didn't have the heart to disappoint Tali. "Sure."

No sooner were the words out her mouth than Tali was screeching with excitement. "It's going to look so good!" She gave Noa a side hug and took off for Alexis and Zahira, who were trying on elegant caped dresses.

Noa reclaimed her pile of clothes from the floor and picked out a second pair of jeans, a pair of leggings, and a few more casual tops. She even found a warm winter cape that she liked—perfect for riding at night under a sky full of stars.

CHAPTER 29

NOA

Zahira, Alexis, and Noa got ready together in the dorms. Alexis drew intricate eyeliner and purple shading on Noa's upper lid, making her green-ish eyes pop with her black outfit. Alexis also donned a monochromatic look in a full-length dress and cape in all bronze with metallic embellishments. Her shaved head and minimal makeup balanced the heavy outfit and made her look like a royal warrior. The vibrant yellow dress Zahira wore was obnoxious on the hanger but looked high fashion on her angular frame.

Jash and V knocked on the door. They wore new clothes from the swap, suits made of a light fabric Noa didn't recognize. They were showered and shaven and Noa thought they smelled good for the first time since they'd left on Skill Trip. They all traded compliments, particularly admiring

Alexis's new shiny head, and strode to the dining hall as one large pack together again.

Noa waited in the foyer as the rest of the group huddled by the bar to grab their drinks. Amar would arrive soon, and Noa couldn't wait to see him.

When he did walk in, Noa's jaw dropped. He was once again dressed in all black but, somehow, looked even sexier than he had the first night. His pants were snug to his body, and his shirt was undone just far enough down his chest to exaggerate the movement of his muscles as he walked. He smiled when he saw her, and her heart swelled.

It was the look and moment she had waited for all day, all these months. The look he'd have when he saw her as a real human being and not just a frumpy Cavalry trainee.

His pace quickened as he approached her and her heart fluttered.

"You look amazing," he said, pulling her in and kissing her.

She shivered. "You look great too."

"We better get in there folks," Jash said, ushering them and the rest of the group along. "I think Decker is going to give out Assignments right at the beginning."

Amar nodded. "He's right. Let's go in. I have to sit at the head table again with Decker, but I'll come find you after you get your post." He kissed her on the cheek before they parted ways.

She couldn't stand how happy she was. Maybe the life she'd find here would be as great as the one Mirai had found with Andrea.

Decker took the stage at the front of the room.

"Good evening, everyone! Welcome. This is supposed to be a fun night, so let's get the posts out of the way and then we can carry on with the celebrations!" Everyone cheered and he waved at individual people in the audience again. "There are four posts, and each is managed by a senior Marshal. Yori manages the North Post, Sai the East, Mirai the West, and Amar the South. They will now each read the new members under their post. New members, unless you're told otherwise by your Marshal, you are posted to the first shift which is dusk to 2 a.m. Try to stay up very late tonight and sleep in because work starts tomorrow."

They cheered at the orders.

The cheering turned into pounding on the tables until Yori took the center of the stage. He rattled off his fifteen names, most belonging to the middle-aged men and women of the new Assignment group.

Next was Sai, who read fifteen more names and, by the murmurs and exclamations in the audience, mainly belonged to the group of Assignments who had worn their sunhats the entire trip.

Mirai called her list which included Alexis and Vitus, but still not Noa.

When Amar stood to read his list, he looked right at Noa and winked. He read her name first and said it with such care and affection, it sounded like magic. Or at least that's how she heard it in her lovestruck brain.

She was a goner. In over her head, absolutely smitten, fallen completely off the deep end in love with Amar. She'd never felt like this before. Nothing had ever made her feel so good.

Except ascending.

She listened to Amar read more names, including Zahira's and Jash's until Decker took the stage again. "We don't have to keep to our route group all night. Gods know you will spend enough time together on duty, but let's start the evening by gathering by post, and meeting our new Cavalry mates."

Amar hopped off the front of the stage while the other Marshals took the stairs. He stepped lightly, clearly in a good mood, and headed right for Noa. She wondered if he'd come to the same revelation she had. Maybe they were both in love.

She had a strong urge to call her sister. It was weird that so much in her life had changed and Sami didn't know. She would call. Soon.

A large group of other Cavalry members surrounded Noa, Jash, and Zahira, grabbing their shoulders in congratulations. Alexis and V were ushered off to another corner of the room to gather with their own post.

"Hello Southerners!" Amar yelled at the ceiling, and the crowd of Cavalry members around them hollered. The other posts were doing similar chants.

Amar had each senior member introduce themselves, and Noa tried to remember all of the names and routes they managed. Then, he read the assigned route legs aloud, "Leg A, four Sections, Senior Member – Deepa: Section One, Zahira; Section Two, Noa; and Section Three, Jash."

After the Assignments and Sections were stated, they toasted a glass of champagne. It was Noa's first but, by the looks of it, everyone else's fourth or fifth. After the crowd dissipated, Amar hugged her from behind.

"Pretty good Section, huh?"

"Great section," she said, turning to face him. She would have liked to make out with him right in the middle of that room, if everyone would have suddenly left them alone.

Instead, they broke apart, but didn't stay too far from one another, as Amar chatted kindly with the other members in the post group. The post groups soon dispersed and intermingled with each other. People moved on from champagne, digging into spirits and beer. Cheeks grew rosier, foreheads sweatier, and the room filled with roars of laughter. Noa put down her fourth drink, she had caught up quickly, and snuck out into the quiet hallway.

She was so happy. *From the champagne? From being in love?* She opened her auto and called her sister. When Sami didn't pick up, Noa left a long, sappy, and sloppy message.

"Sa-a-a-mi," she said, trying to imitate her sister's drawl. "I'm so sorry I didn't call before. I'm so sorry," she teared up. Noa was full of emotions and she wanted to pour them out to her sister. "I didn't want to call until things got better. But they did get better, so I'm calling! I made it to Main Ranch, and you were right that my horse was very difficult. He is also very large. I have a friend, Alexis—she just shaved her head. I won't do that. But it looks great on her. I have so much I want to tell you, but I can't. Not like this." She swayed a bit, and leaned back against the wall, choosing to slide down it and sit on the floor. "But how else am I going to tell you from all the way out here?" She sighed. "I met someone, Amar. He's perfect. And something happened to me. Something big." She rambled on, trying to explain everything with layers of nuance and euphemisms. Speaking in code was hard. By the time she worked her way through the ascensions, and the Library, and blabbering about Jo, she was certain she hadn't made any sense at all.

"But all the bad stuff is over now. And things are better. And Mirai's sister disappeared. That was a long time ago but it made me think that I don't want to disappear. Or you either. Miss you!" Noa ended her call, happy and light. She rose from the floor and wobbled.

No more champagne.

For the rest of the evening, Noa stuck to water and followed Amar around the hall. He was effortless with his Cavalry friends. He was in his comfortable, naturally calm state but more energetic, and his laughter made him radiant. His smile widened from the alcohol, and he grew more handsy with everyone, clapping a palm on a shoulder here and giving a hug to a buddy there. They swirled around the room as a pair, him introducing her to countless people until late in the night. They finally said goodbye, and rode side by side back to Amar's, together.

CHAPTER 30

NOA

Noa checked on Amar to make sure he was still breathing in his drunken sleep. He had managed to ride home, but it wasn't his most elegant ride. He'd stumbled dismounting, dropped the saddle untacking Mozart, and had needed to lean on her shoulder as they walked inside from the stable behind his house.

Now in bed, snoring, he was fine. She laid a cool cloth on his head, turned on the fan, and pulled a blanket over him, leaving him to sleep in peace.

She wasn't tired yet, and lay on the couch for an hour twisting and turning. Every time she dozed off, she thought she heard hoofbeats and woke up, startled. It happened three or four times until she couldn't drift off anymore.

Wide awake, she decided to go for a ride and stake out

her leg of the route. She needed to get used to riding at night anyway.

As she wrapped her boots on the hallway bench, Tali crept around the corner.

"Where are you going?" she asked in a low, sleepy voice.

"Just for a ride to prep for work tomorrow. You can go back to bed."

"I'll come with you."

Noa didn't know what to say. She attached the cape to her coat. It would be cold. "I don't know if that's a good idea."

"I went through training, too, remember." Tali started putting on her own boots and coat. "I don't have my own horse yet, though. So, I'll either need to ride with you, or take Mozart."

"Oh, no."

"Please." Tali clasped her hands together. "I never get to do anything fun."

Noa relented with a shrug, and Tali scrambled to finish dressing. She put on a thick riding jacket, tucked her pant bottoms into the top of her boots, and shoved her hands inside a pair of brown leather riding gloves.

"Oh, gloves are a good idea," Noa said. Even in this mid-summer season, the ranch was cold at night.

Tali dug into a bin near the door. "Here, they might be a little big."

Amar's gloves were loose but fit well enough.

Noa looked at the gloves on her hands and thought about Amar. He probably wouldn't mind her wearing his gloves. He might, however, mind her taking Tali out for a later-than-midnight ride on his horse.

He'd have to get over her doing things he didn't like sometimes. And she would have to get better at apologizing.

TALI

Horses don't sleep much, but Tali thought that both Trax and Mozart looked particularly awake for one o'clock in the morning.

Tali impressed herself by keeping up with Noa's tack speed. Amar had always let her practice getting Mozart ready, or grooming him, or cleaning his stalls—he just didn't let her ride him. He hadn't even let her borrow him for training when they learned there weren't any new horses available to assign to her. He said it was because he was using Mozart to lead his training group, but it sounded like another excuse to keep her from riding. Andrea had thankfully let her borrow Kiffin during the training days.

Noa mounted Trax and looked to Tali. "Ready?"

Tali was tall enough to get onto Mozart herself on the top step of the mounting block, but Noa still gave her a helpful yank from the other side of the saddle. Tali settled in and guided Mozart out of the stable, and waited for Noa to lead them.

They moved beyond the property line at a snail's pace.

"I can go faster, you know," Tali said. Mozart slightly picked up the pace at the nudge of her leg.

"I'm not in a rush," Noa said.

Tali huffed. Noa was cool most of the time but, right now, she was acting like Tali was fragile.

Why couldn't anyone see how strong she was?

"Well, I am." Tali took off, working up to a trot then a canter.

Trax was beside them in no time, but Noa wasn't yelling at her to slow down. To Tali's delight, she said nothing. They rode in parallel under the bright moon, racing past the reservoir where Tali had nearly drowned. Suddenly, the entire experience was hilarious to her.

She started laughing, and Noa got caught in a fit of giggles too.

They rode faster until they reached the pond on the second leg. That's when Tali finally got a stitch in her side and needed to slow. They dismounted at a boulder on the water's edge.

Tali melted out of the saddle with intense bliss and waded through the grass. She threw herself on the ground to look at the stars.

Noa followed suit.

They stared at the stars, and Tali started laughing again. Noa joined, and soon they were both shaking from their bellies. Through tear-filled eyes, the moon and stars began to blur. Tali felt a familiar presence in her belly and looked to where the moon had just been—but it wasn't a moon anymore.

It was a hole in the sky leading to the perfect white nothingness.

Before Tali could, Noa reached up to the moon-sized hole in the sky, grabbed the ledge and stretched it down to earth, offering a hand to Tali.

"Come on. Let's go," she said.

Tali's face filled with excitement. She placed her hand inside Noa's.

"It's you," Noa said, looking down her arm at Tali.

"I told you," Tali said, still giggling and dove headfirst into the sky.

NOA

Tali was the little girl from the teacart.

She was older now, but in the Empyrean space, Noa saw her at all ages at once. Tali was the same girl, Noa was sure of it. She cried at the beauty and excitement of sharing this place with someone so perfect, and innocent, and free. To share this with someone more deserving.

When they plunged into the sea-sky, they floated for a moment, and the woman's voice whispered to them as they swam deeper.

Noa couldn't make out the words and looked to Tali to see if she understood.

Tali wasn't listening.

She was swimming gleefully with her eyes closed, enjoying the icy waters. Noa took a deep breath, and the water filled her lungs. It didn't drown her though. Instead, it felt like a cooling rinse and smelled like fresh air on a cold rainy morning—filled with the scents of mud and worms.

Tali took a deep breath and propelled her body forward with a big push. Noa watched as Tali exhaled and the water in front of her turned to ice and floated toward the surface.

Floating on her back, Noa stared at the shiny surface. It grew brighter every time she blinked. On her fourth blink, a jellyfish floated in front of her face, slowly, lazily.

Hundreds of jellyfish swum around her. Their soft, fabric tentacles floated impossibly far away from their tiny, squishy bodies. They were electric and vibrating. Noa rubbed her eyes, unsure of what she was seeing. They were emanating color. With each pulse of their tentacles, the jellyfish let out a wave of iridescent color, like a pearled shadow cast into the distance.

Noa reached out and touched one. It didn't shock her, but it sent a current of bass so low throughout her body that she knew right away—these weren't fish, they were souls. Noa and Tali chased the jellyfish around the water, bumping into each one and getting a glimpse into that soul's life.

The woman's murmurs became clear.

"Visit them."

Noa's attention focused on a few jellyfish that floated just above her. She reached out and put her lips to it. She took another deep breath and sucked in three jellyfish, like a cloud of smoke.

When she opened her eyes, she was a fat man laughing in his large truck. His friend had told him the funniest joke, and he was crying and turning red, laughing harder at his friend's goofy face.

Noa wiped away his tears and was suddenly at a funeral wiping away a woman's tears.

She was a plain, middle-aged mother who had lost her young son. She was so immeasurably sad, with no words in her head and a hard, beating heart in her chest that filled with pain. It hurt to be alive without him. She remembered who he was. He was a bright young man who loved to play music. She smiled softly and heard his violin, letting herself and the woman smile, just a little bit.

The funeral parlor murmurs turned into roaring fans and the violin's notes shifted into that of a guitar.

Noa listened to the music as it clarified and moved closer.

She recognized the words—she had written the song. She looked down at her hands. They were darker than her own with shorter fingers and gold rings and freckles she didn't recognize. The audience at the concert in front of her sang the words she had written. She beamed with pride.

When Noa exhaled at the concert, she returned to the icy waters and the three jellyfish escaped from her mouth.

Another swam toward her but, just before she could suck it up, a wave tumbled her and Tali away from the school. They both swam up, now suffocated by the pressure of the deep ocean.

When Noa broke the surface, the whitecap of the waves was no longer made of water but of cloud, a soft layer of fog bobbing up and down with the ocean's movement. Noa and Tali both climbed onto the clouds and laid back. They never reached the bottom of the cloud and never reached the surface of the ocean. They just fell, slowly and endlessly. Gently supported by the cottony sky.

After moments of blissful falling, the clouds began to drop off one by one.

They separated from the river of clouds that floated away and into the sky—a sky Noa hadn't noticed. One of orange and yellow and pink and blue. The bed of clouds beneath them grew thinner and thinner with each lost tuft until Noa and Tali both rested on the earth's floor. They stared up, peacefully saying goodbye to the clouds they'd just been lying in.

The dawn sky transformed into more vivid purples and pinks and blues and yellows and oranges. The grass between Noa's fingers was dewy and green.

She sat up, dreamily, and stretched toward the sky.

Tali raised her arms above her head, as well, and let out a sweet, squeaky breath as she relaxed her shoulders and seemed to let the euphoria calm.

Without saying much at all, they both got back on their horses and returned to Tali's house.

CHAPTER 31

NOA

Noa attacked the food on her plate.

Her third ascendant experience was easier to bounce back from than the first two, but it had made her doubly hungry.

On the ride back both her and Tali maintained consciousness, riding blissfully quiet through the early morning. But, as they grew closer, Noa felt her body temperature rise. When she helped Tali off Mozart, Tali was cold to the touch, from more than the cool night air. She was shivering and her lips were pale. Noa supported Tali, walking her inside. She poured her a glass of room temperature water, and got her to stay awake long enough to soak in a hot bath. After Tali's color returned and shivering stopped, Noa tucked her in on the couch and sat in the kitchen, eating everything she could get her hands on, while Tali slept it off.

She checked the comms on her auto as she shoveled food into her mouth.

"What are you doing?" Amar scratched his head, padding barefoot into the kitchen.

Noa stopped eating but it took a second for her to finish chewing and swallow the food already in her mouth.

"I have to talk to you." She kept her voice hushed and pushed the plate of random food she'd pilfered from his kitchen toward him. He grimaced and walked around her to pour himself a glass of water, downing it as greedily as she had been eating.

"Okay." He looked at her with sleepy eyes, clearly not grasping the gravity of her tone.

"It's serious," she said, moving them to sit at the table. He sat across from her, rubbing his tired face. It wasn't fair how hot he was in the morning, especially after what a mess he'd been the night before. Here he was, with disheveled hair and a wrinkled grey tee-shirt, wearing a dumb look on his face still looking gorgeous.

"Have you not slept?" he asked.

She shook her head no. "I couldn't sleep so I went riding. Tali caught me."

"Oh no," he said. "You didn't take her with you, did you? She's not experienced enough yet."

"I did. And she's actually quite a good rider. But that's not what I have to tell you."

She speedily detailed the night, fending off Amar's interrupting huffs of discontent. He wasn't listening the way he had when they'd talked about her ascensions before. She tried to tell him about lying in the grass and the sky opening again. She described the jellyfish and soul hopping but let her story trail when he pushed his seat back from the table.

"Get out."

"What?" He must not understand. "No, Amar, I'm telling you—she came up with me. It was amazing. She can ascend, too."

"Get out. Now."

She stood. "No. I have to be here when she wakes up. We need to figure this out."

"No you don't. I need to figure this out, not you. You need—you need to stay away for a while."

Tali stirred on the couch. "Amar?" She peered over the couch pillows.

"You—go back to sleep. You need to rest. We'll discuss this later."

"She didn't do anything wrong!" Tali said in defense of Noa. "If you would ever listen to me you would know that I've already—."

"That's enough." It was his guardian voice again. It was certain and firm. "You need to go, now." He moved toward Noa, his body seeming bigger and more intimidating than she remembered. He was now herding her backward to the door.

She was cowering. Again.

Noa looked at Tali, who had tears down her cheeks, and then to Amar's belligerent expression.

"I'm going to leave but I need you both to know..." She looked at Tali. "I'm not giving up. This is important and it is so much bigger than all of us."

She glanced back to Amar, but his expression remained

unchanged. Noa stepped onto the front porch with her boots in her hand as the door slammed behind her.

Back at the Main stables, Noa put Trax away and walked to the dorm with her eyes barely open. They were dry and tired from another sleepless night. Despite the heated exchange with Amar, her heart was steady, and her mind was calm. Now that she had another partner in this, it was just a matter of time before she could start investigating again.

Everyone would be on board again. Even Amar.

"Oh, good. Noa, come here please." Sai popped around the corner and waved her over before she entered the dorm.

"Hi Sai, um, I actually haven't slept and—"

"Just follow me."

She rounded the corner to follow him to the side of the building. Decker stood with his head dropped, and his hands on his waist. He looked worried.

It took Noa a second to register that there was someone standing next to him. Someone tall, stiff, and dressed in black and grey. Her body broke into a cold sweat.

Tempsen.

Noa had the urge to run in the other direction but, before she could, Decker heard their footsteps and turned to her and Sai.

"Oh, good. You found her," Decker said to Sai. "Noa, we need to talk."

"What is he doing here?" she asked, infuriated and worried.

"I think we'll need to sit down for this one." Decker looked like he'd also been up all night, with a healthy dose of stress and anger.

"He's a liar, Decker. You know that he got Jo reassigned! He's dangerous, don't believe him." Noa's pulse quickened.

"Calm down," Decker ordered, and she rested back on her heels.

He ushered everyone into his office, and they dispersed into the tiny, pine-smelling room with armchairs wrapped in faux hides. No one sat in the chairs, and Sai stood at the door like a guard.

"Well, it seems you've been doing a little lying of your own, little lady. Ah—" Decker held up a hand to protest her protestation. "I need you to be honest with me. Why were y'all in the Library?"

His bushy grey eyebrows sat pleasantly above kind brown eyes.

"I can't tell you that, sir. Not in front of him."

"I don't know how to be any clearer, Noa." The patience drained from Decker's expression. She did not like this side of him. "You need to tell me, right now."

Noa looked over her shoulder. Decker was in front of her, and Tempsen was behind her to her left. With Sai at the door, she was encircled.

Before she could speak, Tempsen stepped closer. He was tall, much taller than Decker. He towered over her and examined her through curious, dangerous eyes.

"There's no need for her to repeat it. You can believe what I told you." Tempsen studied her carefully, and his snarled face untangled. "Noa, I'm not here to hurt you or report you.

I'm here because I need your help. We need your help."

Noa looked around, he wasn't with anyone.

"I've been working with Jo," Tempsen said, answering her question. "I wasn't behind his Reassignment. I knew what you were looking for at my Library, but I pretended I didn't. I believe you caught onto that."

Noa controlled her expression, trying not to let him read anything from her.

"I figured it was better to downplay it," he continued. "After Jo was reassigned, I realized HQ had figured it out for themselves. I reached out to him, and he told me everything. That's when I put a flag on your comms. When you sent that message to your sister last night, my fear was confirmed."

"What fear?" Noa asked. Her blood was starting to heat. "And you flagged my comms? You listened to my message?"

"You're lucky I did." Tempsen cleared his throat. He seemed immune to her spike in rage. "I was able to delete the record of it before…" Tempsen looked at Decker.

Decker took off his hat and rubbed his brows.

"Well, before it got into the wrong hands," Tempsen concluded.

"Alright, Noa. Can you start from the beginning and tell me your side of things here?" Decker asked.

Noa took a deep breath, considering. "Fine."

She told Decker and Tempsen what she'd felt the first night of her ascension—the race day all that time ago at the beginning of the Skill Trip. She told them about planning and plotting with Alexis and V to make it happen again and then told the story of the night she fell off Trax.

"So, Amar knows too?" Decker asked with slanted brows.

She nodded and his hand found his forehead again, rubbing the tension with more vigor. Noa told them of Jo's theory and their plan to find evidence of hidden reports in the Library's sorting system.

"And you were right," Tempsen chimed in. "Sort of."

He explained how the Library was tasked with identifying and forwarding experiences of ascension to the Variety HeadQuarters. He'd even visited HQ a few times to discuss protocols with a panel of HQ techs and Analysts, but no other Librarians. It had apparently been a strange visit and, when they asked each Library to begin tagging and separating evidence of those flagged experiences and reports, the Library director pushed back.

Tempsen leaned forward with his elbows on his knees. His wool collar gaped around his neck, and Noa wondered how hot he had been standing outside. He hadn't broken a sweat.

"The Library director, Shen, was reassigned the next day as a Mariner, and I received a Variety promotion note. I was made Director in Shen's place." Tempsen leaned back in his chair again. He hadn't fully understood what was happening but didn't want to risk pushing back. As far as he knew, the Southern Library was the only one involved, with all related instances being filtered through them. "Jo was right about that. We have Techs identifying, forwarding, and erasing all traces of reports describing ascension."

"How many reports?" Noa asked.

Tempsen inhaled and breathed out. For the first time, his head hung.

"How many reports?" she demanded.

He met her eye.

"Thousands."

The figure punched Noa into the back of her seat. She had been excited when she learned Tali could ascend, but thousands of others? She knew it had been a possibility, but hearing it confirmed made her feel—invisible.

"But, as far as I can tell, you're the only person who has experienced this more than once, or beyond the first light," Tempsen added. Noa perked up.

Decker tipped his hat. "I'm not sure I understand, Mr. Tempsen, sir."

"Just Tempsen," he corrected.

"Why on Earth would HQ hide important information like this? A computer algorithm can't have ulterior motives. And the entire point of the Variety is to evolve human souls. *If* this was true, I don't think they would have anything to do with hiding it."

Noa didn't like how heavy he leaned on the word *if*.

"We don't understand why yet, but they are hiding it. That's why I need you." Tempsen turned to Noa.

"What do you want me to do?"

"I've been working with Jo and Shen, and we've come up with a rudimentary plan. But we need your help." Tempsen turned back to Decker. "And yours."

Decker held up his hands. "Tempsy," he said, chewing back a proud smile about the new nickname he'd coined. "I want to help, I really do. This all seems peculiar, and I'm sure there is something to be sorted out. But I can't help you. The Variety has stood strong for two hundred years, and it has served me well. I can't take part in questioning that."

Noa shot Decker a look, but she wasn't going to just let her face speak for her. "Decker, I don't know how I can help yet…but I do know we have to understand what is going on, because if something is wrong, we need to do as much as we can to make things right. That is what you do. That is what being a good person is all about. It's about doing what you know is right in your soul. Not listening to what other people or algorithms tell you." She stood up. "You know that right? You can feel it, in here, that something is wrong?" She tapped on her chest.

Decker clicked his teeth and side-stepped Noa. His lips stayed pursed as he walked to the door. Sai opened it.

"Look. You're welcome to stay here at the ranch as long as you need, Tempsy. Noa. I appreciate the pep talk, and you telling me the truth today." He rested his hands on his hips. "Your shift starts tonight at dusk, but your time before and after your shift is yours, as always." Decker left, the door swinging shut behind him.

Sai stayed in the room.

"We don't need Decker," Noa said. "but we do need to figure out a plan."

CHAPTER 32

NOA

Noa stood onstage in Main Hall. She recalled the charisma Decker had brought to it twenty-four hours earlier and tried to channel any residual energy. Her voice was quieter than his, but her presence could be louder. There were only ten people in the room, and she didn't need to be standing on the stage to address them, but the height gave some legitimacy to what she was going to ask. Feet wide, Noa rocked on her heeled boots. Her hands fidgeted, adjusting her shirt.

Tempsen towered next to her in his dark cloak, standing statuesque in his woolen ensemble. He did not sway, or fiddle his hands, or glance around the room.

Noa stopped rocking and tucked in the edge of her shirt. She slid her hands into her pockets to keep them still and kept her eyes on the door, willing more to join so she could finally do something.

Vitus and Jash walked in, and Alexis closed the door behind them. They joined Zahira, Mirai, and Andrea at the table. Decker had not returned, but Sai had followed them into the main room. He stood off to the side, but Noa figured that if he didn't want to be a part of this, he would have left when Decker did.

"Th-thank you everyone for coming," Noa said. Just then, her auto sent haptic feedback into her finger. "One second." She stepped back from the front of the stage and opened her auto. It was her sister, Sami. Noa thought about ignoring the contact but, instead, she answered and put the auto up on a reflective screen, allowing the audience and her to both see Sami.

"Noa, are you okay?" Sami asked breathily. "Whoa, who are all of these people? Hi everyone." Sami finger-combed her messy hair.

"I'm fine. Sami, but, um, I'm about to catch everyone here up to speed, so might as well do the same for you."

"Okay, sure," Sami said. She sat back and adjusted her position for the video feed.

"This is my sister, Sami," Noa told the room, gesturing to the projection.

Tempsen spoke up. "Actually, we can't broadcast like this." He turned to Noa and reached for her hand. "Can you grant me permissions?"

"Sure?"

Noa pulled up the control panel on her auto's projection and accepted Tempsen's request for control. Her auto faded from blue to black, and Sami was almost invisible for a moment. In front of Sami was a screen of code and images of pipelines that Tempsen wrote and navigated from his own auto. After a few moments (and awkward coughs from Sai), Tempsen shut his auto and Sami returned to the bright blue. She shrank in size and, next to her, two more figures popped up.

Both wore pressed and collared blue uniforms. One, she recognized, the other she did not.

Jo blinked on screen. "Hello?"

"Jo?" Zahira replied from the audience, rising to her feet.

Alexis, V, and Jash murmured their surprise. Jo acknowledged them with a polite smile.

"Tempsen?" the other blue-collared figure asked.

"Yup, hello, sir. Everyone, this is my former director, Shen. They will be helping assist us in this mission."

Shen stiffened on the screen when his name was called. Noa took note of them, androgynous in appearance with short, fine black hair, high cheekbones, and an intense focus in their eyes.

Tempsen turned to address Shen and Jo on the screen. "We are in a secure format. I've confirmed with Noa, and we are moving ahead with our plans. Her team is gathered, and we are about to inform them." Tempsen stepped back to give Noa the stage.

As Noa opened her mouth to begin, the door opened once more.

"Amar," she mouthed, almost silently, and everyone turned to watch him enter.

Amar, looking exhausted, stood at the door. Tali wedged herself around him and bounced to the front, nuzzling up to

Andrea, resting a tired head on her shoulder. Amar, on the other hand, entered slowly, not looking at anyone and taking a seat at the end of a table.

"That's Amar?" Sami said from her screen and then clapped a hand over her mouth.

Amar glanced up at the sound of his name and gave a two-finger wave.

Noa started a third time, this time sure of what she was going to say.

"Last night, I confirmed I am not the only one who has started ascending." She looked at Tali, whose head popped up from Andrea's shoulder. "This morning, Tempsen, who turns out to be a friend, also confirmed that there are thousands of us. Thousands."

She paused and paced the stage.

"This should be a good thing, an exciting thing. I've been taught my whole life that the way we live is designed to push us toward this exact thing happening. And, instead of celebrating this wave of evolution, Variety HeadQuarters is hiding it. And," Noa gestured to Shen and Jo, "disappearing the folks who have the capacity to expose them for doing so."

"We have a lot more to figure out, and we need your help to do it. We need to go to HQ and get to the bottom of this."

Silence.

Noa counted her breaths, and her focus scattered across the room before finally landing on V at the movement of him standing.

"I'm following, and I'm with you that we have to do something," he said. "But what exactly do you think we're going to do at HQ?"

"I'll take this one," Shen said from the auto display. "The request for the Library to filter these requests came from a certain group of HQ Analysts, who I believe are being led by a group of Elders."

"We don't have Elders anymore," Mirai said.

Shen nodded, patiently. "That is supposed to be true. But when I received the order, the Analysts gave the instruction in a room with a two-way wall." Shen said this matter-of-factly, as if the short comment explained everything.

Jo recognized his peers' typical confusion and jumped in. "The order came from a group of Analysts who had been instructed by someone anonymously watching over them. Variety HQ doesn't have leadership but, back when it was an Elder-led government, it did. Shen has done more research, and there isn't a lot of proof that the Elders ever died or left the premises. They could still be there, controlling things."

"You all sound like a bunch of conspiracy nuts," Jash piped up. "There's no such thing as Elders anymore."

Vitus spoke over him. "Even if it's not Elders, it's still an issue if someone's there giving these orders, huh?"

Jash dipped his head and held his hands up to say, *You're right.*

V turned back to the stage. "Exactly how are we going to get into HQ—let alone— anywhere near the Variety?"

"They're not just going to let us poke around," Mirai said. "And, if this is as urgent as you say, we'll need to take a jet or jammy, and we'll have to register that travel. They'll see us coming."

"We'll ride our horses," Noa said.

V, Jash, Zahira, and Alexis let out a groan.

Noa held up a hand to cut them off. "Look, it took us two months to get from City Centre to here as trainees, but as Cavalry members, the Marshals make it back to City Centre in five weeks. We could do it even faster without all the extra horses and supply stock."

Her eyes searched for Amar's, but his were trained on the floor.

Sai chimed in instead. "She's right. Without the extra weight and only advanced riders, we could make it back in three and a half, maybe four weeks."

"I'm in," Zahira said. She and Alexis stood, tangled in a side-hug.

Gradually, everyone stood, except Amar and Jash.

Jash finally pulled himself up. "Fine, I'm in but I'm not going anywhere near HQ until we have a way tighter plan than we did at the Library. I am not getting caught."

"You never did," Zahira sniped.

"I'm just saying, we need an insider to help us with this. We can't be running around guessing like we were in Veraccu."

Amar stood, making eye contact with Noa.

She waited, anticipating what he would say. Hoping it was good.

"I was Assigned to HQ before Cavalry. I can get us in."

Noa's hand slipped from a clay rock, and her knee split and bled from the impact of the fall. Not enough blood to warrant a bandage she didn't have, but enough to dampen her skin and cause dirt to stick to her. She added bandages to her mental list of things to bring on the trip.

She'd climbed to the top of Crested Peak. It was the tallest formation near the ranch, the one that faded from black to peach and leveled off with a fantastic three-hundred-sixty-degree view of the ranch property. To a different mental list, she added climbing to the highest point for a sunrise or sunset.

Today, she was climbing to join Yori for his morning meditation—assuming one could call two a.m. "morning".

At the planning meeting, the group agreed to leave for HQ in one week as it would give them enough time to find coverage for the Cavalry routes, prepare supplies, and for Jo, Shen, and Tempsen to organize their own plans to arrive at City Centre within the same time frame. After the timeline was decided, they'd dispersed for their first day as Cavalry members.

Noa had made it through her first shift. It was somewhat boring, full of instruction from Remy, a seasoned Cavalry member who had been on the route for a few years. She'd hoped Amar would stop by since she needed to talk to him, but he'd done a great job of occupying himself supervising all the other legs besides hers. As soon as they were called in for the end of their shift, Noa and Trax sprinted for Crested

Peak to join Yori's meditation.

Amar, Mirai, and Sai were all going on the trip to City Centre, which meant that Yori would have to watch over more of the Cavalry as he had during the Skill Trip. He'd still have Decker, of course. But, even in a few short weeks, Noa had noticed Decker didn't do too much of the actual ranch work.

After the first shift, Decker would receive Amar, Sai, and Mirai's request for travel, and they would ask him to not report it. The Marshals could manage that request on their own, but Noa knew she had to ask for what they wouldn't.

They needed something from Yori, not Decker.

When she finally got to the top of the rock, she found a shirtless Yori sitting cross-legged on a thick woven throw. His long hair was pulled into a ponytail, and its length sat twisted between his muscled shoulders. It seemed odd for someone so large to sit like a pretzel, but he seemed comfortable.

Noa joined, sitting behind him, quietly trying not to disturb him. She settled into a similar cross-legged position and rested her hands on her knees. She'd practiced meditation before and knew what she was meant to do. She dropped her shoulders and aligned the crown of her head over the base of her body. She breathed in through her nose and held the breath. She exhaled through her mouth for longer than she'd inhaled and let her eyes rest on a tuft of frosted wheatgrass growing out of the red rock and glowing in the moonlight. It was enveloped in frozen dew, clinking and chiming as it rustled in the cool midnight wind.

She breathed with the wind of the grass and became lost

in its rhythm. Her eyes unfocused from the single wheat floret only when Yori stirred.

"Ah, at last. You join me," he said. His voice was as flat as it had been the day he'd given the invitation.

"Thanks for inviting me. I needed some peaceful moments after this week," she admitted.

"Mmhmm." Yori raised an eyebrow, curious. "And what else do you need?"

She stretched her arms toward the night sky before dropping them back at her sides. "I have to ask you a favor."

He raised a hand. "I know more than you think."

"I'll need an actual Cavalry," Noa said. "Not ranchers. Cavalry."

Yori grunted, folding his blanket with precision. "Most of the Cavalry needs retraining anyway. They didn't get Yori's training," he said smugly. "We will be prepared."

On her walk home, Noa's eyes stuck at the bottom of her blinks. She'd barely slept in two days, and life felt like a waking dream. Every few seconds, a thought flew through her head that questioned every experience she'd had. At first, she abated the thoughts by relating them to something tangible—another real person involved or a physical element she touched during the experience.

After a while, though, her thoughts wore her down, and it became more difficult to tether her experiences to reality.

The ascension, the white heat burning in her belly, exhaling jellyfish, ungraspable memories. But if the people around her believed her, it had to be true.

What if I don't know I'm lying to them?

She swallowed and ran through her grounding thoughts again. Talking with Tempsen, Decker, and Alexis was real. Riding Trax was real. Lying in the grass with Tali. The fight with Amar. Sami on the auto display. Jo being back. Zahira seeing Jo. Meditating with Yori.

All real.

Until she was alone.

Noa rounded the corner from the main ranch into the hall of her dorm to find Amar leaning against her door.

"I need to talk to you," he said.

"What's going on?"

He nodded to the door.

Noa scanned into her dorm and let them both inside, closing the door behind them. He'd never been in her room. It wasn't exactly a personal space, but it was nice to have him there, seeing where she lived when she wasn't with him.

She pulled out a chair for him and straightened her bedsheets, in which she hadn't slept in days, and sat on her bed.

Amar leaned over his lap and rested his arms on his knees. He stared at the floor and then raised his eyes to meet hers.

He hadn't slept either.

"I can't go with you to HQ."

Noa waited for him to explain but he didn't. His voice was back to the steady, honest cadence of his normal register. It was so far from the annoyed and curt tone he'd stabbed her with as he'd backed her out of his house.

"Amar, I know you're upset with me, but this is a lot

bigger than us. We need your help to get into HeadQuarters." Noa lost control of her own tone, changing from empathetic to angry halfway through her sentence.

"It's not about that," he said. "And I'll tell you everything you need to know to get into HQ before you leave. I just can't go with you. I can't be there. It's too dangerous."

"It's dangerous for everyone. It's scary for everyone. But if you don't go with us, you're making it riskier than it has to be."

He was still in the chair.

Noa gripped the sheets at her sides in a fist. "What about Tali? You must have talked to her by now. You know she's experienced the same thing as me. If there is something this big—this monumental going on—the world needs to know. Whoever is reassigning and hiding people is a danger. They are a danger to people like her!"

"Why do you think I'm not going?" He lowered his voice. "I know you didn't mean anything by bringing Tali out there and, maybe, it would have happened even if you hadn't...but she's not like you. And she's just a kid. If something happens to me, she'll be on her own.

"She's not part of the Variety yet. If they find out about her, they can't reassign her. She's too young."

"Reassignment isn't the only thing they can do, Noa. You know that."

He looked at her knowingly. They could make her disappear.

"Look, we don't know what this is escalating to, but it's only going to be worse if we do nothing," Noa said.

"I don't need you to understand, but my decision is final.

I'm not going."

He stood and left as quick as he'd appeared.

She lay on her bed, rubbing her dry eyes.

Her hands were dusty from riding and climbing rocks. She thought she ought to wash them and shower. She thought she should also go talk to Alexis about Amar and conspire a way to change his mind. She thought about calling her sister, who needed some follow-up after two equally-wild comms. She touched her forehead and thought about Amar's kiss.

But instead of doing any of that, she simply closed her eyes and slept.

CHAPTER 33

NOA

Noa fed Trax a handful of oats and gave him a sympathetic frown. He had no idea the oats would be his last treat for a while. She wondered if he knew they were about to ride harder than they ever had together. Could he sense it, in her energy—in the way her heart beat—that they were about to embark on a great adventure?

He stomped, and her mouth lifted to a pursed smile. She threw herself at his giant body, hugging as tightly as she could. They really had become partners; it gave her hope for the other difficult relationships in her life.

From nearby, Alexis squealed and joined the hug, squeezing Noa from behind.

"Only you could make a fate-of-the-world mission to HeadQuarters feel like a celebration," Noa said.

"You started it. But yes, it's a gift." She flipped her imaginary hair. "We're all packed, V and I. Zahira and Jash are just about done too. Sai and Mirai are saying their goodbyes, but I think they're ready to go after that. So we're just waiting on you and Amar."

"I'm ready, and you know Amar isn't coming."

Alexis tilted her head. "He didn't change his mind, huh?"

"It's fine. We can do this without him. We have the blueprints he went over. Jo and Shen agree it's a good plan. Tempsen's Teaching friend is meeting us at City Centre to give us the HQ uniforms, and we'll have plenty of time on the journey to nail down every other detail—and many, many back up plans."

Alexis's head tilted farther.

"We'll be fine," Noa insisted.

"One more time like you believe it?" Vitus said, walking up and hugging Alexis's side.

"We'll be fine!" Noa pointed to her plastered-on smile.

Someone cleared their throat from behind her.

It was Amar.

"Change your mind?" V asked.

"We'll let you two talk." Alexis said, tugging him away.

Noa straightened her posture and waited for him to speak.

"What?" he asked.

"What do you mean 'what'? Why are you here?" She crossed her arms. "You've told us everything we need to know, right?"

They both knew his instructions were no replacement for having him there when they went into HQ. He was the only one, besides Shen and Tempsen, who had spent time inside. And everyone knew that neither Shen nor Tempsen were as stealthy.

Amar took a step toward Noa, and she took a half-step back, bumping into Trax.

"Do you have everything you need?" he asked. "It's a hard trip to ride that fast to City Centre. You'll need an extra canteen and, at this time of year, a rain cape." He bent his neck around her as if he could see into her closed saddle bags.

"Mirai and Sai created our packing lists. I'll be fine."

"You need to be careful." He took another small step and put his hand on the small of her back. "I need you to make it back." His dark hair fell in front of his eyes and then hers as he put his forehead to her.

She wanted to be very angry, but for once in her life couldn't summon an ounce of rage. "Then come with us," she whispered.

His forehead twisted on hers. "I'm sorry."

"Me too."

He kissed her on the forehead and lifted her chin with two fingers.

They met in the middle, a soft slow kiss—as if they were in no rush at all.

When they finally separated, Noa was dizzy and barely able to keep her eyes open as he walked away.

CHAPTER 34

TALI

Tali hadn't wanted to steal Kiffin.

She hadn't wanted to steal supplies or leave alone in the middle of the night. But what choice did she have? She couldn't stay. Amar was wrong.

Her legs dangled shy of the stirrups, and her toes grew stiff having to press into them. Kiffin, Andrea's horse, was way too big for her.

Ten days of training under Mirai had been grueling, but it served her well. She hadn't learned much, since she'd been hearing the training lessons for five years, but she had proven to herself that she was just as strong as (and better with horses than) most of the new members.

She could handle this.

Plus, she only had to ride alone for a few days. Amar

would catch up to her, or she would catch up to the group.

Thinking about Amar made Tali's eye twitch. The morning after the ride with Noa, Tali had waited for Amar to calm down. She'd been mature, she thought, while explaining everything that happened slowly and clearly. She was so excited to finally tell him about Grandma Dia and Mom, but he shut her down. He didn't want to know—as if she were trying to tell him about a school lesson or a new lemonade recipe.

She hated when he got like that. When he let it be painfully obvious that she was still just a kid to him.

Riding into daybreak, Tali's thoughts got away from her. *How could he be so selfish? How could he not care? How could he be angry at Noa and not her?*

His anger, though rarely directed at her, invaded her. Luckily, Amar had been angry plenty of times before, and Tali had started learning how to guard herself from the invasion. She petted Kiffin and sang to him.

It was a song her mother had sung to her when she was little. Tali didn't remember the exact words—they were long gone—but she would always remember the tune. It was a game of hers to make up words each time she sang her mother's song. Today, the words were:

With pines reaching high,
And winds blowing cold,
We're going to make it, oh.
And nobody knows.

My mind runs wild,
And my hands hold tight.
We have to make it,
Make it through the night.

Tali sang until her throat hurt. She reached for her first drink of water from the canteen. She needed to stay hydrated but also needed to ration wisely until she could find the first water source.

She planned to ride through the night and all the next day, not stopping to sleep until late the next night. Every minute she could ride without taking a break was a larger lead on Amar catching up to her.

Tali led Kiffin to their first water source around noon, dismounting clunkily on a boulder by the creek's edge. She laid back in the sunshine on the creek's bank and drank the rest of her canteen. The sun was warm and, if she held still long enough, felt as cozy as her bed's blanket.

She rested her head against a stone, listening to the wind and Kiffin drinking water. When he was done drinking, she would fill her canteen and they would be on their way.

"Tali, wake up."

A shoe wiggled her shoulder. Her face scrunched as she woke and went blank as she scrambled to her feet.

"Amar," she sighed, letting her defensive stance relax. "How did you—? How did you get here so quickly? Did you not have to work a double today? Damn." Tali shook her head.

"No, dummy. And don't swear. I worked a double." He took a sip from his canteen. "It just takes you ten hours to ride what I can in four." He smiled and leaned down to refill his canteen from the creek. He reached out, gesturing for her to pass him hers.

She filled it on her own. "Four hours? It only took you four hours to get all this way?"

He pumped his eyebrows. "Thanks for the note by the way. Andrea's going to have some words for you when we get back."

"I'm not going back. I have to go with them. *We* have to go with them." Tali prepared herself for his scolding rebuttal, but it didn't come.

Amar shuffled through her saddlebags.

"I know," he said. "But we're never going to catch them at your pace. You'll ride with me on Mozart, and we'll put our supplies on Kiffin. Even with both of us on one horse, I think we can still catch up to them within the week."

"Really?" She dropped her hands from her hips. "Why aren't you mad? I don't understand."

"Do you really want to push it?"

"It's me. What do you think?"

"Just help me transfer the bags. Can you do that now that you're well-rested?"

Tali huffed but smiled as soon as she had her back turned.

They were on their way.

CHAPTER 35

NOA

Finally on flat land and following a route without bath lakes for an extra couple of days, they covered the distance twice as fast as they had on their Skill Trip. By tomorrow, they'd be outside Veraccu with their only reliable connectivity before reaching City Centre.

It had been a treacherous ride through the mountains, and the riding group wasn't able to shave much time off the journey during the first two weeks of rocky terrain. Each day they rode from before sunrise until they couldn't ride any longer at night. Despite the difficult terrain, exhausting schedule, and weighty plans they discussed, the team kept the spirit of the journey high.

Vitus and Alexis had still found time to flirt. Zahira, Jash, and Mirai still found plenty of time to laugh. However, Noa found herself spending her days riding quietly with Sai. His even and optimistic demeanor paired nicely with her depleted energy levels.

"Are you going to call your parents soon?" Sai asked.

"I will, later tonight at camp."

"Tonight's likely the last night for signal, *petit soleil*. You said you would do it yesterday." Sai gave her his own parental look.

"My dad used to call me that when I was little," Noa confessed. It was a common nickname for daughters, but Noa hadn't heard it in a long time.

Sai shrugged. It was a shame he wasn't a father. He was perfectly suited for it.

During a group call, Noa had suggested Sami tell their parents what was going on, so they could use their home as a base. Sami had recoiled at the thought and insisted Noa make the call. Without any other options for shelter in City Centre, the team had agreed before Noa was able to contest.

"I'll do it right after I set up camp."

Sai hummed approvingly.

Noa waved him off and stirred Trax to move faster.

"Hey Lex!" Noa yelled, pulling forward. "Trax wants to race."

Alexis laughed. "I think Luna is up for it."

"Whalen's in," V called, shifting in his saddle and pulling next to them.

"This race is for the big horses," Noa teased.

V scoffed at her and took off with a head start.

The trees blurred past, and Noa cinched her rain cape over her head. Small water droplets hit her face, reminding her of the star that had burned her cheek. She touched a hand to her face. The wind rushed into her cape and knocked her hood off, but she didn't care. She dropped her head back and let the droplets fall on her skin. She soaked up every sting.

The weight of what they were about to do had rarely escaped Noa's mind over the past few weeks but, suddenly, she could see the lightness of it all.

This was bigger than her—than all of them.

Bigger than entire lifetimes and generations.

She'd witnessed it. The next level of consciousness. She'd visited—been part of it. The risk they faced wasn't in getting caught, or punished, or disappeared. It was in failing. The risk was the world never knowing they were capable of ascending, too. If she didn't act soon, she and all the others would stay hidden and disconnected.

With the wind in her face, basking in the lightness, she knew they would be successful.

They had to be.

Alexis hollered as Luna pulled past Trax.

"Catching raindrops?" Alexis mimicked Noa's stance by leaning her head back and opening her mouth wide with her tongue hanging out.

Noa laughed and opened her mouth to catch drops until a chunk of mud flew up from Trax's hoof and landed in the back of her throat. She coughed and choked, and Trax slowed in concern.

V and Alexis surrounded as they slowed and laughed at her.

"And we're supposed to believe you're the evolved one?" Alexis joked.

Noa shrugged. "I try to be a relatable prophet."

Noa smiled as her sister popped up on the auto display. "Hey, Sami."

"What are you going to tell them?" Sami asked. No time for small talk.

"One sec, we have to wait for Jo."

Just then, Jo joined the call. "Hey Noa, can you give me permission again?" he asked, quickly and matter-of-factly.

Noa shared her auto permissions with him. The display flickered before Jo spoke again.

"Alright, you're all set. Just remember it's only scrambled for this call so, if you hang up and start over, it's not secure."

Noa and Sami nodded, and Jo waved before exiting the screen.

"He's really gotta teach me how to do that," Noa started.

"What are you going to tell Mom and Dad?" Sami asked again.

Noa was used to her sister being blunt or crass, but this was different. She was worried.

"I'm going to tell them everything."

Sami shook her head before Noa could continue. "I don't think that's a good idea. They're not going to react the way you think they will."

"You don't have to worry. They're our parents, they're not going to freak out. Now, go get them on your auto, and I'll start."

Noa watched as Sami walked out of her bedroom and into

the living room. Her parents sat next to each other, reading on their own autos.

"Mom, Dad? Noa's here." Sami gestured to Noa on the screen, and Noa waved.

"Ah!" They said in unison and rose to greet her as if she were in the room.

"Noie," Armel said, bowing his head and giving the familiar prayer gesture.

Chemi did the same, a timid smile filling her cheeks. "So good to see you. You look strong!"

Armel gave a flex of his own bicep, and Noa laughed.

"Here, Noie. Let me join from my auto so you can see us more clearly," Chemi said.

"No!" Sami and Noa said.

"Mom, Dad, can you actually turn off your autos? I have a lot to catch you up on, and we have to do it over Sami's feed." Noa said this firmly. She'd never spoken to her parents with this much command before. She'd been bratty to them and angry with them, but never a family leader. Today she had to be.

Noa examined her parents' contrasting expressions: her mother's face was filled with concern and worry while her father smiled with pride and excitement. She hated to think of all the wonderful pieces of news he might be expecting, and the confusing and difficult one she had to deliver.

Noa recapped everything as she'd done so many times before. She was becoming an expert at telling her story, having learned with each rendition about which details to gloss over and which to punctuate. It spilled out effortlessly, not carelessly.

When she finished talking, her mother stood and walked out of the frame. Armel pieced together an excuse about having to follow her and struggled to get out of his seat, getting caught on the chair's armrest.

"Dad?" Noa called as he stepped away. Noa had no words. No thoughts. Blood drained from her. Then her breath left.

He paused and Noa watched her father's shoulders rise and fall in a thoughtful breath before he slumped out of the room.

Noa's eyes widened and welled with tears. Her chest constricted, and she clutched at it to slow her breathing and unravel the binds compressing her rib cage.

Her friends had believed her. Her sister had believed her. *No.*

She believed herself. That was enough. She was enough.

She cried anyway.

"Noa," Sami whispered. "Noa, look at me."

Noa wiped a tear.

Her sister's kind eyes reached through the display and locked her gaze. "They just need some time."

Noa's chest shook, suppressing cries.

"I'll handle them, but we can't bring everyone here," Sami said. "You just need to tell me where to meet you, and we'll work it out when you get here."

Noa wiped at her face again. She could be calm. She could handle this.

"The Stables at the City Centre. We'll be there in eight days."

"Eight days," Sami repeated.

Noa fell asleep that night to the sound of rain and the smell of chilly, water-logged air. She dreamed more vividly than she had in weeks.

She was in the Green Gem House again, visiting the old woman. Though her hair was still streaked with silver, the woman was much younger and wore fewer layers of skirt. She poured Noa tea.

"When?" the woman asked.

Noa walked the room with a warm teacup in her hands and pulled back the curtain looking out to the street.

There was no coffee cart on the corner.

"Eight days," Noa said.

She sipped her tea and, when Noa pulled the mug from her lips, she was suddenly outside, steps away from the coffee cart. City Centre returned to its more recent skyline and young Tali was at the end of her arm, holding her hand.

When Noa looked down to her, Tali morphed from a child to a young teenager, fizzling in and out of her physical body. Noa reached toward her to settle the fragmented form. Instead, her hand was drawn in. The touch had flipped her around until she *was* the child, looking up to a woman who was now free of Noa's occupation.

The woman knelt down next to her.

"Where's Tali?" Noa asked.

The woman tied Noa's shoe. "I thought you knew, sweet girl."

Her face looked carved, with sharp lines softened by thick, dark eyebrows, outlining deep brown eyes. Noa had seen them before on another face.

"Where?" It was all she could manage to say.

"You just missed her." The woman pouted playfully, then pointed.

Noa followed her point and saw herself knocking on the door of the Green Gem House, the curtain in the window still waving from someone's recent movement.

"You'll find us." The woman said, taking Noa's chin in her hand and nudging it toward her.

Noa couldn't help but mimic the woman's sweet smile and found her lips echoing the words.

Find us.

Noa awoke suddenly.

It felt like only minutes had passed, but the light pouring into her tent meant it was sunrise. A fire crackled and beneath its murmur was a girl's voice and someone shushing her.

She hurled herself out of the tent and ran to find Tali and Amar around a fire they'd fashioned in the middle of everyone's tents.

Noa ran to Tali first and hugged her. She was overjoyed that, somehow, they'd caught up and found them. But, with her dream still in recent memory, she had a more important question.

She knelt in front of Tali. "Tali, did you know me?"

"Of course, I know you." Tali laughed like it was a joke.

Amar stepped closer with a confused look on his face.

"Yes, I know. I mean *did* you know me? Like before we

met in person? You recognized me the first day we met at Main Ranch."

"Yes." Tali sounded offended. "Didn't you recognize me too?" She tilted her head.

"Oh my Gods." Noa covered her gaping mouth.

Amar's eyes narrowed.

The rest of the group slowly came out of their tents, checking on the commotion.

Noa rose from her knees, which were now soaked and muddy.

"On my second ascension, the little girl whose hand I held at the teacart. That was Tali. When we ascended together, a few weeks ago. She grabbed my hand just like that little girl, and I knew it was her." Noa looked at Tali again and clenched her teeth in excitement.

Tali laughed, eagerly feeding off Noa's energy.

Amar's eyes narrowed. "That's not new information."

"I know. The rest of it. I didn't put it together until—" Noa stepped forward. "When I met Tali, she recognized me from that day. When she was just five."

"Six," Tali said.

"Six. I visited her."

They all gathered closer.

"What does that mean, hon?" Alexis asked. She stood in front of V, who wrapped his arms around her to keep her warm in the morning frost.

"They see me," Noa said. "When I ascend. I'm not a ghost, invisibly visiting people." Noa had never felt her smile push so wide. She bent over in relief. "I'm visiting other souls. And they knew it was me who was visiting."

"They saw you?" V asked.

"Saw me, felt me? I'm not sure. I haven't been on the other side of this, but they can recognize me. And the others who were around them when I visited—some could see me too!"

"And this is good?" Zahira asked.

"It means we have more friends than we think."

CHAPTER 36

NOA

"Who is this?" Noa asked, petting the auburn horse next to Mozart.

"Kiffin," Tali said, brushing him. They were getting ready to resituate Tali and Amar's bags. Now that they were on flat land, Tali would be able to ride solo with the group.

A heavy bag thudded, and Amar walked out from behind Mozart. "Kiffin is Andrea's. Tali stole him and ran away in the middle of the night to come join you."

"Good on you kid." Noa gave her a wink and turned to Amar. "So, if it weren't for Tali you'd still be sitting at home, huh?"

"Tali, go help Mirai." Amar said. Tali rolled her eyes and passed Kiffin's brush to Noa before backing away.

Noa reached for the brush, but Amar intercepted it and

set it on the ground. He took one of her hands and moved closer.

"I'm here now," he said.

Noa's gaze fell to the ground, willing the brush to jump back to her hand.

Amar's knuckles brushed her chin, drawing her eyes back to his. He had his mother's eyes. "Noa, I'm sorry."

She grimaced.

He smirked. "I thought you liked it when I said your name."

"That face was directed at your apology. You used to be very good at them." She pushed away from him. "It's not enough. It's not enough for you to come now."

He reeled her into him and brushed her hair behind her ear. His eyes ricocheted from her eyes to her lips.

Almost breathlessly, he said it. "Noa, I lo—"

"Don't." She pulled her hand from his. "Don't you dare cheapen that. Cheapen this—" She pointed between them. "—by saying it now. That is not an apology."

The wind blew between them.

"I lied to you," he said. "The first day we met. Do you remember? I made you a promise that it would get easier."

Noa bit her lip. She had made things so difficult.

"None of this has gotten easier," his voice was harsh but not loud. "Raising Tali is one of the hardest things I've had to do. And, regardless of how we ended up there, getting reassigned to Main Ranch was the best thing that could have happened to us. I finally had a break, a good life for her. And we had distance from all the heartache of losing our parents. Then you come along, and you make things so much harder." His jaw clenched as he spoke. It stung knowing that he thought the same thing. "This stunt could take everything away from us. You get that, right? This wasn't an easy decision for me. So, that's not my best apology because I'm not sorry it took me some time to terms with that sacrifice. But I did, and I am here now. I would rather go through all of this hard stuff with you, than live easily without you."

Noa's voice came out small and wavering. "My parents didn't believe me."

Amar straightened, clearly unsure of the connection.

She steadied. "Last night, I told them what's been going on. And they either didn't believe me, or they didn't care. Either way, they're not speaking to me. You're not the only one risking something. You're not the only one risking everything."

"I know."

"And I didn't ask for this." She pointed to the sky, as if any of *this* was actually *up*. "I didn't ask for any of this. I was trying to help them. I was just trying to help. And then I get Reassigned and I have this incredible thing that I can finally share. I finally have something to offer and I can find a way to help in a bigger way, so that no one else has to go through this. So they don't have to lose and risk what we've had to." Noa cupped her face in her hands, though the tears didn't come.

Amar gently pulled her to the ground to sit and knelt in front of her. He separated her hands and placed them around him, resting her head on his shoulder. They sat together, enfolded in each other until they settled back into the grass. They watched the clouds, and he stroked her hair. It felt good to be in his arms again, for them to be on the same team, finally.

Noa counted to five and sat up. She brushed the wrinkles out of her shirt and combed her hair with her fingers.

Amar stood and offered a hand to help her to her feet.

After they rose, he kissed her, and she kissed him back. They left their hands intertwined as they made their way back to the group's camp.

Before they rejoined, Amar held them back a moment. "If we can't go to your house, where are we going?"

"The Green Gem House."

Riding into the City Fields late at night, Noa's chest panged with the same strange sense of surrealism she'd had leaving the city on the first night of her Skill Trip. Colliding with modern life made the Cavalry seem bizarre and anachronistic. Noa obsessively patted Trax's neck as the small group rode into the unoccupied stable.

"Afraid he's going to revert to old habits?" Mirai said as she pulled Reyna, her horse, beside Trax.

"He better not, but I'm going to give him extra love if he keeps being this good," she said, cooing to Trax. "How was this morning's lesson with Tali?"

"Great, she's a natural. Kiffin is way too big for her, but any horse would be too big at her age. Helps that she's been around him a lot at our house."

"Do you miss Andrea?" Noa asked, wondering if Mirai held any resentment for her life being blown-up too.

"Of course. Don't usually do two trips in a year."

"What? You don't usually try to break into HQ during the busy season?"

Mirai laughed. "No, not exactly. But I'm glad I'm here. I've had my own curiosities, and I think I would die if you were all up here risking your lives to get the answers I've wanted for so long."

"We're not risking our lives." Noa second-guessed her statement as it fell from her lips. The truth was, they had no idea what they were up against. Noa's blood pressure volleyed.

"I hope that's true. But either way, there's no turning back now."

They each found a stall as they arrived and took care to give their horses extra attention and full buckets of feed. Sai would stay behind to look after the horses, but it might be a while before they'd return.

In solitude with Trax, Noa's mind wrestled with the repercussions of their actions. Her thoughts were quieted when Amar joined her in the stall. A vignette of their first day together flashed in her memory.

"How's it going?" he asked.

Her mind whirled, unsure how to answer the question.

"Noa?" He prompted again. She hadn't landed on an answer yet. "I asked how you're doing. You okay?"

She heaved a large sigh and stopped fidgeting with Trax. She could be honest with him. "No. I'm not. I'm painfully aware that our plan is up in the air until we know what is going on inside HeadQuarters. I'm excited to see my sister. I'm afraid of what I've dragged her and everyone else into.

My feet are wet and cold. And I have an empty feeling in my stomach."

"So, you're hungry?" He shot her a playful smile.

Her eyes gave way to a full roll, and she laughed. "Sure, yes. Hungry covers it. I'm going to go walk the stable, make sure we're alone."

"Sai already did that, but it's probably good to have another set of eyes." He moved to let her pass him in the stall.

The drizzle in the air cooled the night quickly, and the tips of Noa's toes burned from the wet chill. Without the distraction of riding, the pain grew more severe until she couldn't concentrate. She focused on watching her feet sink into the warm mud. With each footprint her pain calmed— she wanted to bathe in that mud.

Suddenly, she was yanked from behind. She yelped as her feet were pulled from the precious mud.

Sami hugged her sister tight. "I'm so glad to see you!"

Sami smelled like home. Tangled in her sister's arms, Noa gave in.

But even after months of separation, this hug was a little long. Noa stomped to put her boot all the way back on, since it had come half-off from the yank. In doing so, Sami loosened her grip and finally released Noa. They stood examining each other.

Without warning or reason, Noa glared at her sister and flames rose in her chest. She begged her brain to let her be happy but it ignored her will. She knew that she was thrilled her sister was here but, in the moment, she felt only anger. It swallowed every morsel of joy she had wanted for this moment.

"You scared me," she said. "Why are you dressed in all black?"

Sami stepped back and mirrored her sister's attitude. "Why are *you* dressed in all black?"

"There's purple. And my only other clothes are a Cavalry uniform. You watched me pack when I left, remember?" Noa bent over to properly fix her boots in a huff.

"That was months ago, and I watched you pack your plainest sweater and most boring jeans. Not sleek black mission clothes." Sami put a hand on her hip as she dug in her heel. "Also, excuse you—you're mad at mum and dad. Not me. And you owe me some details."

Noa could almost see the poison of her anger infect her younger sister. She relaxed, relieved to know someone had taken on some of her burden. Still, it wasn't fair of her to do. That was the old Noa.

"I'm sorry," she said, taking a deep breath to start over.

Sami watched her with a raised eyebrow.

"Seriously, I'm sorry," Noa repeated. "I'm glad you're here and you're right. I shouldn't have taken that out on you."

"Did Dad's therapy finally work on you?" Sami asked.

"Clearly not, otherwise I wouldn't have to apologize. I don't know how you always know what I'm feeling before I do."

"You're not that mysterious," Sami said as they started to walk together. "Well, except for the last four months. I've had no idea what's going on with you."

"Catch you up on the way? We have to get out of here before someone notices all of us stumbling around."

"Fiiiiine," Sami said with her signature drawl.

Together, they trudged back to the stalls where Noa introduced Sami to Alexis, Mirai, Zahira, and Tali. Every single person gave her sister a nicer greeting than she had. She had to start doing better.

"And this is Trax," Noa said, leading Sami into the stall.

Sami scooped a handful of feed from the box and opened the latch to the stall.

Noa knowingly smirked. "Oh, I wouldn't do that."

Trax turned and towered over Sami. She held out her hand and examined his giant head, cocking her own this way and that. Trax examined her back for just a moment before he bent down and ate out of her hand.

"What?" mouthed Noa.

"This is so cool. He is huge! Like way bigger than I would have thought a horse was."

The rain pounded on the thin stable roof as Amar, Vitus, and Sai jogged by, soaking wet, each carrying a bale of hay.

Amar turned into Trax's stall and dropped the bale just inside the gate. "Alright, this is the last bale, and we're ready to go."

"Hi there," Sami said, dreamily.

Amar nodded, waved, and wiped the wet hair back from his forehead.

"I'm Sami. Noa's sister."

"Amar. Nice to meet you." He gave her a polite smile.

"Oh, I remember." Sami adopted an inquisitive look. "You were on the call a few weeks ago. I thought maybe you weren't coming?" Sami looked to Noa for an answer.

"Tali, the younger girl you met earlier, is his little sister," she explained. "She convinced him to come after all. Tali is…

well, she's like me. She can ascend."

"Wait, multiple people can go? Like you take them with you or on their own?"

Noa shrugged. "We still have a lot to figure out."

"Definitely," Sami said, accepting the partial answer.

Noa had always envied that about her sister. She didn't overcomplicate things. It wasn't that she wasn't curious or that she didn't think about things. Sami just had a stable trust in her understanding of the world. What usually took Noa three or four follow-up questions to accept, Sami took just one.

Amar put his hood over his head and rubbed it to dry his wet hair. "We'd better get going."

Noa leaned out of the stall and stuck her head into the next one over where Zahira, Jash, Alexis, and V were chatting. "You all ready?"

They grabbed Mirai and Tali from another stall and trudged in a single-file line out of City Fields and onto the pedestrian walkway of the City. When the ground changed from dirt to stone, they stomped their feet to shake off the loose mud.

Noa led them through the streets and, eventually, they formed a more normal looking group, clumping into smaller groups making side conversations instead of being overly focused on their directive like inexperienced secret operatives.

Finally, they turned a corner and were in front of the Green Gem House.

"Isn't this the house you were going on about on our walk to Fields?" V asked.

"Oh yeah," Alexis recalled.

"She's always been obsessed with this house," Sami added.

Noa watched Amar. He wasn't examining the house the same way the others were, and he seemed to know where they were going. It occurred to her that this house might mean something to him and Tali, too.

Why hadn't he said something?

"How do we get in? Is someone in there?" Mirai asked from the back of the group.

"What do you think, Tali? Will she let us in?" Noa asked with a knowing smile.

Tali simply returned the smile even wider. Amar winced.

Noa reached for the sparkling geode handle but, before she could touch it, the door swung open.

"Come in, come in. I've been waiting for you."

CHAPTER 37

NOA

Inside the Green Gem House, the rain-soaked Cavalry team melted into the woman's mismatched seating. She'd insisted they remove their shoes once they were inside—not to avoid muddying her rugs—but so they could warm their feet on her heated floor and lay their socks out to dry.

With warm feet, they settled. Feelings of familiarity and comfort washed over the room, despite only Noa and Tali recognizing the woman. And likely Amar, though he hadn't confessed, yet.

Noa watched Amar eye the woman as she sashayed around the room, her heavy skirts following. She couldn't tell if he only faintly recognized her, or if he knew exactly who she was.

The woman tended to each person by handing them a cup

of tea and placing her hands around theirs, to warm their fingers on the mug. She smiled deeply and, like a spell, their shoulders relaxed in her gaze.

Noa had witnessed one other person have this effect on people and wondered if he knew that is where he got it from. This woman's energy was stronger, though. Even snarky Vitus and talkative Alexis were quieted by her aura.

Noa was the only one who refused to sit. Instead, she paced the room to examine the oil paintings that hung in heavy golden frames on the walls. Steamy footprints evaporated behind her as she padded about.

"Is everyone settled?" the woman asked in a croaky but kind voice.

She didn't seem to notice the murmur of responses. She only had eyes for Noa.

Noa must be wrong then. Surely if Amar and Tali were her grandchildren, she'd be tending more carefully to them, not her.

Before Noa could answer, Tali pointed upward.

"Excuse me? Have you been too?"

The woman let out a hearty laugh and moved to Tali, now regarding her as if she were a special gem. "Oh dear, you've been. You know very well it's not up there." The crinkles around her eyes were wonderfully deep. She had smiled a lot in her lifetime. "But yes, child, in a way, that's where I live. That's where I met Noa. Thanks to her, I've always known the two of you would be just fine." The woman tapped Tali's chin and then shifted her focus to Amar. She stared at him, a grown man, with as much childish adoration as she did Tali.

Jash slammed his cup down and stood. "This is all very

cryptic. I apologize that I can't be as cool as everyone else, but what is going on? Who is this woman?"

She looked endearingly at him, as though she had anticipated his outburst before he'd done it. She turned to Noa and gestured, giving her the floor to speak.

"I'm going to sit," Noa said. To prepare to explain everything, she plopped onto the warm floor and put her hands beneath her crossed legs, pressing her palms to the heat.

Jash sat back on the couch too.

"Amar," Tali blurted before Noa could start, "you don't recognize Grandma Dia?"

"What?" Everyone said in unison.

"Your brother hasn't been here in a long time," Dia said. "Your mother stopped bringing him around when, well, when things got complicated."

"I remember," Amar said. His voice sounded typically sure and calm, but Noa could tell his lips were tighter than usual, and his eyes darted across Dia's features. "But I don't know how you do," he said to Tali. "Mom stopped taking us here when you were still very young. And, to be honest, I didn't know she was alive anymore."

Amar looked at his grandmother with something Noa hadn't seen in him before.

Contempt?

"Mom didn't stop taking me here," Tali said. "One of the last days I spent with her was tea at Grandmas."

Watching their complicated family history unfold to an audience felt invasive and wrong.

"Maybe you three should talk privately, as a family," Noa

suggested.

Amar stood. "No. That isn't necessary. We have more important things to focus on. And she isn't our family. We don't have any family."

Deep-seated resentment. That is what Noa recognized in Amar's expression.

"You don't have any family *in the Variety*," Dia corrected. "Not anymore, anyway."

She was either ignorant to or purposefully lightening the mood of the conversation. "I wanted to step in, dear, after your mother and father. But I couldn't, and thanks to Noa, I knew you two would be just fine, and that you'd find me, one day." She raised her hands in a shrug at her sides. "Today."

The room buzzed with hushed voices. Dia had decided she'd explained enough and fell silent again, fiddling with the tea pot on a golden tray table.

"I didn't know she was your grandmother," Noa said to Amar, apologetically. "But it makes sense, sort of. Tali can ascend, so young, so naturally. You said yourself that your Mom's family—" Noa stopped herself; that was something he had told her in confidence. She had no right to announce it to the room. "Look. I've been dreaming about and drawn to this house my whole life, and in my ascensions, I visited her. Dia." Something hollow in Noa filled, putting a name to her guide.

Mirai interjected with her own curiosity. "How are you living here and not part of the Variety?"

Dia twirled around in a way that was reminiscent of Tali's natural rhythm. "Hidden in plain sight. Not everyone is so lucky."

Mirai flinched under Dia's gaze.

"Shoot," Dia said. "I'm all out of tea, and I'll be needing a few more cups soon. Amar, would you mind?" She gestured to the golden tray table and walked into the kitchen.

Amar froze for a few heartbeats but rose, picked up the tray, and carried it into the kitchen.

A knock rapped at the door.

All eyes fell on Zahira, who sat closes to the door. She moved slowly to answer, opening it carefully, as if the Variety itself were going to be on the other side to hand them all permanent Unassignment slips—or worse.

Instead, a soggy Shen and Jo slipped inside as soon as there was a crack large enough.

"Hello everyone," Shen said, standing in front of Jo to stop either of them from traipsing their puddles too far into the home.

Zahira pushed Shen aside and pulled her arms around Jo's neck, burying her head in his shoulder. Jo, who had gotten fitter over the weeks on the Cavalry Skill Trip and even more so during his training as a Mariner, picked her up easily with one arm and held her to his body. They kissed, and everyone averted their eyes.

Dia returned from the kitchen, carrying an armful of towels. "Come in, babies. We must get you dry and warm quickly. You have a lot of work to do." She pointed them toward the bathroom.

"Wait, where is Tempsen?" Noa asked.

Shen and Jo shook their heads.

"He's not coming," Shen replied.

"What do you mean he's not coming? He's the one that prompted all of this." Noa's heat rose. She had never felt her anger in her feet before, but there it was—head to toe.

"Library is under too much surveillance," Jo said. "He said he'd do what he could but it's too risky to link our feeds to his. We thought it would be best if he were left out."

Noa looked around and, since no one else seemed as surprised as she was, she tried to let it go. She told herself there would be a lot of hiccups ahead, and she had to be prepared. Having one less person was not that big of a deal—even if that person was Tempsen.

When everyone was warm, dry, and full of tea and cookies, they piled on top of each other in the living room to discuss their plans for early the next morning. It should have been stressful and intense to sit in that room, but it reminded Noa of when her family would sit together to watch programs or play games together. Jo and Amar studied the map of HeadQuarters, and Jash and Vitus questioned each tiny morsel of the plan. Mirai and Zahira peppered questions about HQ Assignment routing while Sami and Alexis interrupted with side conversations that distracted everyone, especially Tali.

They could do this.

Jo stood at the front of the room, flanked by Amar and Shen, projecting his auto. They walked through the map multiple times, showing everyone the two locations where the Variety might be. They agreed to split into two teams (just as they had at the Library) with a few lookouts for backup.

It was agreed that Dia, Tali, Shen, and Jash would stay

back at the Green Gem House. Dia and Tali to be kept safe, Shen to be the control room, and Jash to act as protection. Although, Noa figured, Amar and Shen had assigned Jash his role based on his inability to fully commit to the plan rather than on his ability to protect.

When they finished running through the plan a final time, Dia arranged for everyone to sleep throughout her home. A few on the couches in one room, a few on the couches in another. Sami and Noa were bunked together on a deep loveseat with a thick quilt. They slept head to foot as they had when they were children sharing a bed for a sleepover. They tugged at the quilt, making sure the distribution was exactly equal, and switched three times before deciding Noa should sleep on the inside with her feet tucked under the cushion while Sami was on the outside with a leg hung over. They whispered to each other for an hour before finally exchanging mumbled "goodnights" as they fell asleep.

Dia woke everyone bright and early, calling them to the living room. To her surprise, Noa's Assignment teacher, Iyan, stood, holding a pile of laundry.

Shen addressed everyone's unspoken question. "Tempsen has connections at the learning Assignment center. Iyan brought us HQ uniforms to help us blend in today."

Noa took a stack of clothing from her previous Instructor. "I appreciate what you're doing, but why?" She couldn't help but grow suspicious of the help from invisible Tempsen.

"I remember you, Noa, and you, too, Vitus," Iyan said.

"Then surely you're not doing this for us," Noa continued. V had not been a pleasant Assignment trainee, and Noa was still a practicing Invisible at that time. She hadn't done anything spectacular to warrant Iyan's commitment to her as a pupil.

"My brother. He was like you, I guess." Iyan's tight, red curls fell to one side when she tilted her head in recollection. "He was assigned as Painter for a while. He'd adventure to the most beautiful places and landscapes of the world, and it brought him more joy than anything he'd ever done. One day, he wrote to me about experiencing something heavenly, but in a literal sense. He'd been on a boat in the middle of the Great Lake and was painting the shoreline when, all of a sudden, his chest filled with a white heat." Iyan's face softened dreamily as she recited her brother's experience: how he floated below his boat and above the clouds at the same time. "He was changed by it. The next day, he was reassigned but he never showed up for his ceremony. I never heard from him again."

Shen caringly rubbed Iyan's back, though, their movements were jilted and awkward.

Dia held her palm to her heart. "Le Grand Lac?"

Iyan's head rose. "Yes, that's where he was for his last painting. The last place I heard from him."

Dia pointed to an oil painting on the wall. It was the one Noa had fixated on in her ascension here. "That is where my husband was, too." Dia gazed at the painting with lovelorn eyes, fingers tracing the frame. "Oh, Charl," she muttered.

"I'm sorry that I can't stay," Iyan said, recomposing herself. "I need to get back. But thank you for what you're doing. Thank you." She bowed and left quickly, shutting the heavy gem door behind her as easily as if it were made of any other material.

As she dressed in her HQ robes, Noa busied her mind thinking about how many others there might be. Tempsen had said thousands, but had he just meant recently? What about past generations? How long had humans been ascending for? Had they always been hidden because of it?

The thought dizzied her, and she had to grasp a nearby ottoman for support. She needed to reset. She sat on the ottoman and crossed her legs beneath her. She breathed slowly, closed her eyes, and released herself into the calm. She stayed that way until she lost count of her breath cycles.

"Um, Noa?" Sami called from the other room, "You need to come here!"

An unfamiliar voice called out, "Oh!"

The door swung open. Noa scrambled to her feet and rushed into the other room, wondering if the entire mission was over before it had even started. But when she peeked her head through the window, what she saw made her laugh.

Trax. Standing on the lawn, grazing.

"How did your horse get here?" Sami asked.

Noa scratched the top of her head. "I might have accidentally called him."

She stifled her laughter greeting Trax on the street corner. In the quiet, early morning of City Centre, a giant horse grazed in front of a Gemstone house. This was, in no way, covert.

Noa led Trax through a gate to the backyard, which (thankfully) had a fence tall enough to hide even Trax's height.

Noa opened the backdoor and called inside to Tali, who came running.

"Do you think you could take care of him for me today?"

"Noa," Tali said, drawing out the last syllable like Sami always did. "I'm not a child. You don't need to keep me busy. I could go with you!"

Noa shook her head. "That got me in trouble last time. Remember?"

"Fine." Tali stomped down the few steps into the backyard, which sat just slightly lower than street level. "It was worth a shot. I'll take care of Trax, but I'm also helping Shen in the control room."

"Sure." Noa smiled.

Returning to the living room, Noa found everyone dressed in their HQ whites and standing around Shen's screen.

"What are we looking at?" she asked.

"We've reviewed the plan for the umteenth time," Alexis said.

"And?" Noa inquired.

"And we're settled," Amar said. "Shen is the control center here. Alexis and I will be opposite-end lookouts; we're both going in alone so that we are less noticeable and more agile to help if needed." He pointed to two midpoints on the HQ map. "We'll have two teams attempt to access the Variety, based on where we think it might be located. Zahira, Mirai, and V will take the east basement. You, Sami, and Jo take the west. Once you're in, you try to find the Variety and connect with Shen, Jo, Alexis, or me. We'll grab as much information as we can and get out of there intact. We'll meet back here for diagnostics and debriefing and ensure everyone is accounted for. Hopefully we'll have heard from Tempsen by then, and he can help us decode whatever we've been able to grab."

"Everyone knows their entrances?" Noa asked, checking around the room. She received all affirmative nods. "And routes?"

"Yup," Alexis said, vocalizing the room full of nodding heads.

"Good." Noa said. "What else are we waiting for?"

"I think we're all just waiting for someone to say go," Vitus said.

Noa dropped her hands to her sides, making a clapping sound. "Go."

CHAPTER 38

NOA

Noa, Jo, and Sami stood in the queue to scan into HeadQuarters. They'd already walked into the public area and were waiting to enter the Assignment-only level where Pastors, Writers, Philosophers, Scientists, and more came to their Assignments each day.

They stood in the white tiled, open-air foyer for exactly twenty-five minutes.

Twenty-five minutes ago, Zahira, Mirai, and V had entered through the north entrance.

Five minutes after that, Alexis had entered at the west entrance.

Five minutes after that, Amar had entered back at the north.

Finally, it was their turn.

Shen was talented. Each of their autos scanned into HQ without an issue.

Jo led Noa and Sami to the perimeter of the west courtyard. It was a busier part of the level and would allow them the ability to disguise themselves in a mid-sized crowd as they moved toward their target—the west basement.

They would only have one chance. The basement entrance was restricted and didn't lead anywhere else. If they got caught, there was no excuse.

Noa spotted Alexis in the middle of the courtyard. She walked with her hands behind her waist, seeming pensive and looking to the ground or to the sky every so often.

"It doesn't look like anyone is going near the entrance area," Noa said after a few minutes.

"It's Geoblocked," Jo said. "That's why everyone is taking such a wide path."

Noa imagined the invisible dome of protection the other, legitimate HQ Assignments knew about and avoided as they walked past.

"We need to break up," Sami said. "We can't be a group anymore. We're going to get spotted."

She was right. Eerily, no one in the HQ west courtyard crowd was paired, in conversation, or walking in a group. It was a sea of individuals in white robes not interacting with each other.

"We can't," Jo said. "We'll only have a second to get past the barrier, and we can only do it once."

"He's right, Sami. We don't have a choice."

"Let's go now then," Sami said, impatiently. "Before someone notices."

Jo waved his hand at his waist and caught Alexis's attention.

At his signal, Alexis dropped to the ground, as if she suddenly fainted. Even knowing it was fake, her performance was so convincing that, for a moment, Noa had wanted to rush to her friend's side.

But, as planned, everyone around them did the same—giving the three of them the opportunity they needed.

They strode for the basement door. On her auto, Noa signaled Shen and hoped he would work fast enough to dismantle the Geoblock and unlock the door.

With only a slight hesitation, the group crossed the invisible barrier and approached the door to the basement. Feedback buzzed in Noa's fingers, and she opened her auto. The projection was a scramble of decile code Noa barely recognized. The door responded to the projection, releasing its lock and opening.

They stepped onto a textured metal platform and the door shut behind them. There was a series of beeps before the floor lowered with all of them on it. As they descended deep underground, whatever natural light had made its way through the ground level entrance disappeared.

Sami reached for Noa and held her arm as they plummeted into pitch black.

When they reached the bottom, Noa tapped her auto and sent a notice to Shen. She nudged Sami and Jo as soon as she felt the feedback in her fingers.

"Shen says we can connect," she whispered.

They stepped off the platform, and the room illuminated in shallow, blue light. The platform rose back to the entrance and, when it stopped, the cavernous space became silent once more.

The three of them circled the room, eventually finding walls but no corridors.

Finding nothing, they commed Shen.

"There's nothing here," Jo said.

"Look for seams," Shen instructed.

Sami was the first to understand and ran her hands along the wall. Noa and Jo quickly followed her lead. Finally, Sami called out in a loud whisper.

"Here!"

"Here!" Noa said in unison from the opposite side of the room.

Jo stood between them and commed Shen.

"There are two doors. Do you have any idea which?"

"No. You'll have to split up. Let me know when you're ready."

Sami waved to Noa and Jo. Noa shook her head, insisting that Jo go with Sami.

"Jo, she can't go alone," Noa whispered.

Even in the dark, Noa caught the face Sami made. Or else she knew her sister well enough to imagine it. All the same, Jo followed Noa's orders.

When Shen unlocked the doors, Jo and Sami left through their door.

At the other end of the room, Noa pushed the door in front of her twice until it popped open, and she entered the dark hallway before her. She followed the walls and dragged her hand along them. Her auto let her see a foot in front of her face, but it would also give her away if anyone else approached, so she decided to move in the dark.

With the next step, her hand fell from the wall into an open space—a crossing corridor. Noa leaned to the other side of the hallway, and her hand fell again. Her only options were right or left. Without anything more than a gut feeling to go off of, she turned left.

For the next several minutes, she ran her fingers along the flat smooth wall. Without reference points or light, it was hard to tell if she was going anywhere. She focused on her feet carrying her forward and realized that it was silent. She couldn't even hear her own footfalls hit the floor or her heart pounding in her chest.

Then, she heard faint, muffled voices.

She tried to discern from which direction they were coming, hoping they might be emanating from the ground-level above, though that was very far away given how far the lift had dropped them. She finally determined they were coming from the direction she was headed.

Far in the distance, the hallway was lit with a soft glow. She made out two individuals ambling in her direction. She couldn't tell because they were so far away, but it seemed like, maybe, they were floating.

She needed to get out of their path.

She started in the other direction, picking up her pace until she was running. She stopped when her hand, dragging along the wall the whole time, fell. She was back where she'd turned in from the entrance.

For a moment, she thought about going back. She could find Sami and Jo and leave HQ. They could go back to the ground level and get out before they were found—before anyone got in trouble.

But that would also be before they solved anything.

She couldn't give up yet.

She couldn't face her friends and Dia back at the Green Gem House having accomplished nothing. She couldn't return to the Cavalry and live the life she had originally intended. One with no clarity, no answers. She wouldn't go back having done nothing about all that she knew or without trying to understand all that she didn't.

If I wasn't meant to do something brave, then why do I have all this courage?

Britt's words echoed in her mind as Noa's feet carried her straight—away from the figures in the light—and into the darkness. Her trailing hands found more intercepting halls, and her instincts reached down each of them. She didn't care about getting lost anymore or going too far. She needed to be thorough, find everything that was hiding in the dark.

She pressed on, giving into the labyrinth nature of the basement—far gone from finding her way back to the entrance and venturing down every hallway she found hoping it would lead her to what she was looking for.

She had no idea what she was looking for.

It occurred to her that the design of the basement must be intentional. That one hall was plain and without branches while the other was intricate, confusing, and broke apart like a fractal.

Why?

Her thoughts were thrown from her head as she smacked into someone and fell to the floor.

"Ouch." She scrambled backward, not able to see the

stranger in the dark.

"Noa?"

It was Jo's voice. He opened his auto, and the light illuminated her face. It was blinding.

"Yes, it's me. Put that away! My eyes were just starting to adjust, and we don't need people seeing us—there are people down here, you know! I almost crossed paths with two of them."

Jo closed his auto and helped her up from the ground.

"Noa…" It was then she caught the disappointed timbre of his voice.

"Jo, where's Sami?"

CHAPTER 39

NOA

"They took her," Jo said.

"Who took her?"

"I don't know. Something weird is going on down here. We have to go."

"No way!" Noa lowered her voice as it reverberated down the hall. "We have to get my sister. Call Shen."

"I've tried but I can't get a response. Noa, we have to get out of here."

"I said no. You are going to tell me what's going on. Who took Sami? We have to go talk to them. Is she in danger?"

"I don't know! They're like these weird, creepy, slow figures. They were off in the distance, and Sami and I split up down a hallway, but the figures sped up out of nowhere and turned down Sami's hall. They were illuminated and I saw them—"

"Saw them what?"

"They knocked her out with something. They didn't touch her, but they aimed something at her, and she collapsed."

Noa spoke through a clenched jaw. "We have to find her."

How could she *let this happen? How could* he *let this happen? He was supposed to be watching her.*

"We have to leave!" Jo insisted. "If we leave, we can get help. Someone can help us sort this out. It's probably a security protocol for intruders. I'm sure they won't hurt her. They'll probably just detain her and call your family."

Noa hoped Jo could feel her piercing stare through the dark. Knocking intruders out cold didn't seem like standard security protocol. But then again, they had no idea who they were up against.

"I'm going to find her," Noa said and took off down the hall Jo had come from. She followed her internal compass at every turn as it guided her into the heart of the basement chamber.

Finally, a light glowed in the distance, and she charged.

"Hello! Please help! Someone took my sister. I just need to explain. It's just a misunder—"

In front of the glowing light, Noa fell silent.

She did not find two shadowy, creepy figures as she'd anticipated, nor did she find her sister. Instead, there was a cylinder of clouds in the middle of a round room, glowing in blues, purples, and deep greens. The fog spiraled and steamed. The cylinder was filled with suspended stars. Synapses fired like lightning in the sample-size universe.

A hand pressed on Noa's shoulders, and she jumped. It

was Jo, out of breath from following her. She swiped his hand from her and looked back at the galaxy in front of them.

"We found it," she said.

Jo was frozen, mouth agape in the glow of their discovery.

"What do we do?" Noa asked and answered herself. "Plug in!"

Jo was still, hesitating at her command.

"Jo, now! We don't have time to marvel!"

Her words snapped him out of his reverence. Jo opened his auto, reading and clicking through tunnels faster than Noa had ever seen. After a few seconds of ferocious programming, Noa couldn't stand the wait.

"What is taking so long?"

"It's graphene vapor."

She bugged her eyes at him, waiting for the explanation.

"Graphene is a liquid metal with intelligence coded into its electrons. This is graphene *vapor*. I've never seen it. I've never even heard of it. There's no way for me to hack it or break into it. It's self-sufficient; self-healing."

The Variety was not an algorithm running through a server, or a code that could be pulled and manipulated by anyone who spoke the language. They had been taught in lessons: *The Variety is unimpeachable.* Noa had heard it a thousand times but only now understood it was unimpeachable not because of its morality, but due to a design that was never discussed, never portrayed, never explained.

Noa circled the galaxy tower and stuck out her hand. She felt the pressure of a Geoblock and, as she neared it, the storm inside lit up near her hand. It gave feedback to her touch. It felt alive.

She stepped back and thought aloud. "We know that someone is corrupting it. Somehow."

"They can't. There is no way to corrupt something like this."

"You don't know that. *Someone* could, if they knew about this. How else do you explain what is going on? If there is no way for anyone to hack into the Variety, how do you explain all the ascendant people getting reassigned? How do we explain all the people being silenced? How do you explain—"

"Shh," Jo hushed. He approached Noa and the storm. His face lit up with discovery and then fell with dramatic sadness.

"What?"

"They can't edit it," he said.

"But I'm saying, what if they can," she tried to continue.

"No. You don't understand. Because it is self-healing, no one can edit it. It would be created to identify and remedy any anomalies."

"Then how?" Noa urged.

"The directives would have had to be built in. From the beginning."

Noa coughed and the room began to darken. Jo coughed, too, as black smoke enveloped him. Noa fell to her knees and pressed her arms against the Geoblock, sliding beneath the smoke. The Variety lit up to her touch and illuminated the room in a gorgeous, stormy reaction.

Two masked figures watched as Jo and Noa lost consciousness.

TALI

"I'm bored!" Tali said, swinging her boot through the top of the grass blades.

"It's only been a few hours," Jash said. "And Shen needs space to work."

"I could help, you know. Doesn't anyone remember I can ascend too? I mean, not whenever I want, but that has to count for something?" Tali swung her boot into a high kick and rounded her body back to square herself with Jash.

"It does count for something. It's very important, and that's why you're here—so that I can keep you safe."

Tali hated when people used their stupid-child voice to talk to her.

Jash seemed to take note of her disdain and changed his tone. "Look, neither of us have the technical skills to be of any use to Shen in there. And both of us got the boot from the ground team. Me, because I had a moment of skepticism questioning everything I've ever believed, and you, because you're young, short, and would stick out. It's not fair to either of us, but life's not fair."

"I'm not that short. And people say that all the time. *Life's not fair.* But it's not true." Tali bent over and picked a stick out of the grass. "Life is fair or, at least, it should be. And when it's not, we should change it!"

"Tali, 'Life's not fair' is not just a cliché people repeat as a cop-out from doing the hard work to make things fair.

It's a cliché people say because there are too many times that making things fair is out of our hands. There is no such thing as natural equity in life. We have to make our own and, sometimes, that means that we try harder than others and we still get less. Sometimes we don't try and get more than we ever deserve. Sometimes, we have every reason to be happy and we're still not. Sometimes, it means the people you care about don't care about you back, and—"

"And sometimes your parents disappear for no reason," Tali said, one-upping him. "But then you have an awesome older brother, and you get to ride horses and experience nirvana." She stopped fidgeting with her stick. "Jash, life is fair."

"Fine. Life is fair."

"But this is not," Tali repeated.

"No."

"Well, what are we going to do about it?"

Jash got up from his step, walked inside, and left her alone in the yard to pick up sticks and keep Trax company.

Tali knew Jash didn't have an answer. The yard was small, but Trax didn't seem lonely, so Tali stepped inside the kitchen.

Something was off about the air inside the house.

"Team One is coming out, but Team Two is still offline. I've lost Amar, and I'm trying to get him back but can't find him."

Tali and Jash stood still, watching Shen navigate the complex comm system.

Grandma Dia spoke first. "Jash, could you please go upstairs and grab the rain ponchos and coats? Tali, run and get your bag too."

"In a minute," Jash said, brushing her off and examining Shen's display.

"You better grab them now. We won't have much time," Grandma Dia said in a firm voice. It reminded Tali of when Amar 'suggested' something that was actually more of a direct order. "And I've left the safety pack by the back door."

Tali turned her head and saw the soft blue bag with a black handle propped by the back steps.

Grandma Dia turned to her. "Tali, dear. The back corner of the fence is weak. It should fall right down, okay?"

Tali looked out the kitchen window behind her at the fence and then back, not quite understanding.

Grandma Dia smiled, softly. "You are brave. Don't let them underestimate you."

Scared, Tali hugged her grandmother. Something felt different, colder.

"Your bag, Tali?"

Tali scurried upstairs and found Jash in the room where her, Mirai, and Amar stayed. Jash was gathering various belongings. Tali grabbed her pack.

A sudden crash sounded from the front of the house.

"Shen said Team One was on their way back," Jash reassured Tali. "They must be in a hurry."

They both knew it wasn't Team One slamming through the front door.

Creeping into the hallway, loaded with bags, they peered out the window to the back of the house. Trax grazed in the middle of the yard, but there was no other commotion out there.

Jash led them to the front of the staircase. From there, Tali had a clear sight line to the front room but not to the living room where Shen and Grandma Dia had been.

Then, Tali saw the presence she had felt.

A shadowy figure inched across the room below. At first, she thought it was a person, but they were moving so slowly. The figure removed its hood and revealed a decrepit, aged face, drained of color. The sight shocked her, and she clasped a hand to her mouth to keep from gasping. The motion caused her bag to fall from her shoulder, crashing into her body and making a noise loud enough to draw the figure's attention.

"Let's go," Jash said, yanking Tali's arm and barreling them down the stairs without hesitation.

The figure raised its arm and held a device in its ailing hand, aiming for Jash.

Jash quickly turned through the two rooms, with Tali flailing behind him. They jostled into the kitchen, and he pushed her in front of him.

As they rounded the kitchen's corner, they both gasped.

Grandma Dia and Shen's bodies lay listlessly on the floor.

In her shock to back away, Tali tripped over something—Jash's foot or the kitchen rug—and fell to the floor. She landed in front of the safety pack Grandma Dia had left and snatched it. She looked back at Jash.

"Let's go," she cried.

Jash was on his knees, his palms pushing into his temples, face red and jaw-clenched, grimacing.

Tali peeled bags off him as he crumpled further to the ground.

The figure crept toward him, the gun still pointed and, apparently, firing something invisible into him.

"Tali, get Trax!" Jash slurred. "Tali!"

She scrambled through the kitchen and outside. She whistled, calling Trax over, and he responded immediately, standing just off the back steps. Tali tucked herself against the house outside of the door and scrambled through the bags she had wrapped around her neck.

In her shaky hands, she found a multipurpose tool in the safety pack. She opened it to the sharp knife point and held it between her thumb and index finger, the blade resting along the line of her palm and into her wrist.

Swiftly, she turned, opened the door, and chucked the blade spiraling through the air, knocking into the hand of the figure, disarming it.

"Jash!"

It took him a second to shake off his pain, but he wasn't completely lost to it. He scrambled up from the floor and ran through the kitchen. He swiped the bags from Tali, hoisted her onto Trax, and jumped on behind her.

Tali pointed to the back corner. "There!"

They held on tight as Trax took off. He could only fit a few strides in the yard, but it was enough. Trax blasted through the weak fence.

Jash leaned over Tali to protect her as shards of wood splintered around them.

They landed on a busy pedestrian walkway. Inside the cozy home and surrounded by tall-fencing, Tali had forgotten they were in the middle of City Centre. Onlookers up and down the block stared at them, frozen and startled by the horse who had just broken through a fence.

"Keep going!" Jash said

Tali directed Trax accordingly. "Where?"

"Stables!"

NOA

Noa sat in darkness. She and Jo had passed out from the smoke, but she had come to when her head slammed onto the floor. She'd been dumped from a cart into the cell where she now sat. Noa had seen the two ghastly figures walk away after locking the cell chambers. She'd yelled to them but, when she did so, one of them pointed something at her that caused her to fall to the floor in agonizing pain.

After a while, the pain subsided and her eyes adjusted enough that she could make out some of her surroundings. She was in a hallway with multiple restraining cells. Her cell was completely empty except for a bowl of water.

When the figures returned a short while later, the hallway illuminated, blinding her. She forced herself to open one eye just a crack and saw they were carting in an unconscious Jo. She shut her eyes again and listened as they dropped him into a cell of his own.

After the figures left, she reopened her eyes to darkness and called out.

"Jo?" She kept trying but minutes passed without a reply.

"Ugh," a voice muttered from a different cell.

"Sami?" Noa's voice cracked and she scrambled to the door of her cell. "Sami?" She could have sworn that was her sister's grumpy wake-up groan.

"Uggghhh." It was definitely Sami.

"Are you okay? Are you hurt?"

"My head hurts," Sami said. "I think I'm okay. Where are we?"

The door opened again, and the lights shone.

Noa shaded her eyes as she peered out her cell. The two figures sulked into the cell block hall with another floating cart bobbing behind them.

"Amar!" Noa yelled, but he didn't move. He was unconscious too.

"Shh," one of the figures hissed.

Noa caught a glimpse of its dirty, wretched, yellow mouth. She continued calling Amar's name and Sami caught on. If they were all locked up, they wouldn't be able to get out.

"Amar! Amar!" they yelled until Amar's eyes fluttered.

The figures shuffled away from the cart and toward the cells, aiming their weapons. In near unison, Noa and Sami dropped to the floor and screamed in pain. Tears leaked from Noa's eyes, and her nose dripped with blood as she clutched her skull.

When Noa regained consciousness, the pain had subdued. She lay on the cool concrete floor, hungover from the intensity. Remembering Amar and Sami, she tried to lift herself from the floor but couldn't.

She shut her eyes again.

TALI

Tali and Jash rode to the City Field stables at full speed, barely letting Trax slow as they dismounted.

"Sai!" Jash called.

Tali saw his familiar face poke up from a nearby stall.

"Yeah?" Sai called back in his typically helpful tone.

"No," Jash said. "We have to go! Right now!"

"The horses are ready. Where is everyone else?"

"There is no everyone, just us. The three of us need to get out of here and get word back to Main Ranch. We need backup. This is way bigger than we can handle on our own."

"That doesn't make sense. It will take forever to ride there and back. I'll just comm Decker."

Sai began to open his auto, and Jash hit his hand away.

"No! And we have to take our autos out. They must be tracking everything, even the comms we coded. They traced us back to the Green Gem House."

Sai balked. "And it's just you two?"

"The others who went into HQ," Jash explained, "We haven't heard from. Hopefully they're okay. But Shen and Dia were at the house with us—they didn't make it."

Tali whimpered.

Sai calmly took everything in.

"I can try to explain more once we get out of town," Jash rushed. "But, for now, we have to get moving. Each on our own horse."

"What about Amar? And Noa? And Mirai?" Tali asked.

"They'll be fine," Jash insisted. "They can handle themselves for now. We'll leave their horses. But Amar will kill me if I don't take care of you. So, we have to go right now, okay?"

Sai didn't let Tali answer. "Let's go then. Knife's here." Sai pulled a sharpened bowie knife from a holster at his hip.

"Um, that's a big knife." Tali said.

Jash rummaged through the med pack, pulling out a pair of tweezers and a bandage. He knelt in front of the mounting block in the stall, laying his arm across it.

"It's okay. Look—I'll go first." Jash said. He took the knife from Sai and, with only a faint hesitation, cut a vertical slash into his left pointer finger.

Tali grimaced, but Jash's face remained impassive. Maybe it didn't hurt as bad as it looked.

Blood gushed from the wound, and he reached the tweezers into his finger, feeling around for the auto. It was awkward and almost comical how long he dug around. Finally, the tweezers came out and a network of threads slithered from the tip of his finger.

Jash laid out the long, filamented device on the block and wrapped his finger in gauze. He handed the knife to Sai, who performed the same cut and removal on himself.

"Tali?" Jash prompted. He was offering her the block, but was holding the knife making it clear he didn't expect her to be her own surgeon.

She stuck her forearm on the block, splaying her fingers and steadying her hand.

"Deep breaths, okay? One, two." Jash cut her on three, and she gave only a small flinch, at first. Unfortunately, the tip of her finger was scarred from initial implantation, which made the cut more difficult. Jash apologized as he took a second swipe.

Sai handed him the tweezers, and Jash reached into her pointer finger. She could feel the metallic tip grind on her finger bone and winced when he finally found the auto bead. He pulled on the material. The tugging sensation carried through her pointer finger, across her palm, up into her thumb, and down past her wrist into her forearm.

When autos were initially installed, they were injected as small beads in the tip of the pointer finger. The organic filaments grew inside of the body as the device got smarter, and the programs updated.

"One more breath," Jash said.

As Tali exhaled, he drew the auto out of her hand and laid it beside the other two. Hers was only about half the size of Jash's and even smaller in comparison to Sai's.

Sai wrapped her finger, and Jash shook out his hands.

"What should we do with them?" Sai asked. The bloody autos sat on a step of the mounting block.

"Leave them," Jash said. "Hopefully the others will see them when they come for their horses and know we took them out ourselves. We're on our own now."

"Are you sure we can't wait for the others?" Sai asked.

"If we wait, it will be too late."

CHAPTER 40

NOA

"Wake," a figure droned.

Noa blinked her eyes open to the horrifying sight of a pale, sagged, and forgotten face. One of the figures had removed their hood as they pulled Sami from her cell and bound her to a chair in the hall.

"Sami!" Noa choked. "It's going to be okay."

"Hush," said the second figure. They took off their hood revealing a second hollowed face. This person, if that's what it was, was beyond anything Noa had ever seen—the ugliest parts of death.

One creature faced Noa, the other faced Amar, who was in the cell next to her.

"Why are you here?" the figures asked.

When no one answered, the figures turned on Sami.

"Why?" they repeated, raising their guns.

Noa hadn't heard anything from the other cells, besides Sami's initial waking. She was likely the only one who was conscious. There was no one to help.

"Why?" They insisted.

Noa remembered the pain from before and flinched as they pulled the trigger on her younger sister.

Sami clenched her jaw and growled in pain as spit and foam leaked from her mouth. Her head fell forward, and her eyes blinked, barely reopening each time.

Noa bit the inside of her cheeks. Watching, waiting, frozen.

When her sister's eyes closed and didn't reopen, she panicked. "Stop! Stop it!"

Noa's fists were white, and her nails dug into her palms as her sister dropped in and out of consciousness.

She answered their questions—she screamed the answers. When she hesitated or held back, the figures pointed their guns at Sami again and put her through another round. Noa confessed everything about her ascension. She let go of every story beat she had perfected and, in panic, rambled off details in any order she could remember. When that didn't stop them, she went on about the Library, trying to describe search pipes she had never fully understood. She told them that they'd found a daily report that sounded like her ascension experience. And that they now knew there were others. Many others. Maybe thousands.

It wasn't enough.

She spilled that their plan was to break into HeadQuarters and investigate the Variety. That they hadn't known how to find it, or what they would do, but that they intended to uncover the corruption, wherever it lived in the system.

She gave them everything she could, trying to convince them there was nothing left. And to leave Sami alone.

When the figures were satisfied Noa had nothing left, they dumped Sami back in her cell and left.

In the dark, lonely, silence, Noa held her own breath, listening for signs of her sisters. When she heard Sami's breathing, she started crying.

Out of fear. Out of anger. Out of relief.

Sami was alive.

And Noa had managed to keep three secrets. *Tali. The Green Gem House. And Britt and Eli.*

She wouldn't let anyone else get hurt.

Another cell stirred.

"Amar?" she asked, stifling her sobs.

"They're Elders," Amar said. Noa could hear the lag in his speech and the dryness of his mouth. He must have been stunned, too. "A sick version of Elders who have been left to rot without the renewal of aging treatments."

For generations, Elders were regarded as pillars of health, wealth, and wisdom. Once designated, an Elder served society as a government leader, a brilliant exploratory mind, and an evolved soul. Elder was the highest status, and earned those dignified individuals privileged rights to aging clinics and the medicines that accompanied prolonged life.

Even in times of historically significant societal equity, Elders were the elite class.

Until the Enlightenment.

With a new understanding of human evolution and the

adoption of the Variety, Elders retained minimal meaningful status. They fell into the shadows of society, dying off almost all at once.

But Amar had to be right. That was the only logical answer for who these monsters could be.

"Are you okay?" Noa asked Amar, before diving in. She confirmed he was, and re-confirmed she could still hear regular and heavy breaths from Sami's cell, before giving in to conversation with him.

"One more thing," she insisted. "Can you hear anything from across from you? I think that's Jo."

"Breathing, but nothing else," Amar said. Satisfied, Noa let him finally explain what had happened on his side of the mission.

Zahira, Mirai, and V had made it to the level they'd needed in the tower but had almost gotten caught. Fortunately, the two HQ Assignments who had caught them were people Amar knew from a while back, when he was also assigned there. He intercepted them, pretending to have been recently Reassigned. He thought he had fooled them until they ended up at the Pastor's Office, all too familiar from his last experience at HQ.

"One thing was new though," he said. He had never believed there was only one Pastor—until today. In the past, it seemed obvious that the Pastor was just a figurehead and unified voice for a system that took several people and intelligences to run.

But today, it seemed that a tall woman with white-blonde hair, who sat behind the Pastor's desk, was the intelligent one running the show.

She was young—or, at least, younger than Amar had ever imagined—his parent's age. She introduced herself and asked if he still had questions about his parents. Caught off guard, and before he could answer, he'd been struck by the weapons' rays and then dumped down here.

He had received a comm just before and was pretty sure Zahira, Mirai, and V had gotten out. They hadn't found anything, but they were safe.

"Would you two shut up?" Jo hissed from his cell. Noa hadn't heard him stir before he scolded them. She shot a confused look into the dark, in his direction.

"They're probably listening to every word," he said.

"Yes, probably. But what else are we supposed to do?" Noa asked. "Sit here and wait for them to execute another round of torture?"

She heard him sigh and plop to the ground.

They sat in their cells, in the pitch black, debating what to do and sharing accounts of everything that had happened. Jo and Noa tried to tell Amar about the Variety with coded language, but it was impossible. And it felt ridiculous. They were locked in cells, Noa had confessed most of everything— they had little left to hide.

Tali. The Green Gem House. Britt and Eli.

At some point over the next few hours, Noa fell asleep and woke up startled when the lights came back on.

An incredibly tall, livelier figure stood beyond her cell's barrier.

"Tempsen?" Her voice cracked, her throat dry from sleep.

He stood in his courtly Library uniform, looking like the epitome of health next to the decrepit Elders.

"Hello, Noa," he said to her. "The youngest girl will be best," he said to the Elders.

One of them opened Sami's cell door. She lay unconscious on the floor, still out from the earlier trauma. Noa's face contorted as the Elders struggled to prop up her sister onto the same chair. Their rice paper hands grabbing at her sister's healthy skin was repugnant. Sami slumped as she was strapped into the chair.

"Tempsen? Tempsen! What are you doing?"

He ignored Noa's cries and carried on with Sami, cracking something in front of her face.

Sami shot awake.

"See, I told you they knew me," Tempsen said to the Elder. The figure remained expressionless.

"Noa, Jo, Amar. You have to tell the Elders everything. If you do, we will only hurt Sami a little. If you leave anything out, we will have to—well, you know."

"You can't do this!" Jo shouted.

The second Elder crept toward Jo's cell, and Jo backed into the corner.

Coward, Noa thought.

"Noa, my colleagues tell me you confessed to doubting the Variety and coming here to ruin it because you think it is corrupt. But you left out the part about how you think you are a God, right?"

Noa was confused, is that what Tempsen had taken from everything she'd shared? That she was disconnected from reality and thought of herself as some divine being? She looked over to Jo, but he was still cowering in his cell. She tried to see Amar but couldn't.

"I told them about the ascensions," Noa said through gritted teeth.

"Right, right, but not about how you think you are the very first, how you think you can help others learn to ascend, if they only follow you. How you have already taught one little girl to rise with you?"

"Leave her out of it!" Amar yelled.

"Nothing to say then Noa?" Tempsen continued. "You don't want to tell them about how you tricked your stupid little sister and persuaded these idiots?"

The accusation came out of Tempsen as phony and forced. She cocked her head at him, and he straightened his jacket.

Was he lying? Noa thought she might know what he was up to.

"You don't know anything about being a God. They are the Gods," he said pointing to the Elders. "They are the ones who ascend, they are the ones who—"

"That's enough," the Elder said, their voice sounding as if it came from sand. A masculine voice, though. He pointed a ghostly finger to Noa and raised his other hand with the gun to Sami.

"Tell me," he said, "about the girl."

Noa was silent.

He pulled the trigger until Sami convulsed, and Noa let out a howl.

"Stop! Stop! Fine! I'll tell you everything!"

Sami stopped shaking, but her head hung motionless. Again. Again, Noa waited. She stared at her sister and waited for her chest to rise and fall with breath.

"Tell me, now!" the Elder hissed.

"Wait!" Noa hushed. He outstretched the weapon again. "Wait!"

Finally, Sami's chest rose.

"Okay, I'll tell you."

Noa told them about her experience with Tali, although she offered considerably less detail than she normally gave the story and left out that Tali accompanied them on this journey. She had only two secrets now.

When she finished talking, she heard Amar crash into his cell walls.

One of the Elders handed their gun to Tempsen. Without hesitation, he aimed at Sami and held the trigger as she seized.

Noa's mouth hung agape, without any screams or cries left in her system. Her sister foamed at the mouth, and Amar continued pounding on the walls of his cell.

She knew nothing. Tempsen was not there to help them. He was there to use them.

"You're going to kill her!" Jo screamed.

Noa stared, readying herself to watch her sister's final breath.

The second Elder raised their hand, and Tempsen released the trigger. He untied Sami from the chair and carried her back into her cell. Without another word they were left in the dark.

Again.

Noa waited for the Elders and Tempsen to come back but they didn't. Amar and Jo had run out of schemes and ideas to break out, and none of them were plausible anyway. Defeated, Noa sank into the corner of her cell and thought through every option, every backup plan, every contact—coming up with nothing.

With no other choice, she prayed.

She tried to keep her thoughts clear but heard only her sister's cries and the thud Sami had made when Tempsen had dropped her limp body onto the cell's floor. She prayed for her sister's life.

She calmed her mind and tried to connect with Trax. Maybe he would be able to pop out of nowhere into her cell and kick the door down?

A laugh escaped from her mouth, and she let it roll out. Her body erupted with laughter, and her eyes filled with feverish tears. From the other cells, Amar and Jo asked if she was okay, but she didn't respond. She let the laughter end on its own and found her breath in its wake.

She was lighter after the fit. A clarity washed through her mind, and a buzz panged in her stomach. She held onto it. Every thought that passed through—about her sister, her parents, Amar, herself—she watched float by. If it got stuck, she blew it away. In the darkness, her breath glimmered, creating a wind that rushed into clouds and painted a skyline that darkened from daytime blue into nighttime pinks and violets.

In her mind, the space around her illuminated, and Tali

sat in front of her, in the grass where they'd landed after their first ascension.

Tali blinked at her. "Noa?"

Noa grabbed her hands; Tali's arm was bandaged. "Are you okay?"

"It's nothing, just don't try to comm me for a while." Tali smirked. "Are you okay?"

"I am, but Sami isn't. We need help."

"I'm with Jash and Sai. We're going for help. Big help." Tali whimpered. "Shen and Grandma Dia are dead."

Noa's face twitched as reality came into focus, but she didn't let it pull her out.

"Dia knew," Noa said, and Tali's mouth cinched, holding back a cry. "I'm glad you're safe."

"Amar?" Tali asked.

"He's fine. He's with me and Jo. What about the others?"

Tali shrugged and picked at her bandage.

"Don't go back to Main Ranch, okay?" Noa said.

"We have to get help," Tali said.

"I've already arranged it. Call Yori."

Tali held up her bandaged arm. "No comms, remember?"

"Call him the way I called you, okay? He'll be ready."

Tali agreed, her hands fidgeting, still restless.

"We're going to be okay," Noa said. "All of us."

"How do you know?"

Noa smiled and, when she blinked, she was back in her cell.

Noa rested on the concrete floor. She chased her sister's cries around in her mind until she was dizzy enough to fall asleep. She dreamed of the frozen wheatgrass she'd seen while meditating with Yori. It clinked and chimed against the other frozen blades in the wind. The sound became more vivid every time she re-woke and fell back asleep until it was all she could hear. The frosted chimes softened as a blanket of fresh snow fell from the sky.

The entire world hushed, and Noa heard it.

The Truth.

She heard it, faintly, and listened again for it to be repeated. But the blanket of silence was gone. The snow melted and dripped, morphing the silken landscape into rough mud and rocks. The snowflakes falling from the sky turned into heavy rain and hail, pelting her. Thunder roared and lightning struck.

She startled awake—and she knew.

"Noa?"

The lights blinded her, but the voice was familiar.

"Hello? Noa?"

"Lex?" Noa asked.

"Thank Gods! Okay, shut up. I need to focus!" Alexis ordered. "How do you open these cell doors? He didn't tell me! Is there another code? They're coming. I saw the light coming down the hallway. We have to run."

"They don't enter a code," Amar said. "When they pull Sami out, they just release the doors with their autos."

"My auto doesn't work down here," Alexis said, "but I bet his does—that's what he meant. Everyone be still!"

Alexis shouted in a whisper and hid in the corner near the door at the opposite end, closer to Amar and Jo's cell.

"Alexis?" Amar whispered.

"Shhh, Tempsen's instructions said to be still."

After an impossibly long time, or possibly just moments, the lights shut off.

"Alexis?" Amar said again. "Are you sure?"

"Amar. Shut. Up. And be ready to run."

"Sami can't run," Noa said.

"Amar will grab her," Alexis ordered.

The door at the opposite end finally shone a dim light. Then came an unfamiliar sound—all four cell doors unlatched.

"Now! Run!" Alexis yelled in her loudest whisper. "Follow me!"

Jo was on her heels as she barreled through the door. Behind them, Noa held the door open for Amar, who had Sami slung over his shoulder. As they ran through the door on the other end, Noa looked behind her and saw the two Elders and Tempsen racing toward her.

She wanted to slam the door in his face, but it was heavy and slow, as though braked by compressed air. Tempsen sprinted and made it through, clutching his forehead and tumbling to the floor at her feet as she finally managed to wrestle the door closed.

"I'm help—" Tempsen huffed.

She understood. He *had* been helping them. Undercover. He'd also almost killed her sister.

"We have to go now!" Alexis yelled, already far down the hall.

"I know!" he said, trying to pull himself to his feet.

They raced and caught up to Alexis at the end of the hall. They followed through a few more turns until they compressed into a tightly knit group, practically running on top of each other.

"Stop!" Noa turned to Tempsen, who chest-bumped her as she veered. "Where is it? You have to take me and Jo back to it. We can't leave without—"

"There is no way to destroy it, Noa," Jo said. "I can't do it."

She stepped further from the group and motioned for them to keep going.

"I can't follow you. I've got Sami!" Amar said.

"Go!" Alexis said, pointing Amar and Jo around the last turn toward the exit. "Straight down, you'll find the door to the platform room. We'll be right behind you. Don't wait for us." Alexis and Noa took off at a walk and paced up to a jog. "Know where we're going?"

"No," Noa said. "But I know what we're looking for this time."

"This way," Tempsen said, running up from behind to join them.

When they found the Variety again, it was no less breathtaking. Alexis, seeing it for the first time, gazed at it from a cautious distance across the room.

"Put your hand to it," Noa said, showing Alexis the small lightning storm that roared near her hand as she reached out.

Alexis stepped forward and did the same.

"So, what is the plan?" Tempsen asked.

"We have to destroy it."

"I know that," he said flatly. "But how? And we have to be quick. They're likely still chasing the others toward the door, but it won't be long before they send someone to check here."

They stared at the storm inside the cylinder, saddened by their need to destroy it.

"I have an idea," Alexis said. From her pockets she withdrew a fistful of bandages, ointments, and a medication pack. With her other hand she sorted through the small items.

Just as Alexis fingered it, Noa saw it. "Medical drops."

"I only have a few," Alexis said, jamming the rest into her pocket.

"Those only work on organic material, like living cells," Tempsen corrected.

"That looks pretty alive to me!" Alexis said.

"But the protective barrier..." Noa frowned, trying to come up with a solution.

"Okay, wait." Alexis fumbled through her pockets. "What about this?" She pulled out a bottle of liquid heat. "I swiped it from the kitchen the other day. Could that work on the barrier?"

Tempsen shrugged, not giving a definite answer.

"It's our only shot," Noa said.

"You want the medical drops or liquid heat?" Alexis offered both to Noa.

Noa grabbed the medical drops.

Alexis poured the liquid heat at the seam of the Geoblock, and they waited.

It fizzled and flickered—and then—nothing. Alexis huffed but Noa stepped forward. She put her hand to the boundary again but, this time, nothing stopped it. Her hand pushed through into the storm. A lightning bolt struck her finger.

"Damn!" She shook her hand. It hurt, but she didn't have a choice. There was no easy way to apply the drops to a gaseous cloud. "Give me the other drops. All of them."

Alexis fumbled to hand her the remaining four tubes of drops.

"How are you going to—" Tempsen stopped talking when Noa stepped into the storm.

Clouds swirled around her in a dense fog, making it hard to see. It was cold and humid, like nothing she'd felt before. Lightning bolts struck her all around. Some were light and playful, leaving only a tingle. Others were forceful and burned like a branding iron pressed deep into her flesh. She flinched as an intense bolt struck her shoulder, catching her robes on fire and leaving her skin smoking and smoldering.

She stayed standing.

Noa reached in her mouth and dragged her thumb nail across the inside of her cheek until she was drooling blood. She poured all four bottles of medicine drops into her mouth as fast as she could and counted the seconds.

She felt the low tingle of the drops sterilizing her mouth, then the numbness of the anesthesia. The next phase was her only chance. The moment she felt the heat of cauterization on her cheek, she spat all the liquid in her mouth up into the storm.

The storm flickered in response, and the stars lit on fire in the spray. It rumbled a loud roar and released a thunderous crack.

"Run!" Tempsen yelled as he and Alexis took off toward the exit.

The storm lit up in a fervorous response to the cauterization drops. The clouds trembled and changed from a dusty grey into a dark purple and rolled into an intimidating bright red.

Noa ran, but not fast enough.

As her foot left the storm's cylinder, it exploded—propelling her into the wall.

She woke moments later to Tempsen's body banging against hers as they ran. She was cradled in his arms and wailed at the rough scraping of his robes on her raw shoulder. Her head fell back.

Noa woke again, this time sitting on the ground, leaning against a cool, Sleekstone wall.

"She's awake!" Alexis's voice called out. "Here, drink this." She passed Noa some water, which she drank.

Someone knelt in front of her; up close she made out it was Mirai.

"Glad you're awake." She brushed hair out of Noa's face. "We need to get you and your sister somewhere now. Where do your parents live?"

Noa mumbled the address.

Mirai asked her something else, but she couldn't hear it. Everything got heavy again. And dark.

This time, Noa awoke in V's arms.

"Down." She squirmed.

"Shh," he snipped. "We're almost there"

"I can walk."

"Fine." V set her down on the ground.

Alexis came up from behind and held Noa steady as she found her footing.

"We've gotta go quick," Alexis said. "Why don't you hold onto me, and we'll walk together?"

Noa took her shoulder. In two steps, she regretted her decision. Pain coursed across her skin and made her feel faint. She recognized a street crossing the alley. They were only two blocks from her parents' house. She could make it.

CHAPTER 41

NOA

Noa woke slowly. She coaxed her heavy eyelids to open more with each labored blink. They didn't want to cooperate, likely from fear of letting too much light in and making her crushing headache all the worse. Even with the pain, disorientation, and limited sight, it was easy to discern where she was. The familiar Soleil Blanc Sleekstone walls (the closest her parents could get to mimicking the bright white color of HQ), the firmness of the couch (as if it were brand new, rather than the same age as her), the lingering smell of her father's cooking—she was in her parents' living room. As if to confirm it on cue, her mother's petite hand patted her forehead with a cool cloth.

It only took those few moments of consciousness for Noa's anxiety to catch up. An icy chill laced with dread descended from her forehead through her body. She sprung to standing, as if gravity would halt the sensation from spreading.

A blur of faces across the long, rectangular living room turned to her. Noa could guess who they were from context—Alexis, V, Mom, Dad, etc.,—but fuzzy vision prevented her from seeing everyone clearly.

She attempted to speak but what came out sounded more like the slurred mumblings of Philosophers after they drank The Tea of Understanding. The blurred faces were speaking to her now. She sort of understood: *sit down, rest, Tempsen explained everything.*

That last one bugged her.

Noa collapsed into the couch. Standing up was exhausting.

Her mother sat next to her, radiating a soft comfort that made Noa well with tears. When warm drops rolled down her cheeks, Chemi brushed them away with her thumb and pushed damp strands of hair from Noa's face. Then, she leaned closer and spoke so just the two of them could hear. "Tempsen explained everything, *petit soleil,*" Chemi said. Their heads were touching now and Noa closed her eyes. She couldn't remember the last time they'd sat this close. "You are okay. Everything will be alright. Just rest."

Noa was only temporarily comforted by her mother. Something about that Tempsen statement got under her skin. No, it was something about the alchemy of her blood. It made her itch whenever she was within the walls of her family home. Even in this weakened state, she could find something to protest.

Tempsen was not the chaperone of some misguided adventure. He was not in charge, and he did not get to explain things.

This was too important. She needed to speak for herself. Unfortunately, the effort expended to lift an arm off the couch and lean slightly forward in dissent was enough to cause another spell of unconsciousness.

When Noa finally managed to remain awake, she stayed sitting on the couch—indignant and deep in thought. Every once in a while, she alternated from annoyance to worry, just to switch it up, but for most of the day, she settled on discontent as her primary resting state.

With Noa up, Chemi's attention concentrated on Sami. Unconscious, Sami lay on the smaller sofa on the other side of the room. Her clothes had been changed, and her wounds tended to, but there was no denying she was in bad shape. And she was dripping in sweat. Her flushed cheeks reminded Noa of hot chilis. Sami absolutely loved them, even though they turned her face red for a full hour after she ate them. "Worth the burn," she'd say. The memory made Noa exhale a small laugh, which then made her condemn herself back to stoic discontent.

Noa decided to focus on Tempsen and scowled at him as he moved from room to room. Rather than browsing the family effects in the living room, he poked around their projection system. In the central room, which housed a few storage drawers, display cases, and their dining area, he sat in her chair. At first it made her angry, but then he leaned back balancing *her chair* on two legs and she decided she was furious.

Noa wanted to jump down his throat, kick him out of this house, and leave him to be attacked on the streets. She was certain that, in his explanation to her parents, he'd left out the part where Sami had been tortured into her current state at his hands.

She wanted to explain it all to her parents, but she couldn't. Whether she trusted Tempsen or not—she needed him.

Armel, Noa's father, removed Sami's auto. It was gruesome to watch, but Noa's arm now had the same scar. She didn't recall the pain of it, so Sami likely wouldn't either. Sami was the last of the group to have it removed except for their parents, who opted to keep theirs in. Her father pulled the chords from her sister's limp arm, and her mother applied the medical drops—*a normal family activity.*

Noa winced, turning to Amar. He sat beside her, a look of worry overtaking his handsome features. Her heart broke. As bad of a condition as her little sister was in, at least she knew Sami was safe, for now. Then, a tidal wave of guilt. Noa remembered how many times throughout the day he had checked on her. Asked how she was doing. Brought her water. Sat next to her. *Had she acknowledged him at all?*

Noa rubbed his back. He leaned into her touch and looked into her eyes.

"Hey," he said, his voice low.

"Hey," she said back. An intimate two-word conversation between them. It was all she needed. The magnetism of his warmth and calm melted her. She was back, she could breathe. She could be there for him now, too.

"Tali's okay," she said. "We connected when I was in the cell. She's with Sai and Jash. They'll keep her safe. They're going to get help for all of us."

His shoulders relaxed and exhaled a sigh, but his relief was momentary. "We can't wait that long," he said. He pulled away from her.

She folded her hand back into her own lap.

"I just need some time to figure out where we can go..." Noa's voice trailed as she caught Tempsen making another lap around the room. "Can you stop pacing? I can't concentrate!"

"Noie!" Armel scolded.

"We do need a plan," Alexis said.

Surprised, Noa tried to look unphased. Not because she disagreed with Alexis, but because she just realized there were even more people she had ignored all day.

"This is a mess, yeah, but we can fix it," Alexis continued. "We were meant to. Otherwise, how do you explain everything, and all of us coming together the way we did? Fate. We can handle this."

"I love your enthusiasm, babe," V said. He sat in one of the comfy U-shaped reading chairs at the front of the room. He ran his hands through his hair, which was long enough to tie back now. "But it wasn't fate that brought us together—it was the Variety."

Alexis threw up her arms and strode across the room to the matching chair opposite V. She plopped down with an oomph. "Well, there's no such a thing as the Variety anymore, is there?"

Chemi opened her auto and projected it on the wall, commanding the room's attention.

"The need for a plan just got more immediate," she said. An incoming message displayed—it was a universal comm from the Pastor.

The Pastor was hooded and spoke with a modulated voice, as usual. But now, Amar, Noa, and (possibly) Jo knew that it was not a man, but a tall woman with white hair.

"Earlier today, a few foolish Cavalry Assignments abandoned their positions and snuck into HeadQuarters," the broadcast started. "Despite our best efforts to detain them, they succeeded in destroying our beloved Variety system." She gave a mournful pause and then continued. "As you know, the purpose of the Variety is to ensure that each life is filled with soul-expanding experiences. It is—was—a refined system that worked for over two centuries. Our ancestors developed it to ensure each human life brought our kind closer to evolution into our true form: a soul species. But, as we know, there are some who are misguided or confused about the importance of the Variety. Those who are flippant toward the system, slow our collective evolution. The Unevolving have been misled by rumors spread over generations and have now caused great harm in their folly."

Almost everyone in the room muttered something sour under their breath.

"The Cavalry is a difficult Assignment," the Pastor

continued. "There is no doubt about that. These new recruits should have experienced great expansion during their time. However, their lack of trust in the system caused undue pressure and added difficulty to their journey, which led to their corruption." The Pastor's hood shook in disapproval. A hand landed over her heart.

Noa imagined the millions of households who were mimicking this motion. Bile rose in her throat.

"What we must focus on now is rehabilitation. Here at HQ, we will begin rebuilding immediately. For the time being, everyone will remain in their current Assignments. However, all assigned Engineers, Scientists, Librarians, Mathematicians, and Explorers will report to HQ first thing tomorrow to assist with the rebuilding of our system. All Service Members will report to HQ, as well, to aid in the recovery of these misguided individuals. Finally, we have also formed a Special Council to oversee the creation of the new Variety and the reintegration of UEs through the work of the Service."

A photo each of Amar, Alexis, Tempsen, and Jo appeared next to the Pastor.

"If you have or learn any information about the location of these individuals, submit a daily report at once. This is a dark time, but we know darkness balances the light. Wishing you all great expansion through this trial."

The display darkened and Chemi tapped her fingers closing the projection.

"Why—" Noa started but didn't finish her question.

She knew the answer.

Zahira, V, and Mirai along with Tali, Jash, and Sai had

gotten away unnoticed, unidentified. Dia and Shen were already gone.

But she and Sami—they were excluded from the roster for another reason.

HQ had no intention of reintegrating them.

They were simply meant to disappear. Never able to speak the truth about what happens in HQ basements.

"We have to go, now!" Noa scrambled across the room to wake her sister. "Sami, Sami we have to go!"

"Noa Lavoie, stop it!" Chemi said. "Your sister is not going anywhere." Chemi stepped between Noa and Sami, but quickly composed herself and softened her voice. "Sami is not going anywhere. But you do have to leave. And all of your friends. I don't want you to, but they will be here any moment, and you can't be around. We will protect her."

"Mom, you can't! Not from the Elders. You don't know what they're like. They'll hurt you."

"They won't, Noie," Armel said, putting his hand on Noa's shoulder. It was comforting until his hand was also nudging her away from Sami. "I won't let them. But your mother is right, you all have to go."

"Dad, how exactly are you going to protect yourself from them? Or Sami? They have weapons and all the technology in the world to find you. They're likely on their way already!"

"Let me help," Tempsen said.

Noa fumed. "You? What are you going to do? You're the reason why Sami can't come with us right now."

"I know. That's why I need to fix this," he said. "I've already hidden your family's home address in the directory system. It should buy us a few hours and, hopefully, by nightfall, Sami will be able to come with us. Plus, I have this." He pulled out one of the ray guns they'd used on Sami.

"Let him help," Jo said. *Another person she'd ignored all day.* Zahira and Mirai were leaning against the wall at the back of the room near Jo. *When did they*—? Noa needed to get her head on straight. And later someone would need to explain what happened after she got blown up and how all these people got here. She was glad they were here, and safe, but the confusion was frustrating. And the headache!

"I don't need to hear anything from you!" Noa snapped at Jo.

Amar stepped in and ushered Noa through the full length of the house, into the kitchen.

She stared daggers at the floor until she needed to lift her chin to hold back tears. He pulled her face to look at his, but she kept her eyes averted.

"We have to go," he said. "Your sister will be okay, I promise."

This time, she didn't believe his promise. It was the first of his promises that sounded shaky and insincere. She resented it completely.

"You're wrong." She pushed Amar away. "Plus, where are we even going to go?" She turned to storm back into the living room but ran into Vitus, who was coming through the swinging door. She tried to maneuver past him, but he grabbed her firmly by her arms, an unsettling move that stopped her in her tracks.

"Noa, stop," he said. "It's going to be fine."

Him, she believed.

"And you know exactly where we have to go."

It wasn't fair that V knew that secret.

Noa looked over her shoulder to Amar.

V followed her gaze, dropping Noa's arms and taking a step back off Amar's look.

"I can't do that to them," Noa said.

"We don't really have a choice," V said.

"You must be thrilled." Noa's lips curled in disgust as she held back a wave of tears. "This is what you wanted all along, isn't it?"

V's face contorted in rage, and his blue-grey eyes pinned her the way he once had in the tunnels underneath the Bowl. Noa thought back to that moment, him cornering her and holding her down. She wished she could do the same to him—to anyone—right now.

She turned from him and pushed past Amar to search through the freezer. She returned to the living room with an ice pack and knelt beside her sister. She replaced the pack under Sami's neck and gave a short kiss at her hairline.

Before pulling away she whispered, "I have to go. Don't give up."

CHAPTER 42

NOA

Noa, Amar, Jo, Zahira, Alexis, Mirai, and Vitus crept out of Noa's childhood home dressed in remnants of her family's clothes. Amar, Alexis, and Jo all had hoods up or hats pulled down covering their face. They needed to get to the western edge of town and couldn't take any public transportation.

"It would be best if we had the horses," Noa said.

"We can't go back to the stables. That's all the way across town," Mirai said. "It's too risky. They'll look for us there."

"Then we need the horses to come to us. First, we need to get off the city streets."

Jo responded. "We can get to the city's southern edge in about twenty-five minutes by taking all back alleys. If the horses can meet us there, we can ride west on the trails."

"And how are we going to get the horses to meet us?"

Zahira asked.

"Shouldn't you know by now?" Mirai slanted her eyes at Zahira.

"I can't guarantee anything," Noa said. "Trax will likely come, but I don't know about the others. Let's get to the city's edge first and then try. We'll need to take those trails regardless of whether we're on foot or horseback."

They snuck out of the city through alleys and broke into smaller groups as they traveled. Each dwelling they passed was aglow with an auto projection or boisterous household conversation about the Pastor's comm. Each street crossing felt like an open field, and every shadowed alley like shelter.

Noa's focus bounced from being annoyed at Jo for walking too closely behind her, to wanting to fight with Amar for convincing her to leave Sami.

She wished Tempsen was walking with them. She would have broken him in half.

At the edge of the city, the groups remerged. Amar and Mirai took the lead and made a path through the woods. After walking a fair while past the Main path, they agreed it was time to call the horses, found a clearing, and situated themselves into meditating positions.

Noa sat with her back to a large tree, wincing when her shoulder brushed it. She rubbed it and tried to peer behind her to get a look at the wound. When she turned around, the group was waiting for her.

"How do we start?" Alexis asked.

"Oh." Noa hadn't thought about this. She was going to be leading them in this exercise. She had never guided anyone along with her before but there probably wasn't a wrong way to do it. So, she followed whatever instruction popped into her mind.

She started with breath cycling instructions and kept her voice flat and uninhibited, mimicking Yori's cadence. The group repeated her instructions, and the forest hushed around them.

"Notice a tingling rising from your belly. Focus on that ball of energy. Let it float upward at its own pace. If you lose it, start again, with a new ball of energy and attach a name to it, if you need to. Think of it as the thing you want most in the world or the person you love most."

Noa imagined her sister, and an image formed of Sami and Tali in the same pearl.

"Now, ask yourself a big question."

Why me?

The image of Yori and herself standing on the edge of Crested Peak came forward in her mind. They looked at the sunset, proud of the land they watched over.

"Yori?" she asked, realizing she was now in his presence.

"Beautiful, isn't it?" He inhaled the majestic landscape. "Ancient peoples have looked after this land for thousands of years. They've destroyed it so many times, but the earth always puts it back together. It's still healing now. But that makes it all the more beautiful. We get to watch her heal right before our eyes."

A timelapse washed over the landscape. Ancient housing developments rose and fell. Tornadoes and fires ravaged the ground. New growth rose from the earth just to be scorched into a desert again. After a blink, the landscape returned to its current state, and the wind danced across it, bringing in breezes from the centuries before and the centuries after.

"Yori," Noa said again, and he looked at her.

His eyes were a deep brown, and she felt secure in his presence—like he knew exactly what was going to happen long after she was taken over by the landscape herself.

"We need your help," she told him.

"We're already on our way."

"How long?"

"We left ten days after you. Thought it best not to wait for the call, given the distance."

Noa tightened her lips and tried to smile, though her chest still felt empty despite Yori's good news.

His eyes rested on her.

"What if I can't do this?" she blurted.

"What if you don't do it alone? What if everyone you never even knew came together to save you, the same way you're trying to save them?" Yori asked, looking to the horizon. "What if you can?"

Noa looked to the horizon and contemplated how long she might be able to stay this time. A few leaves dropped from an overhanging branch, and her eyes followed the branch into the rumples of bark on an old tree.

It looked familiar.

When she blinked, she was sitting on the forest floor once more, but she wasn't facing her friends. She was turned around with her hand touching the tree she had been leaning against.

She turned and found her friends deep in their own meditation. She didn't have the heart to bother them, knowing this might be their last moment of peace for a while. She heard rustling in the bushes beyond the clearing and snorted as Trax's head lazily rose from the dense foliage. She always enjoyed how indifferent he was in her company.

"I did it!" Mirai shrieked, pointing to the horses and then slapping a hand over her mouth. "Oh, sorry, Noa. Of course, *you* did it. It was just too real. I thought I called them. I swear. That is some powerful stuff!"

Noa grinned and shrugged. "Mirai, I didn't call the horses. I think you did it. Maybe all of you together. Apparently, I needed to talk to Yori."

Everyone opened their eyes and joined the conversation, still relaxed from their meditation. After a few toe-touches and forward folds, they were invigorated and ready to press on.

"What did Yori have to say?" Alexis asked.

"The rest of Cavalry is already on their way and should be here in a few days. We'll need to wait on them and try to recruit supplemental troops in the meantime."

"Where are we going to get troops? And what are we asking them to do here?" V asked, gesturing to the empty woods.

"We're going back to HQ. We have more work to do to fix this corruption, and it starts with us taking HeadQuarters," Noa answered.

"We need to figure out where we are going before that," Amar said. "We're going to need somewhere to spend the next few days."

Noa put out an arm to stop the group as they walked to the horses. "I have a plan, and I know where we're going. I need to—before we go—I have to explain. My assignment just before the Cavalry was the Service." Vitus and Amar nodded knowingly, but Mirai, Zahira, Jo, and Alexis leaned in. "There's a UE couple who lives to the west of the city. *That* is where we are going. They were one of my cases, but they're not in the system anymore. I helped them once, and we'll have to ask for their help now. We can trust them."

"What's the plan, once we get there?" Mirai asked gently. "We can't hide for long."

"That's where I need V and Jo's help."

Jo perked up. V switched his weight from one foot to the other.

"We only have a short ride and not a lot of time," Noa continued. "On the way, I need you two to think about how we can broadcast our own universal comm. I have an idea about the steps after that, but I'll need to get a message out first."

V shrugged and raised his eyebrows, agreeing to help. Jo nodded, accepting his task.

They climbed onto their horses and rode, keeping distance from the main trail. After a few hours, they arrived at an odd looking home deep in the woods.

"What is that house made from?" Alexis asked, looking over her shoulder as she tied Luna's lead.

"Wood," V and Noa answered in unison.

"I have seen wood." Alexis scoffed.

"You have seen trees, and you have seen Sleekstone produced to look like treated wood," Noa explained. "Since they don't have access to Variety resources, UEs can't build with Sleekstone. They have to build with whatever they can find or harvest. *That* is what untreated, natural wood actually looks like."

"Hmm," Alexis said, content with the response. "Looks kind of gross."

Noa approached the house alone. It had been her idea, but now it felt weird that her Cavalry crew was standing such an awkward distance behind her.

Three stairs, two knocks on the door, a squeaky hinge and then, on the other side of the threshold, stood the woman she had helped escape the Variety.

"Hi, Britt," Noa said.

"What are you doing here?" Britt looked over Noa's shoulder at the others.

"We need your help. Everything you told me was true."

Britt opened the door wider and stepped outside. "Okay, get in here. All of you."

Noa stepped back down the stairs and waved her friends over, shepherding them inside. They filed in one by one, politely greeting Britt as they stepped in until Mirai froze at the top of the steps. Noa, the last in line, bumped into her and laughed trying to scooch her along until she realized Mirai was stiff as a board.

"Mirai? Are you okay?" She had gone pale with wide, startled eyes.

"Mirai?" Britt choked out the name.

"Rey?" Mirai asked.

CHAPTER 43

NOA

Noa had known them as Britt and Eli, but today she stood in a kitchen belonging to Reyna and Max.

The cramped kitchen—which happened to be the largest room in the house—was brimming with the Cavalry company. At the edge of the room, Noa sat on a coarse yellow couch. She willed herself not to pick its frayed corners, choosing instead to run her hands over the colorful patchwork quilt draped over the back cushion. Instead, she ran her hands over the colorful patchwork quilt that laid along its back. Alexis and Zahira sat on two stools, and Amar and Vitus leaned on opposing walls.

Max offered everyone water, and Noa insisted on sharing hers with Amar, as she'd seen there were only a few cups in the cabinet. As Max passed out cups, he made loud small talk about the horses, hoping to cover up the private conversation Mirai and Rey were having outside the thin walls.

On the other side of Noa, Jo made himself comfortable on the couch in the living room. He worked on an old portal that Max had offered when Jo had asked to borrow "any technology you have" upon arrival. Though portals didn't have the same connectivity or processing power of autos, they did have the added benefit of being workable hardware not implanted under someone's skin.

Jo let out a frustrated grunt that interrupted the kitchen conversation.

"It does fine to keep us up to date on news and other things," Max said, walking toward Jo. "But since we don't belong to the Variety, I just don't have anything better to offer you."

"It's great, it is. If I were doing any normal computing, I could make it work. But trying to get into the main comm line without being noticed is way too sophisticated. Even with the most advanced auto and direct connection, I would have a hard time."

Noa poked her head back into the living room. "Then what else can we do? There must be something. We can't just wait here forever."

"Well, you could try connecting with a bunch of people?" Zahira suggested. "You know, like you did with Yori and Tali?"

"My idea was to get everyone's attention through the universal comm and ask them to do the breathing exercise I asked you all to do. Even if only a few people participated, I could more easily connect with them, and they would spread the word. Then, you know, it would snowball. But without a comm, I don't think I can do it."

"There is one thing we could do," Mirai said, coming in through the door with her sister. Seeing them together made Noa think of Sami and she whimpered to herself. She grabbed Amar's hand who squeezed her back.

"What's that?" Alexis asked Mirai.

"Rey or Max could call their Service person." Mirai looked at her sister, who immediately frowned.

"We can't ask them to do that," Noa said. "They've worked so hard to stay out of the system and, if we asked them to come in now and we don't—well, if things don't go as we planned, they're just as screwed as everyone else. We need to keep as many people out of the system as possible."

She waited for someone to speak up to her, since she had no other ideas, but no one did. Mirai's idea slipped away until Max said something.

"Noa, you risked a lot for us one time. I think I can do the same. Not Reyna, though, just me."

"I can't let you do that," Reyna said.

"It has to be me. They'll run your background and see you have connections to Mirai from the Cavalry. Since we were never formally committed, I'll appear to be a random effie joining."

"What's an effie?" Zahira asked.

"An F-E," Reyna corrected. "Faster-evolving, our counter to that stupid little nickname the Service gave us."

"Jo," Max continued, "if I can get an auto installed tonight and get back here, can you send the message?"

"Wait!" Jo exclaimed. "No one has to do anything—I

figured out a way."

Jo refocused on the portal display. Everyone remained quiet so as not to disturb him. A minute passed, then two, then the group began to fidget.

"Fuck, Jo. Tell us your idea!" Vitus demanded.

"Oh, sorry." Jo pulled his attention away from the portal. "I was just double checking something and it's working. Noa, your parents still have their autos in, and Tempsen scrambled their location. Using the portal, one of your parents can let me into their autos, and I can send out the message. The only thing is, I'm not sure if logging in will override the location scrambler Tempsen applied."

"Then, no. That's not an option," Noa said.

"If Tempsen and your parents are leaving to meet us here tonight, anyway," Alexis started, "then who's to say we couldn't send the message as they leave? They could still get away, and our message could get out. And Max and Reyna won't need to risk contact with the system." Alexis approached Noa and looked at her with the same big eyes she did the first day they met. "It's the only way to protect everyone."

"Except my family," Noa said.

"Tempsen can protect your family," Jo said with his arms still propped up.

"I need to talk to them first."

"I can't do that," Jo said. "Not without unscrambling their location or giving away ours. I have to do it all at once."

"So, they won't know that we'll need them to leave right away?"

Jo shook his head.

Amar strode to the middle of the room and stood between Noa and Jo.

"Noa," he said her name in that way that calmed her nerves. "Tempsen and your family are leaving tonight, that was the plan all along. At dusk, Jo can make the connection and signal them to leave as soon as the broadcast is over."

"How long would they have?" Noa asked Jo.

"It will take HQ just a minute or two to figure out where they are and, my guess, less than five minutes to knock on your family's door."

"They'll need horses to get out of the city that fast undetected," Noa said firmly.

"I'll go," Vitus said.

Everyone looked at him, surprised.

"No," Jo said. "You're the only other tech-savvy person here. I need you in case I need help with the connection."

"I'll go," Mirai and Amar said at the same time.

Mirai continued, "It makes sense for us to go. We're the most experienced riders, and we can get everyone out."

"Two horses won't be enough—none of them can ride. We'll need four horses and to ride two to a horse," Amar added.

"Then that leaves me and Zahira," Alexis said and nudged Zahira.

Zahira looked to Jo, unsure. They exchanged glances and Zahira gave in. She would go too.

Noa felt sick at the idea of not being there when her sister woke up. She felt sicker still at the idea that Sami might not make it through, coming to, only to be shoved onto a horse for a brutal ride through the city and woods all while Noa sat safely in the cabin, protected by the trees and cover of nightfall.

TALI

Sai and Tali left Jash to tend to the fire as they waded through wet woods to find dry kindling. Tali had told Jash and Sai the night before that everyone was locked up in the bottom of HeadQuarters, including Noa.

Jash's face had turned bright red hearing that Noa was in the bottom of a cell, being tortured, and that there was nothing he could do about it. He seemed to think about her a lot, asking Tali at least three times about her since they'd been hiding out.

Tali felt bad for him, remembering Jash's disappointed face that morning she and Amar had caught up to them on the trip up. He seemed nice enough, and Tali figured, when everything was back to normal, she'd try to find him a girlfriend back at the ranch. She was good at those kinds of things.

Tali bent over to pick up a wet stick, but it turned out to be a branch much larger than she anticipated. She picked it up, wiggled it, and followed to its base where it had fallen from a tree. The bark on the tree entranced her and, suddenly, she was on Crested Peak with Yori and Noa.

"You okay?" Sai asked, startling Tali awake.

She was lying in his lap back at the fire. She was freezing and dizzy. She rubbed her forehead and answered, "Yes." After she drank some water from the canteen and warmed her chilled toes, she explained to them that she had connected with Noa and Yori and knew Cavalry were already on their way.

"Everyone's safe," Tali assured them. "The Cavalry will be here in about a week. They left before we called, I guess." She shrugged.

"Oh good, good. That seems normal. Telepathy and now fortune telling." Jash stirred the fire with a stick and adjusted the kindling pile closer to the flames to dry.

"She's the best information source we have," Sai said. "We should trust her."

"She's a child," Jash said. "These could be fever dreams for all we know."

"No girlfriend for you," Tali mumbled under her breath.

"What?"

"Nothing," she said. "But you should know we can't keep heading west. We have to stay here south of the city to receive the Cavalry. Noa and the rest will meet us back here. They have a plan."

"We can't stay in one place," Sai said. "HQ might be looking for us out here, and our horses are too obvious. We need to keep out of sight and move around as much as possible."

"We have to do more than hide and stay invisible," Jash protested. "Noa and the others are doing something. We need to do something too."

"We can," Tali said, bubbling with an idea.

"We are disconnected from the comms, and we have to keep Tali safe," Sai said to Jash. "And we have to receive the Cavalry troops in a few days. We're best to just lay low."

"No," Tali said.

"No?" Jash repeated.

"We can't just sit here," Tali said. "There are more people who can help."

The gears of her mind turned, squeaky with rust from the days of damp woods. They sat near the small fire, listening to the crackle, and ideating off Tali's plan. Once she'd found out that most of the Cavalry was willing and ready to support their mission, it had occurred to her that some of the other far-off Assignments might feel the same way. With Jo and Shen having come from the Mariner Assignment, and the Grand Lake Mariner base nearby, it was a natural place to ask for help.

They argued in the firelight—well, Tali and Jash argued, Sai mediated—going back and forth on details about how to approach the base, what their ask of the Mariners could be, if there were supplies they could borrow, and what this risk meant. If they put themselves in jeopardy, and were no longer able to receive the Cavalry, what would it cost the rest of the crew?

When they finally agreed on a mission, Jash twisted the final embers under his boot.

"Are we ready?" he asked.

"Yes!" Tali cheered.

Sai shushed her, but he nodded emphatically too.

"Let's do this."

CHAPTER 44

TALI

Tali, Jash, and Sai rode to the eastern edge of the woods and stopped just before the beach clearing. The Great Lake might as well have been the sea, it was so expansive. It was still summer season, but the air was crisper at the shore. The dry season meant the beach's water level was low, leaving a longer job between their forest cover and the pier they would approach.

"Are we sure about this?" Sai asked.

No one answered. Of course they weren't sure.

"We don't have time to waver," Jash said. "And, anyways, it's better for us to have something to show for our time, rather than just hide out in the woods for another week."

Tali gave a triumphant nod. She was no coward.

She thought back to her races behind Andrea's garden.

Setting a marker in her mind and rushing toward it—past it, even. She'd have to do that now.

Tali went first, which wasn't the plan, but she'd pulled out all her threads of patience over the previous days. Now, she was a quilt of action.

The Sleekstone pier grew taller above the water line with every step Tali took. At the shore, the waves lapped gently against the stone siding. But now, halfway to her target, the lake thrashed. The wind whipped. The cold stung her cheeks.

She took cover behind a dock box, likely filled with ropes, poles, and other benign Mariner materials. She glanced back. Sai and Jash were scurrying up the pier, both hunched with their coats pulled up, hiding in the shadows. It was lucky the moon wasn't as bright tonight.

Tali skipped ahead to the next marker—a large wooden pole. There were several in a row just where she stood, where Mariners with fishing or patrolling duties would tie their dinghies. On the other side of the pier, Tali noticed a small boat, bobbing with the swells, tied to a pole three up from where she stood.

She let Jash and Sai catch up.

"There," she said. "You two can take that around."

"And leave you where?" Jash asked.

"There." She pointed to the large vessel they were heading toward—there was a small window at the front.

"I can climb through there, then you can meet me on the other side of the deck. I'm sure they have docking things for lifeboats all around. I can find a ladder or a rope and get you onboard from the water."

She knew it was a good plan.

"That's a terrible plan," Jash said. "I doubt you can reach that window—*if* it's even unlocked—and if we take that little rowboat around the pier, the guards will definitely notice us."

"We could take it under the pier," Sai said. "We'd have to be quick to not get caught in the waves, but we could make it."

"And how's she going to get in that window?" Jash pushed. "And what about pulling us up onto the top deck? No one's going to see that?'

Sai shrugged. "Maybe. But if they have the port-side guarded as it's docked to the pier, and it's pretty late, the other side might be more lightly guarded. It could work."

"Got anything better?" Tali asked. If her plan was so terrible, he could come up with his own.

Jash's eyes darted around their surroundings. Tali followed his line of sight.

The end of the pier was lit and at least three Mariner guards staffed the ramp onboard. The large vessel was dark on the top deck, but lights shone from below-deck windows—likely, the members' quarters.

"Fine," Jash grumbled, barely audible. "But you're too small to reach that window. I'll go in first. You row with Sai."

Despite Tali's confidence in her swimming, she found herself praying for her life as she and Sai paddled the small boat under the pier. If you could call it a boat. It felt more like an armful of wood scraps against the crashing waves. On one particularly tall swell, they rose to the ceiling, and both had to lie flat to not rub against the underside of the pier that was covered in sharp barnacles and slimy sea moss.

Finally, out from under the pier, they paddled closely to the large ship, navigating to its darkened side that faced away from shore. They waited, rocking in the waves, for any sign from Jash.

The dark sky twinkled, full of stars. An extra glimmer caught Tali's eye.

It wasn't the sky, but Jash, flashing a light from the center of the top deck. They rowed toward him at full speed.

A full thirty feet below him, they waited as he lowered a rope. Sai anchored the rope to their small boat and gestured for Tali to climb first. The rope was loose at the bottom, making the start the most difficult. Thankfully, Cavalry life was not for the weak, and both her and Sai had the upper body to climb it. Still, Tali was grateful when she came across a large knot every few arm lengths to allow her to grip some rest as she ascended.

Once aboard, Jash pushed Tali toward an outdoor hall that kept her in the shadow of the pier's light that shone from across the hull. She waited until, finally, Sai and Jash joined her.

"Where would they keep the weapons?" Jash asked.

"They're not technically weapons," Sai said. "They likely just keep them in a storage or supply room."

They had agreed to first look for flare guns, knives, harpoons, arrows, any projectile or sharp edge that could embolden the Cavalry's charge. The three of them would work together to get an initial bout of supplies offboard and into the small boat. Jash would take the boat of supplies back to shore. He would be their safety net—ensuring someone was able to receive the Cavalry, and knew about Tali and Sai's whereabouts, should they be detained and need retrieval.

Then, Sai, the most diplomatic of the three, would make contact with the Mariners and ask for help. Tali would hang back to serve as a just-in-case distraction, in case the Mariners weren't as sympathetic to their cause as they hoped.

Tali motioned to a door leading to a stairwell.

Sai agreed to stay on deck while Jash and Tali snuck below. The door opened with a loud creak—the hinges having rusted from the exposure to the lake water over time. The stairwell was white, sterile, and damp. At the bottom of the staircase, they turned and followed a dingy hall with rough grey carpeting. Tali questioned why a ship—of all places—would have carpeting, but she shrugged it off since it was doing them the kindness of silencing their footsteps.

They checked one unlocked door after another to find a kitchen, a control room, and the entrance to the bunks. At the last, they headed in the opposite direction.

They had only made it a few paces past the staircase when someone approached them from behind.

"Hold it!"

Jash and Tali froze.

"Come with me," the guard said. "And don't make any noise or try to run for it. I have ways of catching you."

Tali believed her.

The guard was tall and muscular through her blue jumpsuit. The suit, unlike many Assignments' loose robes, was tailored to her figure with black cuffs at her wrists and tapered at her ankles, tucked into structured, black boots with a shiny metal toe.

The woman forced Tali and Jash into a small dark room.

"Wait," Jash said as the door clanged shut. "Damnit." He kicked the door.

They waited in the dark for who knows how long until the door opened again, letting in a sliver of light. Sai was also thrown in by the arm of the same guard. The guard followed him into the room, and the three of them backed into the corner away from her.

"Why are you here?" she demanded, taking a wide stance.

Jash and Sai looked at each other.

Tali spoke up. "We need your help." Tali had decided that, as in most cases, honesty would be best.

Jash gave her a sharp hush, but she ignored it and stepped closer to the guard.

"Our friends are in trouble, and we need weapons to help them. We thought the Mariners would have some we could, um, borrow."

The guard eyed their clothing. "Cavalry doesn't have weapons?"

"Each Cavalry member has a knife, maybe two," Sai said, placing a palm on Tali's shoulder. "But we were stripped of our arms a long time ago. I've heard that Mariners still practice with their arsenal."

The woman's mouth twitched one way, then another in thought. She turned precisely, closing and locking the door behind her.

NOA

"Thank you," Noa said as she took the hot tea Reyna offered. She held the cup with both hands and put it by her face, letting the steam warm her cheeks. She imagined Dia's hands around hers, helping to keep the warmth in. Her mind flooded with memories of Dia, a woman she'd known for moments; it had felt like so much longer.

"Are you ready?" Jo asked.

"No." Noa had meant to add sarcasm to the word, but it hadn't come through.

Reyna and Max sat on their couch, over-postured and still, while Jo worked on the screen for a few seconds. Noa counted the taps V made with his foot on the floor.

"Armel?" Jo asked into the portal. It was sitting on the coffee table in the small living room.

Chemi, Armel, and Tempsen appeared on screen.

"We're here. What's going on?" Armel said. "Everything okay?"

"Tempsen, your location is compromised starting right this second. I need to use Armel's auto to broadcast, and then you all need to leave as soon as possible. We've sent four horses that will meet you in the alley off 42nd Street."

Tempsen and Armel hesitated, but Chemi did not. "Yes, I know where that is."

"Okay, we're going to broadcast in thirty seconds. Is Sami up?" Jo asked.

Noa peered around him as if she could see beyond the projection's view.

"No, but I'll get her ready. It's time," Chemi said.

"What do I need to do?" Tempsen asked.

"I need you to let me into Armel's auto. Then we're going to sync to the universal comm. I've figured out the code for it. It should process in fifteen seconds. Then we're going to be live with a message from Noa. We need every second of airtime you can squeeze for us. We expect HQ to be at your doorstep in, well, six minutes now. Ready?"

Noa saw her mother move toward their couch to begin waking Sami off screen. Armel sent a control notification, which popped up on the portal display in front of Jo.

"Ready," Noa said. She watched her father helplessly peer on as Tempsen took the controls.

"She's not waking up," Chemi yelled, scurrying back into frame, looking for guidance.

"We don't have time," Jo said. "You all need to be ready to leave. Armel and Tempsen need to stay at the house for as long as they can. Chemi, if you can, carry Sami. Leave now. 42nd Street."

Chemi, looking smaller than Noa had ever seen before, nodded and disappeared. Another few seconds passed, and Chemi crossed again—this time, with Sami slung over her shoulder—marching like a warrior toward the backdoor. Armel kissed his wife on the cheek and held the door as she left.

"Noa, we're live in five, four, three—" Jo stopped counting and mouthed the last two numbers.

Noa sat on the floor again and positioned herself directly

in front of the portal. Her reflection took over the screen, and her mind went blank. Her eyes bounced around the room, looking for something that wasn't there.

Vitus, Jo, Reyna, and Max stared at Noa as her mouth began to move but couldn't settle on one word to say. Vitus moved to sit a few feet in front of her, so that he was just next to the portal screen.

"Talk to me," he whispered. "Just to me. Tell me everything." He waved his hands, ushering her to talk. "Start from the beginning."

Noa's eyes welled, and she pursed her lips to keep tears back. She cleared her throat.

"Yesterday, I destroyed the Variety."

She shook, realizing the weight of her words.

V encouraged her to continue.

"Earlier today, everyone got a message from HQ, and now my life and my family's lives are in danger. I wasn't included in the photo because the Elders don't plan to reintegrate me. They plan to kill me or disappear me, as they have done to many others."

She raised her eyes from V to the camera.

"I don't have much time. They are on their way to hurt my family right now." Noa's voice cracked, and she dropped her eyes back to Vitus.

She hadn't told anyone, yet, what she'd figured out in the darkness of that cell.

But she had to now. They were ready.

"They faked the Enlightenment. That's the real Truth. The Elders of the Advancement Age began ascending over two-hundred years ago. They learned how to do what I can do now—connect with other souls. And, instead of sharing that power, that responsibility, that beauty, and that evolution, they manipulated it. The Elders spoke to all our ancestors, pretending to be Gods."

Noa had so much more to say but was running out of time.

"There are thousands of you, probably more, who can already ascend just like me. Not someday, or generations from now. Today. Breathe with me."

Jo held up a one-minute warning finger.

Noa closed her eyes but had a hard time focusing as the seconds ticked away. She opened her eyes, panicking. Across from her, V sat with his legs crossed, breathing in and out. On the couch, Reyna and Max were doing the same.

She wasn't alone. She could do this.

She focused on her heart pounding. She followed the blood through her circulatory system as she learned in Nursing prep. She imagined a small bead swimming through her veins and then growing into a rope, restricting the flow.

She recalled the feeling of the auto being taken from her arm.

She imagined the rope being pulled from her finger, tugging through her palm and wrist—thick and gritty, at first—like the rope used on a boat. As she pulled it, a greater many smaller and thinner threads came out. The blood started pumping in her toes, then her calves and legs.

Her stomach pooled with blood, and her heart beat with vitality.

Her vision was blinded by white light.

To an onlooker, she was sitting in front of the camera

meditating. But in her mind, she was lighter than she'd ever felt. She felt surrounded by her friends, V, Reyna and Max, Mirai, Amar. She saw Tali and Yori and Dia and Shen and the man in the mirror and recognized hundreds more faces.

She stood, and was in a pebbled stream fed by a waterfall. The water was crisp and clear, reminding her of the arctic jellyfish. She thought she might look for them in the creek, but it was too shallow.

She walked closer to the waterfall, mist splashing onto her skin. She leaned in to examine the droplets as they flew past her face. There were tiny images in each bead. She sat at the mouth of the creek, letting her head fall back, cradled in her shoulder blades, and waited for the water droplets to fall into her open eyes.

The first one fell in, and she visited a young school child. They rolled down a hill together and laughed for an entire afternoon.

Another droplet fell into her eye, and she was working on an old machine with someone's grandfather. She passed him tools as he worked slowly and diligently. She wiped the sweat from her brow and blinked.

Another droplet fell, then another, and another and—like the first time—Noa was in all places at once.

She lounged in a hammock and cooked a family recipe and fell into a deep loneliness and an uplifting joy. She was tired and waking up and alive and dying.

Water poured into her eyes until she couldn't take it anymore.

The light faded and she cried, hating herself because every tear that fell from her ducts meant another water droplet she couldn't catch.

She worried for her sister and her family, like so many of the others she saw, and was comforted by the friends and family who waited for her just over the horizon. She drowned in her own tears and tried to breathe and catch droplets in cupped hands until all faded to black.

CHAPTER 45

TALI

For two nights, Sai, Jash, and Tali remained locked up on the Mariner ship. The first night, they were removed from the closet and placed into three separate holding cells. The cells were far from ideal, but an improvement from the closet as they now had toilets, and a guard brought water and a meal three times a day. Tali could tell the three of them were in the same hall, but the cells must have been soundproofed because, whenever her door shut, she could only hear herself.

She tried again and again to connect with Noa or Yori but couldn't. The first night she'd kept a positive attitude, attempting to write new lyrics to her mother's song or recite the poem she'd written for class so long ago. But after two nights alone, she gave up and cried for a few hours. Her tears pooled under her cheek onto the ground when she realized they wouldn't be able to receive the Cavalry when they came in from the South. They wouldn't be able to connect with Noa and the others. The mission to stop the Elders and their corrupt governance was over. Just because she couldn't sit still.

A wave of noise hit her as her cell door rose into the ceiling. It was Jash jabbering to the guard.

"What do you mean speak?" Jash said. "I'm barely up to speed myself..."

"Come on, Tali. This way," the guard said, offering her hand.

As the three of them were ushered through the corridors, Tali gathered that they were being brought to the mess area for a large event. From the whispers surrounding her, it also sounded like they were asking Jash or Sai to speak. Tali had no idea what they were supposed to be speaking on but was, nonetheless, insulted that she hadn't even been considered. She was an excellent public speaker. Or at least she thought she would be had she gotten the opportunity.

The three of them were first brought to the members' vacant chambers, and Tali was separated from Sai and Jash. She was allowed to shower and offered a fresh set of clothes. After a steamy five minutes with a bar of pine-smelling soap, Tali slid into her new jumpsuit. It was big on her, but she liked the belt and loved her new boots. They made her feel strong and capable of digging herself out of whatever mess they were in.

Tali was brought back to the others and directed through another maze of corridors that led deeper into the ship. They came to a large room that must have taken up half the ship deck where at least two-hundred Mariners sat at tables facing a stage. Jash, in his new blue uniform, stood centerstage with the female guard from before next to him. Tali pulled her long blond hair over her shoulder and held onto it with a firm grip.

"What's going on?" Tali asked Sai.

He shrugged. "It sounds like they've been talking to him without us. I don't know."

Jash stepped up to the microphone, and his voice boomed over the now quiet crowd. "Recently, you all heard from our close friend, Noa. My friends and I...we've been separated from our group since the Elders attacked us. Noa didn't lie to you. But I wouldn't be standing up here if you all didn't already know that."

A sea of high and tight haircuts nodded.

"We came here to steal your weapons," Jash admitted.

Sai squirmed in his seat, his new boots squeaking on the floor.

"Aanah," Jash pointed to the guard next to him, "has offered us more. Now that the HQ Service Members are off your ship, she thinks that more than a few of you might be sympathetic to our mission. That—more than a few of you didn't just watch Noa in her message—you felt her. You went with her."

"What message?" Tali nudged Sai.

He shrugged again, keeping his eyes on Jash.

The front row of Mariners stood, and one spoke. "What do you need?"

"In order for us to evolve, we have to be free from the manipulation of the Variety. Free from the corrupt leadership that held our evolution at a standstill for over two centuries."

Tali's mind spun. She couldn't have given a speech this good. She didn't even fully understand it.

"The Cavalry should be arriving at the Southern edge of the city in a couple of days. Meet us there. Bring every weapon you have. On Sunday, we will storm HQ—together—and put a stop to this manipulation once and for all."

Tali couldn't take it anymore. She let out a holler and started applauding. Jash gave her a stern look until the first row joined, and the others followed. Thunderous applause met them from around the room and, for the first time in days, Tali felt a lightness in her chest.

NOA

"Slowly," Armel said, leaning over his daughter as she awoke.

Noa blinked and glanced around the room. Reyna's small cabin was crowded with faces watching her.

It all came flooding back.

"Sami?" Noa called.

"I'm here," Sami said, grabbing her hand. Sami was lying on the floor just below Noa, who was on the couch.

"Everyone made it back? We did it!" Noa got excited and ignored her father's instruction, quickly lifting her head and swinging her legs around to a sitting position.

"Not yet," Alexis said. "After Tempsen made sure your family got to us, he stayed behind. Some HQ Service

Members were following them and taking shots. Amar went back to grab him, and they haven't shown up yet."

Noa looked out the window. It was still dark out.

"Okay, well they should be here soon, right? They probably just had to go off-trail and had to take a longer way back?"

Armel leaned into his daughter and hugged her tight. "Noie, it's been two days."

Noa's jaw dropped as goosebumps rose across her skin.

"No, we just…I just—I just woke up."

"It took a lot out of you, this time," Alexis said, sliding onto the couch next to her. "You've had a fever for a few days, and it just broke earlier this morning. We were worried about you."

"Where is Amar? Why haven't we gone looking for them?"

"We can't," V told her. "It's too risky. After our stunt, they have Service Members patrolling for us."

"So what? You all have been sitting here doing nothing?"

Sour bile rose from her stomach, and Noa couldn't hide the disgust on her face.

Sami reached for her hand.

"We're waiting for the Cavalry to arrive," Sami said. "And for you to get better. And, well, I've haven't been awake that long…so, also, for *me* to get better."

Noa's vision tunneled. The terrifying chill and dissociation of an oncoming panic attack swept over her body. She stood and rushed for the door, somehow managing not to trip over her sister in the process.

Outside, she was not so lucky. Noa stumbled down the steps, banging her wrist on the hand-railing but missing the opportunity to grip it, and fell on her ass.

Noa had been through this before; panic attacks were sudden and cruel. They never told her what she needed, rather, they were always clear on what she needed to be away from. Right now, she needed to be away from everything and everyone inside. Trembling and lightheaded, she pushed from the ground. With each hurried step, her vision waned, soon able to only make out pinholes of her surroundings.

After either fifteen seconds or thirty minutes of certain death, near blindness, a racing heart, and disorientation, Noa found the exact distance into the woods where *the bad space* ended. She was far enough away from what had caused the panic and could now breathe entire lungfulls of air from *the good space*.

This had to stop.

Noa squatted at the base of a tree in the good space. With each breath, she recovered her vision. Fringes of moss beneath her feet came into focus, green and delicate. When she finally lifted her head and took in her surroundings, Trax and the other horses were grazing in the distance. A small laugh escaped with her exhale. She shouldn't be surprised by that anymore. Nothing should surprise her anymore; she'd come a long way. She still hadn't admitted to anyone how proud she'd once been to be assigned to The Service. How could she have been so naive?

An idea.

She dashed back toward the cabin.

"Hey!" Alexis said, shining a flashlight toward Noa. "We were just about to come looking for you."

"Are you alright?" Reyna asked.

Noa nodded. "But I have to ask another huge favor of you two."

Max looked at Reyna. He reached out and squeezed her hand.

"Whatever it takes," they said.

Noa's plan was executed perfectly the next morning—thanks to her insider knowledge of the Service. She'd given Max as detailed of information as she could recall from memory on the layout and filing systems of the western Service building.

Max had visited this morning and managed to steal at least two hundred appointment files. Instead of hiding out for the three days before the Cavalry arrived, the small group spent the remaining time intervening before the Service Members' planned appointments with UEs.

As Noa had encountered when she was a Service Member, half of the leads were bogus and led to nothing but, of the half that did lead them to an unassigned person, nearly everyone wanted to help with the mission and agreed to meet them outside of HQ on Sunday.

Worries about Amar popped into Noa's mind throughout the day but she forced them away to keep focused on the task at hand. Her worries were always interrupting so she filed them away. Literally. She imagined them quarantined into a zone of her brain reserved for tabled worry.

At dusk, Noa returned to the cabin from her last appointment to find an old man talking with Zahira and Jo. And, in the distance, Mozart. She rushed Trax to the doorstep, slid off, and rapidly fired questions.

"You have Mozart? Where did you find him? Did you find Amar? Tempsen?"

"Noa, this is William," Zahira explained, gesturing a quick greeting between the two. "He is one of the unassigned Jo and I visited. Tempsen found his cabin, and he's there now—with Amar."

William was an aged man with white scruff. He looked healthy enough but moved slowly. Noa didn't think it was possible he could belong to the same generation as Decker, but there were no First Generations still alive. Well, except the Elders.

"What are we waiting for? Let's go." Noa said.

"Do you have any medicine?" William asked. "I have a few relief tablets, but nothing that will make much of a difference."

Zahira put a soft hand on Noa. "Amar's not doing well."

They gathered the medication Reyna and Max had left and rode to William's. Noa busted through the door and found Tempsen sitting in a chair sipping soup, and Amar lying on a couch, covered in ice packs.

Tempsen stood. "I've been doing everything I could to keep him well. His fever is breaking, but it's not the first time it has done so. It keeps coming back. Did you bring anything?"

"We didn't have much." Noa rushed to Amar and felt his forehead, which was freezing from the ice pack. Her hand brushed down to his cheeks, which, in contrast, were roasting.

His eyes opened.

"Amar? I'm here." She leaned over him.

Amar murmured something and closed his eyes again.

She turned to Tempsen. "What happened?"

"He came back to save me, and they got him with the RED ray."

Noa gave him a look.

"Radiated Energy Directed ray weapon—it's the name of those guns. They must have had it turned all the way up because they incapacitated him in the first hit. He might have been fine in a day or two under normal conditions, but I got lost on my way out of the city, and we've been without food or shelter all this time. I've had to keep him moving to try to get to you and…" Tempsen's head dropped. "I'm sorry. It was the best I could do."

Noa swallowed. She could not forget what he had done to her sister, but she couldn't forget that he'd now saved her family and Amar, too.

"Thank you."

Saturday night arrived far too quickly. The groups split between William and Reyna's residences to make for more comfortable arrangements. Noa and her family stayed at William's with Amar.

He'd woken a few times and had even gotten as far as making it outside and sitting on his own, but every night the fever came back. Noa enjoyed every morning with him, and her heart feared every evening. She was comforted when her mother and sister helped care for him. Her heart grew watching Amar and her father have tea outside on the porch in the morning and talk about nothing. He felt like a part of her family, and the routine gave the days some sense of normalcy.

Yori and the Cavalry would be approaching City Centre in the late hours of the night, and they planned to meet in the early morning. Noa had been trying (but unable) to reach Tali. Noa felt lost and wished there was a map or rulebook that explained how and when she could connect with others on that plane of consciousness, the same way she had been taught to understand auto connectivity. She cursed the lack of connection with Tali and not being able to reach her friends and family as she needed. In the same breath, she said a prayer of gratitude in case the connection would ever be lost for good.

Everyone staying with Reyna came to William's on Saturday night. Altogether, they repeatedly went over the plans, vague as they were. Again, they were in a position of not knowing what HQ would do or how they would fight back. Drafting this final plan, Noa reconsidered that, perhaps, all great battles were fought with only a general sense of direction and a commitment to cause.

When Amar's fever came back, Noa called the meeting over for the evening. "We all need our rest tonight because we don't know what tomorrow will look like."

Alexis, Mirai, Zahira, Vitus, and even Jo hugged her before they headed back to Reyna's. Noa said goodnight to her mother, father, and sister before lying on the floor next to Amar. She put her hand on his belly to feel his breathing rise and fall, hoping the rhythm would lull her to sleep.

CHAPTER 46

NOA

Noa sat on the small porch looking out to the empty woods. Trax waited next to her, eager to be in the way and of no help, as usual. She'd sat there since the early morning, trying to connect with Yori. It wasn't a clear connection, but she felt in her gut that the Cavalry had made it and would be waiting for them.

She watched the sun change the sky, and her eyes only tired once she heard stirring in the small dwelling behind her.

Her eyes widened when Alexis bound forward from the woods on Luna. She hopped off and walked to Noa.

"Where's everyone else?" Noa asked.

"We raced and I kicked their ass," Alexis said, just as the others started appearing too. "I thought Luna should have a good sprint this morning to get warmed up." She took a victory bow in front of the others before turning back to Noa. "Are you all ready to go?"

"It's just me from here. My family has to stay. We decided this yesterday."

"No," Alexis said. "You decided this yesterday. Sami insisted she's riding with me, and I don't think you're going to convince Amar—sick as he might be in the evenings—to sit this one out."

Sami and Amar traipsed outside.

"No," Noa said.

Sami held her hand up. "We've made our decision. We're coming."

"Amar, you can't," she insisted, even though the color had returned to his face as it did every morning.

"I'll be fine for most of the day. My energy has been up and, honestly, I feel like I broke through last night. Might have been my last fever. Plus, I need to see my sister."

She couldn't say no to that.

Noa sighed and went back into the house. She hugged her parents goodbye and kissed them both on the cheek, hoping it wouldn't be the last time.

The group rode quickly through the woods. Although the trek to the other side of the city was hours long, it seemed to pass in minutes when distracted by nervous thoughts. Noa's heart dropped when they stopped at a stream. She recalled her vision and suddenly felt surrounded by all the people she had visited.

Alexis pointed upstream, and Noa saw a few horses standing getting water. Then, her eyes adjusted to the camouflage of the woods. Hundreds of Cavalry members and their horses came into focus, speckling the woods like fallen leaves.

Yori approached on his horse and bowed to Noa.

"Hello, chosen one." He winked.

"I'm not the chosen one—" She stopped when she realized he was joking. "Thank you…for everything."

"There's more. Follow me."

On their horses, they trampled farther into the woods, past the other horses and into a large clearing. There were another hundred people sitting and standing around the woods, kicking leaves and sharpening sticks and drinking from canteens. They didn't dress like Cavalry, though. They wore blue jumpsuits and had short haircuts. Most of the Cavalry—men and women—wore ponytails.

Noa spotted Jash and hopped off Trax to run over to him.

"What is all of this? Who are these people?"

Jash introduced Aanah, who explained how many of the Mariners had felt Noa's message all at once. They'd come gladly and with sharp bows and projectiles.

Amar looked healthier than he had in days now that he was reunited with Tali.

An hour passed in those woods as they coordinated their entry to the city and HQ.

"Remember, everyone," Noa said at the front of the group, which flooded with people in every direction around her. "They are dangerous. They will hurt you. But we are not doing this to hurt them. We are doing this to get the Truth."

Noa directed Trax to ride forward. With Sami and Alexis at her left, Amar at her right, and her other friends trailing just behind, they trotted at a quick pace through the city and toward HeadQuarters, shining in the sunbeams.

Pedestrians in the streets opened their autos to capture the scene and find news updates on the Cavalry riding through the city streets.

HQ wouldn't be surprised by their arrival.

At the front of HQ, Noa held the Cavalry's line. In moments, Tempsen and Jo would override the security system—thanks to some autos still in the arms of a few Cavalry and Mariner volunteers. The gates at the top of the pedestrian stairs would fall, giving them full access to HQ grounds.

As they waited for their moment, Noa recognized a few, then several, then dozens of UEs from their rounds in the woods.

Everyone had shown up.

Nearly four hundred strong, they stormed the stairs of HQ and barreled through the dropping gates.

Once inside, the group was excited and hollering, but something felt wrong.

Noa looked around, and Alexis said the thought that was nagging her aloud.

"There's no one here."

"We have to go!" Noa tried to usher everyone out, but too many people were pouring in.

As she yelled, a recognizable intense pain shot through her skull, and she fell off Trax. Through the tears in her eyes and her leaden skull, Noa raised her body and looked around.

Everyone squirmed on the ground, clutching their skulls. Hot tears streamed down her face as she watched Amar, still weakened from the previous attack, begin seizing.

Seemingly less harmed than the others, Sami crawled to Noa.

Noa struggled to maintain her consciousness, fighting the fog in her mind to focus on her little sister. Everything they'd planned was over in an instant because she had no idea what she was doing. She had no right to be leading a revolution.

Sami slid her legs under Noa and rested Noa's head on her lap. She combed Noa's hair back and pointed her head to a still and darkened figure on the stairs of the southern tower.

The Elders were scattered across the tower's stairs, looking down on their bubble of pain as the revolutionaries fell to their knees and writhed.

Sami whispered in her sister's ear, "You have to try," and began to rub Noa's temples. "Breathe and focus, use the pain."

Noa focused and breathed through the pain, eventually giving into it. She imagined it swirling through the synapses of her brain. She remembered seeing the Variety and imagined her mind having a similar constellation. The pain fired through her brain's pathways, and her neurons lit up like fireworks. It sparkled with beauty as it filled her eyes with pressure.

She changed her gaze to one of the dark figures on the stairs and pushed her way inside their mind. All at once, they were a young woman— breathlessly beautiful—and, at the same time, the hollow figure of agedness Noa had seen in the dark basement hallway. A grotesque soul of hatred, greed, and self-loathing.

Noa imagined their pain the same way.

Emotional and physical pain firing on all synapses through her brain. The figure joined her for a moment and stared at Noa, in awe, which scared Noa. She didn't want to invite this figure inside her mind. But she reached out her hand, anyway, and, to her surprise, the figure took it. Noa led them into one of the firing neuro bonds and followed the pathway until they were swimming.

She held the Elder's hand, swimming through the Empyrean ocean and soon the dark waters became crystal clear, changing from chilly to warm and comfortable. The pain was still there, sure, but it was just one of the things she felt, and she shared it with this woman who now joined her. She watched as the Elder became overwhelmed by the soft, temperate water. As if it were boiling.

The Elder shut their eyes and fizzled in form, oscillating between their younger and Elder selves.

Noa's eyes tunneled as she watched the transformation. As her vision blackened, she turned her to her sister, who still held her head kindly. Sami was now wearing down, exhausting herself to protect her older sister.

"Don't let me go. Keep me awake," Noa said.

Sami mouthed an answer, but Noa couldn't hear it as she blacked out.

When Noa came to, she panicked that she had blacked out for days again. But she found herself lifting her head from her sister's lap with squirming bodies all around her.

Some bodies around her began to rise, while others twitched or lay still on the ground. The fragmented commotion confused Noa. Her attention was pulled one way, as someone yelled, "Go, go, go!" and then another when someone cried for help and a few able bodies rushed to assist.

The shadowy figure Noa had started with caught her eye as it collapsed on the stairs. Each Elder standing on a tower had been deploying a device which, in constellation, reached everyone who entered. With one taken down, a few of Noa's people rubbed their heads and found their feet. Then a few more.

"We have to go now!" Noa ordered, barely sitting up.

Jo and Alexis moved slowly, wading through the fog in their brains. They stumbled to their feet as they walked, then jogged, and finally ran toward the back of HQ to the basement that once held her hostage.

Noa looked over her shoulder to Yori, who seemed to be managing the pain better than most.

"Send half of the troops to the streets and out of here. Have them keep people out and spread the word that we will make an address later this evening. Everyone else, the towers! Take the towers!"

Finally, Noa turned to Sami. "Sami, find an auto and call for medicine and Doctors right away."

Yori took off and Sami jumped up.

As the fleet of troops headed to the other three towers, still occupied and firing, Noa set her eyes for the tower she'd already disarmed. Like the others, she moved slowly at first and gained speed as she came back into her body. She ran to the stairs as fast as she could, losing her breath and not caring to find it until she came to the collapsed Elder.

She held the frail body in her arms and decloaked their hollowed and gaunt face. She looked in their eyes, and they peered back at her silently. Their mouth opened and tried to speak, but nothing came out.

Noa whispered. "Why? Why did you hurt everyone?" She raised her voice and brushed the Elder's stringy, coarse white hair the way that Sami had brushed hers. "It's okay. I know. It's not so bad—death. Do you see that now?"

The figure's eyes welled as they let out their final gasp.

A single tear fell from Noa's eyes and glimmered as the sun shone down on the beautiful landscape that was City Centre from the vantage of an HQ tower.

Her spirits rose as she spotted Tali, Jo, and Zahira rising from the ground and sprinting into action.

In a flash, Noa's smile became her last.

Tali was sprinting across the courtyard in a panic. Noa's eyes followed her, and couldn't take in what she was seeing quickly enough. Her throat itched as it choked down involuntary sobs. Sami held Amar as she'd held Noa just minutes before, but Sami's face was crinkled into a small expression. Noa knew that it was over, and that her life would never be the same.

From high on that tower step with the shadowed figure still clutched in her arms, Noa watched Tali—that young girl, who had lost her parents and her grandmother—fling herself across the one person who had always been there for her.

Noa froze.

She didn't want to miss another moment of Amar's life.

She'd only been given such a short time with him already, and she couldn't bear to lose another second, even if it was from afar.

Noa inhaled and closed her eyes. She exhaled a shaky, crying breath, forcing herself to do something she knew was wrong. She pushed and slid her way into Tali's consciousness, struck by a deep and overwhelming sadness. Noa cried, high up on that tower, looking into Amar's eyes through those of his sister. Her grief was compounded—feeling both the weight of Tali's grief (that of a young girl losing the only family she had left) and her own (losing her first love).

Noa knew Tali could feel her too. She'd invaded this last moment Tali had with her brother but, to her surprise, Tali did not push Noa away. She made space for her, crying in unison.

Tali held Amar as Noa listened, quieting herself as she counted his last breath.

CHAPTER 47

NOA

Noa woke in her bed at her parents' house. Three days had passed but, this time, Noa had been awake for them, wishing she hadn't been.

Tali and Alexis had insisted on staying with her, while Vitus and the others had cleaned up and stayed in the Green Gem House. They were all meant to meet there later today for the memorial service.

Amar's last breath had been exhaled to his sister while Noa invaded the moment from a distance. She couldn't keep from reliving the guilt. She'd held the head and brushed the hair of misery incarnated, moments before. A person who had attempted to kill her parents, her friends and family, and her.

She'd sat with them and comforted them as they'd died.

Then she'd violated the last moments of Amar's life.

Noa rolled over in her bed and sobbed, as she'd done periodically for days. Never in her life had tears come so easily and flowed so steadily. She feared that she might never be able to leave her room again. The past three nights, she begged to see Amar in her dreams. She sat in the corner of her room for hours, trying to connect—to be with him for just moments more.

Her grief amplified, knowing that she hadn't been there for Tali, either. Alexis, Sami, and her parents had taken care of Tali while Noa sat in her room like a burden.

Alexis knocked on the doorframe and went to sit on the bed next to Noa. She put a hand on Noa's side to comfort her. Noa buried herself deeper beneath the quilt.

"Hon," Alexis whispered. "It's time."

Noa shook her head, her face buried in pillows. She gasped in her silent cry and sat up. She wrapped her arms around her friend's neck.

"Lex, I can't do this."

Alexis hugged her back even tighter, the way she always did. So tightly it was uncomfortable and choking. Like Alexis could squish away any space between them.

Noa had always thought it odd that her friend held on as tightly as she did, but now it was unthinkable that they didn't all hug each other as tightly as they could at every chance they had.

Alexis pulled away first, for the first time ever. She lifted Noa's chin and wiped the tears from her cheek.

"You can," she said.

Noa waited for Alexis to tell her that she had to, that she

owed it to Tali, that she needed closure—but she didn't say those things. She just left it at that.

You can.

Noa tucked her chin down and played with the crumpled tissue. Alexis kissed her on the forehead the way Amar used to and rose from the bed. She laid out Noa's best whites and helped her get changed. Noa stayed sitting on the bed as her friend handed her each piece of clothing. She was frozen in heartbreak and could barely lift her arm to Alexis's shoulder as she kneeled to lace up Noa's boots.

At the memorial service, hundreds of people gathered and lit candles for Amar.

Mirai, Decker, and Andrea spoke about Amar and filled the room with laughter and quiet sniffles. Noa held Tali's hand for the entire service and squeezed it every time she needed to.

Tali let her, occasionally squeezing back.

When the speakers were finished, Tali squeezed Noa's hand once more before letting go and standing. Tali strode to the front of the crowded room and took her place behind a podium almost as tall as she was. She stepped on a riser and cleared her throat before speaking into the microphone.

"I'd like to lead a prayer because my brother would have hated it, but he would have needed it."

Noa waited for Tali to speak but instead she sang. Loudly, melodically, beautifully:

Dusty palms and an eerie calm,
winds blow, and they only know
where you are.
I'll find you soon,
because I know you won't go too far.

Noa closed her eyes and let Tali's elegant voice transport her to another realm. For a moment she saw Amar, as real as the first day they'd met. Her shoulders relaxed the way they always did around him, and she cried. He kissed her forehead, and she stared into his eyes. It was just the two of them. Together. One last time.

SUNSET

NOA

Noa smoothed wrinkles out of her suit as she stared in the mirror.

"You look beautiful," she said to Tali.

Tali, who stood next to her adjusting her own elegant ensemble, smiled. She looked much older than when Noa had first met her. The year that had passed had transformed her from a gangly child into a young woman.

Since the exposure of the Elders and the destruction of the Variety, the world had been chaotic but more connected.

Noa, Yori, Tali, and many others held connecting ceremonies as often as they could, introducing everyone to the new idea of the ascendence. Noa worked alongside Philosophers, Scientists, and Explorers—but the people who now held these titles had chosen them, rather than been assigned to them. For a year, everyone was free to do and be what they wanted.

For most, the newfound autonomy was intoxicating and intense; daunting but favorable. Corrupting the Variety, however, also meant unraveling all other threads of society. Since its collapse, City Centre and its supported communities had struggled to maintain basic systems: healthcare, food supply chains, waste management, new development and housing, energy supply, and on. As soon as citizens began to accept their freedom, they also noticed the side effects of anarchy.

"Noa?" Tali said. Noa just about jumped out of her skin. It had always been common for her to be in her head, but these days, her thoughts sank her so deep it felt like she floated into different dimensions. What type of world would Tali grow up into?

"Yup, let's go. You've got a world to lead, kiddo."

Today, leaders from the movement would attend an Anniversary Feast at HeadQuarters to broadcast speeches and ideas about how to move forward.

Noa had intended to write out her remarks for the event but had neglected to do so. She had no idea what to propose. Everyone around her commented on how complex everything was, how broken it was. But over the past year, Noa had felt the most whole she ever had.

Even without him.

Noa wanted nothing to do with setting up a government, implementing a new system, or leading society. But she was at the forefront of the movement simply because the stars fell on her first.

People like Alexis, Zahira, Jo, and Vitus had thrived in the spotlight. But Tali and Noa tried to enjoy a quieter life in the background.

Noa hoped the great minds in tonight's room would propose amazing plans, so she'd be able to go back to the Cavalry with Mirai, Andrea, and Tali to train full-time with Yori and become a real Marshal. Maybe she'd finally get to design her own home.

Walking into the grand hall, Noa bumped into Decker, as if fate wanted to remind her of the one reason she didn't want to go back to Main Ranch.

She pulled back, and he remained overly stiff as he acknowledged her with a tip of his hat. "Noa," he said curtly, and moved along.

Noa waved politely to a few others but mostly kept her head down as she paced to join Tali, where they were assigned to sit centerstage at the front of the large hall.

Lights queued the event to start and applause filled the room. Noa knew it was time for her to speak words she had not yet scripted. She stood and stared at her fingers resting on the table, stalling for one moment longer to center herself. Then, she lifted her head and began.

"In each of us, there is a connection that links us to one other. And not just every other person alive today—but a connection to every other being who has lived in the past, present, and maybe the future. Connecting us to the best moments of our lives, the worst moments of our lives, and in all moments of mundanity. I've witnessed it. I've accompanied many of you during such moments, just as you have accompanied me. And we are better for it. We are better for knowing each other's love and pain as if it were our own." Noa gulped, preparing to put forth the idea that had been on her mind for weeks, months, lifetimes…

"But there is the matter of how we marry this revelation about our human nature and our evolution to our history and everyday lives. For too long, we have kept these elements separated for fear they would get corrupted. For too long, we trusted machinery to keep them unconnected and uncomplicated for us. We prioritized the efficiency of living, evolving, and growing. What I have learned from my many visits, connections, and lifetimes is that there will always be more to explore, to live, to love, to be. Always. We shouldn't try to do it all in a single lifetime, and we shouldn't try to be *all people* in a single lifetime. Instead, we must try to follow our own heart and our own soul for the time we are given. To this end, I propose that we extend radical free will."

A silent vacuum filled the space where she had expected a reaction.

Tali whispered, "What is that?"

Noa continued. "The world is full of chaos, and the deliberate actions of humans will do right as soon as the correct causes and conditions are in place. I am proposing no system at all."

"Your proposition is anarchy?" accused someone from the audience.

"No. Anarchy is just the lack of a government. My proposition is that we attempt, in all our actions, as best we can, to abandon all systems. I have seen eons of human souls and, if you can believe me, I promise that they are inherently good. There will be harm, there will be learning periods, but if we evolve to a society dependent upon personal goodwill instead of a system of rules and pressure, we will all rise to the occasion. Under my proposal, the only government that exists will be personal choice because it is the only thing that has ever existed."

Noa took her seat and listened to the room's echoing silence. A few people began to clap but it was reserved and forced. She glanced around the room and waited for someone to challenge the silence.

Tali began to push her chair back, but a louder booming voice took over the hall.

"She said, 'if we can believe her,' and I'm not sure that we can."

It was Decker.

"She says that humans are inherently good just a year after discovering one of the largest scandals and deceptions humans have ever committed. Three generations lived pointless lives under the Variety—under the control of the deviant and harmful Elders."

Decker's tone was charismatic, as always, but devoid of its usual levity. Instead, he was serious, firm, and sounded as though he was scolding her directly.

"I propose that we have a council of leaders who develop the systems that we need. If Noa would like to live a life of leisure and prayer in the woods with her UE allies, then by all means, we should let her. That is where the Variety got it wrong. People who do not want to belong to the Variety, should not have to. If they do not want a life optimized by science, calculation, and the experience of previous lifetimes, then so be it.

"But that is not for me. I propose we rebuild a different life-management system. That we do so publicly and have it checked for any corruption. That we correct the issues from the last system. Life under the Variety was great. Our understanding of the afterlife and our evolution has changed, but our understanding of this life—the one we're living every single day, has not. I don't want that life to be filled with nothingness and selfishness. I want it to be filled with community, togetherness, and adventure."

As the room broke out in applause, Decker tipped his hat to Noa.

Having changed into her Cavalry uniform, Noa groomed Trax in the stables. She cared for his hooves and shoes, for his mane and coat. She had even restitched his saddle mat and lacquered the saddle.

"You look handsome, don't you boy," she cooed to her horse.

"Well, thank you," Jash said, coming in and leaning against the stable's door.

Noa laughed and rolled her eyes, "Hey, superhero. How are you?"

"Ah, so you did read the news articles about me. I'm just one of the many superheroes." He bowed his way into the stable and sat down, softening his tone. "Actually, I need to talk to you about something. The others are going to be here in a minute, but I thought I'd come early to give you some time to react before you had to do so publicly."

"Well, go on. Tell me."

"Decker's taken control of HQ. With most of the Cavalry and nearly all of the city. They all want the new system."

"Hmm."

It wasn't as if she hadn't seen it coming. In the days after the Feast, she and Decker had sent conflicting comms across the country, debating for control or the lack of it. Exactly what Noa had hoped wouldn't happen. Eventually, she stopped responding, leaving Decker to fill the void.

"Don't get too down," Jash continued, "there's more."

Noa sat on a hay bale and leaned her elbows on her knees to listen.

"There is also a not-insignificant part of the population that is in favor of your proposal. Like the Mariners, the FEs, and others…Mainly the people who have experienced the connection firsthand."

Noa waited for more, but he didn't keep going.

"So, those who want to live in the system can, and those who don't, don't have to. It's not exactly what I was going for, but the fact that everyone can choose is kind of the point." She stood. "We just keep doing what we're doing and know that, in time, everything will work itself out."

"Well, not exactly." Jash fidgeted. "Decker has proposed a geographical division between the two parties. He's staked claim over City Centre, including the surrounding cities, Libraries, and, of course, Main Ranch. It's not official, but there's a rumor that he'll offer us Alaska."

"But that space hasn't been redeveloped. There's nothing there."

"His claim is that those who don't want to benefit from

this society's systems shouldn't reap the benefits of its past systems." Jash ran his fingers through his hair. "Surprise, surprise, there is wide agreement among his much larger following."

"I don't have a following," Noa corrected.

"You do."

Tali, Alexis, Vitus, Zahira, Jo, Mirai, and Andrea trickled into the barn. They had obviously been listening just outside the door.

"Shall we go to Alaska?" Noa asked them.

Alexis stepped forward. "You know we're all on your side."

"I don't have a side, but yes, I appreciate that I haven't been hung out to dry by all of my friends and family."

Alexis took more steps, coming in close to Noa. "Not *all*."

Noa scrunched her face in confusion.

Alexis took a deep breath and broke the news to her. "Hon, Sami and your parents…they're not coming. They've decided to stay."

In the muddy stable, Noa was cold and awake. She was wired from the previous year. She had a thousand lives flowing through her—as though that rope had once again been ripped from her veins, letting her blood pump furiously.

"That's their choice. But I think they'll come. Eventually," Noa said.

She started gathering her things from around the stall.

"Are you packing now?" V asked.

"Might as well, I don't think I'm coming back."

ACKNOWLEDGEMENTS

Hey loves.

If you've read this far, you are likely one of the people to whom I owe a tremendous debt of gratitude. If I miss thanking you below, it is likely because I'm tired, not ungrateful. I plan to write many more books which will give me the chance to make up for any missed appreciation.

KATHRYN

Without you, I never would have known I loved writing. I probably wouldn't be bold, or brave, or have gotten through half the shit life threw our way. Thank you for driving me around for little-to-no gas money in high school, for holding me to a high standard in college, for staying my best friend through the longest of distances. But, mostly, thank you for being you — you always have and always will inspire me.

EARLY READERS

Thank you for ignoring the typos, dealing with seventeen points of view, and dedicating your precious time to make this world and these characters complete. Everyone who picks up this book owes you a debt of gratitude, or at the very least, a strong coffee.

JULIE

I will never forget the enthusiasm you have held for my book and writing career since day one. It is rare to meet people who have a good heart and the ability to share their affection so genuinely. Your excitement has kept me working on this novel more times than I can count. Thank you for loaning me that energy. (Bren: Thank you for loaning me your likeness. Let's see how Tempsen fares in book two, huh?)

FAMILY

I'm grateful to have three parents who neither doubt nor pressure me; who care, ask questions, and give generous, unwavering support. I'm even luckier to have three goofy siblings who give me shit and think my achievements are the least important thing about me. Thanks for putting up with the miles between us and the jetlagged visits. I love each of you so, so much.

DAD

You have long shared and encouraged my interests in sci-fi and fantasy. I'm grateful you introduced me to X-Men, Lord of the Rings, iRobot, and Star Wars. Those worlds expanded mine, allowing me to dream of superpowers, epic journeys, inventing technology, and exploring worlds. Thank you for watching with me and making the popcorn.

MOM

I wouldn't love books the way I do without you. I love that you were scared to read my story and I am delighted you actually liked it. Your love for Trax still makes me laugh. Thank you for always reading around me, for letting me skip school way back when to get the latest Lemony Snicket book on release day, for encouraging me to be smart and kind; fierce and compassionate. You have taught me so much.

LITTLE GRANDMA

Thank you for lending me your name.

INSTAGRAM WRITING FAMILY

Oh. My. Lanta. I can't even begin to describe the special kind of drug you all are to me. Funny and wild and real and welcoming. Adri, Jessika, Caitlan, Kelly, Jessica, Nicole, Maggie, MJ, Sarah, Megan, Patty, Nina, Ally, Davona, Morgan, Christina, Rachel, and so many many more. I couldn't name you all if I tried. Thanks for doing this with me.

TAYLOR

Thank you for reading, for encouraging me, for singing praises, and for being a supportive bestie across the country. I'm so thankful for your friendship. I hope we have many more post-movie dance parties in the years to come.

EDITORS: JEN AND BURGEON (SAMANTHA)

Aka the people who made this book readable. Jen, thank you for doing the hard and early work of developmental editing. Burgeon (Sam), thank you for taking on the monumental task of dual editing. Both of you took such great care to preserve my writing style and voice while making it a better experience for my readers. Thank you for all your hard work.

EMERSON

You have not stopped creating gorgeous scenes and elements and vibes for my story since we started working together. I am thrilled that the imagery of my book came to life through you. Thank you for your thoughtfulness and time. You are an incredible artist, and a kind and thoughtful human being, to boot.

JULIA

Formatter extraordinaire. I can (and will) rave about your formatting talents anywhere I'm allowed. Here, I just want to say thank you for your patience and flexibility. I wouldn't have been able to meet my deadlines without you (and this book would look nowhere near as good.)

MADDIE

No one said this journey was going to be easy. Kicking down fences, trying new things, creating worlds – it's not a business for the meek. I'm so grateful for all the effort and expertise (horse and otherwise) you lent me to help make this book what it is. I'm so proud to have grown up in the same author pond as you. Long live all the magic we made.

KIERAN

You begged me to read this book even though you do not read these types of books. When I finally sent it to you, you didn't waste any time. You had it printed before the weekend and read it during your next trip. You asked me a million questions as you read and returned it to me with scribbles on every page and thoughtful notes in the margins, the last of which read, "Thank you for letting me read this, I enjoyed every minute of it. Would you send me Ellory?" I don't think you'll ever know how much that meant to me.

CASSIDY

Critique partner extraordinaire. Blurb expert. Writing retreat bestie. Personal crisis hotline. Fountain of good vibes and solidarity. I don't have the words and I don't know what I did in a past life to deserve a friend like you. But I have one more favor: can you text me? My book is published and I'm probably freaking out. Love you. Mean it.

ABOUT THE AUTHOR

JULIA MARTEL writes stories centered on friendship and adventure. Her debut novel is a YA Dystopian Sci-Fi, blending her passion for exploring human connection and embarking on extraordinary journeys. An avid writer throughout her life, Julia has honed her skills both creatively and professionally, earning an MS in Communication and applying the art of storytelling in corporate settings. When she isn't writing, you can find her basking in the sunshine, traveling, reading, re-watching sitcoms, or enthusiastically cheering on her friends. She currently lives in Laguna Beach, California where the ocean reminds her everyday that you can't stop the waves, but you can learn how to enjoy them.